I0694542

Throne of Sin and Desire

A Dark Romantasy

J.S. RODRIGUEZ

LITERAL PUBLICATIONS

Second Edition, Published 2026

Cover Design by Yosbedesign

Published by Literal Publications, 445 Hwy 46S Suite 29, PMB 151, Dickson, TN 37055.

ISBN: 978-1-970937-05-3 (Paperback)

ISBN: 978-1-970937-06-0

CONTENTS

Prologue   6

1. Chapter One   10

2. Chapter Two   18

3. Chapter Three   28

4. Chapter Four   45

5. Chapter Five   53

6. Chapter Six   62

7. Chapter Seven   72

8. Chapter Eight   84

9. Chapter Nine   88

10. Chapter Ten   95

11. Chapter Eleven   104

12. Chapter Twelve   112

13. Chapter Thirteen   128

14.	Chapter Fourteen	132
15.	Chapter Fifteen	137
16.	Chapter Sixteen	148
17.	Chapter Seventeen	160
18.	Chapter Eighteen	170
19.	Chapter Nineteen	177
20.	Chapter Twenty	188
21.	Chapter Twenty-one	196
22.	Chapter Twenty-two	207
23.	Chapter Twenty-three	217
24.	Chapter Twenty-four	225
25.	Chapter Twenty-five	233
26.	Chapter Twenty-six	242
27.	Chapter Twenty-seven	250
28.	Chapter Twenty-eight	257
29.	Chapter Twenty-nine	271
30.	Chapter Thirty	280
31.	Chapter Thirty-one	288
32.	Chapter Thirty-two	293
33.	Chapter Thirty-three	304
34.	Chapter Thirty-four	308
35.	Chapter Thirty-five	312
36.	Chapter Thirty-six	323

37. Chapter Thirty-seven   330

38. Chapter Thirty-eight   336

39. Chapter Thirty-nine   342

40. Chapter Forty   349

41. Chapter Forty-one   357

42. Chapter Forty-two   368

Note to Readers   382

About J. S. Rodriguez   383

Other Books by J.S. Rodriguez   384

Trigger Warnings

Some content within this book may be triggering or disturbing to some readers. This book is intended for mature audiences only, not for anyone under 18 years of age. Reader discretion is advised.

This book contains themes and descriptions of attempted sexual assault, abuse, sexual acts, profanity, scenes of trauma, anxiety, mentions of domestic violence, murder, torture, graphic gore, kidnapping, captivity, forced proximity, jealous and possessive vibes, and descriptions of death that may be distressing to some readers.

This is a dark romance, not a soft or cozy romance. Please prioritize your mental well-being and do not read if you are sensitive to these topics.

DEDICATION

To my readers who need to drown out reality with fiction. Now, be a good girl and flip these pages.

I got you.

Monsters are made for ruin. For sin. For destruction. Not for love...But when we do love, it's possessive, twisted, and dark.

I would burn the whole damn world and smile as I watch every one of you scream in Hell.

Will I let her go? Or will I be the selfish bastard I've always been and keep her anyway?

She tests every shred of self-restraint I have left. She wants me, but she has no idea what kind of savage monster wants her back.

She has no idea how close I am to snapping. She wants me — thinks she understands what that means. Thinks she can handle the hunger in me. But she doesn't know the truth: if I taste her even once, if I get even one breath of her sweetness on my tongue...I will never let her go. There will be no escape. Not for her. Not from me.

I'll drag her to Hell kicking and screaming if I must...and I'll chain her to my side forever.

PROLOGUE

Three years ago

Rosa

I lie flat on my back in a small clearing, where the sun shimmers through the trees' canopy. Warmth spills over my skin, providing a soothing feeling that I crave. I breathe it in, slow and desperate.

I exhale, eyes closed, letting the stillness settle over me. The birds are singing somewhere above, their soft melody threading through the loneliness in my chest. My fingers curl into the cool earth, grounding me, holding me together.

This is the only place I'm allowed to exist without fear.

He can't take this from me, but God knows he's tried. He hates it when I'm happy, says I don't deserve it.

I don't allow any negative thoughts in this space. I empty my mind of them.

"Thank God!" Cassie's voice cuts through the quiet. I open my eyes to see her jogging toward me, cheeks flushed. "You weren't in your room. I knocked on the window, and I refused to knock on your door, so I was praying you were here."

"I'm sorry," I whisper, sitting up. "I needed some time away from the house."

"I don't blame you. You could've come to my place; you know that, right?"

"Yeah, I know." I don't want to tell her I prefer the solitude here. It's safer. We walk through the woods to get back to my house.

Dread spreads through me the minute I see the blue ranch-style house I live in come into view. My stomach knots uncomfortably. Every second I'm inside, it feels like walking on glass barefoot. One wrong move and the pain comes. We quietly step inside and rush to my room.

"I'm going to take a shower, then we'll go to your place."

"Okay," Cassie nods, lying on my bed, and pulls out her cell, typing away.

My adoptive father doesn't care what happens to me when I turn eighteen as long as I'm out of his house. That has been clear since my adoptive mother died.

I've always known escaping this pain meant getting a scholarship, so school became everything. Thankfully, I got into the same school as Cassie. Her mom, Tammy, helped me through it all.

She'll be the only thing in this small town I'll miss. I'm extremely grateful for her. Without her, I don't know where I'd be. She was my adoptive mother's best friend before she died; I have known them for most of my life.

My adoptive mother took me in when I was six years old.

She wanted a child... he didn't. After she died, he turned into a drunk. He blames me for her death. Sometimes, I blame myself too. He hits me, and I let him. Fear makes me obedient. I just want to survive.

I turn on the shower, slowly removing my clothes, flinching from the sharp pain in my ribs. Jim punched me there a few days ago. He definitely bruised them. Warm water pours over me, and I release a shaky breath as the tears come. I let the water wash away the negative thoughts. I cover my mouth with my hand, so no one hears me. My heart rate spikes, and I start gasping for air. My hand clutches my chest as I look up at the ceiling. I open my mouth and let out a silent scream.

Everything will be okay.

You will be okay.

The promise isn't much, but it's all I have.

I turn off the water and wrap a towel around myself, wipe the steam off the mirror, and stare at my reflection. My light green eyes look washed out, exhausted. I have long, dark, wavy hair, my eyes move to my round cheeks and full, pouty lips. I rarely wear make-up, unless I have to mask a bruise.

I get dressed quickly and step into my room. "I'm ready. Keep quiet in the hall." I remind Cassie.

"Trust me, I know." Cassie nods, standing.

We quickly leave the house. I know he's sleeping; I heard bottles smashing against the walls last night; he was drinking.

When we hit the driveway, Cassie unlocks her pretty BMW. Her family has money and lives in the best neighborhood.

Cassie turns on the car, and the radio is blasting a hip-hop song. My heart rate spikes as she races down the road, driving like a crazy person.

"Loosen up!" she shouts over the music, laughing.

"You're insane!" I giggle, gripping the door tight with my hands.

"But you love me!" She looks over at me and blows me a kiss.

"That I do! Now pay attention, you damn maniac."

Ten minutes later, we pull into her mom's U-shaped brick driveway. It's a two-story white house with a couple of fake balconies on the second floor. I love it here. It reminds me of when my mom and I used to walk down here every day for playdates. I was fifteen when she passed away. I remember that day like it was yesterday.

"Are you coming?" Cassie taps on the window. I smile. I didn't even notice she had gotten out of the car.

We walk in, heading straight to the kitchen, knowing her mom will be there.

"Rosa!" she beams and pulls me into a tight hug. I sigh, melting into her arms. She smells like cinnamon, making my throat tighten with emotion. Cassie and her mom look so much alike with their high cheekbones, hazel eyes, and short blonde hair. Cassie is taller than her, but aside from that, they look the same.

"Good morning, Tammy," I manage as she squeezes me harder. It's like she knows that I need this.

"Today is your big date!"

"Yep." I let out a sigh, trying to sound excited and not terrified.

Chapter One

Rosa

Andrew climbs into the car and turns it on. The car rumbles to life, but the vibration beneath me does nothing to soothe my anxiety. The further we get from town and up the mountains, the tighter my chest gets. My knee bounces uncontrollably, and I stare out of the window as the houses thin out.

My body stiffens when he slides a hand onto my thigh.

"Relax, babe." He rubs my thigh with his thumb.

I blink slowly at the word, *babe...*

"Where are we going?" I swallow hard, inching closer to the door. He doesn't get the hint.

"You like the woods, right?" He grins, tilting his head to the side to look at me. "I know the perfect spot for a picnic."

He slows the car and turns onto an uneven dirt road, causing it to bounce violently.

"It's very secluded here, so we'll have plenty of alone time."

The lump in my throat grows. *That didn't sound creepy at all...*

He parks the car at the end of the bumpy trail and jumps out. My fingers are shaky as I reach for the door handle. By the time I step out, he's holding a basket and a folded blanket.

"It's about a mile hike," he calls over his shoulder as if it's nothing.

I follow, thinking about telling him I'm not feeling well, but Cassie was so excited. I don't want to disappoint her. I look around as towering trees surround us, their leaves forming a dense canopy that filters the sunlight into dappled patterns on the forest floor. It's August, so it's hot, and my skin feels a tad sticky, but I love it.

"So, Cassie says you grew up together and are close, but I've never seen you before."

"I like keeping to myself."

He chuckles, "Yeah. You seem like the quiet type."

I look up when he stops walking and...

Wow, it's amazing. There's a large pond surrounded by trees, and the water is so pretty as the sunlight glitters across it. I should feel calm, but I don't. My gut instincts tell me to leave.

"See, I told ya!"

"Mhm." I walk closer to the water, taking off my sandals and dipping my toes in. It feels amazing. If I were alone, I definitely would take a nice swim. "Would you like any help?" I ask, looking over my shoulder at him.

"Nope, enjoy the view."

I lift my dress to my knees and walk further in.

"If you want to take a swim, you can. It's just us."

"I didn't bring a suit." I tilt my head back as I bask in the sunshine.

"That's okay. A suit isn't necessary, it's just us."

"Oh no, that's okay." I blow out a deep breath of annoyance.

"Maybe later then. Come eat."

I walk back without putting on my sandals. "It looks so good," I say as I sit down, observing everything: some cute little sandwiches, a few different kinds of chips, strawberries, and cookies.

We sit there and eat in a heavy silence. He keeps watching me, his eyes lingering too long, making my skin crawl.

"Here, try some. They're really good."

I look over, and he has a strawberry in his hand. I reach out for it, but he pulls it away. "Open." He pushes it forward and presses it to my lips. His smile drops when I hesitate. So, I open my mouth and take a bite.

"Yeah, they're very good." I start pulling away, but he grips my chin, stopping me. I release a nervous laugh as I try to pull my face away.

"You are beautiful." His thumb sweeps across my lower lip, and I try to pull away again, but he tightens his grip.

"Please let go."

He releases me with a push and grabs his drink. I rub my sore jaw as I watch him.

He takes a long drink from a flask and winces. "Whoa, that's some strong shit."

"What is it?" My brows pinch together.

"Liquor from my dad's bar. He has the good shit." He holds the metal flask toward me.

"Oh, no, thank you. I don't drink." I move away, shaking my head.

"Oh yeah? You're a good girl, aren't you?" The words send a cold shiver down my spine.

"I guess." I shrug my shoulders as I turn to look at the water.

"Let's go for a swim." He jumps up and shrugs off his shirt.

"No, I'm not feeling well. Can we leave?"

His eyes narrow. "Are you serious, right now?"

"Yes," I stand, taking a step back.

He stares at me, jaw clenched, eyes angry. "Stop being so stuck up. You act like you're too good for everyone."

"What?" I raise my eyebrows, feeling confused.

"You walk around ignoring everyone, and now you're acting like you're too good for me?"

"What!" I gasp. "No, I'm not. I just want to go home."

He takes another drink from his flask.

"I think you should slow down on the drinking."

He laughs humorlessly and starts undoing his jeans. He kicks them off and starts walking toward me. I spin around, but he slides an arm around my waist and grabs me with a tight grip.

"What are you doing?" I scream as I try wiggling out of his grasp, but he's stronger than me. "Let go of me!"

He starts pulling my dress sleeve down my arm. The fear crawls up my skin, leaving goosebumps in its wake as my heart pounds hard against my ribcage. "No," he says, his voice low and hungry against my ear. "I did all this work; you need to loosen up." He grabs my breast and squeezes. "Don't act like you don't want it."

"I don't!" Panic rises, nearly choking me. His hand travels down my thigh and starts pulling my dress up, exposing my legs. His fingers are cold against my heated skin.

"Mmm, so soft." His other hand grabs my jaw, harshly lifting my face, and his mouth smashes against mine with a hard kiss. Vomit begins to rise into my mouth, but I swallow it down. The acid burns its way back down my throat. My trembling hands shove the side of his face, pushing him away. "Damn, baby, you are so sexy," he groans, cupping me over my underwear, and I cry harder.

"Stop! Please!"

He shushes me with an evil grin, staring down at me with soulless eyes that make the blood in my veins freeze as I feel the dread twist in my gut.

"Just give me what I want, babe. I promise I'll make you feel really good," he says, not tearing his gaze away as his finger slips underneath my underwear.

No. God, please help me.

"Get off me!" I scream.

My body begins tingling as a strong wave of power rushes through my veins, making me shiver with the feeling of euphoria. I feel alive as the power buzzes through me.

The next moment, my hands begin to shake, and a bright white light explodes through my fingertips. The blast is so strong that Andrew is ripped away, and my body flies through the air. I feel a slight sting against my back as my body hits the water's surface. I hear the water rippling one second, and the next, I hear nothing as I'm being pulled beneath the water. I open my mouth to scream, but the water quickly rushes into my mouth.

I start to swim up, kicking my legs and pumping my arms as hard as I can since my lungs are burning for air. When I finally hit the surface, a large gasp escapes me. I'm in the middle of the pond; I swim frantically to the edge and claw at the mud as I drag myself out of the water.

I look around with wild eyes, looking for him. I finally spot him lying limp against a tree, on the opposite side of me, and he's passed out. Is he still alive, or did I kill him?

Oh God... What did I do?

My head snaps back toward him when I hear him groan. I need to get out of here before he wakes up; I start running, heading downhill to get back to town.

I quicken my pace as the adrenaline rushes through my veins. I feel my feet pounding against the earth as the branches painfully pierce my bare feet.

My foot gets caught on a tree root, twisting my ankle. I hiss at the sharp pain as my hands catch my fall and the thorns slice through my palms. I groan, looking down at my bare feet covered in cuts. I close my eyes and take a few calming, deep breaths. I slowly try to stand, but my dress gets caught and rips.

I tense when I hear a rustling sound. I ignore the pain and keep running due to the fear pulsing through my body and the terror trailing down my spine.

Don't give up.

The fatigue starts to set in, and I finally see my house up ahead. Sweat is beading down my forehead. My muscles and lungs are burning, but I push myself to keep going.

I push the front door open as I stumble inside, dripping pond water. My feet are covered in mud, and my dress is torn up my thigh. My breath comes in short, broken gasps. Jim sits there in his recliner chair right where I knew he'd be.

"Jim!" I cry, falling to my knees with pure exhaustion, the room reeking of alcohol.

"What the fuck!" he shouts, face twisting with hatred. "You got mud all over the damn floor!" I gasp, looking at him in disbelief.

"Jim. Someone just tried to assault me. Please, call the cops."

He stands slowly, beer sloshing. His lips curl into a snarl as he steps closer. I shrink back. "Call the cops? Look at you, you're dressed like a fuckin whore. Whatever happened, you asked for it."

My mouth falls open. "What?" Horror rushes through me. I know he hates me, but I never knew he'd be this cruel.

"What day is it?" He rubs his chin deep in thought. "Isn't it your birthday? No, that's tomorrow. Fuck it, grab your shit. I want you out of the house, NOW!"

"But…" I start to say as he stands up and slaps me hard across the face. My hand flies to the spot he hit, pressing into the sting.

"Get out! You ruined my life! If it weren't for you, my wife would still be alive! I don't give a *shit* about what happens to you. Just get out of my house and my life. I never want to see you again, grab your shit and leave!" he screams and grabs a fistful of my hair, yanking me toward my room. I claw at his wrist. He opens my bedroom door and shoves me in, and I land so hard I crash onto the floor.

Pain shoots up my elbows, and my side throbs; my vision doubles. I try again, my voice shaking, "Please…"

"Fuck you. I want you out now!" he yells, kicking my side. He leaves the room. My eyes are blurring from the tears I'm trying to hold back.

I throw on clean clothes, grab my mom's picture, and run out without looking back.

Somehow, I make it to Cassie's house. I ring the doorbell before I collapse.

CHAPTER TWO

Almost three years later...

Dimitri

"Prince Dimitri. How kind of you to walk into my office unannounced." Alastair's voice drips with arrogance. He thinks because he's my father's right-hand man, he's untouchable, but now that he's broken one of my rules, even my father can't save him, not that he'd try stopping me.

I am the judge, the punisher, and also the executioner.

Being the bastard of the family has its benefits; they leave me alone to do as I please, not that they could stop me if they tried.

"Funny that you think I need permission to enter my domain."

"Does your father know you're here?"

I watch him silently as my blood boils in anger. He sits calmly in his leather chair behind his desk. "My father doesn't control me," I say, voice low and lethal. "And he won't save you. No one will." I smile, slow and predatorily.

The light flickers as I move toward his desk. "I hear you've been enjoying certain activities that are against my rules."

"And do you have any proof of these rumors?" Alastair tenses up slightly, loosening his tie.

"Do you really think I'd waste my time on a rumor?" I bare my teeth, enraged.

"No, of course not, but I wouldn't break a rule of yours. I'd never disrespect you like that." He shakes his head.

I tap my fingers against his wooden desk before throwing myself over it, grabbing his neck, lifting him from his chair, and slamming his back against the wall. I tilt my head to the side and smirk. "Now you dare disrespect me with lies?"

He shakes his head quickly, his eyes bulging as I tighten my grip, cutting off his air supply.

"Now tell me what I want to know." I drop him like trash. He slumps on the floor, gasping for air. "Any moment now, I'm losing my patience."

"Don't kill me, Prince Dimitri."

"Tell me!" I growl, feeling the force of it shake the ground beneath my feet.

"It's true I brought the human down here to hunt her, but it only happened once. I swear it'll never happen again," he grunts out. He's on his hands and knees, catching his breath.

"And my father?"

"No, of..."

I don't let him finish. I grab his head between my hands and twist till his head is torn off his shoulders, his blood spurts across my face, and his body awkwardly slumps forward.

I inhale deeply, feeling satisfied by the scent of fear and blood in the air. I drop his severed head. I watch as it hits the ground.

I step out of his office. His receptionist is standing there, trembling, eyes wide, watching me.

"Alastair needs assistance cleaning up," I say over my shoulder as I walk away, and a moment later, I hear a high-pitched scream. I arch a brow in amusement, for a demon, his receptionist is an easy scare.

Climbing into the back seat of my SUV, the driver nods at me and then starts driving. I sit there with my chin resting on my fist, and my ankles crossed at the knee as I stare out the window.

Before long, we reach my home, and I find a large envelope at my doorstep. I walk into the house, gripping the envelope tightly in my hand. It crinkles when I set it down. I quickly remove my suit jacket and throw it on the couch. Taking a seat, I tear into the envelope.

Inside is twenty thousand dollars in cash. It also contains a ripped shirt stuffed into the bottom and a message.

The note says it is a piece of his shirt, so my Hellhounds can track the demon down. It is signed anonymously.

More information in the letter states that this man is kidnapping runaways and homeless young women to traffic them to men. I growl; this was happening under my watch.

Fuck this.

I need to deal with this now.

I head to the basement, fury shimmering beneath my skin. My Hellhounds lift their heads as they sense me, red eyes glowing with anticipation. They move closer over, sitting at my feet and looking up at me expectantly. They know it is time to hunt; they can feel my emotions rolling off me. Excitement fills me. It's been a while since we've had a good hunt together.

I throw the torn shirt down in front of them, curling my lip. "Hunt the bastard down and bring him to me alive," I snarl. "Alive, Cerberus, do you hear me?" I point my index finger at him. He growls at me in affirmation, his three heads dipping. He sniffs the piece of clothing. When he is done, he looks up at me, waiting for the go-ahead.

"Let's go."

The moment we step outside, the heat slams into me, thick and heavy. Cerberus bolts ahead, his three heads snarling with excitement.

I spread my wings wide, leaping into the sky, wind slicing by as I cross the valley of Hell. Down here, the air tastes metallic, and the sky is a light red, as if the realm itself is bleeding.

After nearly an hour, Cerberus slows, approaching the outer edge, the place where the lowest demons live. The brick houses have patched roofs, some have boarded windows, and the streets are made of stones.

I land hard, wings folding behind me. The demons stop when they see me, bowing their heads, as they should.

Their fear is practically hanging in the air. Cerberus and I continue walking.

A little girl wearing a pink dress skips toward me. "Hi!" she sings, with a big smile. Cerberus steps forward, snarling violently. The girl squeals, shrinking back.

"Enough." I snap, Cerberus obeys, sitting by my side with his eyes forward.

"My name is Lexie!" she shouts. "It's my birthday today. I'm five now." She holds up her hand, five tiny fingers trembling with excitement. I feel myself soften at her big eyes shining with excitement.

"Happy birthday." I force a smile, which feels unnatural and tight.

A woman runs forward, panic in her eyes. "Lexie, you can't just run off. Prince Dimitri, I'm so sorry." She bows, snatches the girl's hand, and drags her away.

The girl looks back, waving bye, a gesture which I return.

When they head inside the house, I walk to their mailbox, slipping the twenty thousand dollars inside, and start following my hound.

A gasp has me look over my shoulder. The mother has the wad of money in her hands. "Thank you," she whispers, looking up at me.

I nod before turning away.

Cerberus leads me to an old two-story home at the far end of the road. I knock hard.

A demon with a swollen belly violently swings the doors open, ready to yell. His eyes widen when he sees me. "P-Prince Dimitri." His face drains of color.

I hear a cry echo in the air, and it has me moving. I shove past him, and he crashes to the ground.

Weak.

The stairs squeak under my weight. The crying grows louder the closer I get. I hit the bottom step just in time to see a man pinning a girl to the dirt floor, his filthy hands tearing at her clothes.

I rush forward as rage pulses through me, snatch him by the back of the neck, and hurl him across the room. His body slams into the stone wall. I'm on him before he can breathe. My fingers wrap around his throat, lifting him until his feet are dangling in the air, eyes bulging as he stares at me.

Fucking pathetic.

I reach into my pocket and pull out the magical chain, an artifact that prevents the person who wears it from using their magic. The metal hums to life when I snap it around his wrists, and it glows.

My phone vibrates in my pocket, horrible timing.

I answer without looking, snarling. "What?"

"Don't use that tone with me."

"...Eleanor." I stop breathing for a moment. I haven't heard her voice since Damion died. She dropped me like everyone does, but I still respect her.

"I need your help," she says.

"Anything. When?" I drop the trafficker onto his ass like the trash he is.

"Now."

Fuck... I didn't expect that. "I'll be there soon." I hang up, dialing Caspian next.

Screams echo in the background on his end. He must be mid-interrogation, and he doesn't bother hiding it. "Dimitri."

"I need you to do this job for me, and you can borrow Cerberus."

"Oh, hell yeah," he laughs.

"I need you now."

"Give me thirty minutes."

I hang up, crouching beside Cerberus. He leans into my touch as I grab his muzzle. "You obey Caspian. Understand?" He whines softly, then bows his three heads.

Caspian arrives in under twenty-five minutes, smelling like blood. His eyes immediately land on the girls huddled in the corner, shaking. They stare at us, pushing themselves against the wall as tightly as possible.

"Why are you all here?" he asks gently, though the fury vibrating off him is strong.

"Our parents sold us," one girl whispers. "The rest of us... We were homeless, and they tricked us."

I step forward. "You're safe now. You'll live under our protection. You'll have a place to stay, and anything else you may need."

The youngest girl's eyes brighten with hope. "Really?"

"Yes," Caspian says firmly.

"Cerberus," I command, "bring me the other man." He rushes upstairs.

I turn to Caspian. "I have to go and handle this."

He nods. "I've got it under control."

"And Caspian?" I pause at the stairs.

"Yeah?"

"Make his death painful." I nod towards the trafficker.

A slow, cruel smile curls at his lips. "With pleasure."

I summon a portal. The darkness swirls together, and I step through it, landing inside Eleanor's living room.

She's sitting on the couch, glass of wine in her hand, waiting.

"Dimitri." She takes a sip of wine before standing and walking over to me.

"What is it you need?" I narrow my eyes and take a step back.

"Always straight to the point. You need to loosen up, boy." She deeply inhales. "I need you to get my daughter here before her twenty-first birthday."

"Daughter? I thought she died?" I look at her, feeling confused. Why would she lie about that?

"I faked her death for her own safety. I have someone keeping a close eye on her."

"So, you lied to me?" I feel my blood boiling with rage. "But you didn't hide it from the person watching her?"

"I'm sorry, Dimitri, but it's not about you. It's about my daughter; Tammy and Cassie are watching over her. I grew up with Tammy, and she was a better fit to watch over Rosa. She's the only one who knows. It's not that I don't trust you, I do, with my life and hers, but I couldn't risk it. I have already lost everything. I can't lose her as well. Please understand."

I stare at her a moment before taking a deep breath and calming myself.

"I will ask Ian to join me if Cassie is involved. They know each other. When is her birthday, and where is she?"

"Two weeks, and she's in Denver."

"Two weeks?" I growl in annoyance. I abruptly make a portal and leave without another word.

I step into my brother's nightclub. He owns a club that caters to the supernatural, so they all have a place in the human realm where they can be themselves. When everyone sees me, they move out of my way. They know who I am, and they avoid me because of my reputation. I walk upstairs to his office, and his receptionist stands when she sees me, bowing her head to show me respect.

"Sir, Mr. Finch is in a meeting," she says. I watch her visibly shiver with fear. "He says that no one is to bother him."

I flash my fangs at her and hiss.

She flinches and rushes to open the door. My brother's meeting is with two naked women grinding on top of him. His head snaps up, and his eyes widen in shock when he sees me.

"Brother," he pushes the women off him as he stands.

"You two, get out," I declare, my hand gesturing toward the door.

"Whoa, now, calm down. There's one for each of us. I'm sure they wouldn't mind entertaining you." He grins at them. "Right, girls?"

"Yes, of course." They both walk up to me and rub their breasts against my arms.

I grab the black-haired woman by her neck, making sure it doesn't cause any pain, but hard enough to get my point across. My patience is wearing thin. "If you both don't leave now, I'll force you out," I snarl.

They both let go of me and rush out of the office, still naked.

"Now, now, Dimitri, that wasn't nice. You need to learn how to treat women." He buttons his pants and walks over to the bar, pouring himself some scotch. "What is it you want, Dimitri? You haven't come to visit me in decades."

"I need your assistance."

"Oh? For what exactly?" He walks to the large window and looks down to see all the dancers on the dance floor.

"It's for Eleanor." I go and sit down in a chair, unbuttoning my suit blazer.

"Eleanor?" He leans against the glass and looks over at me, arching his brow.

"Yes. We both owe her." I lean forward, resting my elbows on my knees.

"That we do." He nods and rubs his jaw. "What does she need from us?"

"She wants us to get her daughter and take her home within two weeks." I pinch the bridge of my nose in frustration.

"Daughter? Isn't she dead?" He sits in the chair opposite me and leans back, taking a sip of his drink.

"Apparently not, she put her in hiding with Tammy and Cassie. I just found out myself and came straight here."

"Cassie? She's with her?" He seems a lot more interested now.

"Yes, she is, and it's about to be her twenty-first birthday soon. We need to get her before that and take her to her mother."

"Is she aware of who she is?"

"She has no clue what she really is. She thinks she's human."

"This is going to be very interesting," he grunts.

"That it is," I agree.

"I'll call Cassie, see where we should meet, and come up with a game plan."

"I think that would be best." I nod, and we both get up. I leave the club and can only hope this will be easy with no complications.

CHAPTER THREE

Rosa

I wake up gasping for air, my hair sticking to my forehead with sweat. I grab my chest, feeling my heart pounding hard against my ribs like it wants to escape. I let out a shaky breath.

"It was just a dream," I mumble to myself, sitting up.

I never get a full night's sleep. The nightmares wake me in the middle of the night with unwanted memories of cold hands trailing my skin, leaving marks no one else can see.

I have worked on building myself, brick by brick, through counseling, self-defense classes, and dancing. The journey has been very emotional and hard, but I never want to feel so powerless again.

The day that dickhead was arrested, I found out I wasn't his first victim, just the first one with enough evidence that his father's money couldn't bury it. It helps that he is behind bars, but it doesn't make the fear go away.

Cassie even started self-defense classes with me, but in exchange, I had to start dance class. Now, dance is the only place my mind feels safe. It grounds me.

I see the time and scramble up; I'll be late if I don't. I shake myself mentally, shoving the haunting memories aside. I put on my workout leggings and top. Cassie and I usually just meet there since she's an early bird and I'm not. I grab my keys and phone off the charger.

After some toast and coffee, I start walking to class, which is a mile away from our apartment.

I walk slowly, enjoying the morning, inhaling deeply to smell the fresh-cut grass, and listening to the birds chirp. It's the simple things like these that take the edge off.

I get to my class, and Jake walks up to me, smiling.

He's not only a close friend but also my self-defense and kickboxing instructor. He's the first guy I've liked, and he's good-looking with blue eyes, cute shaggy blond hair, round cheeks, and a nice body.

"Hey, Rosa," he murmurs, kissing my cheek and hugging me.

"Hi, Jake." I smirk up at him, "Ready to get your ass kicked?"

"I don't know about that, but you are more than welcome to try."

I smirk. "Oh, it'll happen this time."

He just laughs and shakes his head. "Yeah, sure. Get to stretching, and we'll start."

I start stretching as I watch him head to the corner with the boxing bags. He peels off his shirt and glances over his shoulder, winking at me.

I turn my attention away, heat crawling to my cheeks. The main doors open, and Cassie walks in, rushing over to me.

"Why are you late?" I ask, bending over to touch my toes.

"I went to meet an old friend, and I lost track of time." She shrugs it off and starts stretching with me.

"Oh, someone I know?"

"No, you've never met him." She looks away from me. "Oh, look at Jake over there checking you out. He really has the hots for you," she says, changing the subject.

I can tell she doesn't want to talk about it, so I drop it. "Yeah, I think we're going out this coming weekend." I smile, looking over at him. *Yep, he is definitely checking me out.* I wave my fingers at him. I spy a hint of red on his cheeks, and he looks away quickly.

"You ready for me?" I walk over to him; my eyes travel down his slim, muscular body.

"Of course, bring it." He smirks, and I know he caught me checking him out. We start to kickbox, and he, of course, kicks my ass. "Don't worry, you are in the top five in this class, you are doing great. You are definitely fast. I'll give you that. Would you like help up before I go to my next student?"

I'm currently lying on my back because he kicked me down, and my muscles are screaming at me for pushing them so hard. "Nah, I'm good down here."

He laughs, walking away.

Cassie drives us home. We live in a cute two-bedroom apartment that her mom rents for us. Tonight, Cassie and I are going out, and we plan on just relaxing till then.

I'm eating a bag of chips, lounging on the couch as I flip through Netflix.

"Hey." Cassie walks into the living room.

"Hey." I don't take my eyes off the TV.

"Move your big ass over!" She shoves me playfully.

"You bitch!" I gasp.

"You cunt!"

I move over, huffing. "I'm not sharing my chips!"

"Yes, you will. Or I won't make you breakfast tomorrow!"

I gasp at her, putting my hands on my chest, and then put the bag of chips between us.

"Yeah, that's what I thought!"

"You are so mean, threatening to deny me food when you know it's my one true love." We watch *Lucifer* together for the rest of the day.

I'm currently standing in front of my full-length mirror staring at myself.

"I don't know about this dress. If I bend over, the entire club is gonna get a show." I tug on the dress again as if it'll magically grow in length.

"Oh, come on, mine is shorter than that one!" She has a point. I look over at her, and I see her black dress. It's barely covering her ass.

"Fine. I'll see if I can find something sexy for you that's not a dress."

"See, you do love me." I grin, pulling the dress off.

"Got something!" She skips back into my room. I laugh at her excitement. She knows the bartender, and he said even though I'm not twenty-one, he knows I will be in a week, so they won't say anything about me drinking. "A pair of ripped black jeans and a top."

"You consider that a top?" I ask seriously, picking up the red fabric that's supposedly a top but looks more like a sexy sports bra.

"Oh, don't act like you've never seen a crop top." She rolls her eyes at me. "Plus, you said anything that's not a dress, so you're lucky I didn't get my booty shorts out."

I put it on, and damn... I really like it. I smile at my reflection, looking at the cute high-waisted jeans that are like a second skin, and the red shirt is a corset. I'm showing about two inches of my stomach, enough to make me feel good. I have eyeliner on, some blush, and red lipstick.

Cassie exclaims. "You look smoking!"

"*We* look smoking." I turn away from my reflection, grinning like an idiot.

"One last thing!" She runs out of the room and runs back a minute later with two pairs of black stiletto heels. "I got these online. One pair for you and one for me." She hands me mine, and I put them on.

"Ready to rock the night?" She loops her arm around mine as we enter the nightclub.

"Heck yeah." `

We enter a long, dark hall. I scan the area. Couples are pressing up against each other in the shadows, doing things that should only be done behind closed doors. My heart pounds with excitement. I can feel the bass vibrate underneath my feet.

We finally get to the opening, and I start bopping my head to the pulsating music as I look around the large space.

The green, blue, and pink strobe lights are flashing around the dance floor. The tables are nestled by the bar on the left. The dance floor is on the right of the DJ stand, which has a smoke machine.

I want to go straight to the dance floor, but Cassie grips my hand and starts pulling me toward the stairs with VIP written on them.

"Let's go put our stuff down at our table and get some drinks in us, then we'll go dance." All I do is nod. We walk up to the large bouncer who is standing there with his bulky arms crossed over his chest. We give him our names, and he grabs the clipboard hanging on the wall near him, scanning over the list of names. He nods, then stamps the tops of our hands. The black ink reads VIP, and he steps aside to let us through.

We walk by a couple of tables. I gasp, seeing half-naked women giving men lap dances. We get to our table; it's a large, red U-shaped couch with a table in front.

We order lemon drops and margaritas. They're more than I could probably survive, but why the hell not?

The shots taste horrible, but I wash them away with the tasty margaritas.

Warmth spreads through me in a delicious wave. I'm ready to dance and rock the night, as Cassie said.

I look around because, out of nowhere, I start to feel a tingly sensation crawling across my skin. It almost feels like someone is watching me, but I don't see anyone looking in our direction.

And finally, we head downstairs and find a perfect spot in the center of the dancefloor.

My hand roams down my side, and my other hand is in my hair. I start swinging my hips sexually side to side as I close my eyes, getting lost in the music.

I open my eyes when a pair of hands grab me, to find a good-looking guy, but I want to dance alone. I pull myself away, politely declining the dance, and he shrugs and moves on.

"Hey, Cassie!" I shout over the music and lean closer. "I need some water. I'm going to get some. Are you coming?"

"No, but you'd better come back!" She points her index finger at me.

"I will!"

I head towards the bar. I sit on one of the empty barstools. The bartender makes his way over.

"Just a glass of iced water." I smile. He nods and grabs me one.

I thank him, spinning on the stool to look out onto the dancefloor. I drink my water and look up to roll my shoulders.

And that's when I see him.

The entire world around me seems to fade. My stomach drops, and I can't think straight. My breathing turns labored as my heart flutters in my chest.

He's right above me, upstairs in the VIP section. I can see his high cheekbones, sharp, angular jaw, and broad shoulders. He seems angry at the world. He looks like a god standing there scanning the dancefloor with authority and power like we're all beneath him.

My body feels alive. Then he finally stops searching, and I swear he's looking right at me. I lick my lips slowly as they suddenly feel dry. Half of his face is hidden in the shadows, but I know he's staring back at me. His attention is intense, electric. He moves away from the light, but I can still make out his shape.

I quickly look away, heat crawling up my neck. I just got caught staring at someone like I'm some type of creep. I shake my head, then drink the rest of my water, pull a few dollars from my pocket, and leave them behind.

It takes me a few minutes to find Cassie, and when I do, I touch her to get her attention, so she sees that I'm back. She smiles at me, and so does the guy she's dancing with.

One of my favorite songs comes on, and I sway my hips, getting lost in the music again, enjoying the feeling. I look over to the spot where the Greek God was, and he's back in the light. He's further away, but I know he's watching me like he wants to memorize every single detail. It makes me feel confident.

So, I dance very seductively for him, just him, and I don't care if anyone else is watching. I just hope he's enjoying it.

A few men have asked me to dance, and I have politely declined. I'm patiently waiting for *him*.

A guy grabs me from behind, his hands gripping me roughly. He reeks of alcohol. I spin around, and he sways on his feet. He's drunk, drunk.

"Hey, baby," he murmurs. "Dance with me."

"No, thanks."

He grabs my wrist and pulls me forward. "Come on, sexy." His eyelids are droopy, and his eyes are dilated and bloodshot.

"I said no!" I snap, trying to pull away from his grip.

"Why not? You're dancing alone. I am too, so let's dance together, and maybe I'll buy you a drink."

"I can buy my own drink." I push him off, causing him to stumble backward and almost fall.

"Why are you hot girls always so fucking rude? All I asked for was a fucking dance!" He narrows his eyes and grabs my arm tightly. "So fucking dance with me."

"Hey, let go of me. That fucking hurts!" I shout out.

"Let her go!" Cassie comes beside me, fury blazing in her eyes.

"This has nothing to do with you."

"Let her go." A strong masculine voice growls out from behind me, it's low and lethal. It's cold enough that chills snake through me.

"Fuck off." The asshole turns to look behind me.

"If you don't take your hands off her, I'll fucking break them." The way he says it makes me shiver, but the asshole lets go of me finally.

"You can't just keep the hottest girl in the club all to yourself." He narrows his eyes at the man behind me.

"I can if she doesn't want you. Now leave, I won't ask again," the stranger snarls.

"You're not fucking worth all the fucking trouble." He turns and storms away, thank God.

"Fuck you!" Cassie yells at him. She looks up to the man behind me. "Thank you."

"Yes, thank you." I turn around, my chest tightens, making it hard to breathe.

It's the Greek God from upstairs. Up close, he's devastating and intimidating. He towers over everyone. He's probably six foot five or so. His eyes are slowly drinking me in, his gaze lingering on my face before lowering to my chest. Every single nerve in my body lights up, like a Christmas tree. His eyes are bright blue with long dark eyelashes, which'll make any girl jealous.

"I know you are probably tired of being asked to dance." His lips curve into a sinful smirk. "But will you dance with me?"

Lord have mercy... those dimples, they undo me.

"Well?" He lifts a brow.

"Sorry, what did you say?" I laugh nervously. "I mean, yes. Yes, I'll dance with you." I smile, looking at him.

This beautiful stranger grips my hips, strong and sure, pulling me close. He smells oh, so very good.

He leans in close and whispers in my ear, "Good."

The dark whisper sends a burst of electric sparks through every inch of my body. I bury my face in his neck to breathe him in, unable to stop myself. I suck in a deep inhale of his addictive scent, suppressing a moan.

When he straightens, I place my hands on his broad shoulders and plaster the front of my body to his until every part of our bodies is pressed against each other.

At my height, I'm staring at his chest. I slowly lift my eyes and stare at his full lips. My mouth parts when I see him staring at me intensely like he can't get enough. I bite my lower lip, and his eyes follow the movement.

My hips start moving to the beat, my body is rubbing against his front, and I'm enjoying it way too much.

I feel his fingers graze the skin between my jeans and top, and the contact of our skin touching is addicting, like an addict on crack. Heat explodes over my skin in a slow wave.

A deep animalistic rumble comes from deep within him, and it's a very delicious sound. My mind is in a complete haze of pleasure.

He spins me around, my back slamming against his hard frame. I grind my ass on him. His breath hitches, and I feel him grow harder against me.

His strong fingers crawl beneath my top, and I throw my head back, closing my eyes as his other hand moves my hair to the side to expose my neck. I tilt my head to the side, so he has better access. I feel his warm breath against my ear, making me shudder.

I raise my hand, burying my fingers in his silky hair.

His warm lips move across my neck, kissing and licking. Then his sharp teeth graze my skin, and pleasure rolls through me like hot waves. I rub my thighs together. Goosebumps explode all over my body.

"Oh, God," I moan.

"You like that, Malyshka?" he murmurs, voice thick and heated. The thick accent is wicked and dangerous for my pure soul. I can't bring myself to care.

"Mhm," I hum, lowly. It's all I can manage.

I turn around to face him. I miss the contact of his lips, but not for long. They are now licking and sucking on my collarbone. I lift my left leg to wrap around his thick thigh, but he shocks me when he picks me up effortlessly, so I wrap my legs around his waist.

He pulls back to look at me, and I whimper in protest, causing him to smirk. He's a cocky bastard. I stare into his brilliant blue eyes, which remind me of blue crystal water. His dark, shaggy hair and the stubble over his powerful jaw... But oh... those lips are perfectly full and made for sin.

I want to do naughty things to him.

My back presses against something hard, and I look up. We're not on the dancefloor anymore. We're alone in a dark hallway. My heart slams wildly as he cages me in with his body, his chest rising and falling like he's holding himself back.

I swallow hard. This is dangerous, being alone with a sexy stranger, but I can't bring myself to care.

I peek up at him from beneath my eyelashes, and his lips curl up into a sexy, lopsided grin. His blue eyes glint wickedly, making my heart skip a beat.

Maybe I need a little danger.

He's pushing his powerful body against mine, pinning me to the wall. I can feel my own heartbeat thundering in my ears.

His nose grazes my jaw and neck as he takes in deep breaths, almost like he's smelling me. My stomach clenches with pleasure, and sparks spread all over me.

He pulls back slightly, and his eyes are a shade darker, his jaw clenches, and his nostrils flare.

"I can smell your desire, Malyshka," he growls. "You smell... delicious."

His large hand grips my ass. The animalistic action is claiming and possessive.

"I'd like to kiss you now if you'll allow me," he murmurs, staring intensely at my lips. His eyes flicker in a dark, sinful way. I lick them nervously, and he follows the movement with his eyes, in a slow, predatory way.

I part my mouth to answer, but a voice calls out. "Yo, Dimitri." He tenses, and a muscle ticks in his jaw. He slowly sets me down. I untangle myself from him, already missing his warmth.

Dimitri... I like it.

"What, Ian?" he snarls as he runs his fingers through his hair.

"Why don't you invite her upstairs?" Ian tilts his head toward the stairs.

"Nah, why don't we get out of here and get some food?" He looks over at me.

"Okay, but let me grab my friend." I move past him, and he follows close behind like my own personal shadow.

I find Cassie dancing with a different guy; she agrees instantly. Especially when she sees Ian, who's hot too, but less intimidating and less dangerous... *Who knew I was into bad boys?* I blame the spicy fantasy books I read.

We part ways to grab our things from upstairs and pay our bill, but we find out it's already been paid.

"Where are you two lovely ladies going?" Two men walk up to us. "We'd like to buy you both some drinks."

"We're heading out for the night. Maybe next time, gentlemen," Cassie answers.

"Let's exchange numbers then."

"They're with us," Dimitri says, grabbing my hips, pulling me against him, and Ian wraps his arm around Cassie's shoulder.

"Oh, damn. Sorry, we didn't know." They walk away.

"I leave you alone for a minute, and men are all over you," he whispers in my ear. I laugh, and we head for the door. Cassie offers to take Ian in her car, and Dimitri and I drive together after we all agree to meet at a small diner.

The sleek sports car rumbles to life, and I turn up the heat, feeling cold.

"Here, you can use my hoodie if you're cold." He reaches behind him and pulls out a hoodie from the back. I immediately pull it on, and it swallows me completely because of how big it is on me. I roll up the sleeves and then snuggle deep into his leather seats.

"Thank you," I whisper.

He hits the accelerator so hard that I'm pushed back in my seat. I put a hand against my chest. God, please help me. He drives fast and full of confidence. His strong hand is wrapped tightly around the gearshift, and the other is gripping the steering wheel. He looks a little tense. I bite down on my lower lip, looking away. I never knew hands could be so sexy.

"What's your name, beautiful?"

Oh, God. My face heats as embarrassment slams into me. "Rosa," I mumble. I don't know what's wrong with me. It's like I don't have control of my actions, but I don't regret it.

"Rosa," he tests my name, and it rolls perfectly off his tongue. "I like it." He winks, and I nearly melt in my seat.

We pull into the diner, and Cassie is sitting on the edge of her car hood with Ian standing between her legs. It looks like they are having a serious conversation. About what, though? They just met. They quickly pull apart when they see Dimitri's car.

We park beside them. Dimitri gets out of the car, jogs over to my side, and opens the door for me. He reaches out to grab my hand and help me out. Every time our skin touches, I feel an electric shock; it's probably just static.

When I'm fully out, he pulls me close, like he can't stand the distance. I wrap my arms around his slim waist under his leather jacket.

We walk into the diner, and the waitress's jaw hangs open, staring at Dimitri. I narrow my eyes at her, but she never looks my way. We settle into a booth toward the back corner. He grabs a menu and slides it over to me. I pick it up and glance through the options.

"Hi there." The waitress smiles at Dimitri as she openly stares. "My name is Cara."

He never looks up at her. He keeps his eyes on me. "Get whatever you want, okay?"

"Okay. Um, I'll do the cheeseburger with fries and a strawberry milkshake."

"Nothing for you?" she asks Dimitri. "I can help you look through the menu, if you'd like?" She taps his shoulder.

Anger spreads through me. My hand tightly grips the fork sitting on the table. I'd love to jam it into her hand.

Well... that's new. I have never been a violent person, never thought of harming someone.

"Remove your hand and go get my girl her food," he snarls at her.

My girl... For the second time, my insides melt.

Cassie and Ian finally walk in and sit across from us. Cassie waves at the waitress and orders the same thing I did, except with a chocolate shake.

"You guys aren't eating?" I ask, looking at Ian and Dimitri.

"No, we ate before going to the club," Ian says. Dimitri squeezes my waist; I look up at him to find him already staring at me.

He reaches under the hoodie I'm wearing, and his fingers gently brush against my skin. His eyes darken slightly and drop to my lips, like he wants to taste me. His nostrils flare as he tries to control himself. I feel like he's staring deeply into my soul.

Cara shows up with the food, and we pull apart as Cassie and I start eating.

"Mmm, this burger is so good," I groan.

"Yeah, it is," Cassie agrees with her mouth full.

Ian laughs at us. "You are too adorable," Ian says to Cassie.

"Adorable? Don't ever call me adorable!" Cassie gasps, smacking his shoulder. "Adorable is for a baby or a puppy! Me? I'm not adorable. No, I'm sexy or hot, whichever you prefer."

"What about beautiful?" he asks her as he kisses the top of her head.

"Hmm. Well, I guess that'll do." She grins wickedly.

Cara drops off the bill and has written her number on it. Dimitri picks it up, and I'm worried he might shove it in his pocket. She's pretty, after all, with large breasts that are about to pop out of her top that is two sizes too small. I'm shocked when he rips it in half and throws a hundred-dollar bill on the table as he grabs my hand and pulls me up.

"Can I see you tomorrow?" Dimitri pulls me against his body once we're outside in the parking lot.

"Yes," I reply, breathless. He gives me his phone, and I add my number with shaky fingers.

"Time to go, girlie." Cassie drags me away. I look back at him when I open the passenger side door, and he's in the same spot. His hands are in the front pocket of his blue jeans.

Cassie pulls out after I get in, and I turn around in my seat. I stare at him standing there until we turn the corner, and he disappears from sight.

"Oh, my fucking gosh!" Cassie screams.

"What?" I shout in shock at her screaming.

"You! Rosa, you!" She grabs my arm, shaking me.

"Me? What about me?" I ask, innocently.

"I have never, ever in my whole life, seen you act like this with anyone. Let alone a guy! You were pretty much having sex with him in the club back there!"

"No.... no, we were not!" I gasp as I put the hoodie over my head, trying to hide my face.

"Yes, yes, you were! He's smoking hot. I don't blame you. Don't be embarrassed. I'm happy for you, girl, so happy!"

"I've never felt this way before. I don't know what's wrong with me. Maybe I'm going crazy."

"No, you just need some dic..."

"Don't you dare finish that sentence," I cut her off, and she laughs hard. "I feel so bad. What about Jake?"

"Girl, what about him? I know you don't like him like that."

"But he's so nice."

"Apparently, *nice* is not what your heart or body wants."

"How do I tell him, though? I can't go on that date next weekend knowing how I feel about another person, even if nothing goes on between Dimitri and I. I don't want a relationship unless it feels like this."

"Just tell him you met someone." She shrugs like it's not a big deal.

"Yeah, I guess so."

"So, he's coming to pick you up tomorrow?"

"Yeah, I think so." I slowly smile.

"I can't believe my best friend, the good girl, likes bad boys." Cassie teases me.

Honestly, I can't believe it either. I shake my head. "I'm like a different person around him." I look out the window. I don't know if that's a good or a bad thing.

We finally get home, and I take off my clothes, but I put Dimitri's hoodie back on.

It smells like him, masculine and intoxicating.

Chapter Four

Dimitri

When I watched her walk into the club tonight, looking the way she did... I considered throwing her over my shoulder and locking her away, hiding her from the world. I don't want another man looking at her.

I watched her dance, and shit... I almost snapped as rage tore through me when they touched her with their filthy hands like they had the damn right to. I wanted to break their fucking fingers one by one, so they could never touch her again. The anger I felt consumed me, making my blood boil.

Let's just say it's a good thing she declined their offers.

I had no idea why I felt so strongly for her. Is she beautiful? Yes, the kind of beauty that could bring kings to their knees.

Then, when I finally touched her, I knew why I felt the way I did.

She's my mate... my fucking mate.

I don't know what to do with that truth. I know I want her. No, I fucking need her, but I also know I don't deserve her. A demon with darkness in his veins and soul. She's too pure for me, too soft.

Am I going to be selfish and keep her, or do I let her go?

I'm a monster. I don't deserve her sweetness, beauty, warmth, or that kind of love.

Women were just a quick fuck, nothing more.

She deserves to be held, to get everything she desires, someone to shower her with kisses and affection, and that's not me.

I crave violence. I can't love her the way she deserves. Yet that darkness in me doesn't give a fuck… It wants to take her, not giving a shit about the consequences.

"What the flying fuck was that?" Ian shouts. "You were all over her. You aren't supposed to fall in love. Don't complicate it. We take her and drop her off. That's it. Easy, fast, and done!"

I start my car, fingers tightening on the steering wheel. I need to release this tight tension coiling inside me.

"Change of plans. We can't kidnap her. We use Cassie and get her to trust us. She'll come with us willingly." I run my hand through my hair.

"What the fuck are you saying?" he seethes. "I'm not using Cassie like that, plus she'll never agree to that."

"Yes, you will because I said so."

"You forget so easily that I'm next in line to become king of the underworld."

"And don't you forget that I can take that title in a heartbeat." My voice drips dangerously. "I'm stronger than both of you combined. The Hellhounds bow down to me, not you. That makes me in charge, no matter your title; we both know the hounds choose the ruler of the underworld. They only bow to power, dark and lethal power. Just remember, that is me, not you."

He says nothing in response. He knows he pushed me too far. We drive in silence the rest of the way.

When we arrive, I slam the door shut, lean against it, and cross my arms over my chest.

"She's my fucking mate, Ian." When he climbs from the car, I turn to look at him. "I can't hurt her, but I can't be with her. I can't claim her as mine, I don't think." I rub the side of my face with my hand in frustration.

"No fucking way." He leans forward, placing one hand against the open door and the other on the car hood.

"Why the fuck would I lie about that?"

"Why the fuck did you not claim her? Do you have any idea how rare that is?"

"Of course I do. I just can't." I storm away, walking toward the house.

"Why the hell not?" He shoves me hard, and I let him.

I look away, "She's Damion's daughter, Ian."

"So what?"

"Do you really think he wants a monster like me with his daughter?" I finally yell back, the darkness inside rising fast.

"He's dead. Who fucking cares!" He throws his hands up.

"I do. I owe him everything! I won't do that to him."

"I think he'd be honored. You'll love her and protect her. Dimitri, don't be stupid."

"I can't."

"Don't do this. This bond is a once-in-a-lifetime. It's like a dream ... everyone prays for a mate, and you just want to throw it away!" His eyes turn dark black.

"This is none of your concern." I turn to walk away.

"The fuck it ain't!" he growls.

I snap, my hand wraps around his throat, lifting him off the ground as I snarl. "Don't forget your place. You don't want Father to find out." I see his eyes go round in fear and turn to their normal color. I toss him down and walk away.

When I get to my room, I growl and punch a hole through the wall.

I get into the shower and press my forehead against the shower wall. The demon in me is pissed, trying to claw his way out. He's as desperate for her as I am. He wants to mark and claim her.

I close my eyes and think about the way our bodies move together, perfectly so. The way her skin felt against my hand, and the way my whole body lit up and raged with fire. The way the air crackled with electricity, and I could hear the thunderous drum of her heart.

The way her beautiful, long, thick hair moved around her, her dark eyelashes fluttered against her pink cheeks, and those gorgeous, brilliant green eyes that I could stare into for eternity... And *fuck*, those breathless moans. She was made for me, and I for her.

I groan, needing her. I want her, but I can't have her.

This is a perfect punishment for someone like me. I learned how to numb the pain, but I never expected this type of pain. This hunger, the longing is so deep I'm afraid it'll never go away. I feel weak.

"Fuck!" I growl as I hit the wall, and tiles shatter against my feet. I turn off the water, grab a towel, and wrap it around my hips.

I lean my hands against the sink, gripping the sides as I look at my reflection, snarling at myself. This is bullshit.

It doesn't matter anyway. She'll fear me the way others fear me, and I can't handle that...

She has the power to break me, break the demon prince.

And I will let her.

Why would a beautiful angel like her want an ugly monster like me?

I curl my hand into a tight fist and hit the mirror hard. My knuckles start bleeding, but the cut will close in a few seconds.

I quickly pull on sweats and a black hoodie. I throw the hood over my head. After I tie my running shoes, I leave the house and run for hours; the world blurs around me.

When I stop, I'm on the edge of a ledge, and I roar loudly. I hear all the animals scatter away. Like everything else, they are frightened to be around me, too, and soon, she'll be just as scared of me and disgusted by who I am.

My own father doesn't want me, and my stepmother hates me because of the affair my father had with my mother.

My mother and Damion were close friends, and he took me in after she passed and raised me with Eleanor, his mate. She's the only one alive who loves me and is not scared of me.

Even though I know Ian cares for me. I also know he fears the monster inside of me.

The demon inside me is the strongest that has ever lived. Even my father fears it.

I rush to her apartment. I look around to make sure no one is around, then jump to her window and slowly open it without making a noise.

I need her.

I fucking crave her.

She has become my fucking obsession.

I land with a soft thump. She's lying on her back, one leg tucked in her blanket, and the other in view, teasing me. She's still in my hoodie. My scent is mixed with hers, and my demon rumbles with approval, which makes her change positions. I see a hint of red lace between her thighs, but I quickly look away.

I stare at her beautiful face as I step closer.

She looks perfect, her lips are slightly parted as her chest rises and falls with every breath she takes.

Out of nowhere, she whimpers, "No, don't hurt me."

The rage boils within me, my veins are feeling like hot wires, and my teeth are clenched so hard my jaw aches.

I will find them, and I will kill them... But for now, I will comfort her.

With my fingertips, I lightly touch the side of her face, rubbing her soft, smooth skin. An electric shock wave runs through my body, making me groan in pleasure.

She hums and snuggles into my hand.

I tilt my head to the side as I watch the pathetic excuse of a man asleep in a gray recliner, his hand resting on his round stomach, and the other dangling on the side of his recliner, still clutching a beer can.

I kick my leg up and slam my boot on his bare foot. He jolts awake and drops the beer can. I watch as it drops to the floor, and the beer spills out, fizzling.

"Who the fuck are you?" His voice is hoarse.

"I'm your worst fucking nightmare, Jim."

He straightens his shoulders as he stands. "Get the hell out of my house before I call the cops." He quickly pulls a cellphone out of his front pocket.

"The cops won't save you from my wrath." I rush toward him, gripping his wrist and twisting. He screams as he drops the phone. I spin him around and slam his face against the side table.

"What do you want? I don't have any money," he cries out.

"I want nothing from you except your death."

"Oh God, please." He begins thrusting around in my hold.

"God can't save you," I hiss as I grip the back of his neck and throw him hard against the floor. I reach into my back pocket and pull out my knife. He watches me in horror as I throw the knife into the air and catch it.

"W ... why are y... you doing this?" he stumbles on his words as he tries crawling away. I stalk toward him, and my foot slams against his upper back, pushing him down.

"You hurt my mate, and you will pay for your sins."

"No, I swear it wasn't me." I crouch down and grab his wrist once more. His body is trembling with fear. "Who is your mate?"

"Rosa." I watch as his eyes light up with recognition. He opens his mouth to say something, but I swing my knife and watch in fascination as it slashes his fingers clean off. I bask in his screams...

His blood splatters across my face as he screams in agony. I grin wickedly at the sweet sound.

I repeat the action with his other hand as he pleads for mercy. With his hair in my grip, I pull his head back tightly as I position my knees between his shoulder blades and hunch over, declaring, "You will pay for your sins with death, but even in death I will continue to make you pay."

I slice his throat with one clean cut, and I listen as he gurgles and chokes on his blood. I stand and watch as his body convulses for a minute, and then he slumps to his death.

CHAPTER FIVE

I wake up to the smell of food. I groan, snuggling deeper into Dimitri's hoodie, but my stomach growls. I groan, looking at the time. It's too early to get up, but my stomach protests at the smell of bacon and coffee.

Hmmm, food or sleep? It's honestly a hard decision, but my stomach is the victor and wins this battle.

"Fine, you win!" I mutter to my belly.

Sitting up, I rub my face, and when I look down, my hands are smothered in black. I must have forgotten to remove my makeup. My phone dings. I shove it into my pocket. I'll read the message later.

I look at my reflection, and I start laughing at myself. I look like a raccoon. I wash my face and then brush my teeth. My eyes narrow to the spot on the left side of my neck. I grab my hair and move it to the side. There's a bruise on my neck. It's clear as day. And in the center? Teeth marks... A clear claim.

I can't believe it.

My fingers trace the bruise, and the memories slam into me... The way he made me feel when his sharp teeth grazed my skin, and his strong hands were on my soft skin. The way he held me was as if he had already claimed me as his. My thighs rub together as a pulse starts between them. I shake myself mentally. I need help covering this.

"Cassie?" I call as I leave my room, not bothering with pants since the hoodie hits mid-thigh.

Cassie turns with a grin, but my attention is on someone else.

Dimitri stands beside her, looking like absolute sin with his black V-neck top, leather jacket, and blue jeans.

Oh yeah, Ian is here, too, but I'm not too worried about him.

"Oh, uh, hi!" I choke out awkwardly.

"Good morning." He walks closer to me, his nostrils flare. Do I smell bad? I should have showered. He leans into me and whispers, "You look amazing in my hoodie."

"Thanks," I swallow. "It's really comfortable. Would you like it back?"

"Nah, keep it. It looks better on you." His gaze drops to my neck, and he smirks, dangerously slow. "That looks good, too."

My throat tightens, and I swear my soul leaves my body.

"Food is ready!" Cassie hollers.

We all sit at the dining table, and Dimitri sits next to me. His right arm is resting on the back of my chair.

Cassie puts bacon with eggs and toast on our plates, and we thank her.

She and Ian sit across from us.

Dimitri reaches down and grabs the bottom of my chair, drags it until our thighs are touching. Now all I can think about is the warmth of his thigh touching mine.

"Much better." His arm drapes over the back of my chair again.

"Earth to Rosa." Cassie is now leaning across the table, waving a hand in front of my face.

"Hm, what was that?" I ask, blinking a few times to get my brain to focus.

"Did you call Jake? He called me, worried about you." Dimitri tenses beside me. His jaw is clenched tightly, his hand drifts down my thigh, in a claiming way.

"No, I haven't checked my phone."

"Jake has a crush on Rosa. It's so adorable, you should see how he watches her," she sighs dramatically. "He's good-looking, too. He and our Rosa here are supposed to go on a date."

My eyes narrow. *What is she doing?*

A low growl vibrates around the room, his fingers squeeze my thigh, possessively.

"I need a coffee." I stand, pushing my chair back.

In the kitchen, I take a deep breath, trying to calm my nerves. I pull out my phone to see that, in fact, Jake has called and there are a few texts. I'll call him later. I place my phone on top of the countertop.

I jump when I feel a hand slide around my waist.

"Sorry. I just wanted to check on you," Dimitri's deep voice whispers near my ear, his body pressing into mine like he can't help himself.

"Oh, yeah." I let out a small laugh, melting into his touch. "I'm fine. Do you want some?" I ask as I pour my coffee into my mug, stepping away from him.

"Yes, black." He holds his empty mug out, and he adds like he forgot, "Please."

"Of course." I smile and grab his mug with trembling fingers, trying to avoid touching him.

But when I give it back, our fingers brush. I feel the same delicious spark as the night before. I quickly turn away, grabbing the creamer from the fridge.

"So, are you dating this Jake guy?"

"No, I guess...?"

"You guess?" His hand grips my hips, forcing me around to face him.

"I mean, it's not like that..." I stare at the way his shirt stretches across his hard chest.

"So, you're not dating?" He grips my chin, making me look up at him.

"No, we haven't been on an actual date."

"Good," he sounds smug as he walks out of the kitchen.

"Holy hell..." I whisper, fanning my face. He makes me want to sin like some type of devil.

When I sit down, Dimitri leans back, resting an arm around my chair again.

He moves his hand down to my thigh, rubbing his finger in small circles against my skin. Goosebumps erupt across my skin, and I can't stop the moan that slips out.

Everyone looks up...

Dimitri hides his smirk behind his mug, but I saw it.

"Sorry," my face heating as I hold up my mug. "The coffee is good."

"No, it's okay. That was kind of sexy." Ian smiles, and Dimitri gives him a death glare.

We start talking about spring break. Ian takes a drink from his water bottle, and I swear his eyes turn black. I blink, and they are back to their original blue color. Cassie talks me into a short trip with Ian and Dimitri this weekend.

Ian and Cassie leave after breakfast. I clean up as Dimitri watches me.

"I want to take you out for a little ride, if that's okay with you?" Dimitri says after a few minutes of silence.

"Yeah, let me go get changed."

I stand in front of my closet, not knowing what to wear. Something casual or nice? I finally pick a pair of blue jeans, and I wiggle them on. I take the hoodie off, looking for a shirt.

There's a light knock. I look up, and Dimitri is leaning against the door frame with his hands in his pockets.

His gaze slowly travels down my body, and the muscle in his jaw is pulsing as he looks away.

"You left this in the kitchen. Someone was trying to call you." He holds up my phone, showing it to me before setting it on top of my dresser. Then he leaves without another word.

Oh God, I'm wearing a red lace bra, no wonder he rushed out.

I grab a random shirt and put it on.

"Ready," I call out, walking toward the living room. He's leaning against the arm of the couch, looking good enough to eat. "I'm sorry about that back there. I'm not used to closing my door."

"It's okay. I should have waited." His eyes are on my neck, and shoot, I forgot about the large hickey there.

"I'll go cover this with some foundation. I'll be back."

Dimitri straightens, "No."

"No?" I arch my eyebrows in surprise.

"I like seeing my mark on you. Don't hide it."

Warmth spreads through me, settling in my lower stomach.

"Let's go." We head outside, and I follow him to the back of the parking lot.

My heart leaps with excitement when we stop next to a sleek black motorcycle. It's sexy... a sexy beast like its owner.

"Is this yours?" I ask.

"Yes, do you like it?"

"I love it. I've always wanted to ride on one, never got the chance." I smile, walking around to look at it and touch the leather seat. When I was younger, my stepdad had one, and he used to promise me he'd teach me how to ride, but of course, that never happened.

"I'm glad I'll be your first ride." His deep voice dips low, sensual. He comes up behind me, pressing a kiss against his mark. My toes curl in my shoes as my breath quickens.

"Oh, yeah?" I breathed out softly, turning my head to meet his gaze. Our noses are touching. I can feel his minty breath caressing my lips.

"You ready, gorgeous?" His thumb softly caresses my chin.

"Yes..." I want him to kiss me. He smiles down at me, showing me those sexy dimples, making my heart go haywire.

"Here, wear this helmet." He picks it up and is about to put it on my head, but I stop him.

"What about you?" I ask when I only see one helmet.

"Worried about me, huh?"

"Yeah, I don't want you to get hurt."

"Don't worry about me. I'm invincible," he laughs, and I like the sound; it's a deep husky roar, and I want to hear it more.

He pulls the helmet over my head and snaps it.

He climbs on the motorcycle and turns to pat the back. I swing my leg over the seat, pressing my inner thighs around him.

"Hold on to me tight, okay, Malyshka?"

I really need to Google that, so I know what it means. I wrap my arms around his waist, and the motorcycle roars to life as it rumbles beneath us. "Ready?" he asks as he kicks the stand up.

"Yes!"

He starts backing up, and we drive slowly to the main road. As soon as we get on the main road, he presses the pedal, speeding up, I grip him tighter. Not because of the speed, no, because I want to feel him closer. My nails dig into his hard stomach, and his abs clench beneath my fingers.

After a few minutes, I tilt my head back and laugh. The feeling is thrilling. I feel free... good, like I'm flying.

We stop at a red light.

"Are you enjoying yourself back there?" He places his hand on my thigh, right above my knee.

"God, yes."

A motorcycle stops beside us, revving its engine.

"Wanna race?" the man asks.

Dimitri ignores him, tightening his grip on my thigh.

"Come on, dude. If I win, I get your girl to ride on mine."

"Fuck off," Dimitri growls out. I feel his back tense up.

"You scared, bro? Doll face, come ride with a real man."

"I have myself all the man I need, right, baby?" I drag my hands up, roaming his hard chest.

Dimitri exhales sharply, "Damn straight."

The light turns, and Dimitri races off, leaving the other biker in the dust.

Fifteen to twenty minutes later, we slow down and park at a state park.

I jump off, and my legs are a little unsteady. Dimitri hops off, helping me take the helmet off and placing it on the motorcycle.

"That, back there, was very sexy." His hand touches the side of my face, and his thumb lightly grazes my lower lip.

"Was it now?"

"Fuck yeah." He grabs me by the hips, pulling me into him. His gaze drops to my lips. "May I?"

I'm just about to nod when giggling ruins the moment. I pull away, parents are loading their kids into their car, and the mom is giving us a nasty look.

"Let's go." He takes my hand and pulls me forward. We are surrounded by tall trees. This state park is one I have yet to visit. I should be terrified walking through the woods with a stranger, but I feel safe with Dimitri.

We walk for a couple of miles, but then he pulls me off the trail. I'm trying to avoid getting hit by tree branches, and I'm struggling on this rocky pathway. My sandal gets caught on a branch, and I fall into Dimitri's back.

"I'm sorry. These are not the proper shoes for a hike."

"Come here." He bends at the knee. "Jump on my back."

"No, I'm way too heavy for you."

"I highly doubt that gorgeous. Now, come on, I'm not taking no for an answer."

"Okay..."

I grip his broad shoulders and climb on his back. His hands rest on the back of my knees as he starts walking again.

"Are you okay with my weight?" I ask, placing my chin on his shoulders.

"I'm fine, you weigh nothing," he replies.

Chapter Six

Rosa

He walks with me on his back for miles, but I'm not complaining. I look around, feeling at peace. I gaze up, watching birds fly by, singing. The sunlight shines through the trees' canopy. I have always loved state parks; they make me feel... calm. And being here with him just makes it better.

"Are you sure you're okay? I can walk now; it's not bumpy," I ask for like the tenth time, feeling bad.

"Yes," he replies instantly, unbothered. "I've got you."

"You know," I breathe softly, "you're pretty strong if you can carry me on your back this long. Not even out of breath."

He chuckles, "I try to stay in shape as best as I can."

I turn my head, my eyes drinking in the way his muscles flex beneath me. There are black markings on the curve of his neck peeking from beneath the collar of his shirt.

"What's that?" I ask, tracing the little piece going into his shirt without thinking. He shudders violently beneath my touch, and I smile.

"A part of a tattoo." He replies, slightly turning his head to look over his shoulder, his eyes dark, hungry.

"Can I see it?"

"Trust me, you will." His voice is full of confidence, which makes my breath shudder. "When we get there. It's up ahead." He keeps moving, and that's when I hear it, a soft roar of rushing waters. He sets me down gently. We round the large tree, and there it is.

I take off in a run, heading toward the waterfall.

"Rosa! Be careful … slow down."

I stop to look at the edge of the water. From our current location, I can see the summit of the mountain and realize that we are at its foot. I look around in awe, and that's when I see the blanket on the ground with a cooler sitting on it.

"Dimitri… Did you do this?" I spin around.

"Do you like it?" He rubs the side of his neck nervously.

"Do I like it? Gods, Dimitri, it's amazing. When did you even have time to do this?"

"I couldn't sleep, so I came up here early with Ian, and he helped me set it up for you."

Rare emotions choke me, my chest tight. I take a step toward him; I can't hide my emotion spilling from my voice. "It's beautiful, seriously. Thank you." I move forward; my steps quicken as they carry me to him. My arms wrap around him, my face pressing into his chest. He's frozen for a second, and finally, he embraces me back, carefully. It warms my heart. I tighten my grip, needing him closer, my fingers digging into him. He pulls me closer, his face in my hair, my feet nearly off the ground. We stay like that for a while, soaking in the feeling.

Until I ruin it when my stomach rumbles.

He laughs, squeezing me before pulling away, grabbing my hand, and leading me to the blanket.

I slip my sandals off before I sit beside him. He opens the cooler and pulls out some containers and a glass bottle of iced coffee.

"Cassie told Ian you liked chicken salad bagels. I made the chicken salad and the muffins; they are chocolate chip. I hope you like them. The iced coffee is from your favorite café."

I stay silent in complete awe as I watch him open each container for me. He pulls out a bagel and starts putting the sandwich together with so much focus that his brows are furrowed. It melts my heart.

He hands me the plate, our fingers touch, sending a spark up my arm. He grabs the bottle of iced coffee and shakes it, then opens it and hands it to me. Then he starts making his sandwich.

Once he's done, I take a bite. The flavors explode in my mouth, and I groan, rolling my eyes.

"Oh my god, Dimitri. It's the best chicken salad I've ever had."

"Really, you think?"

"Yes." He smiles widely at me.

"I'm happy to know you like it. I only ever cook for myself."

When I finish, I lick my fingers clean of spilled sauce.

"Where did you learn how to cook?"

"I...." he hesitates, voice low. "My mother loved cooking a lot. When she passed away, I kept all her recipes and taught myself."

"I'm sorry." My hand shifts, curling around his fisted one. "How old were you when she died?"

"I was ten or eleven. I can't remember exactly, but I was young." He threads our fingers together and looks away from me, his jaw ticking. The waterfall is the only sound for a while. I decide to open up, even though it's no secret that I don't like talking about it.

"My adoptive mom died too when I was fifteen. I understand how hard it is to lose someone." I say gently, rubbing my thumb against his skin. "Who watched over you when she passed?"

"My father did at first, but then wanted nothing to do with me. I was a mistake from an affair. A close friend of my mom's took me in."

"My adoptive father didn't want me, but was forced to watch me until I turned eighteen. It was a rough three years with someone who hated me. At least you had Ian."

"Ian and I weren't raised together; we're half-brothers. We used to hate each other, actually." He laughs. "But the older we got, we thought it was ridiculous to hate each other for a mistake our father made, but my other half siblings don't agree with Ian."

"I think it's ridiculous to hate someone who has no choice in the matter. It's great you both have each other now."

"I agree." He nods stiffly, and with his free hand, he picks up a muffin and hands it to me. I take a large bite, and oh God... It's perfect, the chocolate melting in my mouth.

"Can I hire you as my cook?" I joke.

"I'll cook for you any time you ask me to," he says, looking at me, eyes shining with amusement. He leans over, and with the pad of his thumb, he wipes the corner of my mouth. "Chocolate," he explains, his hand lingers a moment more than necessary.

"What do you do for a living, anyway?" I ask as I lie down looking up at the beautiful sky. Watch the birds flying above us. Dimitri lies next to me, and I smile at him. He's already gazing back at me.

"I'm a bounty hunter. I think that's the right term. I take bad guys where they belong, so they get the right punishment."

"Oh, do you enjoy it?" I roll to my side to face him and start playing with the zipper on his leather jacket.

"I do enjoy it. The feeling of making people pay for their sins... is thrilling." He smirks.

"Yeah, I think a lot of people get away with shit." I watch a lot of crime shows. I can picture him catching bad guys.

He gets up and slowly pulls off his leather jacket. I have yet to see him with it off, and I'm not disappointed by what's underneath. I knew he had broad shoulders by touch, but lord have mercy...His shirt is tight on his shoulders, and his right arm is completely covered in tattoos.

He then reaches for the hem of his shirt and pulls it off.

I squeeze my eyes shut, but not before seeing sculpted abs and strong pecs covered in ink.

"What are you doing?!"

"You asked to see my tattoo earlier, remember?"

Right... I do remember, now.

"Open your eyes, Malyshka."

I do, and oh God...

His pecs, his shoulders, his abs. God took his time carving him into perfection. He was put on this earth to tempt me, to cause me to sin. The tattoos swirl over his chest and wrap around his shoulder, then snake down his arm. They're dark, beautiful, and dangerous.

I rise and gently trace the dark marks on his chest. He trembles beneath my touch, a shiver that makes me smile. I have the same effect on him as he does on me when we touch.

I slowly walk around to his back, still tracing his tattoos. They stretch across his back. I can see scars all over his back. Long and jagged, they almost looked like whip marks, except for the large V mark in the center of his shoulder blades. I graze them, and sense him tense. My throat tightens as I swallow. I long to kiss away every scar, erasing the painful memories behind them.

Impulsively, I kiss his many overlapping scars, each one gently; they are raised slightly, yet surprisingly smooth to the touch. He exhales slowly, a needy sound as he relaxes and stands still, allowing me to finish. Finally, I stand on my toes, stretching to kiss the back of his neck. His skin explodes in goosebumps.

"Rosa," he groans desperately. He spins so fast, picking me up as if I weigh nothing. The next thing I know, he has me pressed against a tree, his mouth attacks mine.

The kiss is fierce and demanding, possessive, almost as if he's claiming and branding me as his. The heat that floods me is sharp and overwhelming.

His tongue demands its way into my mouth, and I allow it, kissing him back. My head is fuzzy, filled with so much need and pleasure. I'm a throbbing mess.

He lets out the sexist groan from deep in his throat. The ache worsens, so I start to rub myself against him, needing more...*Oh God, please....*

I moan into his mouth. My hands are slowly traveling up his chest and wrapping around his neck, grabbing ahold of his silky-smooth black hair, burying my fingers. My skin feels like it's on fire; my body feels alive and wonderful. I see stars explode in my closed eyes. The wind suddenly stirs violently around us, leaves lifting off the forest floor.

His lips travel to my jawline and slowly down to my neck. When he gets there, he sucks and licks like he's starving for a taste, and maybe he is because I'm desperate for his lips on my skin.

He pulls away, and I cry out. I'm about to yell at him, but he grabs my shirt and slowly rips it off. He looks down at me in my lacy red bra, licking his upper lip.

"So, fucking perfect, Malyshka. You are so beautiful, it blows my mind that you're all mine. You are too perfect for me, and I don't know how I deserve you."

He leans in, kissing my collarbone and down to the valley of my breasts. He grabs my left breast with his hand, squeezing it while kissing my right breast. He bites my nipple through the lace. Burning heat builds slowly in my core. I can't take it, it's too much. I arch my back; the back of my head grazes the tree bark behind me.

"Dimitri," I moan softly. His hand slowly goes down to the button of my jeans, unclasps it, and he quickly starts pulling my jeans off.

Am I ready for this? No...

His fingers slowly enter my underwear, but I grab his wrist.

"I'm sorry, Dimitri, I ca... I can't... I'm not rea-ready for that." I stumble on my words, so worried he'll be mad. He pulls back, looking into my eyes, and his finger gently caresses my cheek. His lips are swollen from our kisses.

"It's okay, love. I'll wait till you're ready." He leans in and kisses my lips softly.

"Really? You're not mad at me?" I blink slowly, dumbfounded; most men get so mad.

"Why the hell would I be mad? Rosa, I have waited a long time for you, and I can wait longer. Now, come on, I need to be cooled off."

He pulls off his jeans and then picks me up, throws me over his shoulder, making me laugh. He runs, and I feel us in the air, and then we hit the water. It's shocking and cold, but somehow, instantly, it warms.

We separate underneath the water. I look around and find him swimming toward me. He grabs me. I wrap my legs around his waist.

We pop out of the water, laughing. His hair is wet. I watch as he slicks it back with his fingers. I bite down on my lower lip.

I place my hands flat on his muscular chest. My fingers slowly trace their way down his six-pack, stopping where his V disappears underneath his shorts. My heart starts beating wildly in my chest.

I feel his rough fingers wrap tightly around my hips, pulling me closer. "You like what you see?" His voice is low and seductive against my ear before he sucks my earlobe between his teeth, causing my body to tremble in pleasure.

"Yes." I hiss as my stomach clenches. I nearly beg him to finish what he started earlier.

I need space. I slip beneath the water, swimming away, putting much-needed distance between us. I spin around. I'm on the opposite side of Dimitri, who watches me.

"Come here." He groans as if the distance pains him. I shake my head. He clenches his jaw and runs his hand through his hair. "I swear I'll be good."

I slowly swim toward him, and when I reach him, he places his hands on my face and intensely stares into my eyes.

"Where are you from?" I ask as I take a deep breath, willing myself to calm down.

"Small town in Russia."

"Ahh, that's where your accent is from. I have always wanted to travel; Russia is on my list. When was the last time you were there?"

"Not too long ago, Ian and I have property there. One day, I'll have to take you."

"Really?" I smile widely.

"Mhm." He grabs me by my hips and pulls me against him. He starts slowly kissing my jawline, making his way down to my neck. He trails down to the tops of my breasts but has to stop because the rest of them are beneath the water.

His groan is loud and full of need, his grip tightens on my hips, lifting me. I wrap my legs around his waist, and he starts kissing and licking between my breasts.

"I know I said I'll be good, baby, but I can't help myself," he mumbles in between kisses. I throw my head back, moaning. I look down, and our eyes connect. His fingers make their way to the back of my head, and he fists my hair, yanking it hard until my back aches as he devours my throat.

"Dimitri," I cry, gripping his shoulders, nails digging into his skin.

"Again, baby. Say it again." He bites my left breast hard near my nipple, making me moan at the pleasure and pain mixed together. "Say it," he demands.

"What?" My brain isn't processing what he wants.

"My name. I want you to say it again." So, I do as he asks.

"That's my good girl." My stomach tightens at his praise. I love pleasing him. He grabs my ass in his hands and squeezes, pulling me into him. I rub myself against his hard cock for some type of much-needed release.

"Fuck, Rosa, we need to stop, or I won't be able to control myself."

I groan, not wanting to stop. I'm fighting a battle between my mind and body, my mind yelling too fast, my body begging for more. I'm having trouble with the tug-of-war between the two.

I was so close.

I pout slightly, but I know it's a smart idea to stop. He pulls me out of the water, then lays me gently on the blanket and lies beside me. He props himself on his elbow and leans his head against the palm of his hand, looking down at me.

"You look so beautiful with my marks all over you." He mutters, tracing the bite mark above my nipple.

And weirdly, I love wearing his mark...

Chapter Seven

When we pull into my apartment building, it's dark out. He helps me off his motorcycle.

"I'll walk you up," he mumbles as he grabs my hand. When we are standing by the front door, he says, "Good night, love."

"Good night. Am I going to see you tomorrow?"

"I don't know. I'll text you tomorrow, but I have meetings and a few things I need to take care of before I leave, so probably not." He gives me a featherlight kiss on my lips.

I nod, unlock my door, and step into my apartment. I wave bye as I shut the door.

I lean against it, sigh, and grab my chest, hoping it'll slow down my heart rate.

I'm running, pumping my legs hard and fast. My thighs are aching in a good way, and I enjoy the burning sensation in my lungs. Just like dancing, when I run, it clears my mind. The pounding of my feet against the cement grounds me.

I stop, bending over, and putting my hands on my knees, taking a few deep breaths to calm my heart.

Glancing around, I realize that while lost in thought, I had crossed the tracks.

"Hey there, sexy." When I snap my head up, I see three gang members standing across the road, smoking. I swallow hard and turn to walk away.

"Hey, ignoring someone is rude!" another one yells as I start walking faster.

"Please leave me alone!" I shout over my shoulder, knowing damn well these guys won't listen.

"Oh, baby, you just wounded me. That's not nice." I yank my cell phone out of my waistband.

"Yeah, we just wanna get to know you."

I hit the call button for Cassie's number, but it just rings. I hang up. I try to fight the rising panic.

Breathe...

Dimitri's face pops into my head, and I pull his contact up on my phone.

"Come on, babe!" I look over my shoulder, and they are a lot closer than I thought they were.

My heart starts pounding against my ribcage. Fear pulses through me. I feel like I'm being hunted down, stalked like prey.

I hit the call button with shaky fingers.

"Rosa," he answers immediately.

"Dimitri," I say, out of breath. I feel like I'm on the verge of having a panic attack. "I'm so sorry to bother you, but..."

"Get your sexy ass over here, baby!" They interrupt me, laughing.

"Who the hell was that?" Dimitri growls harshly through the phone, making me flinch.

"I don't ... I don't know," My throat tightens, feeling sick. "They won't leave me alone. I'm scared, Dimitri." Swallowing forcefully, I try to compose myself. "I tried calling Cassie, but she didn't answer."

"Shh, it's okay. Just tell me where you are." I hear a car door slam shut and an engine roar to life.

"I'm about eight or so miles away from my apartment going east." I trip, my elbows scraping the hard ground, and the phone flies out of my hand. I hiss on impact.

"Gotcha." The idiot laughs as he wraps his fingers around my ankle.

"Get off me!" I kick him with my free leg, but he grabs it before it hits him. I can hear Dimitri's voice, loud and threatening murder.

"Stop, boss man said we're only supposed to scare her."

"Well, he's not here, is he?" the one holding my ankles says. Excitement flashes in his eyes.

"I'm out of here." The third guy shakes his head and leaves.

The second guy slams his boots down, smashing my phone. His partner flips me around, so I'm lying on my back, and straddles me.

Fear threatens to choke me, but I shove it away as adrenaline pumps through me. I will not be a victim again.

I punch his throat, then lift my knee and slam it right into his dick.

His eyes roll back, groaning in pain as he rolls off me.

I scramble up, running.

I turn to look over my shoulder, but I run into something hard–– the second guy–– and I fall.

I sweep my leg, kicking his feet out from under him, and he growls as he falls.

I jump up, turning, but he grabs hold of my ankle. I tilt my body, my foot slamming into his face.

"Fuck!" he screams in pain, and he lets go of me, grabbing his nose.

I run, but he grabs me before I can get too far. His arms wrap around my waist as he pulls me against him, my feet leaving the ground. He rubs his blood on the side of my face like some type of sick claim. "You bad girl, you're gonna pay for that."

"Fuck you." I throw my head back, head-butting him right in his broken nose.

I hiss as pain shoots through my skull, but he lets go of me as he falls to his knees.

Another pair of arms grabs me from behind. "You fucking bitch." He grips my shirt, ripping it in half. His partner is on his knees watching with a sick hunger, broken nose forgotten.

I grab the fucker by his arm and bend forward as I squat; I yank him up onto my back in one quick motion and flip him over my shoulder. He falls next to the broken-nose asshole.

Without hesitation, I spin around and run.

A black sports car races down the street fast. I must look like a maniac running down the street with blood running down my face and my shirt ripped in half, but then I'm tackled from behind.

We both tumble over, and I roll on my back.

He recovers quicker, and now he's standing over me with an evil smirk. He jumps on me, wrapping his hands around my throat, choking me.

In the distance, I hear tires squealing to a stop.

A second later, he's ripped off me.

Dimitri...

I roll to my side, grabbing my throat and coughing violently.

I look up to see Dimitri, his face full of fury as he holds the man in the air by the throat, his feet dangling.

He throws him like he's a rag doll, and his body hits a telephone pole with a sickening smack. He falls to the ground, limp. I swallow hard at the strength he used.

I don't know if I should be scared, amazed, or embarrassingly... turned on. Or all three... *How was he strong enough to throw him like that?*

I look over in time to see Dimitri punch the other guy in the ribs, and I swear I hear something crack. He's not done yet... his fist slams into his face, knocking him out.

From a few feet away, I crawl to him, kneeling next to his unconscious body, and punch him in the face.

"You goddamn asshole!" I shout, my voice full of raw emotion as I hit him again.

"That's enough, Malyshka." Dimitri's voice snaps me out of my anger haze.

Exhausted, I fall on my ass. I drop my forehead to my knees.

"Why?" I whisper harshly. "Why does this keep happening?"

He crouches, grabs my chin, tilting my head up. His eyes narrow at the blood on me. The fury in his gaze is raw and dangerous.

"Don't worry, it's not mine," I whisper.

"Are you hurt?" he asks, touching my cheek softly, his eyes softening, now worried.

"I think so." I shrug.

"Come here." He picks me up bridal style, like I'm made from glass, and I could shatter at any moment. His chest feels warm and safe.

"Wait. What are you doing?"

"What does it look like?" He arches an eyebrow.

"Funny," I mumble sarcastically.

"Don't do that." He looks down at my pout like he wants to kiss it away. He opens the passenger side door, and sits me inside, buckling me in. I take a deep breath, inhaling his scent. It's masculine, and I crave it constantly.

He recoils a bit, eyes me, and traces my lower lip with his thumb, eliciting a moan. The moment the soft sound slips, he pulls away and slams the door, hard enough that the car rattles. I'm surprised it doesn't break the window.

He gets into the driver's side and starts racing down the road. He doesn't even bother with his own seat belt.

I lay my head against the window; my chest tightens with emotion. He stops the car at a red light, and I feel his stare. I turn to find him staring at my chest.

Oh crap. I forgot my shirt was ripped open, my bra on display. I grab both sides and hold them closed as my cheeks warm.

He slams on the gas pedal when the light turns green. His expression darkens like a storm, jaw clenched tight, a deep scowl, gripping the steering wheel hard enough that the color of his knuckles turns.

"I'm sorry for calling you and messing up your meetings," I whisper, low enough that he might not hear me.

"Those meetings aren't as important as you."

"I still feel bad."

He doesn't respond, and I stay silent the rest of the way.

He walks me to my apartment door. He kisses my forehead, his lips linger before he pulls back, not meeting my gaze.

"I need to leave, go and shower, okay?"

"Okay," I nod as I push open the door. My chest tightens even further at his anger. He's barely maintaining control. I just don't understand why.

Cassie throws Ian off her and the couch when she sees me. He falls to the ground with a loud thud.

"Rosa! What the hell happened?" she yells, staring at me, her eyes full of horror as she takes in the blood.

"I was attacked. By three guys..." My voice trails off as emotions tighten my throat. "I just... need a shower. I want to be alone."

I wrap my arms around my midsection as I head down the hall. She follows, asking questions, but I tune her out and shut my bedroom door.

I peel my stained clothes off and toss them into the trash. My mind numb, and my body moves on autopilot. Under the hot water, I break. Sobs fill the small space as I scrub my body hard enough that my skin stings. I watch the blood swirl down the drain. My body finally stops trembling, and the water slowly turns cold.

It's early afternoon, but I sink into bed and pull the covers over my head. I cry until sleep takes me under.

I groan when someone flicks on the lights. Cassie says my name as she steps inside.

"Turn off the lights," I grumble as I push my face into my pillow.

"Dinner is here, Rosa. You need to eat." Cassie sits on my bed and rips the blanket off. "I'm not going to leave until you get up."

"Fine." I move slowly as I pull on a pair of sweatpants and put my hair into a messy bun.

I follow the mouthwatering scent into the dining room, but I stop in my tracks. Jake is here, sitting at the table.

"Hey, Jake," My voice is hoarse. "What are you doing here?" I hug my midsection as I seek some type of comfort.

"Hey, I was worried. You haven't been replying to my texts." He stands and smiles. He's wearing blue jeans and a button-up white shirt. His blond hair is slicked back, and he's wearing his black-rimmed glasses. He looks like a cute nerd.

"Oh, I'm sorry. I've been busy, and I was going to call, but then I lost my phone."

"About what?"

"Our date." My stomach drops as I look away. My eyes land on Ian and Cassie, who are pretending to be busy and not eavesdropping.

"Yeah, I'm excited. I picked out a nice restaurant." His face brightens as his smile stretches.

"Jake, can we talk outside?" His smile falls slightly at my tone. I don't want an audience.

"Sure." Jake nods, and Cassie shoots me a supportive look as we walk out.

It's dark outside, but the lights help. I turn to face him. His brows are pinched together, concern written on his face. I feel awful, he's such a good guy. Sweet and safe, something I should want.

"Rosa?"

"I can't make it on our date next weekend," I rush out, like a coward.

"Why?" he steps forward, but something catches his attention. I follow his line of sight. My heart skips a beat when my gaze lands on Dimitri. He's leaning against his car, arms folded, dark eyes on us.

"Well... I met someone. Someone I really like. We're going out of town."

"You're leaving town with a stranger?" he snaps angrily.

"It's... not like that. I mean, I'll be with Cassie."

"So, he's the reason you've been ignoring me?" He looks back at me.

"I wasn't ignoring you. I was busy." I play with the drawstrings on the hoodie.

"Busy, with him?" he points behind me.

"Yes," I nod, looking up at him. "Jake..."

"Why him and not me?" He cuts me off, voice cracking. "What does he have that I don't? Money?"

"It's not like that. I like you, Jake, but as a friend. You are so sweet and…"

He laughs, void of any emotion. "As a friend? Great."

"Stop, I want to be friends and…"

"No, I have been patient with you. I can't be just friends with you anymore. I wanted us to be more. I could've made you happy."

"Jake, please, don't."

"Call me when he hurts you. Because he will, guys like him love preying on sweet girls like you." He looks down at me, pain in his eyes. "Otherwise, don't contact me. Bye, Rosa."

I stand there, watching him go, gut twisting in guilt.

When he disappears, I make my way toward Dimitri. His shoulders are tense, and those eyes are dark.

"That was so awful. I feel like a bitch." My hands flat on my stomach, feeling sick.

"You're not a bitch, Rosa," he says, voice low and emotionless. Something is clearly wrong.

"Dimitri, are you okay?" I step into him, my hands flat on his chest, trying to soothe his anger. I stand on my toes, reaching up to kiss those full lips, but he turns away, and my mouth lands on his cheek. My chest tightens with his rejection.

The cloud above darkens, the wind stirs around us as if matching my mood.

"Dimitri?" His hands tighten into fists at his sides, veins rising under his skin as if he's forcing himself to maintain control, battling with his temper.

Why is he acting like this… So distant.

So cold.

"I can't do this," he finally says. I take a step back; my hands are still flat on his chest. His words were a blow, a cold sensation spreading through my veins. The streetlight flickers above us.

"Can't do what?" I breathe, even though it was nearly impossible with the hurt choking me.

"This." He grabs my hands that are on his chest and lightly pushes me away. I take a step back, and he continues. "I can't do this with you. I can't be with you," he says roughly, like it's hard for him to get the words out.

I'm in complete shock. I back up until my back hits another car. The sky rumbles, though the night skies are clear, and there's no explanation. My knees shake as I stare at him. My vision blurs, and my breathing turns ragged. It's pathetic, honestly.

His eyes soften, and he slowly reaches out to me.

My head starts spinning, my ears ringing loudly, and in the distance, the sky rumbles again. It's loud and breaks me from my shocked state.

I need to get away from him, so I turn and run.

"Rosa!" he chases me, but I slam the door shut. I start running up the stairs. I falter, but I quickly steady myself.

Somehow, I manage to open my apartment door with shaky hands.

Cassie and Ian look at me in shock, but I run to my room and lock the door behind me.

I lean against it, my body trembling slightly, and the wind slams against the window.

"Rosa!" Dimitri shouts, and something bangs against my door, causing it to rattle.

"What the heck?" Cassie yells. "What's going on?"

"Stay out of it." I hear a hiss. "Open the fucking door, Rosa!"

"Just leave!" I shout, clenching my chest as my heart cracks.

"You need to leave, *now*!" Cassie shouts, her voice sounding different; there's a hint of power. She doesn't know what was going on, but she's quick to protect me.

Karma is a bitch.

CHAPTER EIGHT

A few hours earlier

Dimitri

I leave my mate reluctantly. I feel horrible for leaving her when she needs me the most, but my monster craves blood, and vengeance. It's too strong to ignore.

No one hurts our mate and gets away with it.

I speed off, the tires squealing behind me as I race down the street. People are honking and shouting angrily at me.

Pulling up to the curb, I jump out, only to find that they are gone. I crouch beside the blood, and I sniff. I look in the direction the scent leads to.

I run, following the scent; everything is a blur. I stop in front of a door, sniffing again. Bingo. They're inside.

I kick the door open, the wood splitting in half. Two men are inside, scrambling to their feet.

"Are you the boss's informant?" the one on the right asks. "Tell the boss we scared the Rosa girl, like he asked." I freeze, my muscles tensing. This was a job. They were ordered to scare my mate.

I growl deeply, shaking the entire room. I fly to them, gripping their necks, and my claws come out to play, digging into their flesh.

"Who hired you?" I sound more animal-like than human.

"We can't tell you." One shakes his head, clawing my hand. "He'll kill us, dude." I throw my head back, laughing.

"If you don't tell me, I'll let my Hellhounds play with you like fucking chew toys." My eyes turn black.

"You… you're Dimitri?" he stumbles, eyes wide with fear.

"In the fucking flesh." I choke them until they start turning blue, then I loosen my grip. "Don't make me ask again." These humans are working with a demon. I can smell it on them, but why does a demon want my mate?

"It's Matteo. He wanted to know who this girl was. Someone saw you looking pretty cozy with her."

Rage burns my veins, I break their necks at the same time, and they fall limp onto the floor.

Demons are after her because of me. I've heard of him before, strong and dangerous. He doesn't follow the rules, but the human realm is my brother Xaden's problem, not mine, until now.

My enemies are always watching to see what they can use against me. I let my guard down. A loud growl escapes me.

Before leaving, I call Ian to let him know I'll be a few hours.

I either have to convince him she's nothing to me or kill the fucker.

My car rumbles to life as I call Caspian.

"Caspian, where does Matteo do his illegal drug trade?"

"He owns a strip club; I'll send the address." He sends it a minute later, and I punch it into the GPS.

I step inside the strip club. Naked women are walking around, dancing on poles, or giving lap dances. A few walk up to me, trying to touch me, but I push them away.

I walk to where two bodyguards are standing by a black door.

"You can't go in there."

"The fuck I can't," I hiss at the humans, letting my eyes turn black. When they see I'm a demon, they open the door, letting me in.

I make my way downstairs, my steps slow and calculated. Matteo's men are sitting around a poker table, playing a card game. They freeze when they see me.

"Leave," I growl, and they look at Matteo. I laugh. "You think he'll save you from me? I'll kill you all before he's even on his feet." The smell of fear reeks in the room as they tuck their tails, run past me, and disappear.

I sit down on the chair across from him and lean back, widening my legs in front of me, relaxed.

"Dimitri." He bows his head slightly, showing respect.

"You are messing with my mission, Matteo, and it's pissing me the fuck off."

"Mission? I have no idea what you are talking about." He rests his elbows against the poker table, interlocking his fingers.

"Don't play with me!" I growl and jump over the table. I pick him up by his shirt and throw him against the wall. "You play with me, you'll get my wrath, but if you mess with my mission, you die," I snarl. "I killed your humans right after they told me you hired them to scare the girl. She's nothing to me, but if I don't complete my mission, I don't get my money, so if you fuck it up, you'll repay me with death."

"Yes, Prince Dimitri." He rushes out as he kneels before me.

I leave him trembling with the threat.

I hate myself for what I have to do. I need to push her away until she gets her powers and learns how to defend herself.

When I pull into the apartment, I get out of my car and lean against it. I watch her with him, fighting the urge to grab her and drag her away from him and this realm and to the Underworld, where I can protect her better.

When she leans in to kiss me, I pull away. It's the hardest thing I've ever had to do.

I'm supposed to protect, love, and treasure her, but I did the opposite. I broke her...

Chapter Nine

Rosa

I cried myself to sleep that night, curled in a tight ball, consumed by self-pity. By the morning, I am back to the version of myself I hate the most... the weak, sad girl, all thanks to a man I hardly know.

Why did he push me away? Was it because I didn't have sex with him? He seemed fine with it. Maybe he changed his mind. Maybe I'm too needy, calling him while he was busy. Perhaps he decided I'm not worth it.

He has many women he can choose from. Why choose me? Is this how Jake felt? He was right, bad guys always break the good girl's heart. My chest twists painfully. I did the same to him. Jake would never have done this.

Why didn't I fall for Jake?

Because you wanted the dark, mysterious bad guy.

I get out of bed, stretching my arms over my head. That's when I notice I'm still wearing his hoodie. The scent reminds me of him, which of course makes it worse. I take it off and throw it across the room angrily.

After a long, hot shower, I stare at my reflection—My eyes are red and puffy, and I'm full of hickeys. I cover them with concealer. It doesn't help with the evidence of me crying over a man.

I get dressed, and Cassie is waiting for me in the living room. She looks upset.

"Rosa, I'm so sorry."

"No, Cassie, don't be. It's not your fault." She throws her arms around me and hugs me tight. It's the kind of hug that holds you together.

"I feel horrible knowing you needed me, and I wasn't there. Tell me what happened. Dimitri didn't tell us anything. Why were you in that part of town? And why were you covered in blood?"

"I got lost in thought and wasn't paying attention to my surroundings, until it was too late." I shake my head. "But the blood? You would've been proud. I ruined those guys. I broke noses, did that move from class... You know, flipping someone over your shoulder? I was scared, but at the same time, I felt in control, not weak. Powerful."

"Damn, girl... You're my badass warrior queen."

"I'm glad we took those classes; if we didn't, it would've ended badly." I shiver at that thought.

"And Dimitri? What happened?" She gently tucks a piece of my hair behind my ear.

I clear my throat, my chest tightening. "He told me he doesn't want to be with me." I sigh. "I really don't want to talk about it."

She nods, "Just know I am here for you."

"I know you are, and I love you."

"I love you, too." She pulls away, digs in her purse, and hands me a new phone. "Dimitri did tell us you lost your phone. I added our numbers, even Dimitri's, but delete it if you want."

"Thank you," I whisper, looking down at the smartphone.

Ian walks in carrying brown paper bags. "Please tell me I smell pancakes. I need myself some unhealthy carbs."

"Gods yes, and coffee. From your favorite place," Cassie says excitedly, she grabs the two white to-go cups from Ian's hand, placing a kiss on his cheek.

"You are an angel." I smile and take one of the cups.

We eat together, having a good time, and it helps a lot.

Now I'm sitting in my chair in my room with a glass of red wine, reading my witchy romance book.

I must've dozed off because I wake up to a sound, and I swear I see someone standing by the window. My heart races as I turn on the lamp next to my chair. I look back, but no one is there.

I frown when I see the window is open, letting a light breeze into the room. I didn't open it. I stand, glancing outside, but I see nothing. I carefully shut the window, making sure to lock it.

That's when I hear the sound that must have woken me, and I laugh. Cassie's bed is banging against the wall, and she's moaning.

"Keep it down in there!" I shout, fighting back a laugh.

"Oh, my God, Rosa. I'm sorry!" Cassie squeals.

"No, we're not sorry!" Ian shouts, laughing. I burst out laughing, too.

My phone dings on the table beside me. I grab it, and my heart rate spikes when I see Dimitri's name on the screen.

> *Hey, Rosa, I'm sorry about yesterday. I want to explain myself and why we can't be together. It's not you, I promise. I just don't have time for a relationship, and I don't want to hurt you. Please understand. I hope you have a good night.*

I stare at the message. I start typing a reply, but then erase it, type it again, then stop. Then I put the phone face down onto the table.

I'm not doing this tonight.

The sun peeks in from outside, and I groan as I get up, stretching.

I get dressed wearing a pair of shorts and an old hoodie that a guy friend gave me during a study session.

I look like crap. The deep shadows under my eyes scream "lack of sleep," and I already know, today will require a significant amount of makeup.

I find Cassie in the kitchen making bacon. I grab the eggs out of the fridge, crack a few in a bowl, and start whisking them together before turning on the stove. While I let that heat, I start the toast.

Cassie turns on the music from her phone, and we start dancing in the kitchen while cooking. I start singing along to the music, giggling.

I place the eggs into the pan and begin scrambling them. I sing louder, shaking my ass. Cassie grabs my hips, and we grind against each other, but then she stops moving, looking behind me and narrowing her eyes.

"Can I join that dance?" I hear Ian behind me.

"Funny!" Cassie snorts, stepping away.

"Hope there's enough for us," Ian says, and I turn around, hoping he isn't here, but of course, he is. He stands there looking like delicious sin wrapped in leather. He's wearing black jeans, a gray V-neck shirt, and a leather jacket. His hair is messy as if he ran his fingers through it multiple times. His gaze lowers to the hoodie I'm wearing, and his eyes narrow, turning sharp and possessive.

I turn away from him and pay attention to the eggs I'm cooking. My heart is pounding hard and fast, like a drum.

After finishing the eggs, we sit at the table together. Dimitri sits across from me. I play with my eggs as I try to ignore his intense gaze. It's like he wants to rip the hoodie right off my body and reduce it to nothing but ash.

"What are you guys doing here? I thought you wouldn't be back till later," Cassie questions.

"We weren't, but Dimitri wanted to talk to Rosa."

"In private," Dimitri adds.

"I'd rather not." I take a bite of toast.

"Why not?"

"Because we should keep our distance," I murmur, sitting up straighter. I finally meet his gaze. "You made that crystal clear."

"I didn't want to hurt you, Rosa. I..."

"Stop, okay? It's fine. You don't owe me anything." I shrug, taking a sip of coffee. An awkward silence fills the room.

"So, Ian?" Cassie breaks the silence. "Are there clubs where we're going?"

"Yeah, a friend of mine owns one."

"Perfect, we should go. Rosa needs to get laid." Cassie grins.

I choke on my coffee, coughing violently. Cassie winks at me, eyes shining mischievously.

A deep growl rumbles across the table. It's a low, but dangerous sound. "She doesn't need to get laid." Dimitri snaps, fists ramming into the table, making me jump.

"Yeah, she does." Cassie snaps back. "She told me this morning. She wants to get hot and heavy with a mystery guy because she's tired of doing it herself."

Dimitri slowly turns his focus on me. I swallow, and I swear my soul leaves my body. His eyes are dark and full of burning anger.

Cassie kicks my leg under the table.

I lift my chin. "I did say that. So what?"

Dimitri shoots up out of his seat and storms out.

"Well, ladies, it was a pleasure. Pack for tomorrow. We're leaving at nine sharp." Ian follows Dimitri out.

"Cassie," I glare. She's smirking like some type of she-demon. "You do realize that I'm still a virgin, right? I am *not* losing it to some random guy at a club."

"Oh, *I* know, but he doesn't." She wiggles her eyebrows

"God, you're too much." I pick up my napkin and throw it at her.

"Yeah, I am, and you love me."

"That I do." After we eat, we turn on the music again, make our way into Cassie's room, and I help her pack. We pause to order pizza, paint our toes, and gossip about random things.

I pretend I don't keep checking my phone. I just wish...I wish he wanted me the way Ian wants her.

My thoughts wander, and my toes curl as I remember Dimitri's very consuming kiss. My first real kiss, and it did not disappoint. The way my body lit up and how I felt so alive in a way I never have. I squeeze my thighs tightly as the tingling sensation shoots through me.

God... I want him in a way I have never wanted anything, even though I know I shouldn't. He's bad for me and my heart.

Cassie skips back into the room with a box of pizza. "You should pack some of my clothes. Your clothes are cute..." She says as she takes a pizza slice out of the box. "But not the kind of cute to make a demon fall in love with you. You'll need something sexy to catch a demon's attention."

I snort, grabbing my own slice. "Only because he hurt me doesn't make him a demon, Cassie. He just doesn't want me."

"Rosa, Ian says Dimitri talks about you, and he wants you. He's just terrified of falling for you. He's having trouble staying away."

"Really?"

"I wouldn't lie to you. Not about this. Trust me, he'll break. He just needs a little nudge."

"I don't know..."

"Trust me on this."

"Okay, a few outfits. Nothing crazy, you know my limits."

"Scott's honor." She holds up two fingers.

"It's 'scouts honor,' not Scott."

"Whatever, same thing."

CHAPTER TEN

Rosa

Morning comes too fast. I slept better last night, but even in my dreams, Dimitri was still there. I wish I didn't crave him so much. I glance at where I threw his hoodie, but it's not on the floor. It's neatly folded on my armchair. Cassie must've picked it up. I lift it, inhaling deeply, the intoxicating scent, filling my lungs like a drug, sharp and intense.

I pick up my phone and pull up his contact.

> *Dimitri… I'll wash your hoodie and give it back.*

A ding comes immediately after that.

> *You can keep the hoodie, Rosa… I'd really like to still have you as a close friend.*

Is this a joke? The words I said to Jake are coming back to bite me in the ass. I head to the bathroom, my thumb hovering over the keyboard.

> *I can't be friends with you… Just forget about me…*

I toss my phone face down on the counter, rinse my mouth, and brush my hair. Trying to shake off the ache in my chest.

Remembering Cassie's words, I walk to my closet and grab an unworn black skirt, pulling it on. It's cute and flowy, stopping mid-thigh. I find a sleeveless white crop top and slip it on. The skirt, being high-waisted, shows an inch of stomach. I slip on my white sandals, and I grab my sunglasses, setting them on my head. I check my reflection, nodding. It looks cute, but casual.

"Rosa, it's time to go!" Cassie shouts, letting me know that the guys are here.

"Coming!" I put on some lip gloss, eyeliner, and a little blush.

Cassie locks the door beyond us. I make my way down the steps. The door at the bottom of the stairs opens, and Dimitri steps inside. His gaze roams down my body, slowly and deliberately. The way his eyes darken has my stomach tightening. Is it desire in those dark eyes, or is it lust? Does it matter which...? Nope!

Score!

I slowly walk the rest of the way until I'm in front of him. Cassie walks past, winking at me.

"You look amazing," he whispers.

"Thanks. You don't look bad yourself." I smile at him. "Do you ever not wear that jacket?"

"Why? Would you like me to take it off?" He arches his eyebrows, making my cheeks heat.

"That wasn't what I meant."

Cassie and Ian are waiting next to a black SUV.

"How many cars do you have?" I laugh.

"A few," Dimitri answers, stepping next to me. "Ian and Cassie will be in the back. You and I are in the front."

"Yes, sir," I say, putting on my sunglasses.

I hop in the front seat and turn my head to look back, and I see Dimitri staring at my ass. His gaze moves to my legs, and heat crawls across my skin.

He gets into the driver's seat. I try to act like nothing is wrong, but his being this close to me makes it hard. What am I being punished for? What have I ever done to deserve this kind of horrible torture?

"Can't be too safe." He reaches around me and puts on my seat belt. I look at his lips, so close to mine; he pulls back slightly and stares at mine. They suddenly feel dry, so I lick them, and his eyes dilate as he follows the movement.

"Road trip!" Cassie shouts, making Dimitri pull back. I feel disappointed, but the tension lingers, thick and painful.

"Let's go, brother." Ian pats his shoulder.

Dimitri starts driving as I sink deeper into the seat, getting comfortable and crossing my legs. Dimitri turns slightly, and he looks at my exposed thighs, and I see him swallow hard. I never thought I'd say this, but man oh man, even his throat is sexy. He looks away quickly, putting his sunglasses on as well.

I can hear Cassie giggle in the back seat. I look in the rearview, and they are cuddling, with Ian whispering in her ear. Cassie's hand is inside his shirt, and I turn away quickly.

I lean forward to turn up the music.

I try really hard not to look at Dimitri.

Surrendering, I glance at him. His left hand grips the wheel, his gaze is fixed ahead, and his right arm hovers near mine.

To suppress the groan, I bite down on my lower lip. Why does he look angry? Or maybe he's trying to control himself just like I am?

His arm touches mine, deliberately. I feel a zap of pleasure shoot up my arm, and I shiver. He keeps his arm against mine while his finger rubs the top of my hand. I grind my teeth together.

What is he doing?

Dimitri looks over at me, and I try my hardest not to look back. Is he trying to torture me? If he is, he's doing a damn good job at it.

My phone buzzes. Mark's calling, and his face pops up on the screen with a winky face. He's playful and extremely flirty. Dimitri glances down, his hand tightens on the steering wheel. The air shifts, turning dangerous.

"Hello," I answer, turning my body further away from Dimitri and against the door.

"Hey there, beautiful. I'm having a party next week, you're coming as my date, right?" he always asks me out, but I turn him down. He's too much of a flirt for my liking.

"I can't. I'm going out of town with Cassie, but maybe next time." I grin.

"You'd better," he warns. I've missed him. He's a fun time.

"I will, I'll call when I'm back in town."

"Good, baby girl. I'll catch you later, and no other man can touch you... remember you're mine."

"Sure, whatever you say, sir!" I laugh, shaking my head.

"Mm, I love it when you call me sir. It turns me on." I huff at him, and he chuckles.

"I love that I turn you on."

Dimitri's eyes are fixed on me, stormy, dangerous, and impossible to look away from.

"Yes, baby, and you do it so good, but you're not here to help me do anything about it."

"I'm so sorry, *sir.*"

"You better be. I'll punish you later, you naughty girl."

"Promises, promises." I hang up, and Cassie and I burst out laughing. She knows how he and I joke. Dimitri looks pissed. If looks could kill, I'd be dead. I swallow down my laughter.

"You shouldn't make someone think they have a chance with you," Dimitri mutters.

"He does, though." I look at him.

"You're way too good for someone like that. You deserve better."

"Well, I think that's my choice to make. I'm a single woman." I fold my arms over my chest.

"Yeah, plus Mark is a nice guy and so flipping hot. Right, Rosa?" Cassie leans forward; her elbows are resting on the center console.

"Oh yeah, he could easily be a Calvin Klein model. I have seen him shirtless a few times, and let me tell you...." I start fanning myself.

"You saw him shirtless and didn't tell me? He turned me down once... That sucked." She pouts. "Oh, Ow! Why did you smack me?" She turns and yells at Ian.

"You are literally talking about how hot another guy is in front of me," Ian grumbles.

"See, Dimitri, isn't he perfect for me?" I smile sweetly, batting my eyelashes at him, and all he does is grunt in response.

"You should send him some naughty pictures in that new lingerie you just bought. You know how much he loves red on you."

"Oh yeah, for sure... later, I will." I press my lips together to keep myself from laughing.

"No, you will not!" Dimitri snaps.

"Why not? She's a free woman," Cassie says.

"Because I said no."

"You can't tell me what to do, Dimitri." I huff, leaning my elbow on the center console. "You didn't want to be with me, remember?"

"It doesn't matter. You will not send those kinds of things to. Any. Other. Man!" He growls out. His voice sounds a little different, a little rough, and his accent is stronger.

Wait... Is he jealous?

"Maybe I'll do a strip tease for him," I murmur, heart racing as I tread dangerous waters.

Next thing I know, his hand grips my jaw, tilting my face. "You will not," he growls, "or I'll be the one punishing you. Is that what you want? You want me to bend that sexy ass over my knees and spank it, baby? Want me to paint that ass red?"

I gasp.

He forces my face to turn to look at him, swerving the SUV into different lanes, cars honking at us, but he doesn't seem to care. His thumb brushes my lower lip. My pulse spikes, every nerve on fire. "Maybe you'll like that too much..." His thumb slips between my lips, entering. "Maybe I should shove my cock between those pretty lips." Heat rushes through my body like a storm, and my core tightens. The tension is unbearable, electric. I can barely think. He releases me and slowly leans back, his gaze never leaving mine.

I look away before I climb over the center console, bend myself over his knee, and let him have his wicked ways with me.

"Shit, that was hot." Cassie breathes.

"I fucking agree," Ian says.

I clear my throat as I open my book again, looking at the pages but not actually reading them, and dismiss the conversation. I mean, how dare he?

"Rosa, baby, you know your book is upside down." *Oh God, it totally is.* He grabs it and puts it the right way. I clear my throat, feeling utterly embarrassed.

A couple of hours later, we turn onto a small dirt road. I close my book to look around. The SUV is a little too big for the narrow road that's flanked by trees on each side.

"Wow, it's beautiful."

"It is," he agrees, eyes flicking to me, the corner of his mouth quirking.

The two-story white cottage comes into view, complete with a wraparound porch. Dimitri stops the SUV. He steps out, opens my door for me, and offers his hand. I take it, feeling a jolt.

"Follow me," he says, leading me inside. The old steps creak under our weight as we step up. I look around. The main floor is cozy, two loveseats face each other in the living room, and the walls are white shiplap with blue accents. A small dining area sits beyond that, and a sliding door opens to the backyard.

I can't stop watching him. Every movement is controlled, and every glance he sends my way is possessive.

Our rooms are on the second floor, directly across from each other. He sets my suitcase on the small bed.

"Thank you," I whisper.

"I'll let you settle in." I watch him as he disappears into the other room.

I look out the window. The backyard is nice, but the in-ground pool makes it beautiful, especially the way the trees surround it.

I rush down the stairs in excitement, nearly tripping, to find Cassie and Ian on a loveseat, kissing.

"There's a pool outside! I need to borrow a swimsuit, you're coming right?"

"Sorry, girlie, but maybe later. Ian and I are going for a hike and look around some. You can come with us, and we can swim later?"

"Oh no, I'm staying, but thanks."

I hightail it to their room, digging through her suitcase that she put all her bikinis in. She only has a few, but I find a cute red set that covers most of my boobs. It wasn't easy since my curves are fuller than hers. I grab a swim cover and step outside, enjoying the sun on my skin.

I sit on a lounger and start to rub on sunscreen, looking around and enjoying the view. I try, but I can't reach my back.

"Need help?"

I turn too quickly, nearly falling. Dimitri chuckles, his eyes sparkling with amusement. "Sorry for scaring you."

My eyes drink him in. He's only wearing swim shorts. My breath gets caught in my throat as I stare at his defined muscles; he's perfect.

"You don't mind if I join you, right?"

"No, of course not," I say, but my brain screams: 'Yes, I mind! Go back inside, you sexy beast.'

"Let me help you with that." He holds out his hand, palm up, wanting me to give him the sunscreen as he studies me with an unreadable gaze.

"Oh, yeah. I can't reach my back." I stand, letting my swim cover drop to the ground.

He stands there frozen as his eyes slowly take in every inch of my body.

His Adam's apple bobs with a subtle swallow, and I feel heat pulse through me. Does he like what he sees? His gaze darkens, hungry and dangerous.

I shouldn't let him rub sunscreen on me; it's a bad idea. I am better off getting sunburnt.

I lay face down on the lounger, moving my hair to the side.

He steps closer, his voice low and possessive, a whisper that sends shivers down my spine. "You know, it upsets me that you decided to hide my marks I left on your neck. It makes me want to put my marks all over your body so you can't hide them. So, no other man touches you because they will know who you belong to."

Oh God, that was hot … My lower stomach ignites. I say nothing in response. I don't want words. I just want him to do… whatever he wants, and that's dangerous.

I've always been comfortable in my body. I know my curves are full and curvy. But with him staring at it, I feel shy. His gaze lingers on my ass, my favorite feature, and I feel my cheeks heat.

Finally, after what feels like forever, he starts spreading the sunscreen with deliberate care.

I close my eyes, trying to steady my racing heart, but the tension doesn't fade.

CHAPTER ELEVEN

Dimitri

I stand there looking down at my mate, lying on her stomach on a lounge chair in a bikini, if you can even call it that. It's more like a scrap of red fabric that hardly covers anything. My jaw clenches, and heat slams into my lower stomach. If Ian were still here, I would've ripped his damn eyes out of his head, brother or not. I am the only one who can see her like this.

Mine, my demon growls.

I drag my gaze over her slowly, savoring every single inch, *again*. I can't stop looking. My dick twitches in my shorts. Her body is absolute perfection; every line, curve, and dip was designed to completely ruin me. It's a sinful piece of art that I want to worship and destroy at the same time.

I will kneel at her altar for eternity, pleasuring her, licking every inch.

Every inch of her is a trap, and I am fully caught in her web.

I will do whatever she wants, anything… no matter what it is. She just needs to snap her fingers, and it's done.

"Fuck," I breathe, barely a sound.

I grab the sunscreen and fall to my knees beside her. I've never knelt for anyone, not demons, not even for my father... the king of the Underworld. But for her? I will kneel in fire and ash as I crawl to her.

I squeeze the lotion onto my palm. The moment my skin touches hers, sparks of pleasure storm through the both of us. I know she feels it, goosebumps covering every inch of her.

I start rubbing her back gently, her skin is warm and soft, and a moan escapes her sweet lips. It's enough to make me lose control. My vision turns dark, and my fangs extend.

Every sound that she makes drives a nail of desire through me. She has no idea what she's doing to me.

My hands move lower, and I shift. One knee slides onto the lounger beside her hip. I push my hand in between her sexy thighs, forcing them apart just enough to see more of her. The sight makes me harder than a rock.

A low, rough groan escapes me before I can force it down.

I put my other knee between her thighs.

My gaze hungrily takes in her delicious ass that I want to smack and watch jiggle.

Fuck, it would be so easy to lift her hips and pull her against me as I slip deep into her warmth in one smooth, claiming thrust. To make her forget every man she's ever known. To make her remember only me, my hands, my marks, my voice. For her to only desire me, just as I only desire her.

She'll never think of *Mark* again. I should find the weak human and kill him for daring to breathe the same air as her.

But right now, all I can think about is the warmth of her skin, and how gods damned difficult it is not to drag her ass against me and ruin her for anyone but me.

"Can you do my upper thighs, too?" Her voice is a breathless tease. A smile curls at the corner of my lips. Good, I'm having the same effect on her.

"Yeah..." My hand moves lower, starting on her left thigh. My finger brushes against her panty line. She moans desperately. It breaks the last piece of control I am clinging to. I look up, and the sight of her bottoms... outlining everything perfectly. It nearly fucking shatters me. Grinding my teeth as I switch sides, my hands trembling with hunger as I explore. My hand grazes the swell of her ass cheek, and my nostrils flare.

Fuck...

I give it a little squeeze. I cannot physically stop myself, nor do I want to; I give her ass a smack. I groan, licking my lower lip as I watch it jiggle.

Rosa arches her back, whimpering my name.

Fuck, fuck!

"Are you trying to kill me? I'm going to lose control," I mutter, leaning over her body as my lips graze *my* mark on her neck. I suck her sweet flesh between my teeth. Her scent, *my* scent, wraps around me like a warm blanket, twisting something deep in me.

"What if I want you to lose control?"

"You don't know what you're asking for ... I won't be able to stop."

"I'm okay with that," she breathes, arching her ass, rubbing against me, *daring* me. The temptation is unbearable, nearly painful.

Fuck, I need her, all of her, *now*.... more than I have ever needed anything. I slide my left hand underneath her, grabbing a handful of her perfect breasts.

I am fucking addicted to her. When I'm around her, I can finally breathe again. She is the light to my darkness.

"Fuck, you're making this hard, Malyshka." I quickly flip her around so her back is against the lounger and kiss her. Her lips are perfect and soft. My whole body vibrates with need. My teeth graze her collarbone as I reach between us, and my finger grazes her hard nipple.

My head snaps up. I hear a loud sound, causing my heated train of thought to die out. It's Ian and Cassie, walking into the house.

I slam my eyes shut as I feel them shift in color, darkening. I stand, turning away so she doesn't see my claws extracting. I'm losing control of my demon; he wants to mark her, claim her. I storm around front, without a single word.

"Brother." I spin around to find Ian standing on the porch.

"What?" I snap; I have no patience for him right now.

"I saw you both out there." He jogs down the stairs. "Why are you torturing yourself?" He leans against the railing and crosses his ankles together.

"I don't know what you're talking about."

"You are pushing her away."

"I'm protecting her," I growl between clenched teeth.

"No, you're afraid of what she'll do once she knows the truth about you."

"It's none of your goddamn business." My eyes flash black, an indicator that my demon is close to coming unglued. He's scratching the surface, wanting to come out and play.

"I'll tell her if you don't." He dares to step closer, ignoring the warning signs.

"You wouldn't dare," I growl, flashing my fangs as I grab the fucker by the throat, picking him up and squeezing hard till he can't breathe.

"Oh, yes, the fuck I would." His voice remains calm, not flinching at my violence.

A roar escapes my throat as I throw him across the yard with impossible strength. He slams into a tree, breaking it in half, making the ground shake.

"You want to know why?" My chest caves. "Because I'm a coward. As soon as she finds out what a monster I am, she will hate me." I can hardly breathe at the mere thought. My rage and fear twist through me in a nasty violence I can barely control. "She deserves better than me... but fuck I can't let her go." I grab my hair, pulling it to feel the sharp pain.

"She will accept you; she is your mate. Stop running from fate."

"But she won't, Ian." I turn, facing him as my heart shatters. "Look at me, I'm a demon, a fucking monster." I wave my hand in front of my face, emphasizing my pitch-black eyes, fangs, and demon horns that are on display, along with my black-feathered wings.

"I am telling you now, if you keep pushing her away, she will resent you and run into another man's arms. Another man will touch what belongs to you." He stands, dusts off his pants, and leaves without another word.

I glare at his back, whispering a promise, "No other man will ever touch her without finding themselves at death's door."

I stand there for hours in the same spot, not moving, thinking of what he said until it starts to turn dark. I pull out my phone, needing a distraction.

"Caspian?"

"Yes, Dimitri?"

The next mission is going to be brutal because I need the violence. A man is abusing his family: a child and his wife. Caspian and I move slowly down the halls of their house, like dark shadows. Caspian craves violence as much as I, if not more. It's why he is my right-hand man. It's not just his violence, it's his strength. He can keep up with me, and I trust him at my side in a fight.

We stop when we hear a woman cry. "Please stop! Don't hurt him! I'll do anything! Anything you want!"

"This is your punishment, Trisha! For trying to leave me!" A man growls in response.

"No, Daddy. Stop!" a child cries in pain. I've had enough. I step out of the shadows.

The man is standing in front of a little boy with his fist midair, and the woman stands behind him, hitting his back with her small fist. I rush forward, grab the man by the back of his neck, and throw him across the room.

I crouch, preparing for his swift attack. He strikes fast, a vampire, but I'm faster. I move at the last second, and he slams into the wall, denting it.

Caspian moves in, taking the woman and child away.

"So, you like hitting women and small children? Let's see how you do against a man," I growl out.

"Who the fuck are you?" he snarls, eyes flashing red. "What I do to my wife and child is none of your fucking business."

"It is my business, and you may have heard of me as the punisher or executioner or perhaps, Prince Dimitri."

I see panic fill his eyes. He knows exactly who I am. "No, please don't."

All I see now is a scared little man, and my mouth curls into a cruel smirk as his fear fills the room like fragrance. "Oh, yes, let's have some fun." I chuckle darkly, making my portal, grabbing the man by his hair, throwing him in, and jumping in after him.

He tries to scramble away as his eyes land on my Hellhounds, but there's nowhere to go. "Please stop, I'm sorry!" he cries, his back pressing into the wall behind him.

"Take your punishment like a man; you had no remorse when it came to your wife and child." I stalk toward him, slowly, my lips curling into a sinister smile as I release my demon. My Hellhounds watch eagerly, drooling with anticipation.

The man sobs as he crawls towards me on his hands and knees, reaching for me, but he jerks his hand back when Onyx snaps at it.

"Confess your sins, vampire."

He does every single sin…The list is long.

"Thank you for confessing," I say.

He sighs in relief, shoulders slumping.

"Boys, you can have him." My hounds lunge forward.

I watch as they tear his flesh apart, his screams echoing around the room with the sounds of growls and tearing flesh. Once he's dead, my hounds step back.

"Burn him," I demand. Gwyllgi parts his mouth and releases hellfire, turning the vampire into ash within seconds.

I check in with Caspian. He's taken the boy and mother to a safe location, where they can start over.

I watch the dancefloor as I sip my whiskey. I can't face her yet. It may be cowardly, but my control is hardly intact even after the violence.

The air shifts with electricity, and my eyes snap towards the entrance. She walks into the club wrapped in a dress that's hardly there, clinging to every curve.

My chest caves, and I can hardly breathe as my hands slam against the glass that separates us. I wasn't prepared for this.

Her hips sway seductively as she steps onto the dancefloor. Men turn to watch, and she smiles at them. Jealousy roars inside me; it's dark and dangerous. She shouldn't smile like that for anyone other than me. She starts dancing, her hips move to the heated beat of the music as her hands slide up her body in a slow pursuit. I'm not the only one watching. She shouldn't be dancing for others to see.

My demon roars, demanding I rip their eyes out.

Then she lets another man pull her against him. He touches her body as she leans into him. I watch his hands move along her thigh, hips, and up her waist. Touching what belongs to me.

My teeth grind together. The lights above me flicker as my power surges forward.

I push bodies aside as I move through the crowd, my eyes solely on her. She looks around the room like she feels me coming. Let her sense the danger.

My eyes move to him. He doesn't understand how close he is to death. My fangs extend, pressing against my tongue.

Chapter Twelve

Rosa

Dimitri left without a word. I shouldn't be surprised. I knew he didn't want anything serious, but despite that fact, I still let him touch me, because I needed it, I'm addicted to him. I wish I were stronger, that I could deny it. I called out his name as he walked away, but he ignored me. I don't know how to fight this, but I have to try.

He doesn't want me.

"I'm going to get a bikini. I will be back!" Cassie shouts from inside the cottage. I didn't know she was back. I sit up, wiping my tears away with the back of my hand angrily. I'm angry at him, at myself, and the mess I put myself in.

I jump into the pool, hoping the cold water will wash away the humiliation and the sensation of his touch that's still lingering.

I pop out of the water when I hear another splash. I smile when I see Cassie swimming toward me.

She wiggles her brows, "Tell me, did anything juicy happen with you two, all alone in that tiny bikini?"

"Yeah, a lot." I sigh, looking away. "He touched me, kissed me, and then ran away like his ass was on fire." I roll my eyes. "Is there something wrong with me, Cassie?"

"Hell no... If I were into girls, I'd totally fuck you."

"Then why?" My voice cracks, emotions crawling up my throat. "Why doesn't he want me?"

"Because he's a coward and an idiot. You have men falling for you all the time."

"No, I don't." I swim to the pool stairs, sitting down with my legs still in the water.

"Yes, you do, boo. You just don't notice it because you don't care."

"Let's go out. I don't want to be here when he comes back."

"Good!" She grins wickedly.

"What do you have in mind?"

"You already know, girl!" She sits next to me.

"The club?"

"Yup! Ian is friends with the owner, so free drinks!"

"I need something strong." I lean back and look up at the sky, closing my eyes.

"Girl, I got you. I have the perfect dress, too."

Ian steps outside with a box of pizza, and we climb out to eat.

I walk into the club with Ian and Cassie at my side, eyes turning to look at us. I don't blame them. We look good. I'm wearing a sexy dress that Cassie gave me—a red mini dress with a slit to my hips, and a low neckline. I feel good, and I know I look good.

We head over to the bar, and I suck down three shots in quick succession.

"Hey, slow down," Cassie whispers to me, gently touching my arm.

"Let's dance," I say, not waiting for their reply as I turn away.

I lose myself to the beat of the music, my hips moving seductively.

Ian moves behind me and whispers in my ear. "Don't look yet, but the room to your left with the windows, he's in there, watching. Show him what he's missing."

"How do you know he's watching?"

"He's my brother, I just know." He replies, simply moving back to Cassie, who gives me a *'what is he up to'* look. I shrug my shoulders, because I'm clueless too.

I slow my movements, letting my hips roll, my hands trailing up my body, waist, breasts, and into my hair. Let him watch, let him see what he's missing. I grab a hot guy walking by and pull him to me.

"Hey there, sexy." He smirks like he won the lottery.

"Hi." I smile. "Make me feel good."

"Gladly." His hands slide around my hips pressing me against his hard body, but there are no sparks. I feel sick, wrong for letting someone else touch me. Guilty...

His hands trail down my waist, my back, and he grips my ass. I let myself move against him, let myself forget *his* touch.

The lights flicker above us, and the air charges in a cold, dangerous way. A chill runs down my spine, and I tense. I look up, and my breath hitches.

Dimitri stands at the edge of the dancefloor, glaring. His eyes are dark, cold, and lethal. He looks deadly and dangerous,

I slowly step away from the stranger, and Dimitri tracks the movement. His eyes slowly take me in from the top of my head to my pointy stilettos like he's deciding where to mark and claim me.

My body is on fire, buzzing to life. His anger turns me on, even though it shouldn't...

He stalks towards us, slowly and in control, just like a predator. He shoves dancers out of the way without looking away from me. When he stops in front of me, he shrugs off his leather jacket without a word and drapes it over my shoulders. It feels like a claim. My pulse jumps, but I lift my chin and look directly into those dark, sinful eyes.

"Stop," I whisper, my voice sharp. "Not tonight."

"Hey, man, back off. She's with me, go find someone else." My dance partner steps forward and stands between Dimitri and me.

Dimitri wraps his fingers around the man's shirt, lifting him off the ground so they're nose to nose, and he growls, "*Mine.*"

I do what any woman would do in my situation. I spin around and run.

The stranger is on his own; he should've kept his mouth shut.

I don't look over my shoulder or stop as I'm weaving through the crowd, ignoring the sting of my heels and the burning sensation of his gaze on my back as he hunts me through the club. The music thunders around me, but the only sound I hear is the pounding of my heartbeat.

Escaping Dimitri is my only focus. I make it halfway through the club when his arm snakes around my waist, lifts me, and pushes my back against a hard chest.

"We're leaving," Dimitri growls in my ear, and I swallow hard.

"Put me down." My voice shaky, "I'm not going anywhere with you."

He sets me down, and I turn around, facing him. That was easy, too easy... I take a step to the side.

"Take another step, and you'll regret it, Rosa." His voice is low, but deep and raspy. Will he bend me over his knees like he said back in the car? I hate that a part of me wants it.

"You don't get to tell me what to do." I poke a finger hard into his chest.

He looks away, a muscle in his jaw ticks. When he looks back, there's something dark in his eyes. It's intense, making me take a step back.

Then he strikes. One moment I'm backing away, then the next I'm hauled over his shoulder, the pure strength of it takes my breath away. He starts walking, his hand holding my dress down so I'm not flashing anyone.

"Dimitri!" I hiss, my fist slamming against his back, which does nothing.

Everyone just stands there staring as he carries me across the room. No one helps or even blinks.

We start climbing the stairs. He walks into a room and slams the door shut. It's quiet up here. He finally puts me down, and he starts pacing the room, his chest rising and falling like he's about to lose control.

"Tell me, Rosa," he growls the word in a low, calming voice. "What in the fucking hell made you think that anyone but me can touch you?" I swallow hard, backing up as he stalks toward me slowly, like he's the predator, and I'm his prey. God, help me, every step he takes makes the heat in my core grow. "No one else gets to touch you except me." He slams his fist into his chest. "Do you hear me?"

"You don't own me," I say, my voice surprisingly firm.

His expression is eerily calm, and his eyes bleed darkness. "I don't?" He cages me with his hands on either side of my head, trapping my body between him and the wall. "Because your body melts the second I touch you."

I hate that he's right...

"You're impossible, you can't decide if you want me or not."

He looks away as he confesses quietly. "I want you."

"Then why do you keep pushing me away?"

He closes his eyes, jaw tight. "Just because I want you doesn't mean I'm good for you."

Then he slams his lips against mine. We are both fighting for dominance with our mouths. I moan, and his lips start to trail down to my jaw, all the way down to my neck, sucking the flesh lightly.

"Fuck, Malyshka," he groans, pushing his hips against me. I can feel how hard his length is. "See what you do to me, Rosa."

"Yes," my voice is a low whimper.

He picks me up, and I wrap my legs around his waist. He sucks on my collarbone and yanks my dress down, exposing my breasts to him. He pulls back just enough to admire me before ducking down, pulling my nipple into his mouth.

I shiver at the sensation. I need more. I rip off his top, and the buttons scatter everywhere. My hand slowly trails down his chest, down to his abs, and all the way down to his belt. I feel him shiver under my fingers, and I feel joy knowing he likes my touch.

"Rosa," he groans, throwing his head back, and I take the chance to lean forward, licking his throat, kissing the side of his neck. I hear a deep rumbling sound that is driving me wild. His hand slides under my dress, pulling my underwear aside. His finger starts rubbing my clit in slow circles.

"You are so fucking wet for me." He pulls back and watches me squirm in pleasure.

"Yes, all for you."

"It'd better be only for me," he says. It's a warning and a claim.

"Dimitri..." I moan breathlessly.

"You like that, Malyshka?" He licks the side of my throat before biting down.

"Yes, more."

He quickly gives me what I want, pushing two fingers into my entrance. I feel myself stretch for him, and he starts moving them in and out as his thumb rubs my clit.

The heat in my core keeps building. I'm on the edge of exploding. "Please, Dimitri." I whimper.

He curls his fingers, and the orgasm rips through me, making my body ignite, my vision blurs, and my mouth parts in a silent scream. The feeling is pure euphoria.

"I'm going to bury myself so fucking deep inside of you, and you'll take all of me. Do you hear me?" He grips my hair and yanks it back hard. It stings painfully, but I love it. "Look at me."

I do as he says, and I watch as his fingers move to his lips, and he sucks on them. His eyes dilate as he licks them clean. I whimper loudly. "Fuck, you taste so damn delicious, so fucking sweet." He groans. "Get on your fucking knees and open those pretty lips for me like a good girl," he growls as he pinches my nipple.

Gods, I love his demanding side. I'm about to drop to my knees, but the door slams open with a loud bang.

He quickly covers me and holds me behind him, shielding me from view.

"Where is she?" Cassie storms into the room, shouting.

"I'm okay," I say, quickly fixing my dress and looking around Dimitri's large body.

"*Oh...*" Her eyes widen as she takes in my messy hair.

Dimitri starts walking away, but I grab his elbow, stopping him.

"Don't." My voice cracks. "Don't walk away."

He pauses, but only for a moment, then he walks out. The door slams shut, like a nail in our fate. The silence that fills the room is unbearable and hollow. My knees give out, and I drop to the floor. My breathing ragged as I stare at the closed door.

Then strong arms lift me, it's not him. The scent is different, sweeter. I look up to find Ian, his smile tight.

"I'm sorry, Rosa. I tried talking some sense into him, but he's stubborn. He doesn't let anyone in."

The ride back to the cottage is quiet, suffocating. Cassie keeps looking back at me from where she sits in the front passenger seat, but I can't look at her. I stare out the window, looking at the city lights flash by, my throat burning as I hold myself together. Why does it hurt like this?

We finally get back to the cottage. I slowly climb out of the back seat, and stare at the front door.

"I think I'm going to stay out here for a few minutes. I need to be alone." I mumble, wrapping my arms around myself.

"Okay, let me know if you need anything." Cassie hugs me, then disappears inside with Ian at her side.

I jump on the hood of the SUV, leaning back against the windshield. Inhale sharply, looking at the stars. The night air is cool against my skin. I need to distance myself; I need to go home and work on myself. I can't get over him if he's always there, watching me, provoking me.

Before I can talk myself out of it, I jump off the hood and grab my phone. I'll call Cassie later to explain.

Am I taking the easy way out? Yes.

Do I feel bad? Yes, but I can't bring myself to care right now.

I hop into the driver's seat, and I turn the key that is still in the ignition. The engine roars to life. I don't drive a lot, but I know how. The tires squeal as I pull out, and it smells like burned rubber.

What makes me unlovable?

Not just by Dimitri, but my adoptive father, and worse, my birth parents. Everyone who was supposed to stay. It hurts knowing that I care for them, and they don't care for me.

I wipe my tears away, shaking my head. I need to stop feeling sorry for myself. I have a good life, a great friend.

I need to get off the road. It's dark, and the bright city lights are giving me trouble.

So, the first hotel I see, I pull in. I check in the console next, and thank goodness, there's cash.

I pull down the visor and look in the mirror. I grab the makeup remover from my bag and wipe away the makeup, so I don't look like a clown. In the backseat, I spot the hoodie Ian wore earlier. I snatch it, and thankfully, it covers my whole dress like I thought it would. I grab Cassie's slippers she wore to the club, and took off before we headed in. Now I look like any exhausted traveler, not a girl running.

If they come looking, they'll be looking for a girl wearing a red dress, not this.

I put my hair in a messy bun as I walk into the hotel, and a minute later, a lady with a badge named Ruby comes out, chewing gum.

"Hiya! Can I help you?" she asks with a smile.

"Do you have any rooms available?" I smile nervously.

"Oh yes, we do! One king bed. That's going to be one sixty."

"Is cash okay?" I ask, handing her the money.

She takes it and hands me a key. "Breakfast starts at seven. Check out is eleven!"

I turn away but stop. "Can you do me a favor?"

"Um, sure?"

"If someone comes in looking for me, could you say you haven't seen me?"

Her eyes widen. "Are you in danger? I can call the police for you."

"Oh, God no! It's just my ex. We broke up, and if he comes looking..."

She relaxes, laughing. "No, problem. Us girls have to stick together."

I look for my room two-ten, the card reads. I find it on the second floor. I relax in the chair by the window, finally exhaling. I think I should visit Tammy. That'd be nice, somewhere safe and quiet.

My spine straightens when tires squeal outside. I stand, pushing the curtains aside to peek outside.

A motorcycle pulls up next to the SUV, and a tall figure climbs off. Even from here, I know it's Dimitri. My stomach drops. How did he find me so fast, and how did he get a motorcycle?

Oh God, the SUV has to have a tracker on it. It's the only thing that makes sense.

I watch as he peers into the car, then his eyes scan the hotel I parked in front of across the street, and then he heads inside. I pick up the phone and dial the front desk.

"Hello, front desk!"

"Hi, Ruby, it's Rosa, the girl who just checked in. He's here. Please tell him I wasn't here."

"Sweetie, are you sure you're safe?"

"Yeah, I'm not in danger. I just can't see him right now."

"Okay, don't worry, I got this."

"Hello, welcome! How can I help you, sir?"

"Hi, ma'am, I hope you can," Dimitri's deep voice floats over the line. The sound of it sends chills down my spine. "I'm looking for my girlfriend. She might've come in wearing a red dress, dark hair, she's about this tall. Her car is parked across the street, and I'm getting worried."

I grind my teeth, *liar*.

Ruby doesn't miss a beat. "No, I'm sorry, sir. No one's checked in for hours."

Silence, I can practically feel the tension through the phone, then in a low voice. "The man outside said he saw a woman run over here. Are you lying to me?"

Oh God...

Ruby's tone hardens. "Sir, unless you're booking a room, I have to ask you to leave, or I'll involve the police."

The silence stretches for a moment, then he says, "Thank you for your time, have a wonderful night." A pause, then. "I will see you soon, Malyshka." My breath hitches. He knows I'm on the phone... how? A tinge of fear runs through me. *How did he know?*

Ruby picks up the phone. "Okay, he's gone. Girl, he's intimidating."

"Yeah, tell me about it," I whisper, my mind still not fully processing. There's no way he would've known. I'm imagining things, right?

"Well, have a wonderful night."

"Thank you, Ruby!" I hang up and slowly peek out the window.

Dimitri stands in the middle of the parking lot, staring at this building. He tilts his head slightly, scanning the windows. He looks like a predator on the hunt.

My heart drops when he looks right at me. The corners of his lips curl into a smirk. I jerk away; no, he couldn't have seen me. He's too far away. I stand with my back against the wall for five minutes before I dare to look again.

He's gone...

In the bathroom, I fill the tub, and when the steam fills the room, I peel my clothes off. My mind circling... It's impossible. There is no way he saw me. Tomorrow will be a new day.

I sink my body into the warm water, and once I am fully submerged, I close my eyes and let myself scream underwater, fully letting my frustrations out.

It feels good. I gasp when I surface, something inside feels looser. I lean back and let the water heal my body.

That was long overdue.

I step out, wrapping the towel around my wet body, looking at my reflection.

You will be okay; you have been through worse.

I slip back into Ian's hoodie and crawl into bed, pulling the covers over me. I let out a long sigh.

Beep, beep, beep.

The alarm I set for eight wakes me. I stretch, arms over my head, groaning.

"Good morning, Malyshka."

I jump, rolling off the bed. My body hits the floor with a loud thump. Pain shoots up my back, and I thrash around like a wild animal because I'm tangled in the blankets. "Dammit!" I hiss, kicking my legs free, scrambling upright.

My blood turns cold. Dimitri is sitting in the corner chair, hands folded, chin resting on his knuckles, watching me like he's been there all night.

"How the hell did you get in here?"

I rush to the phone, but he grabs me and throws me onto the bed, pinning me with a terrifying ease.

"Not the best idea," he growls.

"Get off me!" I kick and shove with everything I have. "Get your filthy hands off me."

"You had us all worried!" he snaps, releasing me.

"I don't care. Leave, *now!*"

"No," his voice is calm. "I promised Cassie I would bring you back."

He's calm, too fucking calm, and it only makes me angrier. "Fine," I spit. "For Cassie only. After I talk to her, I'm leaving. Do not talk to me, and you will not touch me."

He flinches, and something flickers in his eyes, hurt. It's gone in a second. The mask of calm snaps back into place.

"Get out of my room and wait in the lobby." I point at the door.

"So, you can run again?" He crosses his arms and widens his stance, lifting his chin. "No."

"Just turn around and leave me alone." I clench my teeth hard enough to hurt. I take my time getting ready as he stands there like a statue, back facing me.

His phone rings, and he answers angrily, then turns. "Cassie wants to talk to you."

"Don't come any closer," I warn, raising my hands. I don't trust myself. "Just throw it on the bed."

He swallows, eyes narrowing, but he throws the phone on the bed, like I asked.

"Cassie," I whisper into the phone, sitting on the chair by the desk.

"Rosa! Oh, my fucking God! Where the hell did you go?" she screams.

"I'm sorry for leaving like that," I whisper, my guilt rising. "I wasn't thinking straight. I just needed to be alone."

"But why?"

"I need to get away from him." I put my slippers on and stand.

She sighs, "From Dimitri? You can't let him ruin our trip. We'll tell him to back off." I squeeze my eyes closed, and my fingers rub my temples. This migraine is brutal.

"He won't listen. Cassie, I'm leaving now. I'll talk to you when I get there."

I hang up without waiting for a reply. Dimitri watches me silently as I grab my things. I toss the phone at him as I walk past, careful not to touch him. I rush down the stairs, not wanting to be in the elevator with him.

When I get to the front desk, I notice that Ruby is gone. A new girl is here, and the moment she sees Dimitri, she lights up, batting her lashes. *What? Is she auditioning to be his next mistake?* I feel an ugly sting of jealousy, but I ignore it.

We walk to the SUV, and he opens the passenger door for me. I ignore him and climb into the backseat. He slams the door, frustration radiating off him.

He runs both hands through his hair, gripping it like he wants to rip it out. I have never seen him out of control like this before.

I wonder for a second where his motorcycle is, but I refuse to ask.

He gets in, starts the car, and looks over his shoulder. "Rosa... Can we talk? Please."

I turn my body toward the door and look out the window. I put on my sunglasses as I feel the slight burn behind my eyes. My chest caving, do not give in.

"Look, I can explain."

The damn audacity... Does he really think I'll forgive him or even talk to him?

"Rosa, please..." he groans out impatiently. His temper snaps. "Goddammit, Rosa, stop fucking ignoring me!" He punches the steering wheel a few times, making me flinch, and the tears finally fall. He exhales sharply. "Shit, Rosa, I'm sorry. I didn't mean to scare you."

I grab my chest as it starts to feel tight. I'm having a hard time breathing as my panic rises.

Chapter Thirteen

Dimitri

I stare at her through the rearview mirror. I can't see her beautiful eyes, but I know she's crying. The knowledge alone rips through me like a blade. My chest constricts painfully until it's hard to breathe. It feels like there's a large, raw, open wound in my chest, bleeding out. I want to drag her against me and protect her from the world and even from myself.

It's a terrifying thought that this little witch holds so much power over me.

I'll be on my knees, ready to kill for her in the snap of a finger. She doesn't even begin to understand how much power she holds in her little hands. I'd rip my own heart out and give it to her if she asked.

Hell, I already have. She owns every piece of me.

It's dangerous for someone to have so much power over a man like me.

"So, what? I'm getting the silent treatment?" I ask, my voice comes out rougher than I intended. She doesn't answer, but I need her to talk to me.

I need to hear her sweet voice. One word would satisfy me. I hear her stomach rumbling, and I latch onto it like a fucking lifeline.

"There's this place that I've heard of," I say carefully, looking in the rearview mirror. "It has the best French toast in the area." She licks her lips. I hate French toast, but hell, I'd eat a thousand slices if it made her forgive me.

She crosses her arms, pouting, and the sight nearly snaps my control. My hand tightens on the steering wheel. I want to taste it, drag my teeth across it until she gasps my name.

"Rosa, you are killing me. What can I do?" I hate how desperate I sound, but losing her is worse. I can face armies, blades, hellfire, my Hellhounds, but this? Her silence? It guts me.

I may be powerful, but I'm not powerful enough to go back and change what I have done.

I really thought I was doing the right thing by walking away. My enemies would use her to get to me, and if they found out she's my mate, they'd rip her apart.

The way she looked at me haunts me.

And what she said... *leave me alone, never touch me...* still echoes like a curse. She doesn't realize that those words broke something in me that has never healed. I felt the tears coming, and it took everything I had to hold them back. The pain in her eyes completely shattered me, but now, they're just empty. I don't know which is worse.

Can I protect her? Not here on earth, but in the Underworld I can. She'd never agree to go.

I crave her so much that I've been going insane. I've been losing my rational thoughts, trying so hard not to mark her and ravish her till she belongs to me. Now all I do is watch her, like some type of psychopath.

I got what I wanted, for her to stay away from me and the danger, but I don't feel happy about it. Driving her away makes me feel hollow, and now there's a big, gaping hole of emptiness swallowing me whole.

Here I thought I knew what loneliness felt like.

When we reach the cottage, she immediately runs inside, like she needs distance to breathe, but me? The distance chokes me.

Ian stands outside with his hands tucked in his pockets, giving me a disappointed look. "Looks like you finally pushed her away."

"I did what was necessary." I shove past him.

"Necessary?" He scoffs, shaking his head. "She's your mate!"

"You think I don't know that?" I growl, spinning around. "She's already been targeted once just from being seen with me. If they knew she's my mate..."

"You are the strongest demon alive," he interrupts me. "Plus, she's not useless; she's a witch."

"Not here on earth. She needs years of training." My voice cracks just thinking about pushing her away for that long. "It doesn't matter now; she despises me."

I grab the nearest vase and throw it across the room as the pain slams in my chest. I can't stop the tears this time. I haven't cried since the day I found my mother dead, not during the centuries of abuse by my father's hand, not for anything. But for her? I fall apart.

"You need to stop this." Ian hisses, gripping my shoulders and shaking me. "Stop making excuses and go to her."

"Mind your business," I shove him away, storming outside.

I end up beneath her window like some pathetic fool, listening to her cry. Every whimper, every sob, punches a hole through me.

Food... She needs to eat.

I rush to the kitchen. I can't believe I forgot that she hasn't eaten since yesterday; she'll get sick.

I hurry as I start pulling out ingredients and whisking the batter for the French toast. I cut the strawberries; it's silly, but I want it to be perfect for her.

Then I'm shoved from behind. I spin around with a growl, ready to kill, but I stop myself. It's Cassie; her fist slams into my chest.

"You fucking bastard!" She screams. "How could you? She is the sweetest person on this planet, and you hurt her? She's been through enough..."

I grind my teeth as I take the hits. Ian runs in and grabs her, arms wrapping around her waist, pulling her away. She kicks, fighting against him.

"Let me go! I'm going to kick his ass for hurting her. She's too good for you, go back to Hell where you belong!"

"You're right..." My voice is a harsh rasp as my chest caves. "She is too good for me. That's why I pushed her away. I had to make her hate me, because if I didn't..." I breathe, "I wouldn't survive staying away from her."

Cassie freezes, breath hitching as she stares at me wide-eyed.

"I know what I am," I add softly. "She deserves better."

Food... she needs food.

I turn back to the stove, and I add the butter. The sizzle fills the silence around us. .

CHAPTER FOURTEEN

Rosa

I hear a knock on the door, but I don't answer. The door opens a little, and Cassie's head pops in.

She frowns when she sees me sitting on the floor, spine pressed to the corner like it could hold me together. My eyes are burning from crying. I feel so hollow, almost weightless. She steps inside, carrying a plate, and sits on the bed.

"You need to eat, girlie," she says quietly, there's pity in her eyes, and I hate it. The kind that makes me feel weak.

"I'm not very hungry, Cass."

"Don't make me force you. I'll get Ian to haul your ass up." She pushes the plate toward me.

I laugh, shaking my head. "Bossy as ever." But I push myself up and sit next to her. The French toast is topped with whipped cream, heart-shaped strawberries, and a chocolate drizzle. It makes me smile. I pick up a tiny heart and eat it. "I need to talk to you about me going home."

"No." She grabs my hand immediately. "Absolutely not."

"I can't be around him, Cass." My voice is thick with emotion.

"Ian said their friend's place is huge. You might not even see him."

I rub my neck. "That's not the point."

She shifts, settling on her knees, her eyes desperate. "We came to get away, to breathe, to have fun! I need you. We'll explore and have fun. Please, don't leave me."

"You have Ian."

"Yeah, I need my sister too. Plus, you can't leave it's your birthday weekend." She clasps her hands and pouts. She looks up at me with so much hope it hurts.

"Okay..." I exhale, caving, completely defeated. Her eyes brighten instantly. I take a bite of the French toast. It's sweet and warm. "This is really good. Did you cut the strawberries?"

"No," she says a little too fast, looking away.

"Did you buy them?"

"Uh, no." She fidgets, acting guilty as hell.

My eyes narrow in suspicion. "Cass, what is it?"

She stands, looking out the window. "It was, Dimitri." It's so quiet I hardly heard it.

My fork slips out of my fingers. I push the plate away. "What? No, tell him I don't want any of it."

She places the plate back on my lap, "He worked hard on it, Rosie. He didn't want me to say anything. You two need to talk."

"I don't want anything from him. Especially not heart-shaped strawberries. It's... romantic." I push the plate away and stand. The anger is still there, but something softens. "I need a bath." I rush out before she can reply.

The tub fills as I sit sideways on the toilet seat.

I pour too many bubbles because I need to feel something warm and soft around me. Praying it'll help with the ache in my chest. I sink into the bath with a low groan; the warm water feels too good.

Why does he keep doing this? Sweet one second and hurting me the next? Better yet, why do I keep letting it? This toxic cycle needs to end.

I feel hollow, like something is missing. My hand clenches my chest like it'll help the emptiness. I rest my forehead against my knees, letting the tears fall silently.

The water grows cold. I stand, wrapping the towel around my body as I open the bathroom door, and his door is open. I can't stop myself from looking.

He's sitting on the edge of the bed, elbows resting on his knees, both hands tangled in his hair, his shoulders shaking, barely, but I can see it.

He glances up, and his eyes are red. He looks wrecked. We stare at each other. Something breaks open in my chest: sympathy, longing, and anger. I look away first, rushing into my room.

I sit by the window, staring out with my forehead against it. I'm angry at myself for being this weak. I pick up my phone, and before I talk myself out of it, I text him.

I need space. Stay away from me.

I hit send, and he answers instantly.

I'll stay away. I'm sorry.

My throat tightens as I type back.

You hurt me, but I'll be okay. I just need distance. Goodbye.

The typing bubbles appear, and I chew my thumbnail as I stare, waiting. They disappear, then reappear. Then nothing.

The silence hits harder than it should.

Cassie walks in a few minutes later. "He left. Well, stormed out. He didn't say a word to either of us."

"Oh." I look away from her, sighing. It's what I wanted, but the ache in my chest doesn't care about the logic.

"He's gone."

"Good." The words taste like a lie. I rub my temples, trying to ease the pain. "Can we get coffee before we hit the road?"

"Of course." She hugs me, her fingers gentle in my hair. "I'm sorry you're going through this."

"It's not your fault. I was stupid. He was a bad idea, and I knew it."

She grabs my suitcase, and we head out. Ian loads the bags into the SUV, his eyes soft with pity.

I look away quickly. I can't handle anyone else's sympathy.

We stop at a busy drive-through. The smell of espresso fills the car, and I take a sip of my caramel latte. The warmth comforts me, and I sigh in relief.

Ian and Cassie are holding hands in the front, and she smiles at him like he hung the stars.

The sting of jealousy and guilt slices through me, and I shake my head, hating it. I'm truly happy for her. She deserves to be happy. I turn, looking out the window.

Two weeks ago, my life was simple, no heartbreak, no Dimitri.

I pull a book from my purse, a vampire romance, desperate to disappear into anything that isn't my own sad reality.

I wish I'd never met him. But even as I think it, my heart knows it's a lie.

CHAPTER FIFTEEN

Rosa

We've been on the road for over an hour. I stop reading as we take an exit, and my gaze moves to the window. It brings us to a small town. It's cute, very cozy, and it's the distraction I need.

Ian groans dramatically when Cassie and I agree to stop. The streets are lined with boutiques, artsy shops, and a couple of wineries. I could use a bottle, or two.

We park at the edge of town, and Cassie links her arm around mine. Ian trails behind like he's suffering through something horrible. Who knew he could be such a whiner? I smile, feeling good.

We step inside a clothing boutique, and I look around, taking my time. I find black jeans, a few tops, and I pause when I see a rack full of leather. A leather skirt and black tank top call to me, sexy and badass, something clicks into place. I need to stop being fragile, and this outfit feels like the perfect first step.

The dressing room door clicks shut behind me, and I slide the outfit on. It's the perfect fit. The skirt and black tank top combo... It hits different. I feel mature and confident in a way I haven't let myself embrace.

I step out, and Cassie whistles. "You're getting that." Her tone is non-negotiable.

"Oh, I know." I grin. "Plus, a few more things."

The sales associate cuts the tags so I can wear the outfit out. We find a pair of heels that complete the look, sleek black stilettos, sharp and dangerous.

As we're checking out, a jacket catches my eye in the display window. It's black, cropped, and leather. I tilt my head toward it. "I want that. Please tell me you have a small."

They don't have any in the back, but luckily, the mannequin is wearing my size.

We leave the boutique with a handful of bags to find Ian leaning against the wall, surrounded by girls. Cassie strides over, arms circling his waist possessively.

"Excuse me, ladies, my girl is here now." He kisses her with the same territorial energy.

We head into a bakery next. I order a ham and swiss croissant with a latte... Yes, another latte because caffeine owns my soul.

"Wait... Did you change?" Ian asks me, confused.

"You just noticed? She looks hot!" Cassie smacks his arm.

"She does, but that's exactly why Dimitri's going to lose his shit."

I take a sip of latte, shrugging. "He can choke on it."

"Yes, exactly. Until he mans up, who cares?"

I point across the street. "Hair and nails?"

"No, let's leave." Ian groans, but Cassie leans over and drags her fingers down his chest in a slow and suggestive promise. His eyes shine, and he shuts up immediately... Smart man.

The salon takes us back, and I ask for a trim, long layers, and a Brazilian blowout. I completely melt as she shampoos my hair. It's relaxing bliss. Then we do a French tip for our nails.

I head into the winery feeling like a new woman. Cassie buys the bottles of wine since I'm still not of age. By the time we're back in the SUV, the tension in my chest feels better, still sore and bruised but not hollow.

"Okay, we'll be there in a few minutes. The person who owns this house is a close friend of ours, don't be surprised, but she's a lot older than us," Ian laughs. "She and her husband raised Dimitri. Don't mention him because he passed away. Her name is Eleanor."

I just nod.

"It'll just be us and someone you haven't met; his name is Aiden. He likes to flirt, so be aware." He looks at me through the rearview mirror like he is giving me a warning.

We turn off the road and stop at a large gate. Ian punches in the code, and it opens slowly. As we drive by, I notice a couple of moving cameras. It's a long, curvy driveway up a large hill with perfectly spaced trees. A minute later, we hit another gate with an excessive number of cameras. Paranoid, but beautiful.

We drive a little longer up the hill, and at the top, there's a mansion that looks like something out of an old-world estate, dark brick, large pillars, and numerous French doors.

"Holy shit." Cassie breathes.

"Yeah…" I agree, not looking away.

We step inside, and the place is spotless. The marble floors look like glass, and there are two curved staircases in the foyer curving to the second floor.

"Over there," Ian points to the left, "is the dining room, and over there," he points to the right, "is the library."

We stop in a sitting area, two couches face each other, but the view is what has my attention. The backyard is breathtaking: a massive in-ground pool, perfect greenery, and beyond that, a large, wooded area.

"Let's go upstairs." Ian leads the way. "The right staircase leads to Eleanor's private space, and to the left is the guest area."

Our rooms are directly across from each other, and of course, the room next to mine is Dimitri's. Just like the rest of the house, it's stunning. A massive bed is on the left, directly in front of a small sitting area with a fireplace. French doors lead out to a balcony with a view of the pool and, unfortunately, Dimitri's balcony.

I find a bathroom that belongs in a high-quality spa, and the closet is full of new clothes, my size.

"We're princesses!" Cassie exclaims as she jumps on the bed after Ian leaves us to go down to the gym with the guys.

I laugh, "It feels like it."

"Let's explore?"

"Yeah, let me change into some flats," I mumble, throwing off the killer heels and digging through the shopping bags for my flats.

We're heading down the staircase when a side door opens.

I stop in my tracks. A man steps out first, shirtless, covered in sweat. Ian's next, then Dimitri.

My lips part as my breathing picks up. His shaggy, wet hair falls into his eyes. His chest heaves lightly, muscles flexing as he runs a hand through his hair.

He commands the room, *me*. He radiates heat and power; it makes me rub my thighs together. The moment he sees me, something in the air changes. His eyes flash when he takes in my outfit, sharp, hot, and something territorial.

The man steps forward, offering a charming grin as he wipes his hands with a rag and takes mine, kissing the top of it. He does it slowly, intentionally, with hazel eyes staring into mine. Dimitri goes rigid.

"Hello, beautiful. I'm Aiden. It's a pleasure to meet you."

"Hi, I'm Rosa."

"Aiden," Dimitri growls, a clear warning.

"I'm Cassie," She steps forward, breaking the tension between the two men. "Rosa is very single," she adds, because she enjoys the chaos.

"Aiden isn't looking for anything." Dimitri snaps, nostrils flaring. It's a bit much, honestly.

Aiden doesn't miss a beat or look away from me. "Maybe I am now."

"We need to talk, *now*." Dimitri steps forward, moving his large body in front of me, and all I can see is his back.

Aiden walks out of the foyer with Dimitri following, stiff with fury. I exhale sharply. *What was that?*

"What's happening?" Cassie asks Ian.

"He's telling Aiden to back off." Ian stares at the closed door as if he can hear.

"It's not his business. I'm not his property."

A few minutes later, they come out. I glare at Dimitri as I push past him, hard enough that my shoulder knocks into his. He doesn't budge.

"Ignore him." I smile. "I choose who I spend time with."

A few hours later, there's still heavy tension as we eat lasagna for dinner.

"Where is the lady of the house, Eleanor?" I try to break the heavy silence.

"She's attending a meeting," Ian answers. My eyes flicker to Dimitri. He's silent, but his eyes are on me.

"Where are you from?" I glance at Aiden, trying for a friendly conversation.

"He's from Russia, same place as Ian and me," Dimitri answers for him sharply.

I grind my teeth. No one talks for the rest of dinner.

When it's finally over, I turn to Aiden. "Walk me to my room? I forgot the way." A bold lie, everyone knows it.

Before he can answer, Dimitri is suddenly behind me, breath tickling my neck. "He has plans tonight, but I'll walk you."

My hands clench as anger shimmers beneath the surface. I don't look at him as he leads the way. He leans against the door frame with a smirk.

"Here's your room." I push past him, careful not to touch as I swing my door open. I'm about to shut the door when his hand slams against it. "No, thank you or good night?"

"Thanks, and good night," I say flatly, then shut the door in his face.

"Malyshka," he groans through the wood, and my heart throbs. I hate that it does. My hand moves to touch the door separating us. Somehow, I can still feel him on the other side.

I push away and change into something comfortable. I head out onto the balcony, sitting on the oversized chair, looking up at the night sky. The night is cold, stars twinkle brighter out here, it's beautiful. I wrap the throw blanket around my shoulders.

I close my eyes, my mind drifting. The way his rough fingers trace my skin, I've never been touched with so much possessiveness. Those firm, demanding, but soft lips.

My lower stomach heats with pleasure as my body craves those hands and lips, my fingertips grazing the marks on my breast and neck. I love the way he claimed me in such an erotic way.

My eyes snap open when I hear something.

My breath hitches. Dimitri sits on his own balcony, shirtless, watching me with pure hunger in his eyes. His eyes lower to where my fingers rest against the mark on my neck.

I stand, leaving without a word.

A minute later, something crashes next door. I swallow hard, trying not to think of his anger.

I crawl into bed and fall asleep.

I'm running and running, and there are a couple of men chasing me. My heart is beating so hard, I swear it's going to jump out of my chest. I feel tears falling down my cheeks. I turn to look over my shoulder, and I roll my ankle and fall, hitting the ground, but I jump right back up, ignoring the pain. They are running so fast, it's almost unbelievable, and they have red eyes.

How is that possible? I run headfirst into a tree branch falling onto my back, and black dots start swirling in my vision. I look up and see the men standing over me, looking at me with evil grins, fangs on full display.

"Rosa! God Dammit, wake up!" Someone shakes me. I gasp as I wake, my chest heaving, and I find Dimitri above me. Without thinking, I grab him, clinging to him like a lifeline. Shame burns over me, but I push it aside. The dream felt so real.

"I've got you," he murmurs, settling in bed next to me as he holds me tight. "You're safe, I promise."

I lay my head on his chest, his heartbeat thunders against my cheek, and eventually, I fall back to sleep.

My eyes blink open with warmth pressed against my back. I roll over, snuggling deeper into it.

That's when I realize I'm straddling Dimitri, his hands are on my thighs, his thumb brushing dangerously close to where I'm already aching, and heat floods through me. The violent waves that slam into me include embarrassment, want, and confusion.

His hand slides up my shirt, and the warmth sends a shiver down my spine. I moan as I lean into it, and he groans with deep satisfaction.

"Do you normally have nightmares?"

"I do, sometimes. I'm sorry about last night." I nod, my chin leaning against his chest to look up at him.

"Never apologize to me, I'm happy I was here for you. Tell me about it."

"It felt real... they were chasing me through the woods. It was dark, and they had red eyes. They were running fast, blurring speeds. Fangs too." I shiver just thinking about it.

He stiffens beneath me, "Red eyes with fangs?"

"Yeah," I breathe, parting my lips. "It was weird."

But my mind wasn't on the dream. No, it's on his hands, rubbing my upper thigh.

He swallows hard when his eyes dip to the mark on my neck. He licks his upper teeth like he's remembering them digging into my flesh. His hand moves up my body, slow and deliberate.

"Look, Rosa..." his voice softens. "I want to apologize for—"

"No. I shouldn't have overreacted. You told me you didn't want anything. I knew that."

"I still hurt you. That wasn't my intention."

"It's fine. Just... stop kissing me."

"I will," he whispers, but his eyes drop to my lips.

"Promise?" I ask breathlessly.

"I promise," he lies beautifully.

We stay there, too close, neither of us moving.

His hand slides to my throat, tilting my head back gently. My legs tighten around his, as my breath shudders. My rational thoughts fly out the window. His eyes go darker, hungrier.

"Maybe," he murmurs, leaning closer, "just one more."

I don't stop him; I melt into the kiss. His hand wraps around me, gripping my ass, pushing me against him. His hardness presses into me, and heat explodes through me.

"Please, I need more."

"Then take it." He growls, "Take what you need, baby."

I push myself up, my hands flat on his chest, moving my hips with slow, hungry insistence. Fabric drags between us, tension winding tight in my body.

He yanks my shirt down so hard that it rips the straps, and the torn fabric falls around my hips. He leans back against the headboard, eyes fixed on me like he's watching something he's been starving for.

"So damn beautiful," he says under his breath.

His hands roam, possessive and sure as he cups my breasts, he pulls me closer, sucking the hard nipple into his mouth, hot and claiming. The heat inside me builds fast, dangerously fast, like a small fire is slowly building deep in my core into something I can't contain.

"Dimitri," I whisper.

His gaze snaps up, and they're so dark that it takes my breath away.

One of his hands slides lower, sliding my shorts aside, thumb pressing against my clit, rubbing in frantic circular motions, pushing the pressure higher.

My head falls back as the sensation breaks through me, sharp and over-whelming.

"Look at me," he says, voice rough. He grips my jaw, forcing my eyes open. "Understand?"

I pull back slightly as I stare into Dimitri's dark eyes, and I scream as my body starts trembling with such a pleasurable sensation.

My body stiffens as I let the fire consume me, swallowing me whole in a deep bliss. The intensity is violent and enthralling, but it ends too quickly. I need to feel more. I collapse against him, boneless, feeling completely satiated and drained.

His hand strokes down my spine, slow and possessive. "Good girl," he murmurs.

My eyes close. My body is still trembling, but my mind is torn in two...Fight him or fall again.

I don't know which one scares me more.

CHAPTER SIXTEEN

Rosa

I reach across the bed, searching for the man who consumes my every thought, but my fingers touch cold sheets. He's been gone for a while.

I exhale slowly. Of course, he left. I shouldn't be surprised, but still, something in me sinks anyway.

No, I won't mope. I grab my phone and check the time. I fell asleep for a couple of hours. I get out of bed, feeling restless. I'm ready to explore this beautiful house, filled with secrets. And there's a library here, somewhere. That alone is worth moving for.

But food first.

I grab my small bag, head to the bathroom, and turn on the shower. Steam fills the room while I brush my teeth. I step under the warm water, letting it wash last night off me.

I get dressed, but instead of the new clothes in the large closet, I reach for my own. I pick something comfortable, black flowy shorts, a white tank top with straps tied on my shoulders, and simple sandals.

I head downstairs following the voices into the dining room.

Cassie waves me over. "Well, hello there, sleeping beauty." I sit beside her, avoiding Dimitri's intense gaze. I'm not mad anymore, but I still feel bruised.

"Good afternoon," I greet.

"Are you okay?" Cassie leans closer. "Ian told me you were screaming last night. Nightmares?"

"Yeah, but I'm okay." I shrug.

"Do you want to talk about it?" She lays her hand on top of mine.

"No, I'm fine." I want to look at him, even though I shouldn't. I risk a glance, and he's already staring. The same look he gave me last night, dark and hungry. I look away before it swallows me whole.

A beautiful woman walks into the room, mid-thirties, and familiar, but I would've remembered her. She's the kind of beauty you'll never forget.

"You must be Rosa. I'm Eleanor." She smiles warmly, her voice soft. "Well, come here and let me look at you."

I stand up, stepping closer. She grabs me by the shoulders, studying me like she doesn't want to forget a single detail. I swear I see her eyes water.

"You, my dear, are gorgeous."

"Thank you," I whisper.

"We ordered pizza before you came down," Eleanor says as I sit down, and she takes a seat beside Dimitri.

"Don't worry, I got buffalo chicken for you," Cassie says, opening one of the boxes on the table. She grabs me a slice and places it on my plate.

"Thanks." I take a bite, praying that it's good. The flavor hits my tongue, and I groan softly, closing my eyes. When I reopen them, I almost choke as I swallow. Everyone is looking at me.

"What? It's incredible." I take another bite as they laugh, except Dimitri. His stare darkens more.

"Buffalo chicken is my favorite, too." Eleanor smiles widely at me, asking Dimitri to grab her a slice, and he does.

"Honestly, Rosa doesn't like pizza that much, but will kill for the good shit," Cassie says.

Aiden leans forward. "I can give you a tour after lunch, if you want?"

"No," Dimitri growls lowly, a lethal warning.

"Yeah, I'd actually like that." I smile at Aiden.

Dimitri slams his fist onto the table, and I flinch at the sound of silverware rattling. "Dimitri," Ian and Eleanor warn sharply.

Heat prickles across my skin, like I can feel his anger. I finally meet his gaze full on. He stares back at me. I can see the storm barely holding together.

"Why?" I ask softly, hopeful.

His jaw tightens. "Because I'm no good for you, but he's even worse." He finally says, and my hopes vanish into thin air. I should've known. His words are calm, but they hurt. I bite the inside of my cheek.

"Well, I can spend time with whoever I want."

He stands, glaring at Aiden as he storms out.

We spend the rest of lunch eating in silence.

After we eat lunch, I stop Aiden by grabbing his elbow. "I'll meet you outside?"

He hesitates, "I don't know if that's the best idea."

"Dimitri made it clear he wants nothing to do with me." The words sting as I say them out loud. "I'm going for a run, give me an hour?"

He nods. I don't blame him. Dimitri is scary. I go to my room, change into leggings and a sports bra, grab my earbuds, and turn on some music.

Outside, I start stretching, and once I'm warmed up and limber, I start running. My thoughts are finally quiet, and I start relaxing.

My feet carry me for a couple of miles until I come across a beautiful pond. I sit on the edge of it, bend my knees, and wrap my arms around my legs.

A splash breaks the peaceful silence. I look up to see someone swimming. He walks out of the water on the other side of the pond, and my heart stops, it feels like I can't breathe.

Dimitri... Dripping wet, muscles flexing as he moves, dark hair slicked back. Gods, he looks sexy. Heat pools low in my stomach with need. Fuck, me... I rub my thighs together, biting back a whimper.

I stand, slowly turning away before I completely embarrass myself.

"I know you're there, Rosa."

I spin around, startled. "I— I'm sorry. I didn't know you were out here. I'm just... running." It's a pathetic excuse, but it's all I have as my eyes devour him. I can't stop them. He's just too tempting standing there. I want to lick every drop of water off him. I look away, clearing my throat.

"Dimitri!" A woman runs out from the trees behind him, long legs, beautiful, like a model. She launches herself into his arms, legs wrapping around him as if she belongs there. My body tenses as jealousy hits me so fast I nearly choke on it.

"Alice," he says, but his eyes never leave mine.

"I missed you," she purrs, clinging to him. "Thanks for inviting me."

"Don't touch me," he snaps, pulling her off. Her eyes turn to me, glaring like I ruined her moment.

I step back, my pulse going crazy.

"Baby, who's she?" Alice asks, laying a hand on his chest.

He grabs her wrist and pushes it away, hard.

"Don't call me that. And she's none of your business." His voice is sharp and lethal.

"You called me," she snaps.

"For a damned favor. Don't act crazy," he bites out.

I turn and walk away. I don't want him to see the hurt or jealousy. It's embarrassing to be envious of another woman, but I can't help it. Is she the kind of woman he wants? I shake my head; it doesn't matter.

"Rosa, wait," he calls, and I hear his loud footsteps chasing me.

"I'm fine," I wave him off, trying to sound bored. I'm really not, but I will be, and I don't want him to know.

A branch catches my foot, and I slam into the ground hard. I hiss as pain shoots up my leg. Dimitri kneels next to me instantly, his large hand carefully wrapping around my calf as he inspects my wound, eyes worried like the small cut is a big deal.

"Are you hurt?"

"Stop, I'm fine." I shove at him, but he doesn't move an inch.

"Please don't be upset," he whispers, looking up at me. "She's not my girlfriend. I only called for a favor, I swear."

"It doesn't matter." My voice cracks, and I move back, trying to put distance between us. I can't think straight with him this close. "It's none of my business."

"I know you're upset."

"I'm not," I lie, looking anywhere but him. I shift so that I can stand, but he suddenly grabs my wrists, pinning them above my head, his body pressing mine into the ground, and his other hand grabs my jaw. It makes my emotions spill out.

"Why don't you want me? Tell me the truth. Is it because I'm not as beautiful as her?"

He rears back like I've slapped him. "Rosa..." His voice is raw. "Don't ever compare yourself to her. You are—" He closes his eyes, breath shaking. "You're on a level she could never touch." Then his knee nudges mine apart, setting his hips between them.

"Dimitri," I whisper, panicked, pushing my back further into the earth. "Don't... Don't do this again. I can't say no to you."

"I know." His lips brush my cheek, kissing my tears away. "I'm sorry, but I can't help myself around you. I need to kiss you." He lifts me like I weigh nothing and presses my back against a tree.

"Malyshka..." He groans like he's in pain and kisses me, mouth desperate. I kiss him back, legs wrapping around him, arching deeper into him, needing to be closer.

His hand slides under my sports bra, thumb teasing my nipple until I gasp. His mouth trails down my neck, marking me even more than he already has. My nails dig into his back, leaving my own marks.

"Please," I breathe. "I need you." My hand drags down his hard abs, reaching into the waistband of his shorts.

He grabs my wrist, halting me.

"I can't," he whispers, forehead pressing into mine, eyes closing, I can feel his body trembling beneath my touch.

"Why not?"

His eyes open, they're dark and haunted. "Because if you know who I really am... you'll hate me."

"I could never hate you," I whisper fiercely. "Whatever you've done, that's your past, and it doesn't change that you're a good man."

"I'm not," he says, voice shaking. "And I won't drag you into my world." Then he kisses me again, like he's drowning, hands cupping my face.

"Stop," I beg, pushing at him with trembling hands. "I can't handle you walking away from me again."

He drops to his knees in front of me, looking freshly ruined and beautiful. His chest rises and falls like he's trying to stay in control, fighting himself.

"I want you more than I want air," he whispers. "But wanting you puts you in danger you can't even imagine."

"Then tell me," I plead, my finger digging into his hair. "Make me understand."

"I can't."

"Then I'm done." My voice breaks. "I'm done letting you hurt me."

He doesn't reach for me. He doesn't stop me, and I won't lie, it hurts.

I walk to the house, anger and hurt shimmering beneath the surface. I look up when a low rumble sounds above me. The skies are clear, but it seems like the weather is matching my mood. I can't stop the words he said circling in my head. No matter what, I'm proud of myself for walking away; this toxic cycle needs to end.

I knock on Aiden's door, and he answers shirtless. It's just what my shattered ego needs, another unfairly attractive person.

His smile is warm when he leans against the door frame. "Hey, you okay?"

"Yeah, of course." I smile, but it's tight.

"Ready for that tour?"

"That'll be great. Can we start with the library?"

"Anything you want." He grins, steps back into his room, and grabs a shirt, leaving the door open. He steps out, and we head downstairs into the foyer, where he swings open the double doors.

My eyes widen. I didn't expect this. It's breathtaking: floor-to-ceiling shelves, full of books, a stained-glass window that's at least fifteen to twenty feet high, a velvet reading bench underneath it, large enough to curl up and get lost for hours, and there's a small sitting area in the center.

"My God..." I whisper, moving forward. My fingers run down the book spines as I read the titles.

"You like it?" Aiden asks as he watches me with a soft smile.

"Like it? More like obsessed with it."

"You're a bookworm, aren't you?"

I laugh, nodding, "I sure am."

"Let's continue the tour."

I sigh as I follow him, not wanting to leave just yet. We head downstairs to the basement, and it's probably the biggest gym I've ever seen. There are a few boxing bags, treadmills, and bikes, everything you could need.

"What's back there?" I point at the closed door.

"Bathroom and a dance room."

"Dance room?"

"Yeah, it hasn't been used in a while. Eleanor used to dance, and she'd be down here every night. She's one of the best dancers I have ever seen."

"Can I go look?"

"Yeah." He walks over and opens the door. "Here, let me get the lights."

The lights flick on. It's a good size, maybe the same as the dance studio Cassie and I dance at, with floor-to-ceiling mirrors.

"Do you think she'd care if I wanted to use it?" I look at his reflection in the mirror.

"You dance?" He arches both brows.

"Yeah. Why do you sound surprised?" I add some sass to my voice, placing my hand on my hip.

"You can ask her. But I don't think she'd care, and I'm not sure." He shrugs.

"Perfect."

"Hungry? I make a mean sandwich," he asks as we step into the kitchen.

"Yeah, sounds good." He grabs everything he needs out of the fridge and turns on the stove. "Do you need help?"

"No, come here, we can talk while you watch." I walk over to him, and he grabs my waist and lifts me onto the counter, right next to the stove.

The back door opens, and Dimitri steps in. His eyes automatically land on the hands resting on my thigh. It's innocent, but his nostrils flare, jaw clenching. I look away, I can't deal with those intense eyes or possessiveness right now.

"So, are you seeing someone?" Aiden asks out of nowhere as he opens the fridge, not bothered by Dimitri's presence.

"No, I'm not."

"Would you be open to it?" He nudges his way between my thighs, and I pull back, but he clearly doesn't see my discomfort, or if he does, he simply doesn't care.

"To what?" I feel bad for only half listening, but my attention is on the man strolling to the couch, and he sits, casually leans back, crossing his ankle over the opposite knee, and spreads his arms over the back of the cushions, showing me that he's not going anywhere.

I lick my lips, and he zooms in on the movement like a hawk.

"Dating."

Dimitri moves, having had enough of this conversation, and he's suddenly standing beside us as if he teleported. Aiden barely flinches, but I reel back.

"I told you to stay away from her," Dimitri growls, his eyes darkening.

"And I told you I don't give a damn what you think, unless you claim her. You don't rule up here." They're chest to chest now, predators circling like they're fighting for the last meal. "Maybe we should let Rosa pick." Both men look at me.

"I will decide who I spend time with," I snap, jumping off the counter. "Not either of you."

"You can, but not him." Dimitri steps forward, his face twisted in pure rage. I shove his chest, but it's like pushing a brick wall; he doesn't move.

"You don't get to control me." I hiss, slamming my shoulder into his side as I push past him.

I step into the library once again, desperately needing peace and quiet. Can't a girl catch a break? I stare at the rows of books towering over me, their spines cracked with age, their pages discolored. The scent in here is of dust and ink, my favorite.

I reach for a random book, trying to read the barely there title. *Demonology: VOL 11...Interesting...*

I go to put it back, but it's like the book is whispering to me, telling me to read its secrets. I move to the reading bench, curl into the velvet fabric, and let the book rest on top of my thighs. My fingers trace the pages as I flip through them. It's full of stories of demons, princes, and dark kingdoms. There are pictures of demons, and some look human with horns and fangs, others have leathery skin and pitch-black eyes.

A chill runs down my spine, *creepy.*

Some of their abilities are shapeshifting, teleportation, speed, and strength. They start changing forms under extreme stress when they lose control, growing larger, eyes darkening, and some even turning black.

My chest tightens, Dimitri's eyes turn dark when he's angry or jealous or whenever he touches me. I scoff at myself, I'm being ridiculous.

I turn a page, and the top says, *Royal Line of the Underworld...*

Only the ruling bloodline is capable of manifesting wings, horns, or full shifts. A demon prince is the most dangerous form, possessing heightened strength, speed, and a near-feral instinct to claim their mate.

My pulse hammers... mates... It says that mates have a pull to each other that is nearly impossible to ignore. They feel each other whenever they enter a room, the air around them hums with the power of the mate bond, and sparks fly whenever they touch each other.

Dimitri's presence is heavy. I guess the air does hum when he's around; whenever we touch, sparks ignite. I turn the page again, and I nearly drop the book.

There's a picture of a royal demon's back, and a large V between the shoulder blades. Just like the V on Dimitri's back. Every demon with wings has this mark. My breathing quickens, demons' strength–like when he threw that man into a pole when I was attacked– or the pull between us, his eyes turning dark, the way he vibrates with anger like he's trying to control himself... this is terrifying.

I'm not a girl who believes in monsters, but... Dimitri has always felt like one. It doesn't scare me, but I feel it in his dark energy. It actually draws me closer, and I don't fully understand, but this is not the answer. *Right?*

No...

I slam the book closed. It's just a coincidence. I'm spiraling for no reason. I can't stop myself from tracing the cover of the book.

I swallow. There's no such thing as demons, there's no throne of Hell, no mate bond that ties your souls together. If these pages were true, I knew what he'd be: a Demon of Hell.

My head snaps up when I feel that same buzz I do whenever Dimitri is around, but there's no one here.

Okay, enough. I gently put the book back in its rightful place.

The one thing I am certain of is that even with his dark, monstrous energy, I still want him.

Chapter Seventeen

Rosa

It's time for dinner by the time I step out of the library; I find Eleanor sitting on the couch, drinking a glass of wine. "The food will be done in ten minutes, dear. Would you like wine?" Eleanor asks as she stands and pours me some wine without waiting for my response.

"Thank you," I smile when she hands me the glass of wine and sits back down, patting the seat next to her.

"You look troubled," she says softly when I take a seat.

"No, I just… I'm having trouble. Boy trouble." I laugh, taking a sip of wine.

"It's Dimitri, isn't it?"

I hesitate for a moment, not knowing if I should be honest. I guess there's no harm in it. "Yeah, he keeps pushing me away. I can't handle it."

She studies me, her eyes warm, not judgmental. "He cares for you. He has trouble trusting people; he's been hurt by everyone who is supposed to love him, parents, his siblings, except for Ian."

My stomach drops. I remember the conversation by the waterfall and the scars on his back. That comes from someone hurting him, not an accident.

"And he fears falling for someone just to be rejected."

"He won't even let me close enough to try." I sigh heavily. I understand, I do, but it doesn't make it easier.

"Be patient, I promise he will. He's unraveling, and it's happening fast. Once he shares his secrets with you..." she pauses, thinking of the right words. "They are hard to process, keep an open mind. It will change everything you know."

"Dinner!" The cook calls, Eleanor pats the top of my hand, and stands.

"Wait, I wanted to ask about the clothes in my closet and if I can use the dance studio?"

"You are more than welcome to use it, and Dimitri ordered those clothes. He wanted to make sure you had everything you needed. He even stocked the bathroom with everything under the moon. She walks off, and I finish off the wine in one big gulp.

After a dinner I barely touched, I rushed to my room, and here I am relaxing in a massive bathtub. The water is perfectly warm, and the Lavender bubbles feel amazing.

My mind is on him, his mouth on mine, his anger, the book, the pictures. My emotions are everywhere tonight.

I also think of the way his eyes darken when he's angry, when he wants me, and when he loses control. I close my eyes, sliding deep into the water until it brushes against my chin.

It's stupid, absolutely insane. I know demons aren't real, so why do I keep thinking about them? It describes him to the T, a demon, the way he moves too fast and silently, like he's part shadow.

Also, what Dimitri did for me: ordered all of those clothes for me and stocked the bathroom. Just for a weeklong trip? It doesn't make sense. He did all of this and didn't even take credit like any normal person would.

He wasn't at dinner, Aiden said he went to visit Alice. Is she the one from the pond? Just thinking about them leaves an ache in my chest. He's in this house, probably on the other side of this very wall.

Or he could still be with Alice. That thought makes it hard to breathe.

I'm being dramatic, I'm too jealous and confused.

"What are you, Dimitri?" I whisper in the empty room, looking up at the ceiling.

An hour later, I'm lying in bed staring out the glass doors. I can't sleep, I feel restless. The questions are circling my mind too much. I throw on a hoodie and slip on a pair of slippers. I'm reading the rest of that book.

I close the door silently behind me and walk to the bookshelves.

But...

The book isn't here. The spot is empty, where it used to be. I blink, staring at the empty hole, but it doesn't magically appear.

The library is massive, so maybe I can put it in a different spot? I look over the other books, fast at first, but slower the second time, and nothing.

A shiver runs down my spine. Someone knew I had it, and someone didn't want me to have it.

A shadow moves past the room, fast, too fast. I almost miss it, then the air hums. I spin around trying to find what or who it was. The double doors are open, but that's not right. I closed them. I remember I did it slowly and quietly to make sure I didn't bother anyone who might be sleeping close by.

Dimitri...?

I take a step back, no...He wouldn't care about a stupid demonology book, unless...

No, I refuse to think about it.

I swallow, rushing out of the library, looking around like something was going to jump out.

Dimitri

I smelled her scent the moment she stepped into the library. I watch as she looks for the book that I have clenched in my hand. She doesn't give up, she keeps looking.

I rush out, opening the door with a slight breeze. I make it to my room and drop the book on my desk. I stare at it, the muscle in my jaw ticking. It's a story of my family. Out of every book in that damned library, why did she have to find this one? My emotions are still a mess from earlier in the day, Aiden's hands touching her skin flashing in my head again, roaring my anger once more.

I flip the book open; it's one of the original copies, one of Eleanor's ancestors' writings about our family. It's too accurate and revealing. She caught a glimpse of the first half, but the second half reveals a lot more and has photos of my father, who looks nearly identical to me. She would've put the pieces together.

I slam the book shut with more force than was necessary, and the cracks snap around the room. She isn't ready yet. I pick up the book, move to my nightstand, and place it inside.

I will tell her the truth in time, after she talks to Eleanor.

I nearly lost control today, nearly shifted right in front of her, and claimed her.

I hear her hurried footsteps rushing down the hall. I smile, she definitely felt me back there, my sweet mate was so close to the truth. If she only knew the demon she keeps begging to love her.

Let her wonder where the book went, she'll dismiss the idea, I know she will.

Because the moment she figures out that I am the demon prince, that I'm her demon, she'll be trapped with me forever.

Rosa

I throw my hair into a messy bun and grab my book so I can read on the lounge chairs, pretend my life is normal for a few minutes, and forget the stupid Demonology book. It was just a creepy book, and I was reading it in a creepy library, mixed with thinking too much about Dimitri.

I will not think about it anymore, absolutely not. I slip on my flip-flops and grab my sunglasses.

I stop at Cassie's door to ask if she'd like to join. It's cracked open, and I can hear voices, low and intense.

"I'm a demon, Cass. You know what that means. If we are going to stay together, I'll have to turn you. Mark you as my mate."

My breath hitches. What the actual hell? There's that word again... Demon. Cassie hisses, but it cracks at the end. "I know that! But we need to talk to my mom first. You know she doesn't agree. And Rosa, Gods, I can't do anything till she knows the truth. I can't do this anymore; she's my best friend, and it's killing me."

"Hey, it's okay. It's almost time, we'll tell her everything."

The truth? The truth of what?

I back away from the door, my hands slightly trembling. *It's all just a coincidence. I refuse to believe it; it's too crazy to believe. I mean, come on! Demons?!* I practically run to the pool like it'll save me from myself.

I shake myself off, exhaling slowly.

You're not going crazy...

She's hiding something, but it's not about that; it's probably something silly... or is she pregnant? No, way. She wouldn't hide something that big. Plus, they only met a few weeks ago, not possible, but what the hell do I know? I barely passed health class. Even though I push the thoughts away, something is scratching at the surface, begging me to put it all together.

I settle on the lounger, rubbing sunscreen on my arms, I twist to do the back of my shoulder, and something in the corner of my eye catches my attention.

Someone is on Dimitri's balcony, not just someone, but him. He's shirtless, leaning on the railing, watching me. I quickly look away, not doing this right now. I'm having a little me time.

"Need help with that?" I spin, looking around to see Aiden by the door.

"Oh, uh, no, I'm okay. I'm planning on doing a little reading." I hold up my book. "So, I don't really need sunscreen on my back. But thank you."

"If you change your mind, I'm more than willing to help." The last time someone rubbed my back... no thanks...

"You don't mind me joining you, right? I was planning on swimming." Aiden asks, walking to the pool's edge and dipping his toes in.

"Oh, of course not. I probably won't jump in any way."

"Okay, cool." I watch Aiden as he removes his sandals and shirt. The flexing of his back muscles does nothing for me. Dimitri damaged me.

I lay down, pretending not to look at Dimitri, while I am definitely looking at him. He's still there, staring at me, and I swear to God my body over-heats. He's too hot for his own good, and the way my fingers roamed those hard muscles... Jesus, no!

His grip on the railing tightens as if he can sense which direction my mind went. I look away and carefully untie my swimsuit cover, letting it slowly slide off my shoulders. I reach for the sunscreen, rubbing it over my chest just a little too intentionally, praying that I look sexy doing it. My body shivers when my fingers glide across my mark over my nipple.

"Come in, the water feels good!" Aiden calls from the pool, and my eyes move to his to see he's also watching me. I pull my cover up. I completely forgot he was here.

"Rosa!" I look behind me. Cassie and Ian walk out; she looks killer in a nude two-piece. They take the lounger next to me, and Ian steals my sunscreen, rubbing it on her back.

I pick up my book and ignore their cute comments and whispers to each other.

"Mmm, Ian, you keep touching me that way, and we'll have to go back upstairs."

"Baby girl, don't threaten me with a good time."

I press my lips together; they are such an obnoxious, perfect couple.

Once Ian is done with Cassie's back, he does a flip into the pool like a showoff. Cassie settles next to me, leaning in and whispering, "Don't think I didn't see your little tease for Dimitri, trying to get him all hot and bothered?"

"I was not!" I gasp, leaning away from her, my face heating, no doubt turning dark red.

"You're playing with fire; you might get burned." She gives me a pointed look.

"Maybe I want to get burned." I wiggle my brows with a grin.

She laughs, "Where did the good girl go?"

I laugh too, standing and taking off my swimsuit cover. "Maybe I'm done being a good girl, and I'm turning into a bad girl."

I jump in the pool, the water is nice and warm, but Dimitri's burning gaze is even warmer. I grab a floaty and lie on it, letting the sun hit just right.

"Stop being a creeper and come down!" Ian shouts.

"Nah," Dimitri calls back. "I'm enjoying the view from up here." He doesn't look away from me, and a blush heats my entire body. Someone flips my floaty, and I fall into the water.

"What the hell!" I cough out, moving my wet hair away from my face.

Cassie laughs hysterically. "Sorry, you looked like you were getting a little too hot."

I flip her off, stepping backward, right into someone's body.

I turn, finding Aiden. "Oh, sorry."

"Don't be sorry, love. I enjoy feeling you against me."

The air crackles with energy, turning a playful moment into something darker. I know it's Dimitri's mood shift.

"Whatever." I shove him, but he dunks me before I get too far. I come back up gasping for air. "What the hell!" I push the hair out of my face, again.

"I'm just playing, babe."

"Don't call me that." I glare at him.

He responds by pulling me closer, and I instantly wrap my legs around him, trying to dunk him underneath. Then his hands roam, and there is nothing playful about his grip.

I try pulling away, but his grip tightens. "Stop, let me go."

"Why? You feel good wrapped around me."

"Aiden, let her go!" Ian snaps, voice panicking. The air around us crackles once more, hotter and darker than before.

Then strong arms yank me back and out of the pool so fast the world blurs. I gasp, clinging onto it instinctively, trying not to fall. I look up, Dimitri. How did he get here so fast?

He cradles me against him like I weigh nothing, anger rolling off him in waves. I can feel him shaking as if holding back. "You touch her again," he hisses at Aiden, "and you're fucking dead."

And he has the audacity to smirk. "She liked it."

I gasp, shaking my head. "I didn't. I told you to stop."

"It's okay, Malyshka. I've got you." He wraps a towel around me. I feel him lean in, inhaling deeply, his breath brushing against my neck. Goosebumps rise on both of us, and his trembling stops as if my scent calms him.

He carries me upstairs, to my room, and sets me on my bed. When he steps back, I instantly miss his warmth.

"It's getting late. Get ready for bed," he whispers, and I nod. He turns and leaves without a backward glance.

Chapter Eighteen

Dimitri

I sit in the chair, my fingers turning into fists as I wait for Alice. The anger I feel is too hot, my skin too tight, and I want to shift and lose control. I don't think I can handle much more. She hurt Rosa by touching me; that is enough for her death. No one hurts my mate, physically or emotionally.

I'm having a lot of regrets, mainly walking away from Rosa that night at the club; now Aiden is all over her.

I lick my upper teeth, my fangs wanting release.

Does she like him? Would she choose him if she knew who I really am? Should I kill the bastard? It'd be easy. Ian is the only reason he's still breathing. I smirk at the thought of me ripping him to shreds, ripping his pathetic heart out.

Ian told me he's falling for Cassie, and he wants to mark her. I don't care, but I did warn him to be careful. She wants a mate. If she finds him, I know who she'd choose.

Rosa fills my mind again, the way she felt in my arms as she slept. I actually slept that night, and I haven't slept.... Not like that, not in a really long time.

Her nightmares worry me. They might be visions, a warning of what's to come. She's too young for her powers, but they are surfacing. I've felt them whenever her emotions are wild. The way the sky rumbles, it's responding to her.

I pull out my phone and call Eleanor.

"Dimitri?" she answers immediately.

"I need to meet you in about an hour. Will you be home?"

"Yes, I will. What's this about?"

"It's about Rosa. I'll meet you in your office, and we'll talk." I hang up.

I need to leave town after her birthday. I am barely hanging on to my control. I need some time away.

I found the courage to pick out a gift, my mother's heirloom, passed down through generations. I want Rosa to have it; it'd mean the world to my mother if I gave it to my mate. I will give it to her, then I will leave.

I don't know how I'll manage it, because it will destroy me, but it has to be done.

Finally, Alice walks in. She steps in here like she owns the place, wearing a smug smile. Alice thinks she's untouchable because she's my father's assistant.

"What took you so long?" I stand.

A few months ago, I stupidly had sex with her, and I regretted it instantly. She's a low-class demon trying to get someone powerful to marry, and she picked me.

"I had matters to take care of, love. Are you missing me? If so, I can..." She slides her fingers down my chest.

I grab her by the wrist, growling. "Don't touch me." I push her back.

"Is this because of that little bitch from earlier? She is nothing, a weakling. I'll kill her myself..."

My vision turns red. She made a grave mistake. In the blink of an eye, I have her pinned to the wall; the force causes the drywall to fall around us.

"Do not," I snarl, slowly, grip tightening around her throat. "Ever speak her name with that filthy mouth. One day you'll be worshiping the ground she steps on."

I cut her airway off, her nails clawing my arm, but I don't let go, not until her eyes roll back and she slumps. Not dead, but when she wakes up, she'll know I'm serious about not messing with Rosa.

I expand my wings, flying to Eleanor's balcony, and step into her office. She looks up and stands. "What's wrong?"

I tell her about everything, the visions, the premature magic. Fear flickers in her eyes, "If she's already getting her magic, she'll be strong. I don't know who to call. The last time a witch received her powers early, she was the leader of witches, that is, before she took her own life. She'll be hunted down. People will want to use her as a puppet."

"You will have to keep a close eye on her. I'm leaving after her birthday." It pains me to say those words out loud.

"You can't leave her," she hisses, eyes blazing. "She will be hunted for her powers, Dimitri!"

"She will be okay, she has you. We're done discussing this." I don't wait for a reply; I'm already jumping off her balcony and onto Rosa's.

It's nearly midnight, she'll be asleep. I push her door open, stepping into the dark room. She's lying on her side, tears on her cheeks, and my chest tightens at the sight. She's having another nightmare, a vision. I brush my fingers across her skin, and her eyes open wide and afraid. I pull the hood off my head so she can see it's me.

"Did I wake you?" she whispers, eyes full of vulnerability.

"No." My thumb lightly brushes her lower lip. "I just needed to see you."

"Will you stay?" Her cheeks redden slightly, and that blush nearly unravels me.

I nod, and she shifts, making room for me. I remove my hoodie, slide under the covers, and wrap my arms around her waist, pulling her closer to me. Her head is on my chest. Her hand tightens on my shirt like she's worried I'll leave.

"Sleep, Moya Lyubov." I kiss the top of her head gently. I inhale deeply, enjoying the scent of lavender.

I don't fall asleep; no, I watch her. Like I always do, I almost got caught once in her apartment.

I have an unnatural obsession with watching her sleep. I am turning into a psychopath, but I can't bring myself to care.

At dawn, I gently press a kiss to her forehead and slip my arms from beneath her, standing. She reaches for me, half-asleep.

"Don't leave me, Dimitri..."

I pause, but she curls into a ball, hugging the pillow to her chest. "Trust me, baby girl." I whisper, "You'll hate me once you know the truth, but you'll always have my heart."

When I get downstairs, Ian, Aiden, and Eleanor are sitting around the bar.

"Are you still being a fucking asshole?" Ian asks.

"Behave, Ian," Eleanor snaps.

"No, he's right." Aiden stands. "He's treating his mate like shit, and when I want to claim her as mine, he…"

I don't let him finish; I'm in his face. "She's not yours to claim."

"She's not yours either because you don't want her."

"It's not that simple!" I shout. My voice is lethal as I threaten, "If I ever see you touch her again, you're dead. Do you understand? My brother is the only reason you're not a pile of ash. I'm leaving tonight, but I have eyes everywhere."

"Don't do this." Ian pleads, standing and gripping my shoulders.

"I don't have a choice, my demon is clawing at my skin, and it's harder every second I'm near her." I shrug him off. "Take care of her." I leave, ignoring them.

I'm in the gym taking my frustrations out on the punching bag, but I ended up breaking all three of them. I turn to leave when the door opens… Rosa.

She opens the door to the dance room, and I wait a few minutes; music begins humming through the walls. I move silently to a dark corner of the room where I know she can't see me.

She stretches, rolling her neck and shoulders as she stares at her reflection, and then pulls off her hoodie, revealing the tight top hugging her curves, the tiny shorts that are more like underwear.

My pulse picks up speed as I stare. She lifts her arms above her head, arching her back, doing a slow stretch. Her breasts lift, and her shirt rises to show skin. I lick my lips as I recall how she tastes.

Rosa starts moving to the music, hips swaying slowly and deliberately, like she's dancing to drive someone insane, and that someone is me, but she doesn't know it.

She drags her hands up her sides, her lashes lower, lips parting as she pants. Nothing about her is innocent. She drops to her knees, still dancing, and fuck…. my cock aches painfully in my jeans. That ass should be worshiped or ruined, maybe both.

I stare at *my* marks I've already left on her body, proof that she belongs to me, but they aren't enough. I'm already searching for bare skin, new areas to claim.

I want my teeth on her throat, her breasts, her hips. I want her covered everywhere, until the world sees her and knows exactly who she belongs to, until she can only feel me, even if I'm not touching her.

She crawls toward the mirror… and my breath stops when she looks at herself in the mirror. Her hand moves up her thighs slowly, disappearing between them, and she spreads her knees farther apart…

Fuck me…

Her hair falls down her back, and she lifts her hips in a slow roll that sends heat straight to my gut.

I shouldn't be watching, but I can't look away even if hell itself opens in the floor beneath us. I can watch her for hours, wishing she'd do some of those moves on top of me.

Naked and sweaty.

She stands, her ass lifting in the air as she twerks, shorts clinging to her tighter than second skin, my dick twitches. She leans forward, circling her hips, biting her lip like she's trying not to moan at herself. My breathing grows ragged as my vision blurs. She has no idea what she's doing to me.

"Rosa…" I groan before I can stop it, and she freezes, eyes locking on mine.

For a moment, she doesn't move, doesn't breathe, but then a wicked smile curves her lips, and she starts dancing more.

It's not shy, it's bolder. Her hand cups herself over her shorts, completely undoing me. Her movements are slower, but sensual; she pats herself like a promise that it's *mine*...

I grip the back of a metal chair in front of me, and it bends. She looks over her shoulder and looks at me; it's an invitation, a challenge, and a plea.

One that every part of me, both demon and man, wants to answer.

Chapter Nineteen

Rosa

I wake up before the sun is even up, feeling restless, my heart pounding too hard to ignore. Everything feels different. It's like something wants to crawl out of my skin, or better yet, explode out of me. I feel like I can do anything. Slipping out of bed, I put on my tank top, shorts, and knee pads. The house is silent as I walk down to the basement.

As soon as I turn on the music, my body takes over, drowning out all of my thoughts.

I move until my lungs burn, and a sheen of sweat covers my body, and I'm panting. I watch myself move in the mirror, and dancing makes me feel confident.

I drop to my knees and sway my hips as I grind the air, touching my body. It's a great start to my birthday, I feel weirdly awakened, new even. It's exhilarating and addictive.

My mind, of course, moves to Dimitri. I wonder what he'd think if I danced like this for him. I almost went to his room this morning, almost... I just couldn't take another wound, not today. One night with him will destroy me in a way I might never recover from.

When I woke up, the sheets smelled like him. My face was buried in the pillow as I held it against my chest.

My fingers slide up my thighs, thinking of his hands on them. Then I move slowly, cupping my breasts before I can talk myself out of it, squeezing and pinching my nipple, the way he does, firm and commanding.

I moan lowly, it's not enough, but it'll do. My lower belly heats with desire. My other hand moves between my thighs, and a low groan fills the room. I hear my name...

I pause my movements, looking up, and gasp when I see dark eyes watching me by the door in the corner of the room. We silently stare at each other, neither of us daring to look away. His chest is rising and falling like he ran a marathon, or maybe he's fighting himself. He looks hungry. A loud snap has my eyes lowering. His hands bent a metal chair.

Instead of covering myself, I turn. Boldly, I keep dancing, letting the music take over once more, my hips moving in slow, sensual arcs. He watches every single movement in a daze, like he's memorizing every curve of my body.

I glance over my shoulder. It's an invitation. I want him to come dance with me, touch me.

He curses, jaw clenching, hands tightening on the metal chair some more. He's fighting the urge. Why? He runs his hand through his hair, exhaling violently and then...

He turns and leaves the room like his ass is on fire.

I stand there, staring at the doorway like an idiot, panting as I try to calm my racing heart. The music is still playing, my body still buzzing, and he just... left me wanting.

I pull my hoodie back on, fingers trembling, turning off the music. My mind spinning, I almost touched myself for the first time in my life, on the floor of a damn dance studio, and he just walked out like I hadn't been practically begging him to take my body.

I sigh, grab my phone, and head upstairs, nearly running. My face is hot, my heart sore as I slam the door shut behind me. I lean against it, trying to catch my breath. Thank God, I didn't run into anyone in the hall.

I need a shower. I turn the water to the hottest setting and strip off my clothes. I refuse to let him ruin my birthday.

I step into the shower, letting the hot water relieve the tension in my shoulders. My muscles are literally shaking from dancing and everything else. I wash off the sweat, but I couldn't get rid of the memory, the way he groaned my name.

Someone starts banging on my door, snapping my thoughts away, and turning off the shower.

"Who is it?" I call from the bathroom, grabbing my robe.

"It's me, bitch, open the door!" Cassie calls out, twisting the doorknob.

I laugh, yanking the door open. She bursts in like her usual hurricane self, screaming, "Happy Birthday!" clapping her hands together, then pulling me into a bear hug.

I squeeze her back, tightly. I've missed her. She's been so engrossed with Ian this past week.

She pulls back, looking me over. "How are you feeling? Do you feel different or weird?"

"Honestly, yeah." I nod slowly. "I feel like a deep part of me that was locked away woke up, and it's powerful. I'm buzzing and restless. It's kinda strange."

Cassie nods as if she expected me to say that. "That's totally normal, but we need to talk later. You'll have to keep an open mind, m'kay?"

I frown, "About what?"

"Nope, not saying anything till we're all together, but just know I love you, okay?"

"I love you, too..." It sounds more like a question. I instantly think of the weird conversation I overheard.

"I know it doesn't make any sense, but at dinner it will, and guess what?" She smiles widely, eyes shining with excitement.

"Hmm?"

"Mom's coming tonight. She didn't want to miss your big day!"

"What, really?" I grin; we've both missed her.

We lay back in bed, staring at the ceiling like teenagers.

"So, you and Ian, huh?" I turn to face her, and we spend the next hour talking about their relationship. She blushes a few times, swatting me with a pillow. They love each other. I end up teasing her, but soon her face turns serious.

"What about you?"

"Me? I'm okay... I don't really want to talk about it, not today."

"It's Dimitri?" She sits up.

"Mhm." I shrug, exhaling. "He looks at me like I'm the only thing he wants, then runs like touching me will destroy his life. He kisses me like he's starving, then leaves me aching and confused." She winces, "He leaves me wanting sometimes, it makes me crazy." I admit in a whisper. "I actually thought about... touching myself, but it feels weird. I don't even know what I'm doing."

"Oh, Rosa, that's normal," she says immediately. "The first few times are awkward, but you'll get used to it."

"So, it's normal? To..." I lower my voice. "Touch myself?"

Cassie nods, "Oh, yeah. I used to do it all the time. Well, before Ian."

I groan, covering my face with my hands. "This is embarrassing."

"No, it's not. Everyone gets horny, especially when a hot, broody man is looking at you like that."

Someone knocks on the door, Ian shouts, "Cassie, open the door. I have breakfast."

She jumps up. "I thought it would be nice just you and me having breakfast in here ourselves. Is that okay?"

"Yes, please, I'm starving." I'm happy that we're having girl time. I really need it.

Cassie opens the door, and Ian steps in, hands full. He places the food on the table, leaning in for a kiss. I look away at the full-on make-out session.

"Okay, time to leave!" Cassie giggles, smacking his ass.

"Fine," he winks at me. "Happy birthday."

"Thank you." I smile, and he walks out of the room, closing the door.

"God, he's so hot!" She fans herself.

"That he is," I agree. "They all are, but Dimitri? He's on another level."

"That he is. He's probably the hottest one, but he only has eyes for you."

"Hey, I heard that!" Ian yells from behind our closed door.

"Well, stop eavesdropping, you buffoon."

I shake my head, picking up the hot drink, and it has me moaning under my breath. "Gods, that's good. Let me guess, a vanilla latte?"

She grins. "Oh yeah, with a splash of cinnamon."

"You know the way to my heart," I tease, pressing a hand to my chest.

"Actually, Dimitri made it for you, remembering it was your favorite. He also made the French toast."

My heart stops. *Of course, he did. How can he break me one moment and then do something like this, thoughtful and extremely intimate, the next moment?*

"Okay, let's get ready for your party!!" She jumps up, clapping.

"Party?" I echo, blinking.

"We're throwing you a birthday get-together," she squeals, wiggling her hips like she's drunk with excitement.

She runs out before I can say anything. I slowly finish the latte, savoring the taste, picturing Dimitri making it in the kitchen. I love that he thinks about me and remembers what I like, preparing something for me with those huge, scarred, gentle hands. *Why does he make it so hard to hate him?*

I stand, rubbing some lotion on my arms and legs, trying to calm the fluttering in my stomach when Cassie and Tammy come into the room.

"Rosa!" Tammy nearly smothers me with a hug. "I've missed you so much."

"I missed you, too." I smile, even when she is squeezing the air out of my lungs.

"Happy birthday!" she sings.

"Thank you. Seriously, it means so much to me that you're here."

"Oh! Mom got you something." Cassie squeals once we pull apart, pulling out a long black dress bag.

"Tammy, you didn't have to..."

"Well, I couldn't help myself when I saw it, and I immediately pictured you wearing it." She waves away my protest. "Open it, sweetie."

Cassie unzips the bag, pulling the dress free.

My jaw drops, "Oh, my God..." I breathe, walking towards it.

It is a champagne silk dress. The front is a low-cut halter. The back is nearly nonexistent, and the slit is high.

"Let's start on our hair and makeup, girls!" Tammy claps her hands, and we all get ready.

Hours later, we're done with our hair, makeup, and dresses, and we look like we belong on the cover of a magazine.

Tammy has on a gorgeous, long, black sleeveless dress with a long slit in the front. Cassie has on a pretty blue silk dress, which is low-cut on her cleavage, is much shorter than ours, and shows off her legs.

My dress is amazing. It flows all the way to the floor with a long slit. The front cuts low on my sternum, showing off my cleavage as well. It also shows a good bit of side boob, and my entire back is bare. It's beautiful, and I feel like a princess in it.

My hair is in a low bun, a few loose pieces framing my face.

Cassie does a slow spin, staring at her reflection. "We look like goddamn goddesses!"

"Absolutely," Tammy agrees proudly, turning to me. "So, what do you think?"

"It's amazing." I breathe, still looking at myself.

Cassie winks, leaning in close. "Dimitri's gonna lose his mind."

My stomach dips. I tell myself it isn't for him, but it is.

"Let's go down, everyone is waiting." Tammy opens the door for us, and we step out.

"Wait five minutes before coming down," Cassie orders, pointing a finger at me. "We want the dramatic effect."

I roll my eyes. "Why?"

"Because I said so." She grins, walking away.

I watch them go down until they're no longer in sight. I wait, nervously, with my heart racing.

"Okay, come down!" Tammy calls out.

I exhale, slowly, then make my way down. I pause on the last step, finally looking up. The room is dimly lit, music humming through the air, and everyone is dressed up, talking, and laughing. My eyes find his. Dimitri is standing toward the back of the room in a black suit. The jacket hugs his broad shoulders, and the collar is slightly open.

His eyes roam down my body slowly, possessively, like he's unwrapping me with his gaze.

It almost feels like the whole room fades. It's just him and me. He's *mine…* I am taking what I want tonight. Whether he likes it or not.

He takes a few steps toward me, but then Aiden appears between us. "Wow, you look beautiful."

I don't look away from Dimitri as I whisper a quick, "Thanks."

Dimitri stops walking and stands completely still. His eyes sharpen when he sees Aiden, and disappointment hits me hard.

Aiden offers his hand. "May I have the first dance?"

I look away, but Dimitri is already turning away, walking toward the door. *Is he leaving?*

"Aiden, give me a second." I'm already rushing away. I catch him as he opens the door, grabbing his shoulder. He turns slowly, like he already knows it's me.

"Rosa." His voice is a rough rumble, and it makes my knees weak.

"Were you leaving?"

"I need some air," he states simply.

"Dance with me?" I whisper, suddenly feeling shy. "Only if you want to."

His eyes blaze as he takes my hand immediately. My hand looks so small in his. "I'd love nothing more."

He pulls me to the center of the room, spins me gently, then dips me without warning, ripping a breathless laugh from me. He pulls me back up, only inches away, but it still feels too far. Out of the corner of my eye, I see Ian spinning Cassie around us, and she is giggling too.

"You look breathtaking."

"Really, you think so?" I look up at him through my lashes.

He leans in, cheeks brushing mine, breath warm against my ear. "I know so."

His hand slides lower on my back, over my bare skin. It feels amazing. It's like my skin wakes up from just one little touch.

I'm going to kiss him until he understands I'm not going anywhere, tell him I know what he is, or at least suspect. He's not going to keep pushing me away; it can't go on like this. I will take charge, I need to.

"Dimitri..." I start, but get interrupted.

"Alright, it's my turn," Aiden interrupts, appearing out of nowhere.

Dimitri growls through his teeth, "We weren't finished."

I tap his chest, "It's okay, I'll be back." I force myself to take a step back.

"I'll wait for you," his jaw tics. He sounds calm, but I know better.

Aiden spins me around the room. He's being charming, but I'm hardly paying attention as I look for Dimitri. *Where'd he go?*

Then I see her, with him, my smile drops instantly. I've never seen her around. She's pressed against Dimitri, hand on his chest, but even as she talks to him, his eyes are on me, watching me closely. It's like he doesn't even realize she's there.

He sees my reaction and smirks, then pushes her hands off his chest. It shouldn't thrill me the way it does. My mouth lowers into a pout without even thinking, and his smirk stretches into a full smile, dimples and all. My heart skips a beat and falls into my stomach.

"Rosa?" Aiden's voice breaks through my daze.

"Yeah?" I force myself to look away from Dimitri. His hand tightens on my waist.

"You look beautiful," he says softly, eyes lowering to my lips. "I hope you know that."

"Thank you."

"I want you to consider going out with me." His eyes fill with hope.

I sigh, looking away. "Aiden, I've told you, I'm not looking for that."

"It's Dimitri, isn't it?" he snaps.

"It's complicated." I shake my head, pulling away from him.

"Why do you even want him? He treats you like crap!"

"I know, but we have a connection."

Chapter Twenty

Dimitri

My fangs extract the second I hear Aiden asking her out.

Will she consider dating the fucker?

He has a death wish. I've warned him what would happen. I move toward him, ready to rip him apart. I can practically taste the violence on my tongue, strong and bitter.

"No, Dimitri." Ian's hand clamps down on my shoulder, stopping me. He must've heard as well. And he knows I'm seconds away from ripping him limb from limb in a very slow death.

"Let go," I snarl, eyes locked on Aiden's fingers resting on her hips. Those fingers will be the first thing I tear off. "You were supposed to keep him away from her. That was his last pass, only because you asked. He dies, now."

"I won't stop you," Ian whispers, "but your demon's out. She doesn't know yet. Do you want her to find out like *this*? You'll scare her. Go outside, now."

"Fine." *Only for her.*

I stalk out to the gardens, dropping onto a stone bench, elbows on my knees, head in my hands.

Am I doing the right thing by leaving? Will it break her? Does she even want me?

Fuck, maybe I pushed her away too many times.

She looks unreal tonight in that dress, like a goddess, no... like a queen, like my queen. That dress hugs every curve of her body as if it were made for her.

My mind drifts to this morning without permission, her hand sliding down between her breasts, then lower, over those tiny shorts.

I was caught staring, but fuck it, I didn't care. I couldn't look away.

I can still hear that soft gasp she made. I imagined it was my fingers on her soft skin, touching her exactly how I want, no, how I need to. I need to be the one who makes her come undone, the one who tears moans from her throat until she's shaking.

I want her screaming my name, so loud that even the Underworld hears it.

My cock twitches at the memory. *Shit, how pathetic am I that a single sound from her can break me?*

My hands actually fucking shake just thinking about it. I should have grabbed her then and ruined her.

I tip my head back up to the sky, and I ask, "Why am I being punished?"

I stand as a decision slices through me. I'm done pretending. I'm claiming her as mine. I don't care if she fights it or if she hates me. No one will dare touch her again. Aiden is dying either way, even if she chooses him.

I'll drag her to Hell kicking and screaming if I have to. I'll chain her to me if that's what it takes. She's mine to protect, mine to claim, and mine to love. And one day she'll understand that there is no escaping me.

I straighten my jacket, jaw set, and head back to the house.

Aiden storms out, furious, kicking a rock across the yard. I smirk. She must have turned him down. Then Rosa bursts out. *What the hell is going on?*

"Aiden!" She grabs his arm, and he spins. "I'm not trying to fight. I just need to be honest about how I feel for Dimitri. I like him more than I should." Heat rushes through my chest. She picked me. She doesn't want him; she wants me.

Aiden exhales sharply, "I understand. It just pisses me off. He doesn't deserve someone like you."

"No, don't say that. He's fighting his past. You don't get to judge him for that." That heat settles low in my gut. Maybe I won't need to force her or drag her to Hell.

She takes a step away from him, eyes looking around. "Wow, it looks like a fairytale."

Aiden steps forward and says, "It does."

"I'm going to get Cassie; she'll love it out here." She turns, but he grabs her arm. A low warning growl escapes me. Of course, he hears it and looks right at me, smirking. If she weren't standing there, I'd slit his throat.

"She's seen it already. No need to go get her."

"Well, I want her out here with us." Rosa tries pulling her arm free.

"I'd like it to be just us."

"I know, but I'm getting uncomfortable."

He moves closer, a hand sliding around her hip. "Are you scared of being alone with me?" He leans in, and another growl rips through me, but it doesn't stop him. Then, the bastard fucking kisses her.

She turns her face, shoving his chest. "Aiden, stop. I can't."

He ignores her, lifts her body, and pushes her back onto a tree, smashing his lips to hers. She starts pounding her tiny fists against his chest.

No one can stop my demon from surging forward, ripping away my control. I don't fight him. I give him full range. He knows who she is; he won't hurt her.

But Aiden? He's about to learn what it means to piss off a demon prince. My body shifts as I stalk forward.

He hasn't been in complete control in a very long time. He stretches and grins, stalking his prey, already imagining the different ways we can dismember him for touching what belongs to us.

My growl tears through the air, deep enough to shake the ground. Rosa's gaze snaps to us, pure terror fills her face, and it guts me. I swallow hard. She's afraid of me, I can smell it, and it fucking breaks me. I never wanted to see that look in her eyes.

I grip Aiden by the back of his neck and throw him away from her. She looks at me with wide eyes, trembling in fear as she takes in every detail. She gasps, covering her mouth, taking in the fangs hanging over my lower lip, the completely black eyes, horns, and massive black wings.

"Dimitri?" she whispers.

"It is me, my mate." My voice comes out rough, deep, and raspy. Her hand rises slowly and gently touches the side of my face. I hold her tighter, leaning in to rub my nose against her neck, inhaling her scent. It's the only thing keeping my demon anchored.

"What are you?"

I open my mouth to tell her, and to reassure her I'd never hurt her, but something yanks me backwards. I spin to find Aiden.

He grabs Rosa and throws her over his shoulder. Her hand reaches for me, desperate.

"Dimitri!" she cries.

"Let her go!" I snarl, the sound vibrating the trees. He turns, grinning as he pulls her off his shoulder, turning her around, wrapping an arm around the front of her chest.

"I can take her. You are no match for me," I hiss.

"I can take you after I mark your mate. You'll be weak from the pain. I'll kill you, take your place in Hell, and keep her. I will fuck her in your bed and on your throne, claiming everything that belongs to you." His chin is resting on her shoulder.

"In your fucking dreams!" I seethe. The rage in me is too much; my hands begin to shake, but I need to think. If I rush forward, he'll mark her before I reach them.

Aiden tilts her head, licking her throat as he looks up at me, and she sobs. "If you come for me, you'll hurt her," he taunts. "You'll just have to watch." My heart starts pounding hard against my rib cage, and a foreign feeling is creeping its way into my chest... I'm... scared?

"Mate? What is he talking about, Dimitri? The book... You took it? It's real?!" Rosa cries.

"Nothing, love, because you're my mate now," Aiden whispers in her ear.

"Dimitri, help me!"

He opens his mouth, fangs extending, ready to bite.

I spring forward, the world blurring around me as my heart shatters. No, this cannot happen!

Ian charges in and grabs Aiden by the face, throwing him backward.

Rosa starts falling, but I catch her, pulling her into my arms.

"You're safe now," I breathe, my eyes squeezing shut as the fear shakes me. That was too fucking close. I bury my face in her neck, needing her scent to calm the demon in me.

"The book... It's true?" she whispers, her body also trembling as she gently touches the side of my face, scared, but also curious.

"I'll take her, Dimitri." I whirl, hissing at Eleanor, clutching Rosa tighter to my chest.

"I won't let anything happen to her. You need to deal with him," she insists, but I step back.

"Hey," Rosa cups my cheek. "It's okay, help Ian."

I nod, reluctantly placing her into Eleanor's arms.

I turn, slowly stalking toward Aiden.

Ian holds him still, and pure terror finally sinks into his eyes. He struggles against Ian, begging. "Please, Ian, let me go!"

I chuckle, shaking my head. "Even if he lets you go, you won't get far. I'll chase you; you'll never escape."

"Wait! We can talk about this!"

"You touched my mate," I growl, and it rolls through the ground. "I'm going to rip your arms off." I look over my shoulder, making sure Eleanor took Rosa. When I don't see them, I grab Aiden's left arm and tear it from his body. His screams echo through the woods. Lightning strikes the ground around us, shaking the earth.

"What the hell is going on?" Ian shouts through the heavy winds.

It's my mate. Her magic is reacting, wild and furious. I can feel her energy in each lightning strike, and in the wind, she's angry. She knows, and she will hate me now that she knows what I am. I roar loudly, grabbing Ian's other arm.

"No, please, Dimitri! Please!"

A cruel smirk curls my lips as I rip it off, and blood splatters over me. My demon revels in it, licking it from my lips, tasting his bitter blood on my tongue. My claws extend, pressing into his chest, and they slowly dig in as I stare into his eyes.

His screams are deafening my ears, but they turn to wet gurgles as his skin grays.

"She. Is. Mine." I snarl, wrapping my claws around his heart, and I rip it out of his chest. He slumps forward, dead.

I stare at the heart still beating in my hands as I enjoy the intoxicating scent of blood. My chest is rising and falling as I breathe hard. Then I crush it, and the blood seeps down my arm.

"Burn him," I order as I turn away. Ian and Cassie stare at me like they're seeing me for the first time.

I hurry my steps as the rain starts pouring down violently. She's crying, is she hurt?

"Dimitri, wait, it's not the best idea to go to her like this," Ian shouts, chasing me. Eleanor stands with Rosa limp in her arms.

"She freaked when I told her the truth, and her magic exploded from pure anger. The storm, it's her. She used too much at once and passed out. Did you feel it? It was intense, unbelievable."

I take Rosa from her instantly. Her scent calms me, quieting the inner turmoil. I hold her against my chest and walk into the house while they deal with the aftermath.

"Dimitri!" Ian calls.

"Let him go," Eleanor cuts him off. "He won't hurt her. His demon knows who she is."

I carry her upstairs, straight past her room into mine. I kick my door shut, laying her gently in bed. I sit on the edge, lift her legs onto my lap, and rub them to soothe myself. He doesn't want to leave her, but he finally lets me take control.

I unbuckle her heels, slipping them off carefully. I watch her sleep for a while. When I saw the terror in her eyes, I decided I needed to leave. She needs time, and I have to give it to her. I place a tender kiss on her lips, stand, and put the letter and gift on the nightstand.

"This is the hardest thing I've ever had to do, Rosa. Don't hate me." Each step I take to the balcony is more painful than the last. I look over my shoulder, feeling completely destroyed. "I love you. Moya Dusha," I whisper as I spread my wings wide. I disappear into the night.

CHAPTER TWENTY-ONE

Rosa

I stare into Dimitri's eyes. He's massive, bigger than I've ever seen him, with black wings that rise behind him, dark as night. His eyes aren't human anymore; they're pure black, cold, and sinister. My heart is racing. Is this really him? It looks like him, but more dangerous, inhuman. Too beautiful to belong to any human.

"It is me, my mate." His voice is different, deeper, raspy, more feral, warming my lower stomach. My hand lifts, my fingers trembling as I brush his cheek. He leans into my touch like he's starving for it. He buries his face in my neck, and the dark horns are ridged, curl from his head like they belong there. Those strong arms tighten around me, like he's afraid I'll disappear. He groans deeply. His chest vibrates, and his wings shake slightly, and then a memory hits.

The Demonology book I found in the library, the drawing, looks exactly like Dimitri's horns, exactly like the wings on his back. It can't be... but it's right in front of me. I can't keep denying it.

I'm scared, but at the same time, I'm not. There's something deep in my soul that whispers, he'll never hurt me.

I'm in complete awe of him. I want to touch his wings, but I refrain from doing so.

He's a demon, but he looks like an angel, only deadlier.

"You're safe now," Dimitri whispers, and I melt into his warmth.

He shifts me in his arms, one under my legs, the other at my back, cradling me in his chest.

"The book... It's true?" I whisper, he opens his mouth, pulling me closer, to tell me.

Then someone interrupts, "I'll take her, Dimitri." He spins around, clenching me tighter as Eleanor comes into view. "I won't let anything happen to her. You need to deal with him."

"Hey." My voice is gentle as I cup his face. "It's okay, help Ian."

He nods stiffly, jaw clenching as he places me in her arms.

Ian is holding Aiden, and Aiden is thrashing violently as he snarls, shouts, and begs. Dimitri moves toward them. I can feel his rage, and I now know it's supernatural.

Eleanor turns, walking away. She's impossibly strong for someone so small. She rushes through the trees—fast—breathing heavily.

When we reach the house, she sets me down on a bench.

"Are you okay?"

"Yes... no. I don't know. I'm confused." My hands won't stop trembling. My body feels like it's going to explode from the inside. "The book... The Demonology one... He's a demon?"

She doesn't answer immediately, but with a sigh. "He should be the one to tell you."

"No..." My voice is desperate and raw. "No more secrets. Tell me now, or I swear I'll go back out there." I stand as my control snaps; the wind violently slams sideways with a taste of magic. Trees bend so sharply they're seconds away from breaking. Lightning crackles close by, and the bright light is overwhelming.

"Rosa, calm down," Eleanor begs as she looks around frantically. "You're creating the storm."

"What? How?" I gasp, looking up at the skies, another bolt slams into the ground so close that the smoke burns my nostrils as it shakes the earth beneath my feet.

"You're a witch. Calm down before you drain yourself."

A witch? No... no, this can't be real. My heart slams against my ribs like it's trying to break out of its cage.

"Tell me what Dimitri is."

"A demon!" she screams over the booming thunder. "He's a demon, Ian is too, and Aiden is a vampire. What the book says is true: you and Dimitri are fated mates."

My heart twists painfully; my knees hit the ground. Lightning slams into the Earth around me in a perfect circle, trapping me inside it like it's trying to protect me. My hair whips around my face as the storm syncs perfectly to the panic in my chest.

Dimitri roars somewhere far away, a sound full of agony and rage. Rain explodes from the dark sky, and everything goes dark...

I jolt awake, gasping. I squeeze my eyes shut, exhaling slowly, letting the panic loosen inside me. *It was just a dream.* I rub my temples. My head is throbbing painfully.

When I open my eyes again, Cassie, Eleanor, and Tammy sit nearby, watching me silently, full of tension like they're ready for me to explode.

"Where am I? And why are you all staring at me?" My voice is groggy as I sit up, confused.

"You don't remember?" Tammy asks carefully.

"Remember what? The last thing I remember is Aiden kissing me."

"You seriously don't remember?" Cassie asks, sharing a look with Tammy.

"No, just the kiss, then nothing," I say, trying to clear the fog in my head. "I did have a strange dream."

"What was your dream about?" Eleanor stands, cautiously stepping forward.

"You'll think I'm going crazy."

"We won't, promise," Cassie whispers, her eyes worried.

So, I tell them about Dimitri's wings, horns, the way he called me mate, the conversation with Eleanor, and it all ended with the storm and the pain. By the time I'm finished, they're staring at me with wide eyes, waiting for something. "I know, it sounds crazy, but you asked."

"Rosa," Eleanor begins, sitting on the bed and grabbing my hand. "It wasn't a dream."

A laugh bursts out of me, hard and full of disbelief. I shake my head, trying to calm down.

"It was real," Tammy states firmly, pacing in front of the bed. "All of it."

Cassie nods with a slight frown. "It's true, we're witches. Ian is a demon. Aiden was a vampire, and Dimitri is... what you saw last night."

"I don't understand," I whisper. "Where's Dimitri? I want to talk to him."

"We don't know. He left." Cassie's mouth opens like she wants to say more, but can't.

"Left? When is he coming back?"

Cassie looks at Ian, who rubs his neck. "I don't know if he's coming back."

"No," I laugh. "No, he wouldn't just leave me like that..." I start panicking. Then again, I truly don't know him.

I stare at them one by one; their faces are pale and serious. It's not a joke. I let it sink in. The book... It *is* real!

"Rosa, honey," Eleanor's voice cracks. "This is going to be hard, and I hope you don't hate me for it."

"Hate you? Why would I hate you?"

"For not being there for you." She cries, "I'm your mother, your biological mother."

"What?!" I jump out of bed so fast the room tilts. "No, no, Tammy, tell me she's lying."

"She's not, it's true."

I stumble back until my back hits the wall, my breathing ragged. I feel trapped, cornered, like an animal being hunted.

My eyes turn to Eleanor, and the resemblance hits me sharply, and it hurts. *How did I not see it before? I knew I recognized her, but this?*

"So, what happened? Did you give me up? How do you know Cassie and Tammy?"

"We were close friends," Eleanor reaches out, but thinks better of it. "We all lived together. You lived here with us for five years. Ian came over often. You two used to play together. You never met Aiden or Dimitri."

"But, why? Why give me up? Why didn't I stay with Tammy?" I feel crazy. My brain can't keep up. *I lived here once? I knew them? How do I not remember?*

"It was a last-minute decision. Your father was killed protecting you. Our house was no longer safe; they knew where we lived. I couldn't leave. The witch council binds us to this area. Tammy couldn't keep you because they knew her too. They watched her for a long time, but she moved away to keep an eye on you. That's why she befriended your adoptive mother."

"My father is dead?" The words slice through me. I'd always hoped I'd find him someday. "And who are *they*?"

"Yes, honey," Eleanor sighs. "And today is your twenty-first birthday. It's the day witches receive their powers. We'll explain everything slowly, I promise."

Yeah, *no shit...*

"I have witch powers?" My voice is barely a whisper.

"Yes," Eleanor nods. "You're a witch, like us."

"I'm a witch..." I repeat numbly. This feels like another dream. *Wish they told me before my magic exploded out of me...*

Cassie steps forward. "Remember how you told me this morning you felt different? Stronger?"

"Yeah..."

"That was your powers unlocking. I felt the same on my birthday," she mumbles, shyly, like she doesn't know how to act.

"Why don't I remember any of this? Five isn't that young. How did I forget everything?"

"I erased your memories," Eleanor admits. "You couldn't remember magic until it was safe."

They stand a few feet away, smiling tightly.

"This is a lot to take in." I rub my forehead, trying to ease the pressure building behind my eyes.

"We know, we'll give you time, but you're powerful. We need to test your magic. Controlling the weather? That's rare."

"I control the weather?" My head throbs harder.

"Yes. Remember the storm last night?" Eleanor asks.

"Yeah..."

"That was you. Your emotions triggered it."

A gasp slips that has me thinking of something. "I have a question."

"We'll answer anything," Eleanor gestures for me to continue.

"What if... what if I had powers earlier... before today?"

"That's impossible," Ian says immediately.

"Oh...never mind." My cheeks burn. I feel stupid for even asking. Maybe I'm the crazy one here.

"No, wait. Why?" Tammy steps forward gently.

God, why do they keep coming closer?

"Well... three years ago, when that guy tried to..." I swallow hard, looking away. "When he tried to assault me... I panicked and kept begging him to get off me. I said it over and over in my head. And then he was just... gone. He slammed into a tree, and the wind knocked me into the pond. He passed out. I... I lied and said I hit him with a rock. Plus, since I've met Dimitri, weird things happen when my emotions are high, like the sky rumbles even though it's a clear day."

Silence.

"Rosa…" Eleanor breathes. "That's incredibly rare. Powers awakening early to save you… It means you're exceptionally powerful." She steps closer and smooths a hand over my hair. "I knew you were special the moment I saw you." She smiles down at me. Her eyes filled with joy and love.

"He wasn't small, either," Tammy adds. "That kind of force is impressive."

"She's strong," Ian agrees. "Unique. Just like Dimitri. He's the strongest demon alive. Even when we were kids, he had power no one else had. Our father feared him. Everyone pushed him away. I was the only one who didn't. He grew up alone… until your father and Eleanor saved him."

My eyes sting. Dimitri has been alone his whole life, rejected and hurt. And he thought I would hate him, too.

"He left you something," Ian says, pointing to the nightstand, to a red box sitting on top of a note.

"Why didn't he tell me?"

"He was afraid of rejection. Witches and demons are naturally enemies; you're meant to hate each other. He didn't think you'd want to be with a demon and couldn't handle your rejection."

My chest tightens. I want him here. I need him to explain this, to ground me, to tell me I'm not losing my mind.

This connection… it makes sense now. It's always been there.

Is this real? Or will I wake up and it'll vanish?

I don't know if I should be happy or furious, feel betrayed or relieved. My mother is here, the thing I dreamed of, yet everyone kept this from me.

"I need to be alone," I finally whisper, overwhelmed to the point that my body is shaking. I need air.

"Of course," Eleanor squeezes my hand before stepping away. "We're right here if you need anything. I mean it, anything at all."

"I'm sorry, Rosa," Cassie whispers before following the others out.

The door closes, and for the first time all day, the silence hits me. I rush to the nightstand and grab my phone, but of course, it's dead.

Of course it is, everything else in my life flatlined today, why not this?

I grab the charger with shaking fingers, plug it in, and sit on the floor in front of the outlet like the world depends on this damn battery symbol. My knee bounces uncontrollably, and I chew on my thumbnails as I wait.

When the screen finally lights up, I go straight to Dimitri's name.

"Come on... pick up. Please, pick up."

I pace in his room, watching it ring and ring and ring.

"Dimitri. Leave a message." Beep.

"Ugh!" I stab the hang-up button and immediately hit call again, and my eyes tear up as I do.

I understand why he kept pushing me away, and I hate it. I wish I had known. It continues going straight to voicemail each time, and I listen to his voice over and over.

The small message sends shivers down my spine.

I grab the folded note from the table, my thumb tracing the edge, but I can't open it. Not yet. I'm afraid of what's inside, afraid it'll make this real. I pinch my arm, hard, and it hurts. *Nope, not a nightmare. I'm a witch. A real, actual witch.*

It feels wrong, like I stepped into the pages of a book and forgot to climb back out. Fantasy is supposed to be an escape, not my life.

Gods, everything I knew was a lie...

I honestly can't wrap my mind around everything. My father died protecting me. My adoptive mom died *because* of me. She'd be alive, and she and Jim would be happy. The painful memory slams into me.

Cassie and I had fought about something stupid, so damn stupid that I can't even remember what it was about. I called Mom, sobbing, demanding she leave work and come get me. I was being a brat, begging and manipulating. Throwing every childish guilt trip, I could because I wanted her attention. Because I was hurt, angry, and didn't understand anything. And she came, of course, she did. She wanted to be the best mother. She left work in the middle of the day because I screamed into the phone that she didn't love me.

She tried to calm me on the drive. She wasn't paying enough attention to what she was doing. I heard everything, the loud crash, her crying out in pain as the car rolled down the hill.

She died on the way to the hospital.

I was depressed for months, but Jim was worse. He never recovered. He just drowned in grief, and he turned it on me, hating me. He blamed me, and the worst part was that I agreed with him.

My throat closes. I hug the note to my chest, too afraid to open it, but too afraid not to.

I don't know what to do or who to trust. Everyone who raised me lied to me.

"Dimitri... please come back," I whisper into the empty room.

I walk to his bed and drop onto it, burying my face into his pillow. His scent hits me instantly, dark, warm, and familiar.

His room mirrors mine, but is darker with charcoal walls and black bedding. Everything is sharp and clean. His shirt from yesterday is still on the bed. I pick it up, pulling off my own shirt, slipping his on. It's massive on me, but it's perfect, soft and warm, smelling exactly like him.

I don't care if it makes me pathetic or desperate. I need him.

I need the one person who didn't lie to me, the one person who didn't pretend to be something else.

I crawl under the blankets and pull them up to my chin. I set the note and the red box on the nightstand beside me. Their presence feels heavy, waiting.

I stare at them until my eyes finally close, and exhaustion drags me back under.

Chapter Twenty-Two

Rosa

I wake up and look at the time. It's one in the morning, and I am starving. I grab the box and note, taking them downstairs with me. Thankfully, no one seems to be up. I don't want anyone seeing how wrecked I am.

When I open the fridge, I see a plate covered in foil with a sticky note that has my name on top. Of course, they're all watching over me now, protecting me like I'm made of glass.

I heat the food. When it's done, I grab a stool, sit by the island, and stare at Dimitri's note. My hand reaches out, touching the edge, and I flinch like it burned me.

"How are you?" I nearly scream as I spin around to find Ian in the doorway.

"Oh God, you scared me. I didn't hear you." I breathe out, my hand flat against my chest.

He shrugs. "Perks of being a demon."

It's the same thing Dimitri would say if he appeared behind me without a sound. I can even picture his smirk.

"Yeah," I say, turning to stare at my food. "Is he really not coming back?"

"He says he won't, but I don't think he can stay away. Not from you, his mate." Ian sits two stools down and watches me carefully. "The bond hits hard. They say it's almost impossible to fight it."

I lean my elbows on the counter, swallowing down the knot in my throat. "You all expected me to freak out."

"You handled it better than we thought. You actually saw his wings, so... that helped." Ian gives a small, sad smile. "He thought you would hate him."

"I could never hate him. I already suspected it." He arches a brow. "Demonology..." I laugh. "You really should keep that kind of information hidden. I just kept pushing it away, telling myself it's insanity."

"Tell Eleanor that. She wants to keep it the way... Damien had it."

"Damien, was my father?"

"Yeah, those were his books."

I play with the letter in my hand. "Is there a way I can reach Dimitri?"

"I could, but it's only for emergencies, and he needs space right now."

"I tried calling." My voice trembles. "He didn't answer."

"He can't. His phone is off. And even if you wanted to go to him..." Ian hesitates. "You can't. He's in Hell. Only demons with wings can pass through, or those who can teleport."

"Oh..." Just like that, my hopes vanish.

"I need to tell him that I love him," I whisper, burying my face in my hands. "I need him to know that I don't hate him for who he is."

Ian's quiet for a moment. "I'm sorry, Rosa. We all tried to stop him. You should read that." He points at the letter. "And don't be mad at anyone. You were in danger, and you still are. They did what they thought was right."

My eyes drift to the box again. It's taunting me, begging me to open it.

"I'm not mad, but I am upset. It's going to take time to process everything."

"Just be patient. He'll come back. We demons are very territorial and very jealous, so just thinking of you being with someone else will kill him. And we understand that you need more time to process, but you need to learn about your powers. It can be dangerous for a witch not to know how to control themselves."

When I look up to say something, he's gone.

I take my plate to the sink, wash it, and head back upstairs with the box and the note. I hesitate outside my room. I keep walking, opening Dimitri's door. Something pulls me toward the balcony. I just need to breathe some fresh air.

I untie the string on the box and slowly open the lid. My heart is pounding in my ears. I'm feeling a little lightheaded, and my hands are slightly trembling. I take a deep breath and exhale very slowly, trying to calm myself down a little.

I stop halfway, closing my eyes for a moment. I'm stalling. I let myself think of what the book said about mate bonds, and how I was drawn to it for no reason I could explain... It was magic. I know that now.

The section on "True Demon Mate Bonds," I read twice, even though it sounded like fantasy.

A demon only meets his mate once in a lifetime. The pull is instinctive, protective, and consuming.

I'd laughed it off then, but now... every word feels like it was written about him.

My hands start trembling as I rip off the lid to the box, unable to drag it out any longer, and I gasp.

A sob breaks free so hard my whole body folds over. The necklace is a dark ruby, shaped as a teardrop, surrounded by tiny diamonds. It glows brightly even in the weak moonlight. Gods, it's... breathtaking.

"Dimitri..." I choke out, lifting my shaky hand to wipe the tears off my cheek.

I reach out to touch it, my finger lightly running across the ruby.

I slowly unclasp the chain, put it around my neck, and clasp it closed, feeling its cold weight settle between my breasts.

Then I open the letter.

To my sweet Rosa,

I'm sorry I wasn't a better man for you. I'm sorry I didn't stay, but I couldn't handle the look of hatred in your beautiful eyes. My love, I just couldn't.

I don't know how to say this, but we are mates. We were made for each other. I am not good enough for you. You deserve way better than me. I love you so much. The short time we spent together was amazing, the best time of my life.

Just know everything I did was to protect you. I hate myself for hurting you. I want to apologize to you.

You mean the world to me. I will do anything for you.

This necklace is important to me, and I want you to have it. It belonged to my mother. She gave it to me when I was young.

> *She raised me and didn't tell my father. Someone found out, told him about me, and came to kill us. She hid me and gave me this necklace. She ran, and when I came out of hiding the next day, she was dead. I was too weak to protect her, but I know deep in my heart she'd love for you to have this.*
>
> *I love you, my beautiful mate,*
> *Dimitri*

I break, every word feels just like him, raw, guilty, and terrified of losing me.

By the time I finish reading, it's raining, cold, and quiet. I clutch the note to my chest. I don't care about the rain. It feels like the sky is crying with me.

I love you too. I clutch the ruby. *Please come back.*

At some point, the rain dies, and I can't fight my exhaustion anymore.

When I wake, my back aches from sleeping on the chair all night. The sky is cloudy, I sit up, and my fingers automatically touch the necklace. I stare at it, and the memory of the demonology book flickers again. There was a small section about witches and their powers.

I'm a witch... The thought still feels unreal.

I remember every line that I read. It talked about elemental witches—the ones tied to the weather. It said overwhelming emotions could trigger storms and be dangerous, especially if the witch is not in control.

It makes sense. The rain last night stopped the moment I stopped crying. I need to deal with this. I don't want to be a danger to anyone, and if I'm going to survive *his* world, I need to learn how to control it.

I grab one of Dimitri's black hoodies from his closet, pull it over my leggings, and walk downstairs. It's time to face my reality. I can't just hide forever. I step into the living room, and everyone goes silent as soon as they see me.

My eyes find Cassie's. She's curled in a tight ball beside Ian. *Are they mates?* Her eyes look tired and slightly red. I can tell she's hardly slept. My fingers find the necklace since it calms me.

"I'm ready to learn more about what I am."

Eleanor stands and reaches for my hand. "Okay." There's this soft smile on her face. "I want you to know, I have always loved you, Rosa. I knew everything about you. We talked about you every single day. I begged for pictures, and I watched you grow up from a distance. I never truly left you. I missed you every single day."

I swallow hard, "I haven't fully processed it yet," I admit quietly. "You being my mom. I'm not mad, I'm just... overwhelmed. I feel upset, sad, and happy all at once. But I do understand why you did it, and I want to know about him, my dad. I want to know everything."

"Of course, darling." Her eyes soften. "I have pictures of him, and of you when you were little. You have his eyes." She touches just beneath mine, and I feel my chest tighten.

"I can't wait to see them." I walk toward the kitchen, and Cassie immediately wraps her arms around my back. I turn around, hugging her tight.

"You hungry?" she asks, pulling back with tears in her eyes.

"Yes, please don't cry." I pout, and she wipes her tears away.

"I don't want you to hate me!"

"I don't hate you. I know you were only protecting me. I love you like a sister, even if I do wish you had just told me! It's insane, I'm a witch."

She laughs and turns away. "Being a witch is cool and fun. I knew you'd be happy. I know how much you love that kind of stuff."

I hop onto the counter, watching her pull things out to make us a BLT. "So, tell me something. I overheard you and Ian talking one day. He was saying he wanted to mark you. Are you guys mates?"

"No," she sighs. "We're not mates, but he wants to mark me, and I said yes."

"What if you meet your mate in the future?"

She sets the bread down, turning to look at me. "Rosa... meeting your mate? It's nearly impossible except for werewolves. I'm okay with that because I love Ian. He and I have always had a connection."

"If you're happy and love him, that's all that really matters. When he marks you, will you turn into a demon?"

"Yes, but I'll still be a witch." She smiles as she hands me a bag of chips.

"Will you change, like your personality?"

"No, I mean yes. I'll be different, but stronger, and I'll become immortal like him."

"Shit... as in you'll live forever?" I raise my brows in shock.

"Yes," she laughs. "But witches live a long time. They age more slowly."

"Well... what if Dimitri ever marks me?" I ask, feeling heat rush to my face.

She pauses and looks at me, her tone serious. "Would you want that?"

"Yes." I bite my lip. "I love him. Do you... Do you think he'll come back?"

"Yes," she says with no hesitation. "He loves you, Rosa. The way he looks at you... Ian told me he never thought Dimitri would ever care for someone so much." She gives me a pointed look. "I'm honestly surprised. He's very scary."

"He's not scary."

"Oh, he is. Just not to you. You're the only one he softens for." She laughs, sitting beside me. "If he marked you, you'd be part demon too, immortal. We'd be actual sisters." She eats a handful of chips.

"If he comes back."

"He will." Ian walks in, stepping between Cassie's legs, kissing her.

"So why don't you have wings like Dimitri, if you're a part of the royal family? I thought the book said every member of the royal family has them."

"Only powerful demons have wings, not just the royal family," he says, carefully watching me as he rubs Cassie's upper thighs.

"Not to be rude," I say, taking a bite, "but if your dad is powerful and Dimitri is your brother, why aren't you?"

"I'm strong, just not like them. The firstborn inherits most of the power. But my father doesn't want him taking over. He wants me to."

"But why not Dimitri if he's the firstborn and powerful?" This whole thing is confusing.

"My father wants nothing to do with Dimitri, Rosa."

"That's awful. It's not Dimitri's fault your dad cheated on your mom." Anger rises in me. "Your dad is the one who messed up."

"I know, and I've tried to fix it. I don't want the crown. It doesn't want me. The throne selects who sits on it, and I cannot sit on it because the power declines me. That is why Dimitri does the judgments."

"The judgments?"

"Yes, that is where souls go after death. Dimitri is in charge." Oh, I see. That's what he meant when he said he punishes bad guys.

I look down at my hands. "When I get my powers... can I contact him? Send a message? Something? I don't know how Hell works."

"You can't find him unless he wants to be found," Eleanor says, stepping into the kitchen. "He disappears a lot."

"I need to see him. I need to talk to him." I pull my necklace out from under my hoodie.

"He gave it to you," Ian says softly. "He never went anywhere without it."

"I love it," I whisper, rubbing the pendant.

"It'll mean a lot to him that you wear it."

"He called me his mate..." I clutch the note.

"You are his mate," Ian says. "He knew the first night he touched you."

"He knew all this time?" My eyes widen. The hurt stings, but the sympathy outweighs the anger.

"Yes."

"I wish he had talked to me."

"We asked him to," Eleanor says gently.

"Then you should've told me!" I snap, looking at Cassie. "You especially. You knew how I felt about him. You knew how confused I was."

"I'm sorry!" Cassie throws her hands up. "I couldn't tell you without revealing everything. And if Dimitri told you, he could protect you. I couldn't. I'm not powerful, Rosa."

I breathe in slowly, trying to steady myself.

"I'll be back in a few hours," Eleanor says, walking out of the room with Tammy.

I take a deep breath. "I'm going for a walk." I hop down from the counter and walk out without looking back.

Chapter Twenty-three

Rosa

I walk around for hours, the weight of everything pressing down on me, and I have no idea how to even process it all. I don't want to be weak, to break down over something I can't control. What good would that do? None. Absolutely nothing would change. I could crawl into a hole and disappear, but it won't rewrite the past, and it certainly won't change what's to come.

I promised myself I wouldn't be that scared girl anymore, the one who hides from the unknown. But here I am, standing in it, and I can't stop the feelings from growing. I don't know how to handle this, how to react to the emotional storm that's brewing inside me.

I wish there were someone who had walked the same situation before me, someone who could tell me how to survive it, how to breathe through the chaos. I wish I had my stepmom. She always knew how to steady me when I was lost.

Somehow lost in my thoughts, I ended up at the pond, the same one where I saw Dimitri swimming.

I sit at the edge, remove my slippers, and dip my feet into the cool water. I lie back, staring up at the sky. It's overcast, a dull grey hanging above me, mirroring the crazy storm inside. I wonder if I'm somehow the reason the cloud above me is dark.

I think about my father. *Was he a witch, too? What was he like? Was I anything like him? Was he kind, strong, brave? They said he saved Dimitri, so he must've had something good in him. But how? How does someone risk everything for another?*

I want to make him proud of me, but I'm the reason he's dead. Would my life be different if he hadn't died that day? Maybe I would've grown up here, knowing that I'm a witch. I would've known how to use my magic instead of this... not having control of anything, it's like I'm riding passenger, and I keep screaming at the driver to turn, and they never do.

This would've been my home the entire time, and Dimitri, I would've met him earlier. On the flip side, I never would have met my adoptive mom. I don't need to think of the what-ifs or would-haves. I am proud of who I am and the horrors I survived.

"It's time you stop feeling sorry for yourself and take control," I whisper to myself, standing after lying here on the grass for the last few hours. I decide to leave my slippers off since my feet are still wet, and it'd ruin them.

I walk barefoot, enjoying the view and feeling the grass beneath my feet. It's silent and extremely peaceful except for the birds chirping in the distance. It takes a while since I'm moving slowly, but the house finally comes into view. I slip my slippers back on and step inside.

"Rosa." The voice comes from out of nowhere, and I nearly trip when Ian is suddenly in front of me. He looks me over as if looking for injuries. "We were getting worried."

"I'm sorry," I look away. "I went on a walk to clear my head. I didn't mean to worry you guys."

"It's okay, we understand."

Everyone else walks in behind him. I straighten my shoulders, inhaling deeply. "I am ready to embrace this new side of me. I'm not running scared anymore. Is Eleanor back?"

"That's wonderful news," Tammy and Cassie say at the same time, exchanging a happy look.

"I'm here," Eleanor steps into the room. "Let's get started in the library."

We follow her in silence and sit in a circle in the sitting area. I'm next to Tammy, who gives me a supportive smile, while Ian and Cassie sit across from us. Eleanor is to my right, her expression soft but serious.

"So," Eleanor begins, breaking the silence. "We know you're powerful when it comes to the weather and that your emotions seem to trigger it, but we need to see if you have another ability. Can you move things with your mind?" She glances at Cassie. "Normally, witches either have control over elements or telekinesis, but I want to see if it was the wind or telekinesis that threw that boy off you."

"Okay." I nod, nervous knots tying in my stomach.

"We'll start simple and work our way up." She turns to Cassie. "Please demonstrate and move that candlestick across the room."

Cassie narrows her eyes as she focuses all her energy on the candlestick. Her hand shakes as she stretches it toward it. With a small grunt, she lifts it an inch off the table, but it immediately drops, landing with a loud thud. She groans in frustration.

"It's okay, honey," Tammy nods at her. "You're doing fine."

Eleanor smiles. "It takes time, Cassie. It's rare to be able to move something on the first try. Even if you have natural talent, it takes months of practice to move objects consistently. Cassie has been working hard for nearly two months." She turns to me. "It takes hard work and a lot of it. Weaker witches use spells, but our family comes from a strong bloodline. Cassie and Tammy's coven comes in second. I would like to see you lift it."

I glance at the candlestick, my fingers curling into my palms as I try to clear my mind. Tammy moves it slightly, setting it upright. Her voice is gentle as she speaks. "Alright, sweetie, all you need to do is relax. Just picture the power coursing through your body, you'll feel it, like a hum, and then guide it, and direct it."

"Okay." I take a deep breath, feeling slightly nervous with everyone's eyes on me. I close my own eyes and try to concentrate, just like they said. I call to the magic within me.

At first, I feel nothing but a slight tension in my chest, but then there's something I felt before, the day I was attacked. It's a flicker, a pulse, like something inside me stirs. A buzzing starts at the center of my chest. The energy spreads outward, making me shiver as it trickles down my arms to my fingertips. It's like an electric current shooting through me. The feeling coursing through me is intoxicating, like I've unlocked something in my body that it has been craving, like I can finally breathe. My fingertips tremble lightly as the buzzing intensifies.

I open my eyes, my hand stretches in front of me, palms facing the object, fingers spread wide, they start trembling, but then the candlestick rises.

The whole room gasps, but I don't break concentration. I move my hand, swinging it to the other side of the room, but instead of moving slowly like my hand, it flies across the room with a force I didn't intend, slamming into the wall and leaving a dent.

"Oh, shit," I hiss, my eyes wide cin shock. I rush over to it, bending down to pick it up. "I'm so sorry, Eleanor. I didn't mean to break it."

No one answers me; Cassie and Tammy are wide-eyed, Eleanor's hand is over her mouth, and Ian's brow furrows in thought, like he's trying to make sense of what just happened.

"What?" I ask, lifting the broken piece. "I said I'm sorry. Don't be mad. I think I can hot glue both sides together."

"No one cares about the damn candlestick, or the hole in the wall." Ian finally says, his voice flat. "That's not the point."

"Then what is?" I ask, looking at Eleanor for help. "Did I do something wrong?"

"You did nothing wrong, sweetie." Eleanor stands. "You did something that no one else has ever done. No one has ever moved anything on their first try, let alone across the room with that much force. Normally, it takes months of constant practice just to move a candle, but you did it in seconds."

"Well, you did say we are from a strong line of witches, right?"

"Not that strong. I was the fastest to be able to move and lift, and it still took a couple of weeks of non-stop practice. Even then, everyone was dumbfounded. It's also rare to have more than one ability. That is extraordinary."

"Why make me try if it's never been done before?"

"We wanted to show you how it feels so you can practice, and out of curiosity, like I said before, with you moving the boy."

"I'm a freak," I mumble to myself.

"You're not a freak. You're a total badass!" Cassie jumps up, throwing her arms around me. "You're the strongest witch alive! Hell yes!"

"Alright, alright," Tammy says, laughing. "Let's try again, but maybe not break anything this time?"

I roll my eyes. "Funny, but I didn't mean to do that."

"They're just things. They can be replaced. Let's move that chair," Eleanor encourages me.

I lift my hand once more, focusing on the chair as I let the power course through me and visualize it lifting. It floats a few inches off the ground, and I slowly swing my hand to the side, but instead of moving slowly with me, it crashes into the wall, leaving a large hole in the drywall.

"Holy shit!" I gasp, "Sorry, sorry!" I rush to the chair, but it's stuck in the wall. "Maybe I need more practice."

"Holy shit is right." Eleanor is staring at me with wonder. "You need to learn control, and I need to call the rest of the council. They'll want to know about this."

"The council?" I ask, confused. "I thought you said we shouldn't tell anyone?"

"We're the most powerful beings in each faction: witches, werewolves, vampires, fae, and demons. We enforce the supernatural laws." Eleanor's eyes soften as she looks at me. "I trust them, but for now, this stays between us."

"So... werewolves and fae are real, too?"

"Yes, and they might want to meet you, but for now, this does not leave this room. You need to keep practicing, but maybe outside, and with smaller things. Being in nature will help with control."

"Is that the reason I love being outside, especially in the woods?"

"Yes, that is the witch side of you."

"Just wait for the full moon. It feels the best." Cassie grins.

"Dimitri has a very powerful mate. You may surpass Dimitri's power in the magical department." Ian laughs. "I wish he were here. If he were, he'd be proud of you."

"Wait, Eleanor, can I ask you something before you leave?"

"Of course." Eleanor pauses at the door to look at me.

"Was my father a witch, too?"

"No, I mean, yes, but men are called warlocks, not witches."

She leaves, asking Tammy to follow.

I'm processing everything as I look around the room for something that isn't breakable, and I find a wooden table lamp. I walk up to it, unscrew the shade and light bulb, and pick it up.

"You think this will be fine?"

"Yeah. I'm coming with you. Just don't take my head off." Cassie laughs.

"Haha." I let out a fake laugh. "Very funny, Cassie."

"Thanks, I thought so too."

"I need a coffee before we start."

"I saw how Dimitri made your latte. It won't be as good, but I can make one for you," Ian suggests.

"That'd be great."

"Aw, babe, that's so sweet. Make me one, too, please, we'll be outside." Cassie smiles, fluttering her eyelashes at him. He nods, turning to leave, but before he gets too far, she spanks him.

"You'll pay for that later." He looks over his shoulder at her.

"Can't wait." She giggles.

"I am still here."

"Sorry." Cassie gives me an innocent look.

"Sure, you are." I sound annoyed, but there's a smile teasing my lips.

"Fine. No, I'm not."

We find a good spot, far enough that we can't see the house.

Ian meets us out there after about ten minutes, and I sip the latte. It's good, but it's not as good. I think it's missing cinnamon, but I appreciate the attempt.

"He made it look easier than I thought. The maid is going to be mad when she gets here; I made a big mess." Ian says, shaking his head.

"Thank you, babe. I'll reward you later." Cassie gets on her toes, kissing him.

CHAPTER TWENTY-FOUR

Rosa

We've been sitting out here for about an hour, and I haven't made any progress. The damn lamp keeps slamming into the tree. The one time it missed, we spent a good twenty minutes looking for it. The frustration is eating at me, gnawing at my patience. I cross my arms over my chest, grinding my teeth.

"This is so frustrating," I groan under my breath, staring at the damn lamp.

"Let's try making it rain," Cassie suggests, being her cheerful self.

"Rain?" I stare and frown, skeptical. "I've only ever done that while crying, but fine. I can give it a shot. How do I?"

She shrugs, "Maybe imagine it?"

"Okay." I nod. Breathing deeply and closing my eyes, I picture it raining and imagine how the rain feels, the scent of it. I try to will it into existence. The power rushing through me feels electric, like a high, and for a moment,

I swear the entire sky is moving because *I told it to.* Then a little raindrop hits the tip of my nose. It starts slowly, but as I keep pushing, it turns into a steady downpour.

Oh, God, I did it...

"Oh, my gosh, you did it!" Cassie jumps up and down laughing as she spins around with her arms stretched wide, not caring that our clothes and hair are getting drenched. I can't help but spin as I laugh, too. It feels good and powerful. I don't know how I'm doing it, but it felt like I unlocked something inside me that had been buried.

"This is awesome!" I shout over the sound of heavy rain. I want to see how far I can go. My mind starts focusing on lightning, and a zap of energy rushes through me; it's fast and electrifying. The air around me cracks, my hair standing like static; everything in me buzzing as I push, and then a lightning bolt slams right into the ground a foot away from Cassie with a loud crack.

She screams, jumping back, eyes wide.

"Shit, sorry. I didn't mean to, but you have to admit that was a little funny." Laughter bubbles up inside me that I can't stop. This whole situation is absurd.

"No, no, it scared the crap out of me." She narrows her eyes, though her lips are twitching as she tries not to laugh. "Maybe we should take a break? I'm cold and wet."

"Fine," I agree, wiping the wet strands of hair from my face.

We head inside, dripping wet, laughing, and shivering. The three of us are sitting around the table eating. Tammy and Eleanor are still gone, and there's still no sign of Dimitri yet. My insides are empty; it hurts. I've forced myself not to think about him, but when my mind isn't busy, it's hard not to. I need to keep moving and pushing myself. I sit here trying to eat, hoping it'll fill the hollow space, but it doesn't ease it.

Ian and Cassie are keeping the conversation going, but I'm not listening. I shift my attention to the magic. It was powerful, and I can still feel it pulsing behind my ribs. My skin is tight, and I feel like I'll burst if I don't release it.

Dinner ends, and everyone grabs a glass of wine, drinking and relaxing, but I can't sit here anymore.

"I'm going back outside. I need to keep practicing."

"Are you okay?" Cassie asks, scanning my face. "I can come with you."

"Yeah, I'm just feeling restless. I need to figure this out. You don't have to come. It might help being alone."

I leave them in the dining room, lamp in hand, as I step outside, the air cool and fresh. I decided to name the lamp since we are going to spend a lot of time together.

"You need to help me here, James," I say to it as I place it on the grass in front of me. "This can't just be on me. We're in this partnership together." I lift it off the ground, but once I flick my wrist, it disappears through the trees. I groan as I stand to find it.

I talk to him as I walk back to the house. "I'm doing all the hard work. I'll let you rest tonight, but tomorrow you'd better be ready to work hard."

"Oh, there you are!" Eleanor stands from where she is sitting with Tammy and a man that I don't recognize, but he gives me the heebie-jeebies as he slowly takes me in with his dark eyes. My stomach twists as I study him. He's tall, around six feet tall, and he's in his late twenties. It's his piercing eyes that throw me off, mixed with his aura. His power feels off and creepy. His gaze lingers long enough to make me feel uncomfortable.

"You must be Rosa," he says smoothly. Then he takes a step forward, his eyes darkening with interest as he extends his hand, taking mine, lips brushing the tops of my knuckles.

My skin crawls. It feels like he's marking me. My instincts scream at me, making me shiver and not in a good way. For a second, my power twitches beneath my skin like a warning. My pulse quickens, and I pull my hand away before he can linger any longer. "I am, and you are?"

"Oh, yes," he chuckles darkly. "Where are my manners? My name is Julian."

I take a step back, not bothering to hide my discomfort. "Pleasure to meet you, Julian."

"The pleasure is all mine." His eyes drift over me again, narrowing at the sight of my shirt. His nostrils flare, and his jaw clenches. I cross my arms over my chest, feeling exposed and suddenly cold.

"Rosa, this is Julian the vampire on the council," Eleanor explains, smiling, not noticing the tension. "He wants to be here tomorrow to see your magic firsthand and see how it manifests."

"Yeah, of course, that is no problem." I give him a tight-lipped smile.

"Wonderful." His smile doesn't reach his eyes. "I'll be back tomorrow." He turns, and then he's gone, leaving a lingering, uncomfortable silence. There's something about him that I don't like.

"How did practice go?" Tammy asks.

"Honestly? Frustrating but also good. I have the weather side of things down. I can manifest rain and storms. But the other stuff? Moving objects? It's not getting better, maybe even worse."

"You need to clear your mind." Tammy taps her fingers on the table as she thinks. "Maybe, try meditation."

"Yes, that might help." I nod, agreeing. It seems simple enough. "That guy Julian? He gave me the creeps," I finally say.

Eleanor and Tammy both nod knowingly. "Yes, he has that effect on people. He's very powerful. He's the vampire prince." Eleanor explains.

"A prince?" I blink, not expecting that. It does make sense with the way he carries himself. "I've never met a prince before."

"Yes, very powerful, but not powerful enough to take the throne. Even with his royal blood, his father will not allow it until he finds a powerful queen to rule at his side. He's been beaten in battle by two different beings."

"And who are the two?" My curiosity grows despite my unease.

"One was your father, and the other was Dimitri." The weight of the words smacks me in the chest. *Dimitri?*

"The council wanted Dimitri to take over until they found a vampire powerful enough to lead, but he declined."

Now, this vampire prince is interested in me? And Julian is looking for a queen, someone powerful. My stomach twists. This is getting worse by the second. "What does this mean? What if he doesn't find someone?" I narrow my eyes, not liking the way the dots are connecting.

Tammy hums. "Maybe that's why he took an interest in you. If he doesn't find a queen, the vampire king in Russia has a few sons. The youngest one might come over to take control."

"Yes, maybe indeed," Eleanor agrees.

"No," I snap, shaking my head. "I have a mate."

"Not one who has claimed you," Tammy argues, voice sharp. She seems to be the only one who is mad at Dimitri for leaving.

My anger and frustrations grow. "I'm not just going to fall for someone just because it's a convenience."

Tammy frowns, tone softening. "I'm not saying you have to mate him, but maybe consider going on a date or two before writing him off completely."

I shoot her a look before turning away, feeling the weight of their expectations. "I'll think about it," I sigh. "But I'm not ready to give up on Dimitri. I'm going to bed."

Eleanor stops me before I can leave. "First, you should know that you have met a prince, Rosa," she says gently.

I pause my steps, "What do you mean?"

"I don't know if we should tell her." Tammy shakes her head at Eleanor.

"I'm right here, and no more secrets." I turn around, facing them.

"She's right, no more secrets. Ian and Dimitri are both princes. Ian is next in line to rule the Underworld."

"Wait, their father is the Devil?" I gasp. The thought is overwhelming. Dimitri's the prince of the Underworld? If he's the one the Demonology book talked about, then he's one of the seven sons. He's stronger than the Devil himself. That alone should scare me, but my stomach heats with pleasure.

I know that Ian was talking about the crown and a throne… but I didn't think it was because they're the princes of the Underworld. I just thought they were a part of the royal family.

"Yes," Tammy answers, clearing her throat. "There is one more thing you should know."

I groan. I don't know how much more I can handle. "What now?"

"I think she's had enough; we'll tell her another day." Eleanor steps in.

"No, now I want to know." I sit in a chair as I wait for the next thing. I'm drained both emotionally and physically.

Tammy hesitates as she looks me over. "Jim is dead."

My blood turns cold. "What?" I whisper, shooting up from my seat, hands trembling. "How? And why didn't you tell me?"

"It happened recently. We didn't want to ruin your birthday."

"Tell me what happened," I demand. I don't feel sad. That man was horrible to me, but I'm shocked.

"He was murdered," Tammy answers softly. "It was violent."

"Who did it?" I hold my breath, bracing myself for the answer.

"We don't know if we should be the ones to tell you." Tammy rubs her upper arm with her hand. She looks uncomfortable.

"It was Dimitri," Ian says, stepping into the room. I stare at him as I slowly let the words sink in.

"Dimitri? But why?"

"He protects what's his," Ian says, casually leaning against the door frame. "Jim hurt you, and Dimitri wanted him to pay for his sins. He would kill anyone who touches you."

I stand frozen, the words suffocating me, my mind spinning. The words echo, *Dimitri killed Jim because of me...* I become lightheaded, and my ears start ringing. My breath catches. I'm stuck somewhere between relief and horror, but God help me. I feel more relief than anything, like part of me has always known he'd do anything to protect me, and that terrifies me more than the murder itself.

"He'll kill anyone who touches me," I whispered, trying to process it all. I lean my back against the wall behind me to support my weight.

"In a heartbeat," Ian confirms.

Tammy nods. "That is who he is. I know he's caring toward you, but he is a sinister man. He'll murder without a second thought."

"You make my brother sound like a monster." Ian snaps.

"He is, and he's the worst of you all. Rosa, he's a dangerous and unforgiving man. I have heard awful stories of him." Tammy rushes out.

"That's enough, Tammy," Eleanor growls. "He doesn't just run around killing everyone. He only kills those who have sins to pay for."

"And what of Aiden?" Tammy pushes. "What so-called sin did he commit?"

"Aiden assaulted Rosa after she very clearly rejected him." Ian snarls.

"Having a crush on a girl is enough for him to kill? In that horrible manner. Yes, I agree he crossed the line and deserved punishment, but a painful death?"

As they fight, I try to let their words sink in. My back slowly slides down the wall. He killed Aiden because of me.

"Not just a girl, she is his mate. Dimitri warned him, but he didn't listen." Ian growls, growing angrier by the second.

"Unbelievable!" She looks over to Eleanor. "You let him murder Aiden over something so trivial. I need some air. Rosa, think about what I said. He is an evil man." She walks out of the room.

"Rosa." Eleanor kneels in front of me. "Dimitri will never hurt you. He does have blood on his hands, but he isn't an evil man. He'll protect you at all costs."

"Aiden didn't deserve to die," I whisper. "I need to be alone."

"He touched you. He was warned, so yes, he did deserve to die," Ian says, walking out of the room with Eleanor.

CHAPTER TWENTY-FIVE

Rosa

I walk upstairs, numb and hollow. I feel like my mind will explode from everything I have learned. He murdered for me. What the hell am I supposed to do with that? How am I supposed to feel?

When he told me he made people "pay for their sins," I naïvely assumed he meant he dragged them off to prison or something. Not this violence or death, and blood. I walk into the bathroom and turn on the shower. I stare blankly at the tile floors as the steam rises around me.

Aiden is dead because he liked me...

I'm not saying Dimitri is evil, but he is absolutely unhinged. I now understand why he got so angry all those times anyone would touch me. He's overly possessive of me.

I quickly remove my clothes and step in. I stand under the warm water, with both palms against the wall, bowing my head as the water runs down my back. My emotions are scattered around like a thousand-piece puzzle, and I need to sort them out.

After the shower, I toss and turn all night, barely sleeping, not able to clear my thoughts.

This wasn't the Prince Charming I had always dreamed of. No, this is a deadly prince.

I wanted to scream, to cry, to make sense of it all. But there was no sense to be made.

I'd prayed for a prince, but what I got was the prince of death... a killer.

"No! Please NO!" I scream watching Dimitri stare at me with cold, cruel eyes.

"I reject you as my mate, Rosa. I don't want you." He hisses. "Why do you think I left. You think I want a witch as a mate?" He starts viciously. "I don't need you; I have someone else."

The woman from the pond steps beside him, smiling like she won something. "He wants a demon, someone powerful and beautiful. Not someone like you."

Their laughter echoes. My knees hit the ground.

"Please, Dimitri."

"Please, Dimitri." The woman mimics me, laughing.

"No, no, no," I cry, shaking my head. The wind slams into me, violently swinging my hair all around.

"How pathetic."

"Very pathetic, my love, isn't she?"

"Yes." She turns toward him, rubbing her hands across his naked chest. He picks her up and starts kissing her while watching me.

"No! No! No!" I wake up, screaming and tossing around the bed. I sit up covered in sweat, chest heaving. I blink around the room. I'm in Dimitri's room, not in the nightmare; it wasn't real.

"It was just a dream," I whisper, pressing my palm to my chest, trying to slow my racing heart.

I lie there a long time, replaying everything that happened last night. I've been sorting through every emotion until the pieces finally fall into place.

This unhinged psychopathic murderer has killed twice to protect me. He has blood on his hands because of me, but even though that is all true, if I am honest, no matter how disturbing this may seem, I still want him. Even worse? It turns me on.

The fact that he will kill for me, his obsession, and protectiveness. It's dark, and twisted... but it's mine.

Who needs Prince Charming when I have a deadly prince who would burn the world down for me?

He is my unhinged, deadly, psychopathic prince.

I stretch in bed until my back pops, then finally force myself up. I walk outside onto the balcony. The sun is bright today, warm, and steady. I tilt my face up, closing my eyes. The sun-rays feel good against my skin. I stand here for a while just enjoying the feeling and letting myself breathe.

I love hearing the birds sing; it's beautiful and magical. When I open my eyes, my gaze goes straight to the broken tree. The one Dimitri smashed Aiden into, the world has moved on, but the small violence is still there.

I head inside, needing to eat, and I get dressed in black leggings and a white tank, slip on my slippers, and go find Cassie.

I knock. "Cassie!"

"What?" She opens the door, her hair is a mess, sticking up everywhere, and behind her, Ian is half naked, trying to shove pants over his ass.

"Oh, my God! I'll... see you downstairs!" I turn away, laughing.

When I walk into the dining room, Tammy looks up. "Good morning. How are you?"

"I've had an eventful morning, saw things I can never unsee."

"Like what?" she asks, confused.

"Ian's bare ass."

She spits coffee everywhere. I laugh as I sit down, grabbing myself a cup of coffee.

"I wanted to apologize for last night, my outburst. I'm just worried about you. Deep down, I know Dimitri won't hurt you, but... his world is dangerous. That's why he left."

"It's okay," I say softly. "You just want to protect me, but I refuse to turn my back on him. Not yet."

"Just stay safe, that's all I want."

"Good morning." Eleanor walks in, picks up a piece of toast, and spreads grape jelly on it.

Tammy immediately hugs her from behind. "I'm sorry about saying those things I said last night. I know he's like a son to you." Eleanor gives her a warm, tired smile.

"It's okay, dear. We'll always have different opinions on Dimitri. Just know I'd never let Rosa be in a dangerous relationship. He'll take care of her."

Ian wanders in a couple of minutes later, half asleep, and that sends us into another round of laughter.

"Am I missing something?" His voice sounds groggy, eyebrows coming together with a frown.

"I don't know what's going on with those two," Eleanor answers him.

"I'm just grabbing breakfast for Cassie," he mumbles as he piles the plate with pancakes.

"Yeah, you two looked very cozy this morning. She definitely needs her energy."

"Behave, Rosa!" Eleanor hits my shoulder. Ian leaves the room, shaking his head.

Eventually, the chaos dies down, and Tammy clears her throat.

Eleanor turns to me. "Julian should be here in a couple of hours. I was hoping you'd come with me to see pictures of your father. Maybe answer the questions you have."

"I'd like that." I nod with a smile.

We head to a hallway that mirrors the guest wing. At the very end is a door that Eleanor hesitates to open. "This was your father's office."

There are dark mahogany shelves filled with ancient books and a massive desk in the center with four leather chairs.

"I haven't been in here for such a long time." Eleanor walks inside slowly. She runs her fingertips across the table, then picks up a picture frame. She turns it over and smiles down at it. A single tear slides down her cheek.

My heart breaks a little. I walk to her, touch her shoulder, and she hands me the frame.

It's a picture of a man carrying a little girl on his back. They are both smiling at the camera, their eyes filled with laughter. The little girl is me.

He has shoulder-length hair, the same color as mine, dark brown, almost black. We both have the same pale skin. He has a stronger jawline and high cheekbones, where mine are a little rounder.

"Here is a close-up of his face." Eleanor shows me another picture; it is of her and him smiling at a camera in a selfie. They look so happy, a man who adored his mate and daughter. I can't help but notice I have his eyes, and that makes me feel so freaking happy. I have a piece of him.

"What happened exactly?" I ask quietly. "Why did they kill him?"

Eleanor exhales shakily. "There's a secret society. They want the council gone... they want control for themselves. They broke through my protective ward that day; it was war, bloody, and many died. They killed the fae ruler and captured your father. They couldn't overpower us in the end. So, I did what I had to, hid you away with the humans so they couldn't use you against me. I had already lost your father; I couldn't lose you."

"No one knows who their leader is?" I sit, gripping the picture tighter.

"No one," she answers, sitting across from me.

"That doesn't make sense. You have the strongest beings alive, yet you can't find a small society? Are you sure it isn't someone on the inside?"

"No," she straightens, shaking her head. "There's no traitor on the council. I've known them all too long."

"Are you sure? Because the best way to keep a secret society a secret is to have someone on the inside. Have you conducted an investigation?"

"No, of course not. There's no need to do that."

I shake my head in disbelief. Who has not at least conducted an investigation? Something in my chest settles cold. I have a feeling I know... But how can I figure out for certain who the traitor is? I want revenge for my father. Not just that, they need to be punished for stealing the life I could've had.

"If they failed to overpower you, why didn't you come back for me?"

"Believe me, I wanted to," she says softly, sitting beside me and taking my hands, "but I think you're still in danger."

My stomach knots. "Why? What makes you think that?" My knees bounce with anxious energy.

"There's a rumor..." She hesitates, choosing her words carefully. "The leader of the group wants a powerful mate at his side. Everyone knows you're the only daughter born into the council in this generation. We believe he'll try to take you and force a mate bond to gain access to your power. With you beside him, he could take over everything."

My breath catches. "But why would he think I'm powerful enough? And how can he force a mate bond when Dimitri is already my mate?"

"Dimitri is your soulmate," she says gently, "but anyone can claim a mate. It's our version of marriage, except these bonds are permanent. And you'd be powerful because your father and I lead the council. Those roles and our magic are passed to you and your future mate when we die." I swallow, heart pounding. "We always knew you'd be strong because of your bloodline," Eleanor continues, voice shaking slightly, "but you are far more powerful than we expected. Which is exactly why no one outside this house can know what you can do until you learn to control it. You are the only key to the kingdom he desires since he failed to overpower us."

"And is Dimitri aware of this?"

"He is…"

He is, and he still left me to deal with this alone…

Everything about Julian feels wrong, cold, and hungry. It has to be him. Plus, the stories match… the leader needs a powerful mate… Julian needs a powerful queen. If he's the leader, it means he already knows I'm back. People like him will do anything for power, even if it means turning their back on their own people. They can't see it because they are so close. They can't see the darkness in him, but I do. That means I'm in danger.

I look down at the photo again. "We seemed happy."

"We were. He loved being your father. He never missed tucking you in and reading to you at night, no matter what, even if he had to leave after." Her voice breaks slightly. "He adored you."

My throat tightens. "I can't believe I forgot you both," I say, feeling angry that this beautiful life was taken from me because someone out there is so desperate for power.

A loud doorbell cuts through the silence.

"That must be Julian," I say breathlessly.

"Yes, it must be." Eleanor nods and pats the top of my hand before standing.

I hold the photo to my chest. "Can I keep this?"

"Yes, of course." She smiles at me.

"Thank you." I return her smile as I stand. "I'm going to go get changed and put this away in my room, okay?"

I start to walk away, but stop, turn around, and wrap my arms around her waist. She gasps in shock for a moment and then hugs me back.

Walking down the hall, I already know what I need to do. The only way to confirm Julian's involvement... is to play his game.

Make him think I'm interested. Use myself as bait and get close enough to see the truth. Even if it puts me in danger. I go to my room, open my closet, and grab the outfit that makes me feel powerful. Black leather pants and a fitted black top paired with deadly stilettos.

I pull them on, look in the mirror, and lift my chin. The pants hug my body, and the top shows a perfect amount of cleavage. My necklace settles right between the girls.

Julian wants a queen? He's about to meet one. A dangerous one.

Chapter Twenty-six

Rosa

I walk down the stairs slowly, each step steady and controlled. I've already decided that if Julian is the threat I think he is, then showing any hint of fear would be my first mistake.

Halfway down, Julian looks up at me. His eyes slowly take me in, and his smile grows wide.

"Wow," is all he says. The others turn to look at me.

Cassie's brows pinch together, and she frowns in confusion. I wink at her more for reassurance than playfulness.

"Okay, since everyone is here, let's get started," Tammy says.

We follow her to the living room. I can feel Julian's stare burning into my back. I glance over my shoulder; he isn't pretending not to look. His eyes are glued to my ass. I slow my steps and sway my hips, just enough to bait the prince who thinks he's the predator here. Let him think I'm soft and easy to read. It'll make me more dangerous.

In the sitting room, we all sit except Julian. He stays standing in the center of the room like he's in charge.

"I want to see what you can do and how strong you are," Julian starts. "There are witches who can hurt someone using their mind alone. It's rare, but I want to test to see if you can."

I tilt my head, pretending to hesitate. "But who will I hurt? I don't want to hurt anyone."

"Me, little one." He touches my shoulder, his fingers staying longer than necessary.

"But..." I act as if I care.

He cuts me off. "I'm a vampire. Hard to hurt or kill, it'll be okay, I promise." He squeezes my shoulder before taking a step back.

"Okay, but how do I even do that?" I ask, my eyes turning to Eleanor.

"Just like you made yourself think of rain and thunderstorms and made it happen. Focus, think of him in pain." Tammy answers. I suppress a smile. *Now that I can do.*

He widens his stance, bracing himself, staring at me like I'm his next obsession. I pretend to chew my lip nervously.

"Are you ready?"

He nods, so I picture him in pain, and nothing happens.

I stand, inhaling deeply, letting my hatred guide my magic, and I narrow my eyes at him. He took my father, stole my life. In my head, I scream angrily, *pain.*

My magic rushes through me so intensely that it slams through me, throwing me back onto the couch as the air blasts out of my chest. I'm panting heavily; the power in me is pure ecstasy. I feel alive, *good*. My hands are trembling from the force.

Julian's screams rip through my daze. He's gripping the sides of his head tightly and drops to his knees. Blood spills from out of his ears. Everyone panics, but I don't. My revenge is right there.

My heartbeat is pounding, my eyes glare, and I push harder. I want to smile, but I keep myself steady. I can't believe I have the strength to bring such a powerful man to his knees.

"Stop, make it stop, Rosa!" Eleanor shouts as she drops to her knees and grabs Julian's head.

"How?"

"Tell the pain to stop."

I nod, looking back at the screaming Julian. In my head, I cut the cord with a sharp *stop*.

He collapses forward, hands flat on the floor, panting, body shaking.

"That was the worst pain I have ever felt," he says between breaths. "It was like burning alive."

"Gods, I'm so sorry. Are you okay?" I move to him, kneeling in front of him, masking my face with concern.

"I will be fine." He looks at me; his eyes are blood red.

"Here." Tammy rushes over with a rag. I take it, cleaning the blood from his ears, keeping my hands steady even as he studies the side of my face.

"That was extraordinary." He breathes. "It's unlike anything I've seen."

"Yes," Eleanor agrees. "Very few witches have that ability."

"I am curious if you can kill someone, too." He lightly grips my wrist, stopping me from cleaning the blood, and stands.

"I am not testing that," I say firmly. I take his outstretched hand, and he helps me up.

"No, of course not. I don't think any of us want to die," He chuckles, but it isn't a joyful chuckle; it's creepy. I knew in that moment he would let someone die just to test it.

"Your eyes," Cassie gasps.

I rush to a mirror and stare at my reflection; they are the same color, but they're glowing. I lean in closer, and my pupils are nearly gone.

Julian moves to stand behind me. "It's normal for powerful witches who use strong magic."

"They're beautiful, will they fade?"

"Yes. In a few moments."

He eyes me with a deeper hunger now, and it makes my skin crawl. I don't step away, even if I want to. "May I talk to Rosa alone for a moment?"

"Of course." Eleanor nods, and everyone walks out of the room. Cassie is the last to leave; she throws me a worried look. I nod, telling her I've got this.

Once we're alone, Julian steps even closer, lowering his face until his chin nearly touches my shoulder.

"I find you very beautiful, little one."

I give a small, but cautious smile, then look away. "Thank you."

He grips my chin gently, but firmly, turning my head until we're face to face. I can feel his warm breath against my lips. "I must take my leave now, but I'm hoping you'll come to dinner with me?" he murmurs as his thumb rubs my cheek.

I blink up at him, keeping my expression naïve. "Really?" *This is my chance to get close to him. I may figure out if he's the leader of the secret society.*

"Yes." His lips curl into a slow, predatorial smile. He likes my innocent act.

"Okay," I whisper.

"Perfect. I'll pick you up around six." He kisses my cheek, then disappears.

I exhale slowly before walking to the library.

Cassie jumps up and rushes to me. "What the hell was that?"

"He... asked me to dinner tonight."

"What did he say when you said no? I wish I were there to see his facial expression. I'm sure he doesn't hear the word no from women very often," she giggles.

I look away, "I said yes."

"Wait, what?" she shouts.

"You aren't going out with him." Ian snaps as he stalks over, looking pissed.

"Why not? He's handsome and a prince."

Ian's jaw clenches. "He wants you as a mate."

"At least someone wants me," I snap, letting the jab land where it needs to.

Cassie freezes, and Ian goes silent. *Good. They buy it.*

Tammy steps in. "Let her go. She knows what she's doing."

Not exactly, but I know what *I* need to do.

Upstairs, alone, the fear crawls up my throat. I could get hurt; he could kill me.

No. He won't kill me; he needs me and my power. He has to impress me. I know I don't have a handle on my magic, but if I need them, I could use them. I crush the fear; this is something I have to do for my father and the revenge I crave. I sit at my desk and pull out a piece of paper.

> *If I didn't come home, I wouldn't have gone willingly. I went looking for the truth, and he forcefully took me. If something happens to me, please tell Dimitri I love the necklace. Tell him that I'm not afraid of him. I don't care what he has done in the past; nothing will make me think less of him.*
>
> *Love,*
>
> *Rosa*

I stare at myself in the mirror. I look good, most importantly, I don't look breakable. I'm wearing a black silk dress with a slit that shows off my right leg. I swallow the nervous lump forming inside my throat and rub my sweaty hands down the sides of the dress.

The magic pulsing beneath my skin gives me the courage I need. I am not going to be bait; I am setting a trap.

"You know you don't have to go, right?" Cassie asks, watching me from where she's sitting on Ian's lap.

"Yes, I'm aware," I mutter, adjusting my dress, not able to look her in the eyes. She knows me too well.

"Dimitri will be furious."

"Well," I smile coldly. "He's not here, is he?"

Cassie looks taken aback and worried, not by what I said, but by how I said it.

Let everyone think I'm moving on because I'm hurt, not because I'm hunting my prey for revenge.

The doorbell rings.

My pulse spikes, but I ignore it. Fear isn't going to help me. I turn my back on my reflection.

Downstairs, I release a shaky breath before opening the door.

Julian stands there in a black suit, gripping a bouquet of roses in his hand. "Wow. You look good enough to eat." He smiles widely.

"Thank you." I point at the flowers. "Are those for me?"

"Yes. Beautiful roses for a beautiful woman."

I giggle, "Thank you. Let me put them in a vase." I take them, and he follows me into the kitchen, close enough to touch. When I nearly slip, his hand curls around my waist fast, too fast. It sends a shiver through me, though not the kind he thinks. It's pure disgust.

"Be careful, beautiful," he whispers.

I step forward, grab a clear vase, add water, and place the roses in it, letting the simple action ground me.

He leads me outside to a limo and opens the door for me. I climb in, and he settles beside me. The interior has black leather seats with blue lights on the floor, canister lights on the ceiling, and blue LED light strips. I can't see the driver since the black window is heavily tinted.

"Champagne?" He hands me a tall flute glass filled with a clear liquid.

I take the glass, eyeing it. One, he could've poisoned it, and two, I've never drunk champagne before.

It's okay, don't panic. I take a slow sip, watching him over the rim.

I enjoy the way the bubbles dance on my tongue as I savor the mouthwatering flavors, a wave of strawberry, cherry, and pops of vanilla bean with an acacia honey finish. He places his hand on my exposed thigh, thumb stroking me. I give him a coy smile, but in my mind, my thoughts are full of anger. If he is the one who murdered my father...he just placed his hand on the person who will destroy him.

"So, you're the Vampire Prince?" I ask casually.

He smirks. "Yes, I am."

I tilt my head. "Did you know my father?"

He holds my eyes, a beat too long. "Not well, but yes, I knew him."

Chapter Twenty-seven

Dimitri

I stand in a dark corner of an alleyway, the hood of my black hoodie pulled low over my head, eyes scanning for my next target. I can feel the blood pumping in my veins from the excitement of the violence and the hunt. This is what I do. I find those who have committed sins in the world, and I make them pay.

Tonight, I'm dealing with a man who murdered his wife and kids, and I can't wait to drag him to Hell. The idea of his screams echoes in my head, and I smile. He'll meet my Hellhounds, and they'll rip him apart, piece by piece.

It's not a job, not really; I've been doing this to keep myself busy. Keep my mind off of her. Keep my mind off the fact that I haven't claimed her. I can't stop thinking about her, no matter what I do. No one told me it'll be this fucking hard to stay away from her. Every moment I'm not near her, I feel like I'm suffocating.

I can kill this bastard within seconds, and no one will stop me. I'm the best. I've been honing my skills for years, and the fact that I do this for fun makes me feel invincible. I guess I have my father to thank for that.

I can make people pay for their sins, bring them to justice. I'm addicted to the power and control.

I shouldn't be here, though. I should be with Rosa, but it's safer this way.

I can't drag her into this; she's too innocent. My father's kingdom isn't for someone like her. I've tried very hard to make him proud for the longest time, doing things his way so I can win his approval, but I'm done. I just don't give a shit anymore.

I could kill him, my father, with my bare hands if I wanted to, and I do for what he did to my mother.

If I do, I'll become the King of the Underworld, and I don't wish to become its ruler. I need to wait until Ian takes his place; that's when I'll strike. I have made it clear to him that I will kill him if he ever slips up, and I don't care if I become king or not. He heeds my warning and stays out of my way.

I pucker my lips and begin to whistle in a low, deadly tone as I step out of the dark corner.

The human stiffens and glances back. "Fuck, dude, get the hell out of here before I fucking kill you," he snarls, but I chuckle. "Ya think that's funny, buddy?" He pulls out a gun and points it at me. "What about now?" He has yellow teeth, brown eyes, and reeks of alcohol.

"Yeah, I do," I say, still walking. He fires his gun, and the bullet punches through my shoulder. I look down at the torn fabric. "You put a hole in my favorite hoodie; you'll pay for that."

He fires again and again. The bullets hit my stomach and chest, but it's useless. I barely feel the little holes. The blood he expects never appears. Panic enters his eyes. "Wha... what the fuck!"

"Enough games," I growl, letting my demon face slip through. His heart rate speeds up as he recognizes real fear for the first time. He turns to run, trips over his own feet, and falls face-first into the concrete.

Pathetic.

I grip the back of his neck, dragging him upright as I open a portal to get back to Hell. I step through it, and we're standing in my basement. My Hellhounds lift their massive heads, red eyes gleaming when they see me carrying dinner.

"Hey, boys, we're going to have a little fun tonight." They start snarling.

I pause, feeling a little flicker of energy.

"Dimitri." I hear a voice behind me.

I turn to find Ian's spirit there, flickering in and out of focus. I immediately know something is wrong. We don't use this type of communication unless it's an emergency.

The spell is rare and painful. Only one witch knows how to take a soul out of the body to travel here for only a limited time.

"It's Rosa, Dimitri. She's in danger." Right then, my heart stops beating. My breathing quickens, and my eyes turn black as my demon lunges inside me. They had *one* fucking job.

"I'm coming," I growl, my voice no longer fully human.

"Hurry, Dimitri," he says, then disappears.

"NO!" I roar out so loud it shakes the floor. My Hellhounds whine loudly at my distress, bowing their massive heads. "Take care of him," I push the murderer toward them. "Gwyllgi, you are coming with me."

He leaps to my side instantly.

I make the portal back to Earth. It's very dangerous to bring my Hellhound, and I normally don't, but for her, for my mate, I don't give a shit about putting humans in danger. Let them scream in fear, as long as she is safe.

How could I be so reckless? How did I think she'd be safe without me? I thought she'd be fine with Eleanor and Ian, but I was wrong. I fought this bond for her safety, but it didn't matter, did it?

I should've just claimed her. I should've brought her here with me. Yes, that's what I'll do. I'll bring her with me.

Do I force her to come?

Yes, if it keeps her safe. Anything to keep her safe.

She's mine whether she likes it or not. Whether she hates me or not. I don't care.

Whoever touches my mate will pay heavily, and when I find them, I will rip them apart slowly, enjoying every second of it.

We step through the portal into Eleanor's living area, and they are all standing there waiting for me.

"Tell me," I grind out. "What. The. Fuck. Happened,"

My demon is pushing to take control, and I don't think I can hold him back till we find our mate.

"She went on a date..." Tammy starts. I look at her, and she immediately steps back.

"A date?" I ask slowly. "With whom?"

Looking at Eleanor, jealousy burns like fucking acid. The thought of Rosa smiling at another man makes my demon slam against my ribs. The next time I see her, I'm going to fuck her and show her who exactly she belongs to.

"You brought a Hellhound with you?!" Ian screams, eyes wide.

He has always feared the Hellhounds, having seen the kind of damage they can cause. "Do you not understand the danger you put the humans in by doing that?"

Gwyllgi growls and is ready to rip him apart for disrespecting me, not caring if he's my brother.

I step closer, eyes pitch black, "I fucking did. If you have a problem with it, Ian... then fuck off. I'll scorch the world with hellfire if that is what needs to be done."

"Let him be, Ian. It will be okay," Cassie whispers, rubbing his upper arms.

"Gwyllgi, down," I demand, and he immediately stops, sitting by my leg.

"I won't ask again. Where the fuck is she?" Looking at Ian, he looks away, not wanting to tell me. Cassie starts crying by his side.

"Julian, he declared he found his mate," Eleanor finally answers.

Everything around me goes deadly still and cold.

Through clenched teeth, I ask. "What does this have to do with Rosa?"

"He's forcing Rosa to be his mate," Cassie snaps, tears falling. "He wants her. Now he's going to mark her against her will, and this wouldn't be happening if you hadn't left!" Her power lashes out, making objects fly across the room.

"She is mine!" I roar, losing control and causing the house to shake. My demon surges through me, breaking through the surface. My body expands, muscles tightening, vision sharpening. I slam my fist into the granite island, shattering it in half.

"Dimitri," Eleanor speaks softly, stepping closer. My eyes turn to her, and she flinches when I do.

"Why did you allow her to leave with him?" I hiss, glaring at Ian. My chest heaves as rage heats my blood. I'm seconds from burning this entire estate.

"I couldn't stop her, but we also didn't think she'd be in danger. I came for you as soon as we heard what he was planning."

"Bring me something she's worn recently," I order. When no one moves, I shout, "Now!" I'm ready for a hunt, to kill.

No one will dare stop me because I'm going on a warpath, and I'll kill anyone who tries.

Cassie jumps up and runs out of the room like her ass is on fire.

"She's strong," Eleanor says softly. "She'll fight. I know it. She made a hole in my wall with a chair. She's special, Dimitri."

Pride cuts through my fury. Of course, she's strong. She's my mate and my equal.

"She also knows how to cause someone excruciating pain with her mind, not lifting a single finger," Tammy adds.

I smirk. *Good girl.*

That kind of power will come in handy. That's why the bastard wants her, because she'll get him the crown he has always desired. I won't let him have a chance. I will kill him first and take back what is mine.

Cassie rushes back down, holding a black shirt and leather pants.

"She had these on this morning," Cassie mutters. "But here is a note, too; it was on her bed."

I take them from her, and my demon stills as we inhale the scent, sweet lavender. My eyes roll back in pleasure, groaning at the relief that hits me like a drug.

Goddess, I fucking miss her. I want to see her green eyes.

I open the note and read it. She wrote that she wasn't afraid of me. My monster side drops to its knees inside me, and my human side aches.

Gwyllgi nudges my hand.

I will get her back and never let her go again.

"Gwyllgi, find her." He growls low, sniffing the clothes in my hand. "He's going to find her, and I'll be going with him."

"And then what?" Cassie asks.

"We prepare for war." I pull out my phone. "Julian wants a queen? He picked the wrong fucking girl. I'll call a close friend of mine. He'll help us." I say as I turn on my phone.

"Dimitri," he answers.

"Julian has my mate," I say.

"I'll be there," he replies instantly.

I hang up and dial two more names, demons who owe me favors.

I will destroy anyone who thought they could touch what's mine. But before we go on this warpath, I need to get her away from Julian.

Chapter Twenty-eight

Rosa

Dinner has been a blur. He reserved the whole restaurant, so it's just us here, and I can feel Julian's eyes on me constantly. They've been glued to me all night, and I can't stand it. The way he looks at me is... predatory. It irks me, but I don't show it. I keep smiling, laughing, trying to make this night feel normal.

He wants to take me somewhere special after we eat, but I declined. I blamed it on a headache, which changed his demeanor. I can see the small change in his eyes, and the way his smile fades, the way he grows tense. He's not happy with my response.

I keep trying to talk about my dad, but he dodges my questions. Honestly, I shouldn't be surprised. I'm tired and want this night to end.

I'm not getting anywhere with him.

"Do you want some dessert?" he asks, voice low and smooth, dripping with something sensual.

I open my mouth to decline. But just as I do, two of his bodyguards rush into the room and whisper something to him. His eyes flicker to them, and I can feel the shift in the air. Something's wrong.

"Sadly, we have to skip the dessert," he says as he stands, holding out his hand. I place my hand in his, too tired to care how his skin touching mine sends a wave of disgust through me.

Julian leads me outside quickly with a hand on my lower back. He's rushing me. Something is definitely wrong.

As soon as we get outside, I feel a sudden coldness in the air. He pauses, inhales deeply, and releases a low rumble of annoyance as his hand tenses against my back.

"Give me a moment," he says, voice tight as he opens the limo door and rushes me in. He seems panicked.

"Is everything alright?" I ask, as I climb into the back.

"Yes," he hisses before he shuts the door. I glance back at him, watching him talk to one of the guards, but the limo starts to roll forward.

What the hell is going on? Before I can think too much, I hear a growl, deep and familiar. My muscles tense.

"Are you having fun on your little date?"

I don't have to look up to know who it is. The voice alone sends shivers down my spine. He's sitting across from me, eyes narrowed, black as night, and I feel the heat of his anger radiating off him like a furnace.

I bite my lip, trying to hold back the overwhelming mix of emotions passing through me. A part of me wants to scream, to demand answers, but another part of me feels an unsettling thrill that I only get when he's nearby.

"You're angry because I'm on a date? You *are* un-freaking-believable," I snap, pushing the words past my clenched teeth.

He doesn't flinch. No, his gaze hardens. "You learn that you're my mate… and you *still* go on a date." The words drip with possessiveness, but there's something else in his eyes, something that makes my breath catch.

"You left!" I shout, pointing my finger at him angrily. "You don't get to be angry when you are the one who walked away. Let me the fuck out!"

"Did you let him touch you?" He looks and sounds so calm, almost too calm.

I feel my body freeze, and my blood runs cold. "If he did, it's none of your business." I snap, but inside, a knot tightens. I can't stop the sick feeling building in my chest. The jealousy in his voice is unmistakable.

The next thing I know, he's right in front of me on his knees, grabbing my jaw, his grip tightening as he seethes with barely contained fury.

"I'm not playing with you. If he laid one finger on you, he's dead." His eyes are pure black, his fangs are sharp, and the horns on his head look deadly. "I'll tear him to shreds and feed him to my hounds."

My body goes rigid, a mix of fear and something I can't quite place rushing through me. The danger in his voice is overwhelming, intoxicating even. I should be terrified, but all I feel is heat pooling low in my stomach. I feel like I could drown in his anger, in his raw need to control me, to claim me.

"I didn't let him touch me," I whisper, my lips part as I begin panting. I know I'm crazy, I'm sick and demented for feeling completely turned on by his demon side, the possessiveness, the violence, knowing he'd kill a man in such a violent way just because he touched me.

I stare into his black, hatred-filled eyes, and a small whimper escapes. My gaze lowers to his hands fisted on his thighs, and I lick my lower lip, thinking of how powerful they are and the way those hands killed for me. Gods, I need him to touch me.

"Dimitri." Without thinking, I grab his suit jacket, yanking him toward me, and smashing my lips against his. He groans, and his hands tightly grip my hips, pulling me against him.

"Rosa," he mumbles as he grabs the top of my dress and pulls it down, exposing my breasts. His other hand wraps around me and slowly dances up my spine. Then he reaches up, fisting my hair and yanking on it until my back arches.

I close my eyes as I release a long-satisfied breath. Then his mouth is on me.

The electrifying sensation runs straight to my core as his tongue swirls over my nipple, and I gasp, my body arching instinctively toward him.

"Oh, Gods…" I moan breathlessly, feeling the fire of pleasure shoot through me as my hips grind against him, desperate for more.

He growls low in annoyance, pulling away. My body aches from the loss, and my chest tightens in a way that has nothing to do with desire. He pulls my dress back up, covering me. I stare at him, confused and frustrated.

Why did he stop?

My heart sinks, my chest squeezing painfully. I blink, trying to keep the tears at bay.

Without a word, he reaches behind me and opens the door. I can barely process what's happening before he's pulling me along with him. I try to look around, to make sense of my surroundings, but his grip tightens around my waist, and before I know it, he's lifting me, effortlessly pulling me against him. My legs instinctively wrap around his hips, and he grabs my jaw, forcing me to meet his gaze before kissing me roughly.

The kiss is harsh, a demand. It makes my pulse race. Then, in the next breath, I'm thrown into the air... *what is happening?* I gasp as I land on something soft. I lean up, resting on my elbows, trying to steady my racing heart.

"Did. He. Touch. You?" Dimitri's voice is a guttural, dark growl. His eyes are burning as he begins to remove his suit jacket, his movements slow and deliberate, like a predator about to claim its prey. I watch him, every muscle in my body tense.

"No, not in the way you're thinking." My voice shakes as I shake my head.

"Good, you'll regret provoking my monster," his voice a low growl of approval. "Because *now* you belong to me, mate."

His words slam into me, raw and final. I don't know if they're meant to comfort or command, but either way, they send a shiver through my entire body.

"Yes, I'm yours." I nod, the words foreign, but there's no denying the truth. I can't stop myself from looking at him, my breath hitching as he undoes the buttons of his white shirt, taking his sweet time, his eyes never leaving mine.

"Please, Dimitri," I whisper, my voice trembling. I don't even know what I'm pleading for exactly, but the need inside me is so intense, I can't contain it. Every part of me is calling out for him.

"Please, what, little mate? Please touch you? Please eat your sweet little pussy? Please fuck you?" he tilts his head, licking his upper lip like he already knows the answer, like he's savoring it.

His vulgar words hit me low in the stomach, heat rolling through me in one delicious wave. The way he lists every possibility steals the air from my lungs. I hate how much I want him. I hate how much he knows it.

"Yes," I breathe, barely audible, but it's honest, painfully so.

A slow, wicked smile curves across his mouth as he shrugs out of his shirt. He doesn't rush. He wants me to watch. There's a soft hiss of leather as he unthreads his belt.

"Don't worry, *mate.* I'm gonna fuck you to show you exactly who you belong to." His pants fall off, and he's standing there in black boxers. I swallow hard.

He steps closer, grip firm as his hands slide behind my knees. With one effortless pull, he drags me to the edge of the bed. I gasp. His eyes never leave mine as his fingers push the fabric of my dress higher, and he then pushes my dress up to my hips. I watch him intensely as he hooks his fingers around my panties and slowly pulls them down my legs.

His nostrils flare once he completely removes them and grabs the tops of my knees, spreading my legs. But I immediately snap them shut as heat floods my cheeks, and embarrassment runs through me.

He stops, lifting his gaze to mine slowly and deliberately. He tsks, a soft click of his tongue, it's a warning.

"Don't hide from me," I stare at him, pulse pounding, then I slowly reopen my legs, spreading them wide for him. His eyes drop, and a low groan escapes his throat. He runs his tongue across his upper teeth, his expression turning hungry, and... absolutely unhinged. "Fucking perfect. Prettiest pussy I have ever seen." I squirm as his gaze admires me.

His hand leaves my knee and makes its way down my thigh, slow enough to make me tremble. He knows exactly what he's doing. He doesn't stop until he reaches the area where I crave to be touched the most. His thumb slowly rubs against my swollen clit, and I gasp at the sensation. "So, fucking wet for me. You're such a good girl."

"Please," I whimper. My hips move without permission, grinding against him, needing more friction.

"Don't worry, baby, I'll take care of that ache." He drops to his knees, and I watch as his head disappears between my thighs.

The first brush of his tongue steals the air from my lungs. His mouth sucks my clit between his lips, teeth scraping against the sensitive skin. My head falls back against the mattress as a breathless moan slips free. A rush of heat sweeps through me so sharp and sudden it makes my eyes sting.

The window shakes as lightning slams into the ground. The sensation is all too much, so my fingers grip the sheets, needing something to cling to.

Oh God...

My body starts squirming under him as heat coils low in my stomach, tightening with each second. I don't know how to breathe, don't know how to handle the way he's unraveling me so effortlessly.

"You taste like fucking heaven." He groans lowly as he devours me like he's a starving man. I grip his hair tightly with my fingers, trying to lift my hips, but he grabs my hips firmly. He keeps me exactly where he wants me.

"Dimitri..." I whine his name, desperate, breathless.

He pulls back just enough to look at me, not my face, but all of me, and the hunger in his eyes nearly destroys me. He watches himself as he runs a finger down my slit, rubbing me, teasing me, before he pushes his finger into me. He quickly removes it to add another, moving them inside of me, stretching me. He lowers his head once more, and his tongue swirls around my achy clit. He curls his fingers, hitting the perfect spot. A dizzying sensation builds. It's sharp and overwhelming. The pleasure comes fast, too fast, curling tighter, rising higher, until I can barely speak.

Holy shit...

"Dimitri... oh gods, I think...""Yes, baby, cum for me." His voice is a rough command, and the words alone push me over. I slam my eyes shut as the rush hits. My body trembles, my mind goes blank, and for a moment I feel weightless, undone, lost in pure, overwhelming euphoria.

Stars dance behind my eyelids as I cry out his name. I can barely remember my own name, let alone remember my own body while Dimitri watches me like he's witnessing something sacred. My lips part as I pant heavily, and the aftershocks ripple through me. He drags his gaze over me like he owns every inch of me.

"I need to shove my cock in this tight pink pussy of mine, claiming what belongs to me." He removes his fingers and licks them clean, not once removing his gaze from mine.

He stands, removing his boxers, and the hunger in his eyes grows. His cock jumps out, slapping his stomach. It's huge. The veins are large and angry. His girth is wide, and the tip is wet with precum.

"It's okay, I'll be gentle, baby." He whispers, leaning down to kiss my lips softly; I can taste myself on him.

He sits me up with gentle hands, yanks my dress off, and then reaches around me, unclasping my bra, making my breasts bounce free. His fingertips graze my skin as he sucks my nipple into his mouth, and he gently pushes me back onto the mattress.

He braces himself above me with one elbow beside my head, holding his weight and caging me in the most intoxicating way. Threading his fingers into my hair, his other hand grabs ahold of his cock, and he starts rubbing the tip against my clit.

"Ready, baby?" He looks into my eyes.

"Yes." I nod, biting my lower lip nervously.

"Look at you," he murmurs, voice low. "Nervous, but desperate." His smirk is slow and dangerous. "So damn needy for me."

"Yes…" I nod quickly because it's true. Every part of me is trembling for him, reaching for him, aching for more.

"Good," he whispers, his forehead lowering to mine. "Let me take care of you. It's gonna hurt, little mate, but I won't stop." His voice drops into a warning growl. He shifts his weight, and then he pushes into me with a forceful thrust and unforgiving claim. I feel myself stretch, and it burns painfully. The shock of it rips a gasp from my chest. My body fights him, but he pushes harder, forcing his way in. I squeeze my eyes shut, holding my breath.

"Open your fucking eyes," he snarls.

My eyes snap open at the command, meeting his dark, burning gaze. His jaw is tight, his brows pinched together, every muscle in him is trembling with restraint.

"Fucking hell…" he hisses when he completely fills me, my eyes are welling up with tears. "You're… goddamn tight, baby. So damn tight."

"Are you okay?" He lowers his forehead to mine, breathing hard. He presses his lips against mine in a sweet, gentle kiss.

"It hurts." I whimper, blinking through the sting in my eyes.

"I know, baby. I'll make it feel better. I promise," he whispers against my lips and then starts moving again. His movements slowly ease the ache; it grows until heat spreads like fire low in my stomach.

"Oh God, Dimitri!" I moan, throwing my head back against the mattress, pleasure overtaking the last of the discomfort. "Yes…"

"That's it, baby. I'm your god," he growls, a dark, sexy sound. "You're such a good girl."

His voice alone sends a pulse through me, and my lower stomach clenches tightly with pleasure. He pulls back a little to look between us where our bodies are connected, and he watches himself thrust into me.

Then he drags his gaze back to mine, eyes full of undeniable pleasure, he bites his lower lip, and that alone nearly unravels me.

"You're mine." Dimitri's voice is a low, feral growl so deep it vibrates straight through me. He grabs my jaw, and his fingers tighten, digging into my cheeks, forcing my eyes to lock onto his. The fury and obsession in them... should terrify me. "Say it," he snarls, breath hot against my lips. "Tell me you belong to me. Tell me this tight, pretty pussy is mine."

A desperate sound escapes me, and my legs wrap around his hips on instinct, pulling him closer, needing more.

"Oh, God," I gasp, my nails digging into his shoulders as my body arches into his. Pleasure crashes over me in waves I can't control. He starts thrusting faster and deeper.

"Say it," he demands again, more brutally this time. He looks so deadly, it's fucking sinful. The sick, shameful truth is that I love it. I crave the darkness in him almost as much as he craves me.

"I'm all yours, Dimitri. My pussy is yours... oh God, please!" His hand lowers to grip my breast, and he pinches my nipple. The sensation becomes too much; it cripples me.

"That's it, baby, cum all over this cock. Cum for me like the good little slut you are." The praise is wicked and fucking addicting as he starts pounding into me harder.

The pleasure builds, spiraling, my vision starts blurring with stars. My mouth opens in a silent plea, and I explode. He growls and starts pounding faster. The headboard is banging hard against the wall.

It's mind-numbing, intoxicating. I thought the feeling of my magic flowing through my veins was addictive, but this is pure ecstasy. It's as if my soul left my body and went into an alternative universe full of pleasure.

Outside, the thunder roars violently, and the wind slams into the house as the room brightens with lightning sparks.

"Fuck! I'm gonna cum in this tight pussy." The veins in his neck pop, and I see his jaw clench so tight I'm surprised his teeth don't break. His body tenses above mine, and I feel him give in, every ounce of his restraint breaking. He throws his head back and releases a loud roar, and I feel his cock throbbing as he spills his cum into me.

He collapses against me, breathing heavily, both of us trembling. I reach up in a daze and brush the damp strands of hair from his forehead. He stares into my eyes, and I watch his eyes slowly turn to their original color. I'm still worried he might regret it and run off like he normally does. I'm terrified because I won't recover from this.

He cups the sides of my face and gently kisses my lips. "I'm sorry I let my demon take over me with pure jealousy." He squeezes his eyes shut, shaking his head. "Did I hurt you? I know I was rough."

"I actually very much enjoyed your roughness." I lick my lips, and he smirks, lying down and pulling me with him.

"When your demon side takes over... can you still feel? Are you still in there?" God, I sound ridiculous. But I need to know.

"Yes." His thumb brushes my cheek. "I feel and know everything that's happening. Trust me, I felt everything just now."

Heat floods my face, and I bury my head in his chest. He presses a soft kiss to my forehead, surprisingly gentle for someone capable of ripping a man apart.

"I'm sorry, Rosa," he murmurs. "I'm sorry I left you. I was afraid you'd hate me or leave me. I've never been afraid of anything, not even dying."

I put my chin on his chest, looking up at him. "It's okay, I understand."

"I won't leave you again." His voice darkens. "But understand this, I won't let you leave me, either. Now that you're mine, nothing, not even you, will keep me away. You can't hide from me. I'll gladly chain you to me if I have to."

A delicious shiver slides down my spine. His eyes burn into mine, intense and dead serious, and I know he means every word. I should be scared, but the truth hits me hard. I'm not scared. I want this, and I never want him to let me go.

"I want you, Dimitri, all of you."

"Good." He gives me a quick kiss. "We need to talk, but first, I'm starting a warm bath for you."

He stands, and I can't stop the smile that pulls at my lips as he walks, completely naked, toward the bathroom. I can't look away. The water begins to run and sit up. I lean against the headboard, pulling the blanket over my naked breasts.

When he returns, he has a towel wrapped around his hips. Without a word, he pulls the blanket away, lifts me bridal-style, and carries me to the bath. Steam rises around me as he lowers me into the warm water.

"You're going to be sore, so you need to relax. I need to deal with something. It can't wait, it's just too important. I'll be back in a couple of hours. Make yourself at home."

"Okay." I smile softly, nodding. He cups my cheek and kisses me before leaving. I lie my head back against the tub and smile. That was mind-blowing.

Later, he returns fully dressed in jeans and a grey T-shirt that stretches across his chest and arms. He looks painfully good. His eyes are on me as he walks straight to the tub, sits on the edge, and pulls me in for a long, melting kiss. I grab the back of his head, threading my fingers in his hair.

He groans. "You make it impossible to leave. I'll be back fast. Don't leave the house." His voice lowers and turns serious. "I love you, Rosa."

My mouth parts, the words stuck in my throat. His gaze drags down my body, a low rumble escaping him before he disappears.

"Why didn't you say it back?" I whisper to myself. "Fuck, Rosa…"

I can't believe that just happened. He left me, came back out of jealousy, and then we had sex. We do need to talk about everything, but I'm not worried about him running off after what he said. I repeat it in my mind: *he loves me.*

I sink deeper in the water, smiling like an idiot.

Cassie is going to lose her mind when I tell her.

I still feel like I'm on cloud nine.

Eventually, warmth drags me under, and I drift off.

When I wake, the water is ice cold, and my body is shivering. I scramble out, wincing at the soreness, wrapping a towel around myself, and heading back into the bedroom. I slip into my dress again, wrinkling my nose as I put my underwear back on. Everything aches, and my legs are shaky.

I slowly take in the room I was in. It's dark and masculine. The walls are a dark grey, the chairs by the large window are black leather, and the bed has black silk sheets.

My stomach rumbles, and I leave the room. There is a short hallway before I reach the living area, which resembles the bedroom: dark grey walls and black leather furniture. The very modern kitchen has black cabinets and white countertops. I walk to the fridge, and it's empty except for water, so I grab one and start looking in the cabinets. Those are empty as well.

He's been gone longer than he said. He should be back soon.

There's a sharp knock at the door. I walk over. I try the peephole, but I'm too short. When the knocking intensifies, I decide to open it.

"Can I help you?" I ask cautiously. The man is tall and dark-skinned. His hair is in a low bun, and he's huge with nothing but solid muscles.

"Prince Dimitri told me to take you home. That'll he'll meet you there."

My stomach drops. No, this isn't right. Dimitri said he'd come back.

"Sure. Let me grab my purse." I lie as I try shutting the door, but his hand stops it cold. He gives me an evil smirk, grabs a fistful of my hair, and slams my head into the door.

Everything goes black.

Chapter Twenty-Nine

Groaning, I slowly sit up, squinting into the dim, unfamiliar room around me, confusion setting in as I try to piece together where I am. The events hit me in one big wave... that man slammed my head against the door. Panic rises, but I take a deep breath and look around.

My fingers tremble as I reach up, searching my neck for the pendant. I let out a small sigh of relief when I feel its familiar cool metal against my skin. It's still there.

Thank God.

I stand as I take in my surroundings. The walls are a bright red with black trim, dark hardwood floors that creak beneath my feet, and a large bed in the center of the room, near the single window that overlooks... nothing but dark woods.

I rush to the door, my hands shaking as I turn the knob, but of course, it's locked. My heart races, the dread sinking deeper. I rush to the window, trying to gauge the height. I think I'm three stories up, maybe four... It's hard to tell with the darkness outside.

Frustration rises in my chest, and the panic claws at my throat once more. No, no, no. I'm trapped.

Before I can think any further, the door creaks open behind me, and I freeze, my pulse skipping a beat. Julian steps into the room. His cold black eyes lock onto mine, and a smile creeps onto his lips, but it's not comforting, not even close. "What? Are you not enjoying your room?"

"What the hell am I doing here?" I ask, trying to add a bite to my voice, but I think I already know the answer. I step back, trying to put some distance between us.

Julian's smile widens as he steps forward. "You're going to become my mate tonight, my love. We'll have a little ceremony. It's invite-only, too bad your family isn't on the guest list. Don't be mad, I'll make it up to you," Julian says smoothly, his voice sweet as he moves closer.

My stomach twists, and I fight to keep my composure. "No." My hands ball into fists at my sides. "I have a mate. I won't—" I begin, but my words are cut off as his hand shoots out, gripping my chin roughly and jerking my head up.

"Yes, I know, too bad he hasn't marked you." His lips crash against mine in a forceful, bruising kiss. I push against him, my breath quickening in panic, but it's no use.

He lifts me off my feet with one hand and throws me onto the bed. I scramble to push him off, but his weight pins me down. He's smirking down at me now, his voice low and dangerous. "Tell me, Rosa, has he claimed you? Really claimed you?"

My heart flares with anger, my body shaking with the need to fight. "Fuck you!" I snap.

He chuckles, his fingers tightening around my wrists as he kisses my neck, biting down sharply. Pain shoots through me, and a cry of pain escapes me. My mind is scrambling to find a way out. I won't let him take me without a fight. His hand slides down my dress, lifting the hem slowly, before pushing aside my underwear. I freeze, the dread suffocating me as the color drains from my face.

Gods, no...

"Please stop. Don't do this," my voice fills with terror. It feels weak, pitiful. I hate myself for it, the fear claws its way up my chest.

"Yeah, you are right, my queen. We should wait till tonight. Make it special after our ceremony." A sick grin plays across his lips. Then he puts his finger into his mouth, sucking it. "Baby, you taste divine, and I can't wait to have more tonight. Get some rest."

He pulls away and looks at me like he's savoring the moment, enjoying my terror.

"Please, don't," I beg, my voice breaking. The cold fear inside me has me begging.

Julian tilts his head, considering me. "You're mine now, Rosa. There is no turning back." His words send a cold shiver down my spine, and I realize that I'm trapped.

"I will not mate you." My voice dripping with venom.

"That's cute; you actually think you have a choice in the matter." He tsks, shaking his head slowly, frowning like he's disappointed in a child.

I scream in my head, *Pain... Pain!* Come on, come on, *COME ON!*

Nothing. I feel a slight buzzing beneath my skin like it's trying, but it's trapped.

Julian's amusement shines in his dark eyes as he watches me. "I can feel you trying. Impressive, even collared. You're making my head hurt. The collar is meant to stop witches from accessing their powers." His finger brushes my throat. I jerk away as my hand snaps to it—a thin piece of metal digs into the skin around my neck. I try removing it, but it's too tight, and now that I know it's there, it's suffocating.

"I put that on your father, too," he says, so casually that it makes my stomach dip, and I feel sick. "Witches always think they can overpower anything, but magic craves freedom, and cages, or in this case collars, take that away."

My mind is swirling with confusion as I try to keep up... The collar is blocking my magic and... He put one on my father?

I swallow hard. "You're the leader of the secret society, and you kidnapped and murdered him. I knew it."

"Murder? No." He grins widely, like he's proud of himself. "But I do have him. Look at you, so smart. I was always shocked that no one suspected me. I thought I'd have to hide, but everyone was too stupid to look." He laughs. "You're going to be a perfect mate for me." He leaves, shutting the door behind him.

He's fucking delusional.

My father is alive?

I need to get out and warn Eleanor.

Dimitri will come for me. I know he will, but I'm not going to sit here like prey waiting for some mating ritual that makes me his property. I'll get myself out, or I'll die trying.

I scan the room again, but there's nothing helpful, just the bed. I drop to my knees and look beneath it, searching for anything I can use as a weapon. I don't see anything, just dust and a small piece of metal.

I sit on the corner of the bed, my hands gripping my hair. Fucking think. Do something, anything. Panicking won't save me.

I stand and look at the window. I can't jump. It's too high, and I'm not breaking my legs only to get dragged back in. Screaming is useless because we're surrounded by woods.

Okay, I'll move the bed against the door. It's not much, but it'll slow them down. I place my hands on the bed and shove it toward the door. I'll break off a leg and hope it's enough to stab someone's eyes out.

But as I push it, my eyes land on the metal on the floor. I gasp—it's a latch! I push the rug aside and stare in complete shock. It's a hidden door.

"Holy shit," I breathe.

I tug the handle, and of course, it doesn't budge. I grit my teeth and pull harder, using all the strength I have, arms shaking. It pops open with a groan.

Cold air rushes out. I look down to find a narrow staircase that descends into complete darkness. I can't see where they lead. The hairs on the back of my neck and arms stand. I swallow the nervous knot in my throat, pushing down the fear.

I look back at the door. Julian can walk in at any moment.

You got this. Remember, you're not weak. You're not that girl anymore. You're a bad bitch.

I slip into the opening, pulling the door shut behind me, engulfing myself in darkness. I press my hands onto the walls, steadying myself. The walls are rough, slick with dampness, and my legs tremble as I go down each step. My steps echo. My fear rises even more the further down I get.

I count... five, six, seven... then ten, and finally I reach a landing and inch forward, hands out in front of me, since I can't see shit. My fingertips scrape stone, then emptiness. Finally, a faint glimmer of light beckons me forward. It seems as if I've hit the end. I think it's a door because the light seeps through all around it.

I press both palms to the surface and lean to peek through the small gap. It's a small room, and it looks empty.

I place my ear against the door, trying to listen for movement, but my heart pounding in my ear is making it difficult. My sweaty hands reach for the small handle and push it, but it doesn't budge. I look over my shoulder, staring into pitch darkness.

Not knowing what horrors are on the other side causes terror to strike into me, and it slowly creeps up my spine.

I can't go back.

I need to get out. I press my back against the door and push with all my strength.

Please...

The door slowly opens, making a long creak. Dust falls over me in a soft cloud. I swallow a cry of relief.

The door slams shut behind me with a bang that makes me jump. Stifling a scream, I squeeze my eyes shut, holding my breath, and pray no one heard it. I look at how the door was hidden. It blends into the wall.

I face the room again and notice a door out. I go to leave, but stop short of the exit. Maybe I should look for some type of weapon, just in case.

This room looks exactly like the one I was just in, except it has a black dresser and a smaller bed, with nightstands on either side. It's messy and lived in. I look in the dresser and see nothing but men's clothes. Next, I go over to the nightstand and open it.

"Jackpot," I mumble as my fingers wrap around the knife handle. It's sharp and has a little curve, deadly, just what I need.

I grab a long-sleeved shirt from the dresser, use the knife to cut off a strip of fabric from the sleeve, and tie it around my thigh, securing the blade snugly beneath the fabric.

Okay, let's move....

I suck in a deep breath and slowly push the door open; it's an empty hall. I look left to right, not knowing which way to go. I decide to go right.

There are too many doors, all of them closed. It's a creepy design made to confuse someone. I move down the hall, noting every detail. The white walls with black doors feel like walking through a haunted house. I stop when I reach a staircase, one up and one down.

Of course, I choose down. My shaky hand tightly grips the railing, and I stand there paralyzed with terror. I let out a long, shaky breath as I stare down the stairs.

Fear is racing through my veins as my blood runs cold. Who knows what kind of danger awaits me down there? I carefully continue down the stairs. I hit a landing, and it looks exactly the same as the hall I was just in. Why are there so many doors? I keep going, passing another landing.

I finally hit the last floor, and I look around. I'm in a large wooden kitchen with black and white tile floors, and servants rushing around, all wearing blank expressions, all dressed the same. It's too controlled and quiet; they seem like robots, slaves, or vampires. Neither option sits well with me. If they are slaves, I will have to find a way to get them out. They shouldn't be here living like this.

No one notices me, so I move in the shadows. Every kitchen has a back door. I finally find a large wooden door, and I make a run for it, turning the handle. As soon as I step outside, the cold air slams into me, and I breathe in the fresh air like it's a drug.

"Can we help you?" I turn slowly, seeing a man standing outside smoking a cigarette. His friend is leaning against the wall and tilts his head as his eyes trail down my body like he's undressing me. They are wearing the same clothes as the people inside.

"Yeah," my voice was spuriously calm. "Can you point me in the direction of the main drive? I was visiting Prince Julian, but he got an emergency call, so I have to leave now."

They both straighten up, buying the story instantly. "Follow the path," the smoker says. "Leads right to the garage."

"Thank you, gentlemen." I wink; they both grin. It's a good thing men don't think straight when they see a pretty girl.

I move slowly so they don't see me rushing and catch onto my lie. It's a stone walkway; the left side is the stone wall of the house, and the right is nothing but trees.

Once out of view, I run, but I don't continue on the pathway. I go through the woods.

It's a dark and foggy night, but luckily, the silvery light of the full moon illuminates the trees, creating a pathway with its magical glow.

For a second, I look up, my heart swells. I take a moment to admire how the ethereal light of the moon gives an otherworldly glow to the otherwise dark night.

I can feel the magic in the air, and I know it's the moon calling to me. I want to dance in the moonlight and embrace its magic. I can feel the moon's magic coursing through my body. It feels alive and electric. I hum in appreciation before I begin running. There is no time to embrace the moon's energy.

I reach a lamp post and stop, my feet throb. I rip off my heels, making it easier to move, and keep running barefoot. I try to stay low and quiet. My heart is pounding so hard I think any vampire close by will hear it, so I try to calm down and slow the erratic beats, but it's not working.

"Hey, you there!" I freeze, blood draining from my face. A warrior steps into view, dressed in all black with brown combat boots and weapons strapped to his belt. He's tall and pale, with red glowing eyes and a large beard covering half his face, ugly as sin.

I spin around and try to make a run for it.

"Hey, stop!" he shouts and chases after me. A second later, he tackles me from behind, slamming me into the ground.

I roll and jump to my feet.

We're facing each other. He tries to come at me, but I kick him in the stomach with everything I have.

Magic buzzes through my body, just a flicker, but enough to send him flying into a tree. He hits it hard.

I stare completely stunned for a moment. The moon... I believe the magic of the moon coursing through me is helping me even with this collar wrapped around my neck. The full moon heightens a witch's magic.

He gets up, faster this time, and blocks my path.

"I just want to go home," I plead, but my fingers hover near the knife under my skirt. "Just let me go."

"No can do." He shrugs. "Prince Julian wants you brought back, princess."

"So, you don't care he's holding me against my will?"

"Nah."

CHAPTER THIRTY

"Well, I'm not going down without a fight!" I shout and run into the shadows, running as fast as my legs can carry me. I can hear my heartbeat roaring in my ears. *What will happen if they catch me? I don't even want to imagine it.*

Up ahead, a figure looms, blocking the path. Tall and broad... a man, or at least, something human-shaped... but his red eyes gleam like fire in the darkness. I freeze for a split second, panic tightening in my chest.

His hand rises, and I gasp. A ball of flames forms above his palm, twisting and dancing in the moonlight.

My feet move on instinct, dodging the fireball. It scorches a tree nearby. I turn to run when another ball of flame passes by my head. I watch as it hits a large tree with vines and red flowers wrapped around its trunk. Flames slowly rise, and I watch as the red flowers curl and blacken, ash drifting downward like snow. It's a beautiful thing to watch with the full moon in the background.

Another flash of fire passes my head. I scream, stumbling over my own feet, my ankle twisting sharply. Pain flares, but I force myself up and keep running. Déjà vu strikes me like a lightning bolt. *This moment... I've seen it before. Was it a dream?*

"Help me! Someone, please!" I scream, desperately. I look over my shoulder, and the two of them are chasing me, grinning, teeth glinting in the dim light.

Yes, I've dreamt of this before... But how? Was it a glimpse of the future?

I turn back around, and my face hits a tree branch. I slam into the forest floor hard, vision spinning as black spots dance across my sight. My fists slam into the dirt, fury rushing through me. Both of the vampires come into view and stare down at me with evil grins. I shake my head fast, but they both laugh and start reaching down to grab me.

A loud growl stops their movements. They both turn to look over their shoulders. "Oh fuck! Hellhound!" They both take off running, leaving me on the ground.

Relief floods me, but it's short-lived when I see it. He's a huge black wolf, or I guess Hellhound, its eyes glowing red, its fur bristling. A growl rumbles from deep in its chest.

I scramble to my feet, my legs trembling, and run in the opposite direction.

Up ahead, I see a small cave in the hillside. I'm small enough to slip inside. I grab a large stick as I rush in. Maybe I can make a stake. My dress rips on the way in, exposing my underwear, but I don't care. Every movement is survival. I sink against the damp wall, gasping, tears stinging my eyes.

There is no escape. I can't outrun them forever. If they catch me, Julian will force this mate thing on me. I swallow bile, holding my knees to my chest. *I will not give in without a fight. I have to survive.*

I may not get out of here, but I can make it hard for them. I can make them regret it. I will kill Julian if he forces me to mate him.

I grab the knife I had forgotten about and start carving the end of the stick to make a stake with a deadly point. My hands shake, blood thunders in my ears, but I finish it. Weapon in hand, I inch toward the cave's mouth. I'm ready, or as ready as I can be.

I hate the idea of killing someone, but they leave me no choice. I have to fight for my freedom. I start running. The first vampire is there, waiting, red eyes fixed on me.

"Bring it," I snarl, knife in one hand, stake in the other.

"Put that down, little girl. You'll hurt yourself," he says, voice smooth, almost amused. "There's a Hellhound out here. You'd be safer inside the castle."

"I'll take my chances with the Hellhound," I snap, running forward full speed.

He moves toward me with an impossible speed that I wasn't prepared for. He drops down and spins, kicking my legs from under me. I hiss in pain. I look down to see the knife sticking into my side, the pain striking through me like a lightning bolt: sharp and intense, burning my insides like lava.

I scream out in pure agony. The sound echoes through the woods. I slowly move onto my knees, clenching my teeth to keep myself from crying out again. I inhale deeply, regretting it immediately as another strike of burning pain shoots up my side, leaving me breathless as tears fill my eyes.

He kneels beside me, grinning. "See, told ya you'd hurt yourself. Should've listened, you naughty girl." He grabs my jaw tightly with one hand. With the other hand, he rubs the blood that is pouring out of me. I watch him raise his fingers to his lips and suck them clean. His eyes roll back, and he moans, "Witches' blood tastes the sweetest."

I gag, weakly. "Get off me!" My voice is pathetic, frail.

"My partner and I will enjoy punishing you," he says, leaning closer. I smell him, iron, and rot. I scrunch my nose, looking sideways to get my face away.

His nose grazes the side of my neck as he smells me. I spot the stake lying just beyond my reach.

Desperation sharpens my focus. I call for my magic, every ounce of power straining against the collar. It starts buzzing, but it is weak. I narrow my eyes at the stake and push harder, *please.* The stake shudders forward, landing in my hand.

"Fuck you!" I snarl, drilling the stake into the center of his chest. His eyes widen in disbelief, lips parting as life leaves him, and he collapses onto me. I shove him off, every muscle trembling. A growl erupts behind me—the Hellhound. My heart nearly stops.

No.

For a moment, I freeze just staring at him, not knowing what to do. *I'm going to die. It's going to kill me.* I shake my head as I slowly drop onto my butt and start backing away.

It steps closer, slowly and deliberately. My back presses against a tree; there's nowhere to run. He stops about a foot away from me. "No, please." I cry out, he cocks his head to the side, and then steps even closer to me. His snout rubs the side of my neck, sniffing me. I squeeze my eyes shut, mind screaming as I hold my breath. After a tense moment, he leaves...

From out of nowhere, the second vampire appears, looming over the dead guard. "You fucking bitch," he growls. He rips the knife from my side, sending agony through me. My hands clench the wound as he cuffs my ankles and drags me. My dress rips further, exposing more of me, but I grit my teeth, refusing to give him the satisfaction of my screams.

Ignoring the pain, I turn so my stomach is on the ground, trying to grab onto something. He flips me around, throws me over his shoulder, and begins running at full speed. Everything around me blurs. I start getting sick to my stomach. I clench my teeth tightly as every bump he hits makes my wound dig into his shoulder.

He slows once we get to the castle, and I can see the Hellhound following from a distance, gripping the knife in its jaws, blood glistening on its fur. I whisper a hoarse, "Thanks, boy," and it cocks its head as if it hears me.

"Who the fuck are you talking to?" the guard asks.

I ignore him. Inside the castle, maids watch in horror.

We stop in a large sitting room, and Julian's voice cuts through the room. "That was an impressive attempt. Too bad you're inexperienced. Put her down."

He does, and I hit the floor hard, gasping.

"She killed one of ours," the vampire snarls.

Julian crouches beside me, eyes gleaming as he traces the blood along my side. "Did she now? I am very pleased with you. You are the perfect queen for me."

"I will never be your queen," I spit, and for a fleeting second, it lands on his eye.

He backhands me, teeth clenched. The pain is sharp and instant, causing me to cry out. "Disrespect me, and next time it'll hurt more." His hand grips my jaw painfully. I whimper as the metallic taste of blood fills my mouth.

He stares at my mouth and leans closer, tongue darting out as he licks my lips. When he pulls back, I see my blood on his sharp teeth, his eyes turn red, his nostrils flare, and he looks feral. "You taste so fucking perfect. I killed my mate for you." He rubs my cheek in such a romantic way, smearing my blood. "You should feel special."

"Why would you do that?" I gasp. I can't believe someone would hurt, let alone kill, their other half.

"She was too weak to be a queen. At first, I didn't care. I was going to put my dreams of becoming king and leading the council behind me, but then you came along at the perfect time. It was fate. Thank you for that."

"No," I whisper, horrified. *She died because of me.*

"You'll be thanking me soon enough when the kingdoms bow, and we control everything."

"I'll never thank you, and I will never be your queen. Dimitri will come for me, and he'll kill you for touching me." I shout, glaring at him with pure hatred. He is nothing but a soulless man, and I cannot wait until *my* own monster makes him pay.

"You don't really have a choice, do you? He'll be too late. Punishment for running, you'll be in the dungeons till our ceremony tonight."

"Wait... dungeons?" Of course, they have fucking dungeons.

"Take her down and don't clean her up until I say so."

The second vampire picks me up again and throws me over his shoulder. He stops to open a door, and then he starts carrying me downstairs. The smell hits me, piss, blood, decay, making my stomach twist.

We pass a few cells, and he finally opens one of them and throws me inside. My back slams against the cold concrete wall hard. I cry out in pain, and waves of agony course through my body, making my head spin.

I can't take this pain anymore. I crawl to a corner, my arms wrap around my legs for warmth, and I lean my back against the dirty wall, feeling completely drained.

The floors are concrete and dirty, and there's a small window in the corner of another cell that lets the morning light shine through.

I glance around my cell, and it has nothing except a dirty mattress on the floor and a bucket. Most of the cells are empty except the one across from me. I see someone sitting in the corner, and their back is facing me.

I look down at my wound. I can't tell how deep it is; there's too much blood. I rip the bottom of my dress off, make it into a ball, and press it tightly against the wound. I hiss in pain as tears start filling my eyes.

I touch the bars close to me that are connected to the other cell, and they are freezing cold. I rub my arms and close my eyes, thinking of being wrapped in Dimitri's warmth and feeling safe in his arms. I think of his stunning blue eyes and full lips.

"Hey..." My voice cracks. "How long have you been here?" I ask the person in the cell across from me. He doesn't answer, he barely even moves. "Okay," I whisper, swallowing hard. "Not a talker. That's fine."

I don't know why I keep talking, maybe to stay conscious, maybe because the quiet presses on me like a weight. "I got grabbed by Julian," I murmur, more to myself than him. "Dragged down here like some... thing he owns. I ran and fought. God, I fought. I managed to kill one of them." My eyes burn, unfocused. "Didn't get far, though."

The man exhales, releasing a low grunt, but it's something. A reminder I'm not alone in this tomb of stone and rotting air.

I begin feeling lightheaded, fatigued, and weak. I lean my head back against the wall as my breathing increases.

The door opens with a slam. I hear heavy footsteps coming our way. My head tilts to the side weakly as I lick my dry lips, feeling extremely dehydrated.

The guard from earlier stops in front of my cell, staring down at me with an angry expression on his face.

"I'm here for payback. You killed a very close friend of mine," he spits, his fist tightening around the bars like he wants to tear them apart.

"You were the ones chasing me," I manage, but my voice is slurring, thick with pain. "I had every right to defend myself."

He snarls and swings the cell door open so hard it rattles against the stone. He steps inside... and my stomach drops.

Gods, please no. I can't take another hit. I can't even lift my arms.

"I don't give a damn," he growls, unbuckling his belt with slow, deliberate clicks that echo far too loudly in the cramped cell. "But don't worry... he'd love this punishment. Consider it a tribute."

My spine shoves back against the cold wall instinctively, even though every movement sends sharp pain through my ribs. My head won't stay upright; it drifts sideways like my body is giving up piece by piece.

"No, stop, please..." The words come out raw, barely more than breath. My hands tremble uselessly in my lap. He laughs at how powerless I am.

"Hey! Leave her alone!" The person in the other cell shouts out in a raspy voice that sounds like he hasn't talked in a long time or had anything to drink.

The guard whips his head toward the sound. "Shut it, you old bastard!"

The man coughs. "Touch her, and you'll regret it. Even down here."

Chapter Thirty-one

Three hours earlier

Dimitri

I land with a soft thump, my Hellhound shaking out his fur beside me before curling up to sleep. I look around my room, clutching a bag of warm food, but she's not here.

I grin, shaking my head. There's no way she's still in the bath, but she could have fallen asleep. However, when I enter the bathroom, she's nowhere in sight.

"Rosa!" I shout her name as I step into the hall towards the kitchen, where she is probably searching for food. "Baby, I brought food."

My guilt flickers hard in my chest. I shouldn't have left her. We were hunting Julian. What a waste of fucking time, especially when I could have spent time with my mate.

I lick my lips, as I relish in the memory of her body arching under mine as I knelt between her thighs and worshiped every inch of what belongs to me. She tastes like my new favorite drug, and fuck, that pussy feels like my new addiction.

My cock twitches, hardening fast. Fuck, no one has ever felt like her. No one has ever made me lose myself like that. I could drown in her pussy and die a grateful man. She's the closest I've ever come to heaven.

I need to feel her spasming and choking my cock again. The way she said my name, gasped it, claws its way down my spine.

This is beyond obsession, but she needs time to recover. I'd been too rough, too desperate.

Do I deserve her? No, definitely not, but she's mine anyway, and she wants me. For the first time in my miserable life, I feel happy. She's my fucking miracle. Rosa isn't just mine, she's the only thing in this world that makes me human.

"Rosa?" I call again as I reach the kitchen, and a cold feeling slides down my spine. *Something is wrong.*

I open the front door where the guards are supposed to be, but I see both of them slumped dead on the ground. Throats ripped open with blood drying on the floorboards. For a single second, I can't breathe.

The blood pumping through my veins begins to boil from the rage I feel. Magic slams against my skin, my body shaking with the violence of the rage begging to be unleashed.

I tilt my head back and let out a monstrous roar that rattles the windows. Gwyllgi rushes to my side and

I bare my teeth, ready to kill.

Someone took her, touched her, and thinks they can survive that. My vision darkens, and my breathing turns feral.

"Rosa..." Her name breaks out of me, desperate, and murderous. I slam the food bag against the wall, the contents exploding across the stone.

Then I rip open a portal with my bare hands, snarling through my teeth, and hurl myself into it with Gwyllgi close behind.

Eleanor will know something.

Let the gods look away. I'm coming for what's mine, and I won't be leaving survivors.

I've been pacing for hours. My Hellhound has been gone too long, and every second he doesn't return, my chest tightens another inch. The living room is packed with ten of my men and the witches Eleanor called. Everyone is silent and waiting. Except for me, I can't stop moving.

"You're going to leave permanent marks on my floor if you keep pacing!" Eleanor shouts, rubbing her temples. "Goddess, Dimitri, you're making me dizzy."

I ignore her. My body feels wrong, too hot, too tight. Like my skin can't contain what's underneath.

Caspian stands and approaches me. "We'll find her. I can't believe you found your mate and didn't tell me."

"What if we're too late?" My voice cracks on the last word. I aggressively rub the side of my face. My heart aches with fear. I need to release the rage that's pulsing like fire through me.

"We won't be. He won't hurt her. He needs her," Eleanor says next.

"If he marks her?" I choke on the thought. If Julian touches her...

"We will kill the bastard slowly," Caspian growls.

Ian steps up behind me, gripping my shoulder. "He can't mark her yet. Not publicly, they need the ceremony in front of the king's court. He isn't prepared. Worst case, it's tonight, but we'll reach them before that."

"If I didn't leave, this wouldn't have happened," I hiss angrily.

"Brother, you cannot think like that. What is done is done."

I push him off, slam my hand against the window frame, and stare out at the full moon. The pain in my chest is unbearable.

"It's easy for you to say. It's not your mate out there." I scream. "I'm done just sitting here waiting. I am going to go look for her myself!" I sent my Hellhound thinking he'd be faster than me, but I was wrong.

She fucking needs me.

"Dimitri," Cassie whispers.

"What?" I snap, harsher than intended.

"He's back." She points out the window on the opposite side of the room with her index finger.

I don't reply. I spin so fast the floor cracks under my feet, and there he is charging across the lawn. His fur glows, his eyes burning red, a knife clamped between his teeth. He bursts into the room and drops it at my feet. It's covered in blood. I lift the knife, holding it up, and inhaling deeply, my body tenses. The fear races through me, poisoning my bloodstream, almost crippling me.

It is Rosa's blood.

My nostrils flare. I turn to everyone, and they all take a few steps back.

"Is... Is that her blood?" Cassie whispers, her hand covering her mouth as she sobs.

"Yes." Ian grabs her gently, and she starts crying.

Tammy forces herself to breathe. "That does not mean she's dead."

"Let's go get our girl back!" Eleanor bares her teeth. I haven't seen her this angry in a very long time. I let my demon fully take over my body.

"Yes," I rumble, voice no longer entirely human. "Let's go find my mate."

"Yes!" Everyone in the room growls.

"You stay here." Tammy turns to Cassie.

"I will do no such thing." Cassie cries, shaking her head.

"You will. You don't know how to control your magic. You'll get hurt, and we'll be too distracted protecting you."

Ian cups her face. "She's right, love."

"But…"

"Enough!" My roar makes Cassie jump. "Do you want us to bring Rosa home, or do you want us babysitting you while she suffers?"

Tears spill down her cheeks. "I… I understand. Please bring my sister back."

I nod once, then crouch in front of my Hellhound. I grab his muzzle, meeting his glowing eyes.

"Take me to her, *now!*" I growl. He turns and rushes out the door. I follow him with the group of killers behind me.

CHAPTER THIRTY-TWO

Rosa

We run for what feels like miles, the forest whipping past us with the cold air blasting against my face. My Hellhound finally slows, shoulders hunching as he sniffs the air. The night feels heavier. When he stops, he stares forward with a low rumble in his chest. I follow his gaze. A massive stone castle rises in the distance, jagged against the night sky. Its towers are dark, built from old stone.

A smile stretches across my face, wide and violent.

At least a dozen men are surrounding the grounds, maybe more, but it doesn't matter. They will all die. They must be guards, black uniforms, brown combat boots, weapons strapped across their backs. They look like shadows waiting to charge.

"Kill as many as you need to kill and have fun, boys." My voice drops into a dark, eager growl.

"We'll have fun, don't worry." Caspian flashes me a wicked grin, his eyes turning pitch black like he's already tasting blood.

I crouch low, gripping the thick fur around my Hellhound's neck. "Kill whoever you want. Just don't touch my mate, not a hair." My Hellhound snarls, sharp and eager, then runs ahead.

A few seconds later, screams erupt mixed with growls.

I stand and start running, adrenaline pumping hard in my veins. Every step brings me closer to her and to killing anyone who touched her. My men run beside me, all of them wearing the same twisted grin I know I'm wearing. Guards rush toward us, shouting.

My heart slams in my chest with the thrill of the hunt.

My claws extend with a crack of bone, and I slash through the first line of men, heads flying, bodies dropping in halves, blood drenching the dirt. It is gruesome and bloody. My demon wants to savor the kill, to tear them apart slowly... but I don't have time. Not tonight, not when she's somewhere inside those walls.

I'll never let her out of my sight again.

The castle doors burst open, blown off their hinges by a blast of magic. I turn to find Eleanor standing in the center of the battle with her witches using magic, tossing men through the air like ragdolls. Her eyes are glowing like wildfire. She winks at me before flinging another body.

The courtyard looks like a battlefield, blood everywhere, screams echoing off the stone, bodies piling like a second floor. It smells like death.

Good. Let them choke on it.

"Go find our girl. I'll find Julian and kill him myself," Eleanor shouts over the chaos. I nod, knowing she won't hear me through the deafening screams. Even though I want to be the one to kill him, finding my mate is more important.

I whistle sharply. "Gwyllgi!"

My Hellhound appears in seconds, coated in blood, tail high with the thrill of killing. We enter a large sitting room with black furniture and red walls. It looks like someone decorated using their ego alone. I inhale deeply, smelling her scent in the area. She was here recently.

"Take me to my mate!" I grab a guard by the throat and twist until his spine snaps, blood spraying across the red wall like it was made for it. I lick my lips, enjoying the metallic taste of blood.

My Hellhound tears into another guard, ripping out his throat in one swift movement.

"Good boy." I wipe blood from my face with the back of my hand. He sniffs the floor and takes off. We move down a hallway lined with old portraits. Julian's ancestors stare down with cold eyes, painted in tones that make everyone look half-dead. The air here is stale and damp.

Farther down the hall, guards rush toward us. I don't wait. I shove my hand into his chest and yank his heart out as I twist the second one's head off in the same motion. They crumple at my feet. They never even had the chance to cry out.

Gwyllgi leaps, tackling the third one; he finishes his kill with a crunch of bone.

We keep moving, passing through a massive kitchen and into a dining hall lit by flickering gold sconces. The long wooden table is set like someone expected guests tonight, silver plates, wineglasses, candles burning low.

That's when I see Julian, and I grin widely. He has a phone pressed to his ear, back turned, panic in every tense line of his body.

"We are under attack, Father. Where are you? I have no guards. They're outside fighting!" His voice cracks.

Fucking idiot.

Gwyllgi growls, deep and lethal, and Julian slowly turns, his face draining of color.

"Prince Dimitri." He bows stiffly. "Why have you brought a war here?"

"You have something that belongs to me," I snarl.

"I don't know what you—" I'm already on him, dragging him by the neck and slamming him into the wall.

"Where is she?"

"You don't deserve her," he spits. "You already have power; you don't need a mate as strong as her. My mate was weak. I killed her so that I could take yours."

Wrong answer. "She belongs to me," I roar, but he kicks my chest. My body flies through the air, and I land on the table, wood splintering beneath me.

"Now she belongs to me, and she tastes divine. Have you ever tasted her juices? She tastes like honey, sweet and innocent. I can't wait to have more." He licks his upper lip.

He touched my mate.

He fucking touched her.

Rage tears through me, and he turns to run. My wings burst free with a crack, filling the room as my body grows in size. I fly after him, but before he gets too far, Eleanor blasts him across the hall.

"I'll kill you for touching my daughter!" she screams from the doorway, magic burning hot around her.

Julian screams in pain at whatever she is doing to him.

"I'll take care of him. Go get Rosa," she says without looking at me.

Gwyllgi stands by a heavy iron door, muscles tense like he already knows what's waiting behind it. I shove the door open and take the stairs two at a time, stepping into darkness. The air changes immediately, damp, rotting, hopeless. A dungeon meant for breaking people.

The motherfucker kept my mate in this.

"Please... stop..." Rosa's voice slurs, faint and full of pain. My chest burns with anger, and we sprint down the corridor. At the end of the hall, a guard is on top of her, his filthy hands groping her breasts. Her dress is torn, soaked in blood. Her skin is too pale, and she looks fragile.

"MINE!" My roar shakes the fucking walls.

The guard jerks his head up, eyes wide.

Rosa's eyes flutter when she sees me. "Dimitri?" she whispers before her head drops sideways, her body limp.

"I'm here, love." My voice is filled with violence and relief all at once. "I'm here."

I drag the bastard off her by the throat, my claws slicing into his skin. "I wish I had time to torture you," I snarl, slamming him against the bars hard enough to rattle the entire cell. "But I need to get my mate to safety."

"I—I didn't know she was your mate," he chokes.

"Do you think that saves you?" My claws lengthen. "You touched what's mine."

He whimpers. I dig one hand into his scalp, the other gripping his shoulder.

"No, please, don't—"

"Didn't you beg him to stop, Moya Dusha?" I look to Rosa. She's trembling, trying to cover herself, bruised, lip split, cheek swollen.

Her chin wobbles. "Yes."

"Did he stop?"

"No," she sobs.

"Why would I grant you leniency?" I yank, hard. His scream tears through the hall for a single, pathetic second before it snaps off as his head rips free, blood spraying across the walls and all over me.

"Dimitri!" she gasps, shaking.

"I'm sorry you had to see that," I say softly, stepping slower now so I don't startle her. Her eyes are wide and focused on me.

"Don't be afraid, little mate," I whisper. "I was made to protect you, but them?" My voice drops darker. "I'll burn every last one of them alive and watch the ashes fall between my fingers if it means you're safe."

"I know," she says quietly. "I'm not scared." My gaze drops to the blood seeping from a wound on her side. She tries to move and winces.

"I need you to drink my blood," I say, voice low and rough. "It'll heal you, Malyshka."

I kneel in front of her, cupping her face gently, too gently for the violence that's still burning in me. She licks her dry lips, breath shallow, trusting me completely.

Fuck, the way she trusts me almost brings me to my damn knees. I raise my wrist to my mouth and bite, fangs slicing skin, dark blood welling up instantly. She stares at it, nervously trembling.

"All you have to do is drink, love," I whisper, sliding my hand to the back of her neck and guiding her head into my lap, holding her like she's something breakable.

"Are you sure?" she asks, looking up at me with those green eyes and pouty lips that ruin me.

"Yes, Malyshka," I growl softly. "Take what I give you."

She wraps her full lips around the wound and sucks, and fuck... my head snaps back as pleasure shoots through me. "Fuck, Moya Lyubov." Her mouth works against my skin, soft and hungry, and she grips my elbow, pulling me closer like she needs every drop of me. My pulse stutters, my demon snarls with pleasure, and I swear I almost come undone from just her mouth on my wrist.

When she finishes, she lifts her head slowly. There's blood on her lips, pupils blown, and she kisses me softly. That soft and gentle kiss nearly ruins me.

I scoop her into my arms. She wraps her legs around my waist, instantly clinging to me. Her warmth is everywhere on my chest, my arms, and my neck. The pendant my mother gave me rests between her breasts, glowing faintly against her skin like it recognizes her as mine, and fuck... she looks made for me.

"Damn, baby," I groan, capturing her mouth in a deeper kiss. She moans, breathless, making my cock throb hard enough to hurt.

Then she whispers. "I love you, Dimitri."

The words hit me like a blade to the chest, sharp and shocking. I laugh, wild with relief and something close to joy. "Say it again."

"What?"

"Tell me you love me again." I rest my forehead against hers. I used to crave those words as a child.

"I love you, Dimitri. So freaking much."

"I love you too," I whisper, cupping her face with both hands. "I'm so fucking sorry I left you. I thought you were safe."

She runs her fingers through my hair, nails grazing my scalp. A deep, involuntary rumble vibrates from my chest. My demon is purring under her touch.

"How did you find me?" she asks softly.

"My Hellhound tracked your scent." I tilt my head toward him, waiting outside the cell like a shadow.

"Hellhound?" she gasps. "I saw him. He was trying to help me. I ran from him, though. I killed the first vampire, but he took my knife, so I couldn't use it on the second."

I pull away to look at her, stunned. "You killed a vampire?"

She nods. My chest swells with pride so intense it's almost painful.

Fucking perfect woman.

I lift her into my arms again, burying my nose in her neck. "Mine."

Then I spot a metal collar clamped tight around her throat.

My vision turns red. "What is this?" I growl.

"Oh... I don't know. It stops my magic."

"You killed a vampire with no magic?" I whisper, my feelings a mix between awe and fury.

"I was a total badass," she says, smiling a little.

"Yes," I breathe. "You were." I kiss her neck. "And you're all mine."

"I'm all yours," she says back. My fucking heart nearly combusts. She hesitates, fingers curling in my shirt. "Can I ask you something?"

"Yes. Anything."

"Can I see your demon side again?"

"You want to see him?" My demon surges forward instantly, claws dragging against the inside of my skin.

Her cheeks flush that delicious shade of red. "Yes."

A wicked smile tugs at my mouth. My demon practically puffs his chest at her attention, stretching inside my ribs, eagerly. "Later, my love. He'd enjoy that," I whisper, brushing a kiss against her forehead. "He likes it when you ask for him."

"And your wings..." She swallows hard, eyes flicking down my back. "I want to touch them. If that's okay. They're... beautiful."

A groan rumbles out of me before I can stop it. Fuck, she has no idea what that does to me. "Of course it's okay," I breathe against her ear. "You can touch anything you want. I'm yours."

She fists my shirt as I carry her, clinging like she never wants to let go. "Let's get out of here," she whispers, breath ghosting across my throat. "It stinks."

"First, we cover you up." I set her down gently. Her wounds have healed, but she's covered in dried blood.

She looks like sin, like temptation covered in blood.

Hell, she looks like something a demon should worship and ruin. That demon? Is me...

My cock throbs painfully at the sight. I drag my shirt off and pull it over her body. It drops to her mid-thigh, hugging her curves, swallowing her in my scent, making a possessive shiver race through me.

I shouldn't be thinking about bending her over right now, imagining her legs shaking as she sinks down on my cock again, or fantasizing about where I'll sink my mark into her, her throat, her breast, or thighs so deep she'll think of me every time it throbs, but fuck... I can't help myself.

I run my gaze down her body, slow and hungry, mapping every inch I plan to claim. A groan tears out of me, and I drag a hand through my hair, trying and failing to calm the ache between my legs. "Fuck." I rumble, biting my lip.

Her eyes widen. She presses closer, innocently, and entirely unaware she's pouring gasoline on a demon's fire. "What?" she whispers.

I drop my head back with a low, dark chuckle. "Don't be frightened, little love," I murmur, cupping her jaw and brushing my thumb across her lips. "It's nothing."

My eyes drag down her body again, covered in my shirt, her bare legs, cheeks flushed. "It's just…" I lean close, lips brushing her ear. "You look too damn good wearing my clothes, and all I can think about is what I'm going to do to you when we're finally alone." I scoop her into my arms before she can reply and start to walk—then freeze.

"Dimitri…" A hoarse voice echoes down the hall.

Rosa cups my face. "What is it?"

"Shh. Someone's here."

Her eyes widen. "Oh God. I forgot. Someone is in the cell across from mine."

Someone who knows me. I turn back and head to the cell. I place Rosa down before I rip the door open, and someone slowly crawls out and lifts his head, looking up at me.

"Dimitri," he rasps.

My stomach drops. *No fucking way.* I stare in shock, breath stalling. "Damien?" *He's alive!*

"Wait," Rosa says, looking between us. "You two know each other?"

"Yes."

"How? Who is he?"

I look down at her, swallowing hard. "Rosa... he's your father."

Chapter Thirty-three

Rosa

Dimitri stares at the man who claims to be my father like the world just tilted sideways. I don't know how to feel. Shocked, angry? Maybe a little of everything. None of it feels right. He's kneeling on the filthy stone floor, breathing like it hurts. His face is half-buried under dirt and an overgrown beard, but those eyes... I've only ever seen them in pictures.

It's impossible, but I can't deny the facts.

Dimitri's Hellhound growls, and it pulls me back to reality. The cries and screams of the battle happening up above rush back in.

"Put me down," I whisper, avoiding the man's gaze.

"No," Dimitri looks down at me, and his grip tightens around me as if he's afraid of letting me go.

"I'm okay, put me down. We need to get out of here, and he's the one who needs to be carried." He shakes his head, such a stubborn man. "I'm here, I won't leave your side. I swear. Please, he can't even stand."

"Not happening," he says firmly, leaving zero room for negotiations. "Gwyllgi!" Dimitri shouts. I hear the pounding of Gwyllgi's paws hitting the stone floors as he rushes over. He moves with such a lethal grace, perfect for a predator.

"Damien, you need to climb onto Gwyllgi's back. Can you do that?"

I feel Damien's gaze on the side of my face before I see him shift in my peripheral vision as I watch Gwyllgi shift his large body to sit down. Holy shit, he actually understands Dimitri's demands. The hound is terrifyingly huge; he can easily carry a man plus more.

Dimitri doesn't wait to see if the man can actually climb up. He turns and strides toward the stairs, tightening his grip on me like he's worried I'll disappear. I try to look around his broad shoulder, but he locks me in place.

The door at the top of the stairs is already wide open. Eleanor is there, pacing alone, looking pale and frantic. The moment she sees me, her mouth opens in a sob, and she runs forward, eyes trailing over me, looking for injuries.

"Thank the Gods, Rosa. Are you hurt? Are you bleeding? Does anything feel wrong?"

"No, I'm okay now." My eyes roam the room, arms gripping Dimitri tighter, afraid of something else happening.

"Eleanor," Dimitri starts, jaw tightening. "There's something you should—" He doesn't finish, his Hellhound comes into view, standing beside us with Damien lying on top of him.

"Who…" Eleanor begins, but Damien lifts his head, eyes connecting with hers.

"Eleanor," he rasps.

Eleanor's knees wobble before giving out; she collapses hard enough that the sound echoes.

"Is that–– is he…?" She looks at Dimitri, her eyes filling with tears.

"Yes, it's him." Dimitri nods, but his attention is elsewhere.

I follow his line of sight. He's staring at Julian's body. His body is twisted and broken; limbs are bent in angles that shouldn't even exist, and his mouth is open in a silent scream. Whatever killed him didn't bother to make it clean.

Something in Dimitri darkens, his lips lifting in a snarl. It's as if he's imagining different ways to kill him.

"We need to get out of here." A man with shaggy blond hair bursts into the room.

"Tell everyone to retreat," Dimitri growls, his eyes growing dark. Something clearly set him off. I can feel his anger hot on my skin. The man turns and disappears from sight.

"Let's go." Dimitri lifts his hand and opens a portal. the air swirls as it splits with a violent snap. It leads to nothing but swirling darkness. He turns to Eleanor, who is crying as she clenches Damien's face like she's afraid he's just in her imagination.

"Eleanor. *Now.*" His tone is too harsh, and I want to smack him. Her mate, who she thought was dead, is here and alive. She deserves a damn second to breathe, but now isn't the time to argue. He forgets that not everyone is built like him.

Eleanor nods, pinching her lips into a tight line as she stands, wiping her tears with the back of her trembling hand without releasing Damien.

The Hellhound jumps through the grey swirling portal without any hesitation.

I honestly don't think I would have jumped willingly if Dimitri weren't holding me. Without any warning, he steps through. My grip tightens around his shoulders, and my eyes slam shut when everything blurs, and it's nothing but grey and black swirling around us, causing me to feel dizzy. It feels like someone pushed us off a cliff, my stomach drops, and my hair swings violently around us. I'm happy I haven't eaten because it would have ended up all over his chest. It's like we're dropping into a pit of nothing, just falling and falling.

The violent winds finally stop, and the feeling of falling does too, but I refuse to open my eyes.

"It's okay, we're here." Dimitri's voice is low, warm, and annoyingly amused.

I loosen my grip, my eyes snapping open. The first thing I see is Dimitri's piercing blue eyes that are sparkling with amusement.

I narrow my eyes at him. "You could have warned me first!" I smack his chest and twist out of his hold, turning to take in our surroundings.

We're in Eleanor's family room.

For the first time since this all started... I feel safe, like maybe we might actually survive.

Chapter Thirty-four

Rosa

My knees bounce with anxiety. I can't tell if it's the exhaustion, the nerves, or the fact that my brain still feels like it's spinning from everything that happened. I can't wrap my mind around it all. Cassie attacked me the second I stepped into the house with a million questions, then hugs and rapid-fire kisses all over my face. Normally, I'd laugh, but Dimitri's expression darkened like she'd committed a crime.

Possessive bastard... it is cute though.

Now the two of us sit in Eleanor's living room, waiting for an update, while Dimitri talks outside with Caspian, the man with blond shaggy hair. The glass doors are cracked open, letting in the faint scent of smoke. The battle must still be going on somewhere in the distance. I can feel the low hum of magic; it's a strange vibration in my bones.

Cassie is sitting across from me, staring at the large Hellhound sitting beside my feet in a protective stance. I can feel the tension radiating off his body; every sound has him jumping with alertness.

Dimitri commanded him to watch me, even though he's only a few feet away on the other side of the glass. His gaze keeps moving toward me, like he can't help himself. It's sharp and territorial, burning through the glass like it's nothing, but his intense gaze branding my skin is more than welcome. He's unfairly handsome, standing there, arms crossed over his chest. He's now wearing a shirt, but he's still covered in blood. His face is hard and serious, but those blue eyes soften each time they meet mine.

"I think it wants to eat me alive," Cassie whispers, her eyes wide as she stares at Gwyllgi. His large head slowly turns and narrows his glowing red eyes at her like she's an annoying insect. Then he bears a canine the size of her index finger. It does sort of look like he'd love nothing more than to eat her. I find it amusing that every time she gets close to me, he growls and snaps his large mouth at her.

"Don't be silly, he won't eat you." Gwyllgi makes a sound between a huff and a snort. *Okay... maybe he does want to eat her.* "At least I don't think he will."

Cassie makes a strangled noise. "Super reassuring, Rosa."

I can't help the small laugh that pushes out, but it dies quickly. My eyes drift to the library doors again, where Damien is being treated.

"Do you think he'll be okay?" My voice sounds small, even to me.

Cassie sighs, tucking her legs up in the chair as if she's trying to make herself smaller. "Yeah. My mom said he was severely malnourished, barely kept alive. They wanted him weak, not dead." Her face twists with disgust.

I rub my eyes with my hands in exhaustion, desperately needing some sleep and a shower. I almost dozed off earlier, but the idea of not being here if something happens to him... my father... He's in bad shape. Eleanor got hold of a healer, and they're working on him. It's been an hour, and we still haven't heard anything.

"I need to go check." I stand, and Gwyllgi leaps up beside me instantly. Dimitri's gaze snaps to me instantly. I point to the library doors, and he nods.

"Okay, I'm going to go check on Ian." I pinch my lips together to keep from laughing when Cassie lifts her knees to her chest as Gwyllgi walks past her and keeps his crazed eyes on her.

His eye contact game is good, just like his owner's. Intimating as hell, I guess being a badass Hellhound does that. A part of me thinks he's enjoying the reaction he's getting from her.

"He seriously has issues," she mutters.

"He's just... protective." I smile, just like Dimitri.

I reach the library door, but I don't knock or move to open it. I just stand there staring at the carvings in the wood. My heartbeat is slow, but heavy in my ears.

Gwyllgi startles me when he rubs his nose against my hand, which is tightly clenched together. He releases a low whine as if he can sense my uneasiness. He's surprisingly sweet for a murderous Hellhound

"I'm okay, boy," I whisper, rubbing the top of his head. He presses into my side, comforting me, which shocks me. And yet again, just like Dimitri, he's a complete asshole to others but sweet to me.

Courage runs through me with his help. I lift my hand and knock on the thick wood.

A second later, the door opens. It's Eleanor, her hair wild, and her eyes red. She offers me a small smile. She widens the door but takes a startled step back when she sees Gwyllgi.

"How is he doing?" I ask, my eyes drifting to where he lies on the sofa. He's clean of dirt and looks to be in a deep, peaceful sleep.

"Better." She replies softly, moving toward him. "Healing will take time. They nearly starved him to death." Her voice cracks on the last word.

My throat tightens. "Can I do anything? Can Dimitri give him blood?" The corner of her lips lowers into a frown, looking confused, so I explain, "Dimitri gave me some blood when he found me in the cell, and it healed me."

"Oh, that doesn't happen," she shakes her head. "He only did that for you because you are his mate. He won't do it for anyone else. It's okay. I have the best healers here. Your father is already showing signs of healing. Why don't you go shower and get some rest? It'll make you feel better."

"Okay," I look down at myself. I'm still covered in dirt and blood. Dimitri's shirt is clinging to me, helping me stay calm with its warmth and scent. "Let me know if you need anything."

I turn to leave, but before I make it too far, she says, "Thank you. If you hadn't put yourself in danger, he would still be down there, alone and weak. I should've listened to you."

"Anyone would've done it," I say as I open the door and both Gwyllgi and I slip out.

Chapter Thirty-Five

Rosa

The hot water cascades down my sore back, stinging where the bruises haven't fully healed yet, and I watch dirt and dried blood swirl down the drain.

I have the bathroom door cracked open because every time I try to close it, Gwyllgi shoves his massive body between the frame and me, snarling like the bathroom is dangerous. His glowing eyes track every movement I make, protective and unyielding.

I grab the bottle of body soap, rubbing my entire body hard until my skin is red, like if I scrub hard enough, it will help wash off the horrors from me, and from my memories. I know it won't, but that doesn't stop me from trying. I still haven't even had time to fully process what happened.

Julius kidnapped me and had full intentions of forcing a mate bond on me... A ghastly shiver runs down my body at the thought of being forced into something like that, being forever trapped. He's dead, I remind myself once more.

I hate to say this, but I'm glad he is, and I'm glad I saw his dead body with my own eyes, because if I hadn't, I don't think I would actually fully believe it. I mean, he wasn't just anyone. He was the Vampire Prince, a powerful man, and Dimitri overpowered him. It means he is stronger than I ever imagined.

And then there's the man in the cell across from mine. The one who could barely stand, barely even breathe, and he still tried to save me. I can still hear his desperation as he shouted at the guard and pleaded for me. He didn't even know who I was, and he still tried to help me.

My chest tightens. If he ever wakes up, I'll be proud to call that stranger my father. *He has to!* He can't just give up after years and years of fighting to survive; there is no way he can just stop.

I shut the water off with a shaky exhale. I step in front of the mirror, and my hands grip the sink so hard they hurt as I blink my eyes rapidly until the room stops spinning. The shower did nothing to ease my thoughts like I had hoped. My body doesn't understand that we're safe now, out of danger. I refuse to stare at my reflection; the marks on my skin that he left behind are ugly, painful, and not just physical.

The bathroom door creaks open, and Gwyllgi's massive head pushes through. He presses against my hips, knowing that I need something to ground myself.

"Hey," I whisper, my fingers tangling with his fur. "I'm okay."

He knows I'm lying, and I do too.

I honestly could fall asleep standing here. I dry off quickly, throwing on an oversized t-shirt and some shorts. My body is moving on autopilot

Groaning, I crawl into the soft bed. I faintly feel Gwyllgi climb into the bed and land his heavy body on my feet. I should be annoyed, but I'm not. I actually like it, and it makes me feel safe, maybe it's the warmth or weight of his body. He's like a dark protective shadow wrapping around me.

I feel protected just like I do when I'm with Dimitri. My sigh is full of contentment, and I pull the dark comforter up to my chin, and I'm asleep as soon as my head hits the cold pillow.

I blink my eyes open, but I groan with annoyance and immediately slam my eyes shut once more. The bright sun is making my eyes feel a sharp discomfort.

Something feels wrong. I sit up, forcing my eyes open when I don't feel the heaviness of Gwyllgi on my legs. I find him sitting on his backside, his back straight and tense as he stares straight ahead as if on duty. Behind him, lounging in a black leather chair as if it's a throne, is Dimitri. He looks arrogant and deadly; it suits him.

He's leaning back against it, his ankle resting on the opposite knee, one arm resting lazily on the arm of the chair, and the other is fisted, resting his chin against it. His eyes are sharp as he silently stares at me, completely consuming me with his heated gaze alone. I move to sit at the edge of the bed closer to him. I almost forgot how intense his eyes can be when he's watching me.

"Are you hurting anywhere?" he asks, eyes moving over me like he's checking for injuries.

"No," I breathe, shaking my head. "I'm just tired."

His jaw flexes, like that answer doesn't satisfy him.

"Why are you looking at me like that?"

He closes his eyes, looking away. "Because I thought I was going to lose you."

My gaze lowers as heat stings the back of my eyes. He rises from his seat, slowly, and steps closer, but keeps his distance.

"You're trembling," he says lowly, and steps closer, like he's afraid he'll spook me.

I swallow, meeting his gaze. "I'm having trouble telling myself I'm no longer in danger. My body still feels their touch on me. No matter how hard I scrubbed my body, it's still there." My hand reaches to the mark on my neck where Julius bit me, a reminder of the pain.

Dimitri's expression shifts a mixture of dark possessiveness and protectiveness.

"Come here," he pleads as he sits beside me, leaving space. He's letting me decide if I want his touch, but Gods, I hate that he's being cautious with me. I love it when he takes control. I move without hesitation. I crawl closer, my fingers gripping his shirt as my body collapses in his warmth, and everything inside me shifts. He exhales deeply like he feels the same need, and his arms wrap around me slowly. It's soft and full of safety, letting me know he's here for me. His lips brush the top of my head.

"No one will ever hurt you again, I swear it on my life." He whispers against my hair, and a sob releases from my chest. It's a relief, because I believe him.

I need him and his touch to replace the horrors. I tilt my head back to look at him as his warmth slowly melts my fear in my body into something else: want and desire.

My face heats when I remember the last time we were alone together, how our sweaty bodies rubbed against each other in a heated, desperate rhythm. The way he moved above me was like he was completely desperate for me, like he was trying to ruin me for all others. I'm praying he doesn't notice the change in my expression, but he, of course, does.

"I love it when you blush for me," he groans in a deep raspy voice as his hand lifts, and he brushes his calloused fingertips across my right reddened cheek. My heart rate spikes to an unnatural rhythm, and my thighs rub together as my pussy starts throbbing like it has a pulse of its own.

I lean closer, just an inch, and he follows, but pauses as he searches my face.

"Tell me what you need," he whispers. He won't touch me unless he knows I'm ready.

"I need…" My eyes move to his lips. "I need you to erase their touch with your own. Help me forget."

He rumbles, cupping my face. "Are you sure?" My teeth sink into my lower lip, my eyes begging.

"Fuck it." He growls, standing and spinning us around so I'm sitting on the corner of the bed and he's towering above me. There he is, my monster that takes control, handles me with the roughness my body craves.

A couple of different things happen. Dimitri reaches behind him, yanking his shirt off. At that exact moment, Gwyllgi rushes forward just as Dimitri's lips touch mine and forces his large body between me and Dimitri's. Dimitri jerks back, startled, as the Hellhound snarls and pushes him away from me.

My hand moves on its own, rubbing the top of Gwyllgi's head. My fingers are threading through his dark fur as I whisper, "Shh, it's okay, I'm okay."

"Leave, Gwyllgi," Dimitri snaps. The command cracks through the air with demonic authority, making me flinch. Gwyllgi's growls stop as he leans against me, but he keeps his eyes locked on Dimitri like he'll rip his throat out if necessary. "*Now, Gwyllgi.*"

Gwyllgi slowly peels himself away from me and follows Dimitri, who opens the door. The Hellhound looks back at me with an uncertain glance before walking out of the room. Dimitri slams the door shut and turns to me.

"What the fuck was that?" His voice is low and dark. "You turned my own hound against me." He crosses his arms over his naked chest as he towers over me, muscles shifting with the movement. His expression is twisted with disbelief. I force my eyes to stay on his because all I want to do is memorize every single ridge of his hard abdomen.

"I did no such thing. It's not my fault he likes me more than you." I grumble, my lips lower into a frown.

Shock slams into me when Dimitri starts laughing. My eyes widen; I can count on one hand how many times I've heard him laugh. I'm also shocked to know that he's not angry.

He bends at his hips, caging me in as he plants both of his hands on the mattress on either side of me, his nose nearly touching mine.

"What am I going to do with you?" he mumbles against my lips.

"I'm not sure," I breathe, "but right now, you can start by touching me until I can't handle it anymore."

I take myself by surprise when boldness slams into me, but I should not be that surprised. Dimitri brings out a side of me that I never knew existed. It's a side of me that I'm slowly falling in love with. I love being confident and bold.

I grab the hem of my shirt, pull it over my head, and toss it off to the side. I watch as he pulls back and his eyes drag over my naked breasts, nipples hardening under his stare, begging to be touched. Desire flashes his features, and his groan lights every nerve in my body.

He gently pushes me down until my back is flat on the mattress. His mouth is on my neck, sucking and licking my sensitive skin. One of his hands slides up my sides and teases the underside of my breast before cupping it.

"I'm not sure where I should mark you." Dimitri's voice is deep with desire, "here," he gently bites the curve of my neck right above my collarbone before moving lower. "Or here." He bites my left breast, right above my nipple.

My head tilts back, eyes fluttering shut as a moan escapes me. He licks my nipple once before lowering his body while leaving small trails of heated kisses on his way down.

He settles his upper body between my thighs, teeth grazing the sensitive skin on my left thigh. "Or here. What do you think, mate?" His eyes meet mine, full of dark hunger.

"I don't care, mark me anywhere you want. Just put your lips back on me." I tilt my hips upwards, hoping to get his mouth against my clit. I still have my shorts on, but any little touch will do.

"Such an impatient little thing you are. So desperate for me." The roughness of his voice sends heat straight to my core. "It's so damn sexy."

"Please, Dimitri. Touch me."

A low, dangerous sound rumbles out of him. He pulls back only long enough to hook his fingers in the waistband of my shorts and slide them down my legs. He hisses between his teeth when he sees I'm completely bare beneath.

"Fuck." His eyes flare, darker than the room. "I love it when you beg. Can't get enough of it. I need you, every part of you. You're an addiction I'll never get clean from." He sits up, unbuttoning his pants with a slow hunger that makes my breathing quicken.

His gaze sweeps my body like he's memorizing a sin he's proud to commit. "You look like an angel, but you're a devil, such a naughty little devil hiding in plain sight, stealing souls, but I will gladly give you mine. As long as you're *my* little devil, you can suck my damned soul from my chest. Now get up, I want to see you on your knees," he commands. Without hesitation, I do as he demands, dropping to my knees before him.

He shoves his pants and boxers down to his ankles and stares down at me through his black demon eyes. His demon in him is watching the show as well. "You look so good on your knees for me."

He grips his large, achy cock, stroking once before tapping the thick tip against my lips and says a single command, "Open."

My mouth parts, and my tongue slips out as I stare into his eyes. The corners of his lips curl into a snarl, and he pushes his cock into my mouth. He's not gentle, not that it surprises me. One of his hands wraps around my jaw, and the tips of his fingers dig into my cheeks until my mouth opens wider. My eyes water when his cock touches the back of my throat.

"Come on, my little devil, relax that throat for me. Let me in." His low guttural voice makes the pulsing between my thighs worse, and chills rack my entire body. It sounds so desperate, and it eggs me on. I want to please him; no, I *need* to please him.

I breathe through my nose, relax my throat, and widen my mouth further, forcing him deeper into my mouth, causing me to gag, but I push through it.

My eyes flick up just in time to see him toss his head back, and the harsh groan he makes is long and deep; his lips are parted, and his Adam's apple bobs.

He looks extremely sexy; the unadulterated pleasure in his face excites me and drives me forward. I've never seen anything like this, and I will do anything to keep it there. I pull back halfway, wrapping my hand around the base, and then push forward. I repeatedly do this over and over, my hand moving in sync with my mouth. I lift my other hand to cup his balls. The room is filled with pleasurable grunts and groans.

"Fuck, stop." His fist tangles in my hair and yanks.

I wince at the slight sting. "What did I do wrong?" I ask in a hurry, blinking rapidly, trying to clear the haze of pleasure.

"Gods, baby, you did nothing wrong." His pupils are blown wide, his chest rising fast. "You were absolutely perfect. I don't want to come in your mouth. I want that sweet pussy."

"Oh." That's all I managed to say. My eyes trail after him as he kicks his pants away and turns. I get a clear view of his firm ass as he walks away.

Damn.

He drops into the large leather chair and pats his upper thigh underneath his large cock.

"Climb on top, my sweet little devil, and sit on my cock with that tight little pussy." His dark eyes pin me in place.

I swallow nervously. The last time we were together was my first, and I've never been on top. "It's okay, Malyshka. You can do nothing wrong. I will love every second, and I will show you how to move those hips." His tongue darts out, licking his lower lip.

I step in between his thighs, and he grips my hips, lifting me. My legs are on either side of his hips as I straddle him.

One hand slides to the back of my neck, pulling me forward, wrapping his lips around my nipple, and his other hand disappears between my thighs, fingers separating my pussy lips, rubbing circles around my achy clit. I jerk my hips forward and arch my back as much as I can with his grip still tight on the back of my neck. His fingers are relentless, stroking fast.

My fingers dig into his broad shoulders, tightening in a death grip, and I cry out. The heat in my lower stomach builds fast. I'm so close to coming undone.

I scream his name in frustration when he slows his strokes.

"Use your words, my naughty girl, tell me what you want. Do you want me to fuck you so deep that you feel me in your ribs?"

"Yes, please." I nod eagerly, keeping eye contact.

"Good girl." He reclines further back and grabs his cock, and his other hand grips my hip, pulling me down until the tip is pressing against my entrance. "What are you waiting for? Take it, *use* me."

I place both hands flat on his chest, using him for support, and lower myself down. Taking it inch by inch slowly. I can tell he is struggling with the need for control to push me down harder by the tension in his jaw.

But me? I'm struggling to keep going, my thighs trembling. The stretch burns; it hurts.

Out of nowhere, he snaps.

His hands clamp my hips and pull me down.

"Fuck..." he moans, it vibrates through me as I cry out. He throws his head back and growls. He doesn't give me a single moment to breathe; he pulls me up and slams me back down again, taking what he wants.

The pain subsides, and I'm a moaning mess. Soon I'm moving on my own, rocking and rolling my hips, fast and hard, chasing the sensation that destroys me. He releases his grip on me and cups my breasts, pinching and swirling my nipples with his fingertips until I'm gasping.

"You look perfect riding my cock," he mumbles when he leans back and watches me, his eyes roaming over me as I work my hips.

I don't reply, I can't. My vision blurs, and the pleasure becomes too much as it slams into me. "Oh, God," I moan, my head tilting back.

"I decided," Dimitri rasps. I hardly hear him over my orgasms shattering through me. "I'll do it here." My body is a quivering mess, and I hardly feel the heated lick on my skin right above my left nipple, right where my heart beats beneath. Then, I feel sharp pain so intense I nearly black out.

He's marking me.

But as immediately as the pain comes, it disappears, turning into something euphoric and exhilarating. I mumble Dimitri's name, and I feel his grip tighten around me as he pulls me impossibly closer, claiming every piece of me. He groans as he thrusts up hard, his cock throbbing as warm come fills me.

His grip loosens, and his body slumps back against the chair as he slowly pulls his fangs out of me and licks the mark clean, fangs still visible, my blood at the corner of his lips, and his tongue snakes out, wiping the blood clean. He stares at me through hooded eyes, looking completely and utterly satisfied.

"We're fully mated," I state the obvious, looking down at my left breast where his teeth mark is permanently embedded in my skin.

"Yes." He grins, dimples winking at me. "You are completely mine, soul, mind, and body."

"Such a possessive demon."

"Your possessive demon." His grin widens.

I smile. "Yes, mine."

Chapter Thirty-six

Rosa

I dress myself in a pair of blue jeans and a simple tank top with spaghetti straps. I took a shower while Dimitri went downstairs to grab me some breakfast.

We have a lot to discuss, he says, but he wants me to eat first.

I open the closet door, and a massive dark blur rushes towards me. I laugh when Gwyllgi's front paws collide with my chest, pushing me back a few steps with his weight. His tail thumps wildly against the wall.

"Did you miss me?" I scratch the back of his ear and he… Purrs? *And people say Hellhounds are soulless and cruel.*

"Down, Gwyllgi," Dimitri growls when he comes into view with a plate of food. My stomach rumbles in response. He immediately drops to the floor, though he sneaks a final lick to my hand.

"You are so mean to him," I grumble at Dimitri, taking the plate from him, leaning up to place a kiss on his jaw, and walking out to the balcony.

"He's a trained warrior, not a *pet*." He spits out the word 'pet' as if it is gross and unnatural. His gaze drops to our mark, which is partially on display. You can see the top half of it peeking out of my tank top. The corners of his lips curl slightly up, and his eyes shine with something dangerously close to joy. It almost makes me lose my train of thought.

"Well," I say as I settle into the balcony chair. "Trained warrior or not. He deserves some playtime, Dimitri. It's not all about killing things."

"Yes, it is," he says, flatly standing beside me in that manly way of his, arms crossed.

"Oh, really?" I raise a brow. "Says the demon who used to be an uptight warrior all the time until I came alone. Are you telling me you prefer the before and not this?" His eyes narrow, and I smirk. "Exactly." I dig into the French toast that I know he made me by the heart-shaped strawberries. I have never felt so content. I feel loved. I have a family, a mom, and a dad, even though I haven't officially met him.

"I talked to Eleanor in the kitchen, and she says Damien is responding well to the treatment. His vitals are stronger."

"That's amazing," my words muffled due to a mouth full of food. "I can't wait to officially meet him. You know he tried saving me down there, even though he was barely able to stand, he still tried with the last of his strength." Relief crashes into me.

"He's a good man." He looks away, eyes distant, staring at the blue skies.

"Dimitri?"

"Hmm?" He answers but doesn't look back.

"Did you really kill him? Jim?" He turns back to me, eyes searching my face, maybe searching to see if I can handle the truth. "Tammy told me when you left."

"I did."

"But why?"

"Why?" He snorts. "You think I'd let someone who hurt you walk away breathing?"

"But you didn't know me then."

"I don't care. I won't let a person who harmed you roam this earth. I'm the demon who punishes for crimes committed, and he never answered for his heinous ones. I judged and executed. It's what I do, and it's who I am, especially when it comes to what belongs to me." He turns to me, his voice lowers, and darkens. "If that upsets you, I can live with that. Because even if you are, there's nothing you can do about it. You're mine now. You're not going anywhere."

"No, I'm not upset." I want to say more, but I'm not sure what to say to that. He's more possessive than before, and there's a part of me that likes it.

"Good." He nods, shoulders losing some tension. "There's something I've been wanting to talk to you about."

I say nothing as I take a sip of my coffee.

"We're leaving, and..." He looks at me as if he wants to tell me something, then shakes his head like he decides against it. "Never mind."

My mind brushes over the never mind and straight to the we're leaving. "What?" I sit up straighter. "Where are we going? What about Eleanor and Damien? I thought Eleanor couldn't leave because of the council. Will Ian and Cassie come with us?" The questions spill out of me. I know I need to ask one at a time to get a better answer, but I can't stop it. It's like word vomiting when I'm nervous.

"A lot is going on with the vampires. Prince Azrael is coming to investigate, and it's not safe. The other question I don't have answers to those." He shakes his head. "I haven't talked to anyone but Caspian and Ian about this. You have to remember I'm new to this. My instinct was to take you while you slept. But Caspian reminded me that I need to discuss things with you before I take charge and allow you to say goodbye."

"You're making it sound like I don't have a choice in the matter." His stare hardens, and I know that I'm right with that stare alone.

"When it comes to your safety, Malyshka, you do not have a say." My pulse spikes. "I am telling you instead of dragging you because I respect you, but that does not mean I will not force you if it comes to it."

"Dimitri, no." I stand abruptly, toe-to-toe with him. "I haven't met Damien yet. I'm not leaving him until I know he's okay. You can't force me to go."

"Rosa…" he rubs his face with the palm of his hand. "What if…" He exhales sharply. "What if I bring you back when he wakes up? You two can meet and make plans once a week to get to know each other."

"Okay, that's reasonable," I whisper. "Are we going far?" It could work. Dimitri can teleport, and we can come whenever I want.

His jaw works. "Far enough."

"Okay, then I'm okay with it. I want to be wherever you are."

"Good." He bends to kiss my forehead. "I will go and talk to Ian and Eleanor. Gwyllgi will stay here with you."

"Okay." But he's gone before I even finish the word. I drop back down into the chair, picking up the cup of coffee, taking a sip as I look at Gwyllgi, who is sitting across the table from me. His calculating eyes roam the area as if he's looking for threats.

"Come here, Gwyllgi." His large tail wags, but he takes another look around before bouncing happily towards me, tongue hanging loosely out the side of his mouth. "Good boy." I rub the top of his head as he places it on top of my knees, and I lean back, resting against the chair.

A couple of hours later, I am ready to leave. Dimitri has already packed for me. We're standing in the library, and I'm staring down at my father.

Eleanor left, giving me privacy to say goodbye. He looks so much better. Someone, and I'm guessing Eleanor, shaved his overly grown facial hair and gave him a nice haircut, and of course, he's clean of dirt and sweat. He looks exactly like he did in the photo I have of us. Except, well, he's asleep.

"See? I told you he's doing well. He'll be up and walking any day now, and if he's doing well, I'll be able to come get him." Dimitri whispers behind me and wraps his arms around me. His chin rests on my shoulder as his hands slide down my arms until they reach my tightly clenched hands, and he unravels them.

"Where are we going?" I ask softly. "You still won't tell me." His arms tense around me. I tilt my head to the side to meet his gaze.

"No, but I should warn you that the teleportation will be longer than before, and the drop will be worse."

My brows pinch together, and I ask, "Why? Where are we going that'll take that long?"

He takes a few minutes before answering. "Because we're going to my home."

"Oh? As in Russia?"

His lips twitch, fighting a smile. "Something like that."

"What––" I'm cut off when Cassie's voice booms behind us.

"You're leaving?"

Dimitri sighs in annoyance, making me pinch my lips together to stop my own smile. I know he finds Cassie annoying and loud, even though he's never actually said those exact words. He turns us both, but doesn't release me. She looks between us, tension tightening her features.

"Yeah, we are, and you should come with us. Dimitri says it won't be safe here." I step forward and out of Dimitri's grasp, who releases a low growl.

"I don't know…" she mumbles. "Ian mentioned something to me, but I'm not comfortable going there."

"Why? What's wrong with Russia?" I frown when Cassie's eyes flick to Dimitri. Cold dread rushes through me. "What's going on?" I snap, my arms crossing over my chest when I turn to face him.

"Nothing is going on." His eyes stay on Cassie with an intimidating glare.

"I won't hide this from her." Cassie steps forward, voice full of confidence, regardless of Dimitri's glare. "Yes, he's taking you home, but it's not to Russia." She turns to face me. "He's taking you to the Underworld."

"The Underworld? As in Hell?" My voice is so high-pitched as I shout, I hardly recognize it. "What the hell, Dimitri?" My voice rises, "You weren't going to tell me something that massive?"

"It's not that important," he says lazily, lifting his shoulders in a shrug that absolutely infuriates me. "We're going regardless, and it's my home just as I said. You'll be safe."

"Not important?" My shout turns into a full-on yell. "I'm not going anywhere with you. You're being an unemotional asshole."

"Don't disrespect me," he snarls, eyes blazing black. "You are coming with me. Don't make me drag you."

"You wouldn't dare." I lift my chin and ball my hands together into fists, widening my stance. His jaw flexes, and his eyes flicker; it looks like fear.

Suddenly, his voice drops, too deep and emotional, "I didn't tell you because I was afraid you'd say no. And I can't lose you." My breath catches, and for one impossible second, he looks almost... human, but then his fear fades into something dangerous. "Gwyllgi!" Dimitri commands, and heavy paws come from behind me.

I frown. How is he involved? Whatever he's planning, I know I won't like it. I step back and whisper a quick. "Don't."

And with a small, arrogant smirk, he says, "You asked for it." My hair whips violently around me when the wind picks up, ripping papers from the tables. I turn to find the swirling grey and black hole to nothingness. "I told you that you'll regret provoking my monster."

"No," I shake my head, but the violent winds swallow the word.

I watch Gwyllgi walk into the teleportation hole, and then strong arms wrap around my waist, my back slams against Dimitri's strong chest.

"No, Dimitri, stop!" I scream, turning to see Cassie's face full of panic as she rushes forward, but Dimitri is faster as he jumps into the portal, and the portal seals behind us with a violent snap.

Chapter Thirty-seven

Rosa

After what feels like hours, though I know it's only been a few minutes, my eyes snap open as the violent wind fades to a slow breeze. My back is still pressed to Dimitri's chest, his arms locked around me with an iron grip. Gwyllgi is nowhere in sight, but the world around us steals my breath.

The dark clouds are an angry grey with a red tint to them, like someone smeared blood across them. No sun in sight. This is no nightmare; it's the Underworld.

Below us is a forest that spreads farther than my eyes can follow. The trees are wrong, beautiful, but wrong. Their bark is pure black, polished like obsidian. The leaves are entirely grey, and the forest floor is the same muted ash color. Even the grass... if it is grass, is dark grey.

My body shivers as I stare, not from cold, no, from how colorless and dark the Underworld is, but it's hauntingly beautiful.

I turn my head, chin brushing my shoulder, to look at Dimitri. His jaw is tight, eyes burning straight ahead, wings beating rapidly to keep us high in the sky. He's angry, tense, and absolutely refusing to meet my gaze.

I turn back around; the forest is coming to an end, and I see nothing but black rolling hills. *How am I going to survive this? I love the sun and being outdoors, in a green, lush forest. I'm a witch. Even though I just found out, it has always been a big part of me. With how the fresh earth calls to my blood, the way it calms me, and feels like a warm hug welcoming me home, I need that feeling. Not this...*

Staring at this forest, it doesn't call to me. It doesn't welcome or comfort me. It's not fresh. It's dead and unalive.

The dark rolling hills start to flatten, revealing a massive river with black, raging waters. We fly past it, and a town comes into view.

There are three separate rows of homes. At the end of each row is a market area, and overlooking all of it, sitting on a hill is a dark, intimidating castle that dominates the land.

The first street we pass has small brown-brick cottages in a neat line. The second is filled with medium-sized homes, gothic in structure. The third street has massive, elegant, wealthy estates, and is unnervingly perfect.

"That is where my father lives," Dimitri whispers in my ear and points toward the looming, midnight castle.

Of course, the Devil himself lives there.

"It's beautiful," I whisper. "But it's a dark, dangerous kind of beauty."

We fly over the town and toward another forest, but between the rolling hills and forest is a three-story house. It's built of smooth black bricks, but it's mostly dark windows, with a black iron fence surrounding the entire property. It's elegant yet grim.

I wouldn't be surprised if the Grim Reaper himself lived there.

As we get closer, I see that even though the house is mostly windows, you cannot see inside. The windows are too dark, more like mirrors. My heart shutters in my chest when Dimitri lowers us to the ground.

Is this Dimitri's home? I can't believe I'm here, Hell or the Underworld, as Dimitri calls it. I'm beyond overwhelmed. A couple of weeks ago, I was a normal girl trying to get her degree. Now I'm a witch, my mate is a demon who marked me, and our souls are tied.

I'm pretty sure that means I'm part demon, but I could be wrong. I need to ask some fucking questions. I mean, shit... why haven't I?

A sigh of relief escapes me when Gwyllgi comes running into view.

Dimitri sets me down, and my legs nearly buckle. I cling to his arm since my knees are too weak to support my weight, and my other hand digs into Gwyllgi's fur for mental support when he steps beside me.

"We're home." Dimitri's eyes are on the black glass house in front of us. "What do you think?" He turns to look at me like my approval means everything to him. I don't look at him. I'm still angry with him, and also terrified, confused, overwhelmed, and fully captivated by this world. He chose for me. He took away my freedom, like it was nothing, and yeah, my heart doesn't know whether to run or reach for him.

"It's dark and unemotional, but breathtaking," I answer truthfully.

Dimitri steps forward, his wings are gone. He pushes open the iron gate and beckons me forward with a single curl of his index finger. Gwyllgi and I follow him to the front door.

My breath gets stuck in my throat the second we step inside.

White marble floors that have black and grey streaks throughout. Dark grey walls with thick black trim carved in beautiful hand-cut swirls. A grand staircase that spirals to the second floor is also black with the same hand-carved designs. To the left is a glossy grand piano, and to my right is an arched opening leading to a modern living area furnished with grey leather furniture and ash-toned wood tables.

"Wow," I breathe, turning to see Dimitri watching me closely, and I'm surprised to find that he seems almost... nervous? He's shifting from foot to foot and is tapping his fingers against his thigh. I smile, and he visibly relaxes. "Your home is beautiful, Dimitri."

"Our home," he corrects, in his grumpy asshole way, like he doesn't give a single fuck. I used to think I'd get used to his nonchalant way; he acts like he doesn't care, but he does. I can see the edges of vulnerability he tries so hard to hide. I just wish he'd open up, at least when it's just us. I'm trying to be patient, but it's harder than I thought.

He turns away and walks through the archway, leading into the living area. I follow him, and my feet stumble on each other.

The back wall is entirely glass, floor to ceiling, which makes you feel like you're walking into the dark forest. It's like there's not even a wall, and you can walk out and be amongst the trees.

"Rule number one." Dimitri's voice cuts through my awe, and I turn to find him leaning against the wall, watching me, a glass of dark whiskey in his hand. His shoulders are tense. His gaze is hard. "Never go into that forest without me and my Hellhounds, so we can keep you safe from the beasts."

"Beasts?" My heart shutters, and my skin crawls. Of course, there are beasts in there. We *are* in the underworld after all, it's where beasts and monsters run free.

"Yes, but as long as you are within the fence, you are safe. The wards are strong. You can go to the edge of the forest, but not deeper. Do you understand, Rosa?" His jaw tightens, and a flicker of fear appears in his eyes. It softens my anger, but then it's gone, replaced by his emotionless mask. "I mean it. I can't lose you here."

"So, I'm your prisoner." I cross my arms.

His entire body tenses, he inhales sharply, nostrils flaring, then looks away, running his fingers through his hair like he's grounding himself. He sets the glass of whiskey down and walks to me. "Rosa, you are not my prisoner. I just need you safe." He cups my face, letting his emotions show; he looks vulnerable and worried.

"I thought you said I'd be safer here."

"It's the underworld; you are not safe outside these wards." His eyes beg me to understand. "These wards are safer than Eleanor's house; there's a tear somewhere in her wards that Julian made, but no one can find it."

"If you ask me to take you into town or outside the wards, I'll try. I swear it. Once you learn to wield your magic, you'll roam freely, with my hounds." His thumb brushes my cheek, eyes begging me to hear him. "I know it's a lot for me to ask of you, but it's only for now. Please understand."

"Okay," I nod, resting my forehead against his chest, and he wraps his arms around me.

"I have a surprise for you," he says after a moment. His tone lightens, cautious, like he's afraid I won't like what he did for me.

"A surprise?" I pull back, brows raised. I know I shouldn't melt because he shows me a little softness, but I do.

"While you were asleep earlier, I came home with one of Eleanor's friends, and she helped me." He grabs my hand with a genuine smile that's overly contagious.

"I'm guessing you threatened the poor girl," I tease.

"Only a little." He winks, and I laugh, the sound breaking the heavy tension in my chest.

We pass the kitchen; the cabinets are dark grey with gold handles, and the marble countertops are the same type as the floors.

He stops at a door and squeezes my hand as he opens it, and a gasp rips out of me.

The room is enormous, and it's like stepping into a slice of the world I left behind. The walls are glass, showing the dark forest outside. But inside? It's like being in the forest back home, full of color, with tall trees growing from the dirt floor. I drop to the ground and dig my fingers into the soil. Warmth pulses through me. It's alive; a feeling of calmness wraps around me.

I look up to see a few butterflies dancing around each other as they fly past me, and I hear a beautiful melody that I know is from birds singing. The back wall has a running fountain that resembles a pond with stones surrounding it, big enough for me to sit on and put my feet in the water.

"I know it's not enough," Dimitri says quietly behind me. "It's not a real forest. Not the kind you're used to. We made it as large as we could, but..."

I stand and cut him off. "It's more than enough." My voice breaks, tears sliding down my cheeks. I'm not sure what he's talking about. This space is as big as mine and Cassie's apartment.

"Those are happy tears... right?" He steps forward, cupping my face once more, looking worried. I laugh, and I nod, rising to my toes and kissing him softly on the lips.

"Yes, happy," I whisper against his lips. "I love it."

"I wanted you to have something that felt like home."

He dragged me to Hell, but he built me a slice of heaven...

My anger is slowly turning to forgiveness.

Chapter Thirty-eight

Rosa

"Let's finish the tour. The hounds are getting anxious and curious since they can feel your presence with me."

"You can feel their emotions?" I step away, looking longingly at our surroundings. I have plenty of time to enjoy it another time. He places a hand on my lower back and guides me out of the room.

"Yes, they are bound to me, and I am them, which makes them bound to you, but it will take some time to feel them. You'll need to be around them and get to know them, and that'll slowly strengthen the bond."

"I do have questions about our bond. I know our souls are now intertwined and we're a part of each other, but is what Cassie said true? Am I part demon now?"

"In a roundabout way. I am part of you, and you are part of me. You're not going to turn into a demon, but you will gain some of my abilities..." he says it like a fact, a permanent one. "You'll become immortal. You won't fully feel the change yet. Not until you consume my blood, and then once you do, the change will begin. You'll be able to see in the dark and have sharper, clearer hearing. If I were a lower demon, you probably wouldn't get anything, but since I am a higher demon, you definitely will. That's why lower demons want to be with a stronger creature; it's all about gaining more power. We demons find power sexy. No one will know exactly what abilities you will gain, but you're already powerful. It will not matter. The most important part is that you will live as long as me."

I will become immortal... forever with him. The thought should scare me, but my pulse quickens.

"Consume your blood? But I did in the cell."

"You did, but I hadn't marked you at the time. It has to be done after the mark has been placed."

Without thinking, my hand moves, and I thread my fingers with his. His lips lower into a frown as he looks at our hands. For a moment, I think he'll pull away, but he tightens his fingers around mine and smiles at me before turning away. It's like he needs the contact more than he wants to admit.

We head up the grand staircase in the entryway; my free hand slides up the wooden railing as I look at the designs curved into it.

At the top, you have a choice: turn right or left. He turns left and shows me three rooms that all look the same. We head to the right, and there is only one door, like the others, black. Dimitri turns the handle and pushes the door open, motioning me to go in first.

I step into the room, and my lips part.

I've never seen a room so big, even at Eleanor's. The king-sized bed is covered in black silk sheets, and chairs are facing the bed by the double glass doors and fireplace, but there's more. There is an archway that leads into another room. It looks big too, but I can't see much. I move forward needing to see more.

And wow, I'm yet again breathless. I stop in the center of the room and spin around, taking it all in. It's a library, with black shelves, gold hardware that holds a gold ladder to reach the upper shelves, and a curved velvet couch in the center. There are so many different kinds of books, and I can't wait to read them all. Yet again, it has zero personality, like there is no emotional attachment to anything.

"I knew you would love it here. The shelves were once empty, but I took notice of your love for books and asked Caspian to fill the space."

He notices the small things, things no one else ever has, and always makes sure I have whatever I need or want.

"Are you ready to meet my other Hellhounds?" Dimitri asks, coming up behind me.

"Yeah, I am, but I'm not ready to leave. Can I look around first?" I turn to meet his gaze from over my shoulder.

"Whatever you want." He kisses the top of my head and sits in the center of the curved couch and reclining back before his eyes settle on me once again.

I move closer to the shelves, reading the titles of each book: some are old and very worn, judging by the cracked spines, but some appear newer. There's a lot of romance, my favorite.

I take my time looking around, and once in a while, I pick up a book to look at the cover and read the summary of what it's about. Dimitri's eyes are on me the entire time, and he never once complains, even though we've been in here for at least an hour. He seems content just by watching me, like I am the only thing worth staring at.

My eyes widen, and my steps falter. Dimitri glances over his shoulder at me, brows furrowing in concern, but my gaze is locked on one of his hounds, a massive creature with three heads, and each pair of red eyes is fixed on me, tracking my movements. He's bigger than Gwyllgi, and I feel nothing but fear crawling over my skin. Something is urging me to run, but there's something else that draws me closer.

"Don't be worried," Dimitri's voice cuts through my panic, calm but firm. "I know Cerberus is intimidating, but he won't hurt you. Just like Gwyllgi, he feels our souls are intertwined, which makes your soul attached to theirs as well."

Our souls are intertwined... another thought that should terrify me more than it does. Yet, the knowledge of these creatures being bound to me through him brings a strange sense of comfort.

Gwyllgi steps towards me and rubs his head against my leg, sensing my uneasiness. Cerberus growls lowly, but not in an ill-intended way, more like a whine of caution, and the head in the center lowers, a reaction to my fear. His movements are slow, like he doesn't want to scare me.

"My other hound is Onyx," Dimitri continues, "but he's with Caspian. Onyx is the calmest one out of the bunch." He turns away from me and moves further into the room, then bends at the knee, "Come, here." He curls his middle and index fingers at Cerberus. The three-headed hound shifts slowly toward him. "He senses you're afraid and doesn't like it, so he's moving cautiously to avoid spooking you."

I swallow my fear; I know that if there was a chance of Cerberus hurting me, Dimitri wouldn't let me anywhere near him. I think. A flicker of doubt creeps in, and I can't help the shiver that runs down my spine.

I look around the room as I try to calm my nerves. We're in the basement, and the floors are padded mats, like the ones you see in gyms. The back wall of windows offers a haunting view of the dark, endless forest. There's a door in the back corner that you just push, and it opens. Three large cots covered in dark fur line the back wall. It smells of smoke, earth, and something wild. It's oddly comforting.

"They come and go as they please," Dimitri continues, his tone casual but heavy with warning. "They know not to get close to town, not that they would. Almost like me, they hate being near crowds or anyone, for that matter. I do want to warn you, though: they have access to the house, so you may see one of them upstairs occasionally."

I only nod in response. He holds out a hand for me to grab and says, "Please, come closer."

I take it, and the warmth of his skin sends a calming sensation through me. His hand is steady, and reassuring, and I hate how safe I feel in it. He guides my fingers to Cerberus, who sniffs them carefully, each face exploring, assessing, and testing boundaries.

"Hi there," I whisper, moving fully in front of Dimitri and kneeling in front of Cerberus, giving him my full attention. My hands reach out, one to the center head, the other to the left. I scratch behind the ears, and the hound rumbles, a deep, vibrating sound that shakes the floor beneath me. Dimitri leans over my shoulder, gently stroking Cerberus' right head.

"You look so damn sexy kneeling in front of me," he murmurs, lips grazing my ear. A shiver races through me, from the intimacy of his touch.

"Really, not here," I reply, smacking him playfully, though laughter escapes me despite the tension. Cerberus chuffs, almost like he agrees with me. I swear he looks amused.

Dimitri's gaze lingers on me, a dangerous mix of pride and possessiveness. He lets me focus on the hound, but the weight of his eyes reminds me that I'm never alone in this world and never entirely safe, either.

Even as I kneel, I feel his pulse under my hands, the steady heat of him grounding me, and a strange, thrilling sense of connection binds us all: me, Dimitri, and the creatures that live in this house. These Hellhounds are terrifying and beautiful. They are mine now, in a way I don't fully understand yet. And I am his.

CHAPTER THIRTY-NINE

Rosa

After dinner, Dimitri had to leave for an important meeting. And I stand frozen, staring at the gift Cassie must have slipped into my luggage without Dimitri noticing.

Black leather corset and a pair of tiny thongs. My fingers trace the smooth leather, and a shiver runs through me. How is this going to cover me? There's a part of me burning to try it on, to see how it hugs my curves, lifts my breasts, emphasizes my waist, but another part of me hesitates. I feel... exposed. I shrug, trying to shake the nerves away. Just try it on; if you hate it, take it off.

What will Dimitri think?

I slip into the bathroom, the soft click of the door echoing in the quiet house. I tug the corset over my torso, feeling it tightly cinch. My hourglass shape looks more pronounced, and it lifts my breasts beautifully. I tilt my head, staring at my reflection. My chest rises with each breath, my skin tingling from the heat of it, and a flutter of confidence coils in my belly.

Hell, I look sexy and confident and a little dangerous.

I would definitely fuck myself if I were Dimitri.

I look towards the bedroom when I hear footsteps on the other side of the door. I left the bathroom door wide open. My heart skips a beat as I quickly fix my hair before stepping into the bedroom, and at the same time, the bedroom door opens slowly.

I don't know if I should be posing or trying to do something with my hands, maybe touch myself, but I don't. I stand here with my shoulders back, waiting for Dimitri to come into view.

But when the door fully opens, it's not Dimitri.

Panic slams into me like a wave. I step back, and the back of my knees hit the mattress, my chest heaving. I inhale deeply, mouth opening to scream for Gwyllgi, but then a voice, calm, smooth, unnervingly controlled drifts across the room. "Shh, it's okay."

Something in that voice makes my panic hesitate, my muscles partially unfreeze, but my fear doesn't vanish; it simmers beneath my skin like flames.

I take in the man before me. Extremely tall, almost Dimitri's height, with broad shoulders, radiating power in a dark, tailored suit. Hair buzzed close to his head, full lips, blue eyes that somehow remind me of Dimitri's. Every step he takes screams authority, yet there's an unsettling softness in his movements.

The man lowers his gaze, staring down my body in a slow pursuit. It should make me feel disgust, but I just feel calm. I know I shouldn't be, and I want to be afraid, but it's like my feelings are paralyzed, and somehow, I know they're not my true feelings. My fear is there, right beneath the surface, trying to fight its way back in.

He steps further into the room and whistles, "My bastard brother is one lucky man. I don't think he'll mind if I have a little taste. What about you?"

My head nods, but it's not me. Not truly, my mind screams no, but my muscles betray me, which earns me a devilish smirk. He knows.

"I am glad you agree." He sinks into Dimitri's velvet wingback chair. "Come here, beautiful. Let me smell your scent."

I try to shake my head. It doesn't listen, neither do my legs. I stumble forward, panic clawing at my chest. My voice dies before it leaves my lips, and every nerve feels almost numb. My panic is pushing through the invisible border. The twinkle in his blue eyes lets me know that he's enjoying my struggle.

I step in between his parted legs.

He reaches out, grabs a hold of my hips, turning me, seating me across his thigh, then lifts my legs and rests them over his other thigh. My heart pounds in my ears. My body trembles, stiff as a board. Every instinct is screaming fight, but I am caught in invisible chains.

His eyes are on the movement of his hand as it moves down my thigh, but he does stop before going up too high. Which I'm grateful for.

"These legs are magnificent," he whispers, hand tracing along my thigh. "How did such an oversized bastard deserve this?"

He tugs my upper body forward with his hand on my upper back until his nose touches my collarbone, then travels up my neck, and licks me. The groan he makes is deep and more like a rumble.

"You smell delicious. Tell me, does my bastard brother treat you right? If not, I'll gladly take you away and hide you from my beast of a brother."

My emotions might be calm, but my body is trembling softly. "Relax, beautiful. I'm not going to hurt you. I am not a rapist. I mean, look at me. I don't need to force myself onto women. I'm just merely curious, and I don't want you triggering those Hellhounds. Offering you a way out."

Footsteps sound from outside the door, and I feel his lips stretch into a smile against my neck. He leans back and glances at the door as soon as it opens. I do too.

Dimitri's entire body tenses when he sees me. His eyes darken when they latch onto his brother's hand on my bare thigh and then move to the corset hugging my body.

"Long time no see, brother. You didn't answer my calls, so I came by. Look at what I found! This magnificent creature. I have never felt so envious of the bastard in the family. But gods, Dimitri, she is stunning."

Dimitri growls low, deep, and menacing. "Come here, Rosa." He holds his hand out for me to grab without looking away from this psychopath holding me against my will.

He booms, "NOW, ROSA!" His black eyes burn into mine, tremors of rage coursing through him. His horns poke out, and his muscles bulge. He's larger and more intimidating than ever. I try communicating with my eyes, but he's too angry to notice.

"She likes me, bastard. I don't think she wants to leave just yet. Maybe she likes my touch." His hand slides higher up my thigh and stops at my hip, thumb making small circles on my exposed skin.

I shudder in disgust, but Dimitri's eyes are what kill me. They flash with uncertainty and possessiveness. I try to say something, I try to move away from the psychopath, but I can't.

Gwyllgi and Cerberus charge into the room. They can feel his unforgiving anger.

Gwyllgi looks at me first and then to the demon holding me, and his growl is low and deadly. I break through the calming pressure, and a small whimper escapes my throat.

I can see Dimitri's mind working, and when it finally clicks, "You're using your thrall on her," he states confidently. "Release her, Alastor, or I will kill you." The Hellhounds take place on either side of Dimitri; their teeth snap as they growl violently at the psycho holding me hostage.

The psychopath-- Alastor clicks his tongue, "Always so violent. Calm down, bastard, I'm just having a little fun."

Then I feel it. The invisible pressure that held me snaps, loosening strand by strand like untangling a web. When the last strand loosens, my legs obey me again. I spring forward, and he gently pushes me behind him, hiding me with his large body.

I grip the back of Dimitri's shirt with my fingers, and I bury my face into the fabric. My forehead slams into his spine on his lower back. Heart hammering, I feel his solid, warm body steady me.

I knew he had grown in height, but standing next to him makes it more noticeable.

"I know you like your mind games, Alastor, but my mate is off limits. The only reason you're not dead is that it'd throw everything off balance. Don't think for one second, I won't kill you if you ever mess with her again." The threat hits its mark, and Alastor nods stiffly.

His eyes flick to me. "I apologize for scaring you, darling. I just wanted to mess with my bastard brother. I took it too far, but I did lose my mind finding you in that little corset. The image will forever be ingrained." He stands. "I can see I'm no longer wanted. We do have a lot to discuss with Ian; he needs to come home. He can't pretend to be human with zero responsibilities anymore. We gave him his space for the last decade, but it's time for him to come back."

He opens the door, but before he steps out, he turns to look over his shoulder, meeting my eyes with a smirk, and I don't look away. "It was a pleasure, beautiful." He winks and then shuts the door behind him.

Dimitri doesn't move a muscle, just stands there, body tense and anger still radiating off him. I don't dare move either; he's angry with me.

"Why are you walking around the house like that?" he finally asks, voice calm but low, and dangerous.

"Wh–what?" I stutter, heat rising in my face. "What do you mean? I wanted to surprise you! I didn't think a nutcase would break into our room. I didn't know—what the hell was that? A thrall? I... I couldn't control my movements! I didn't even think something like that was possible! I knew vampires use compulsion."

I'm breathing heavily, he turns around and looks down at me, and my anger grows. "I mean, how fucking dare you! If you're going to point fingers, then I can, too. You could have warned me. You know this world is new to me."

"He fucking touched you and saw that." Dimitri's voice is a low snarl as he gestures to my barely clothed body, jaw clenching hard enough I hear his teeth grind. "That—" his hand cuts the air sharply, "—belongs to me. It's for my eyes only."

"You think I wanted him to touch me? To see me like this?" My voice cracks, anger flaring in my chest. "I couldn't control my movements!"

He steps forward like he might tear the world apart for letting something like that happen to me. "Yes, you could if you had control of your powers." He stops himself, shoulders rising then slowly falling. "It's not your fault. I'm mad at myself for not warning you... for not protecting you. Gwyllgi would've blocked it if he were with you. I didn't think my brothers would dare come near you."

His eyes search mine like he needs proof I'm truly okay. My anger softens under his guilt.

"Don't be so hard on yourself." My voice lowers, and I take a few steps toward him, and I press my hands against his warm chest, feeling the rapid beat beneath it. "It's new for the both of us."

He's still tense, shaking with rage. "Hey, I'm here, it's okay." My thumb slides up his clenched jaw, trying to soothe him with my touch.

That's when the tension in him melts and changes to hunger. I know he wants to replace Alastor's touch with his own. His gaze drops to my body, and his pupils dilate with need. He licks his upper teeth, nostrils flaring.

"Set everything aside, do you like it?"

His eyes stop on his mark, which is on full display. "Fuck, Rosa. Do I like it? Nah, that's too much of an understatement. It's everything, and you look absolutely delicious in it."

"Oh yeah?" My voice drops, dripping with sex as heat pools between my thighs. I push him back, and I know he allows me. He falls back onto the mattress. I step between his strong thighs, but I don't touch him, letting him ache for me. His fingers curl in the sheets like he needs something to grip or he'll lose control.

"Say it," I whisper. "Tell me you want me."

His throat works as he swallows. "I always want you, every damn second of every fucking day. Shit... come here, *please*. I need you." I step closer, and he watches every move, but before I settle on his lap, he growls, grips my hips, and spins me around.

Chapter Forty

Dimitri

I spin Rosa around, and my eyes fall onto her perfect, round ass. I capture my lower lip between my teeth, and a low hiss rumbles from deep in my chest. Every inch of her is absolute perfection.

My hands lift with a mind of their own, and gripping her hips, squeezing her ass cheeks like I'm trying to memorize the shape of her body. Rosa releases a moan that has my cock harden painfully, demanding her.

"Touch your toes, baby. Let me see you." I command, my voice rough with need.

She hesitates for a moment, and it's unbearable, a tiny spark of resistance that makes my hunger worse, making me want to punish her. Then she does as she's told and touches her toes.

"Fuck me…" I groan as my right hand moves and slaps her ass cheek, leaving my red handprint on her, and she shivers at the sting. "Such a good girl, you're my naughty little devil, aren't you, baby?"

"Please…" she whimpers, pushing her ass back.

I stand, bending over her, my hands sliding along her sides until I grip the back of her neck, pulling her flush against my front. My lips brush her ear as I whisper, "Please, what?"

"Touch me," she breathes, and those two damn words ruin me. My cock jerks enough that it hurts.

Fuck, she will be the death of me one day, and I will die a fucking happy man. She grinds her ass against my hard-on, slow and sinful. A pleasurable shiver crawls its way down my spine, straight to my cock. My balls ache, desperate for release.

"Touch you where? Tell me what you need," I growl, breath hot against her neck.

Her fingers find my hand and guide it lower. "Here," she whimpers, sliding it off her hips until our combined hands press against her wet, dripping pussy. With a single flick of my wrist, I rip the flimsy thong. I groan as my fingers spread her soft, glistening lips until I find her clit. I rub in slow, but controlled movements, teasing her as her body jerks and her back arches into mine.

"So, fucking wet... such a naughty girl. Mine, for me and me only," I rasp. She nods, murmuring something I can't quite catch, her body trembling.

"Do you want me to bury my cock in this tight little pussy?" I ask, hips already pressing against her heat.

"Yes, Dimitri. Please..."

I keep my hand between her thighs, trying and failing to undo my jeans. Frustrated, I growl, and without warning, I lift her effortlessly and toss her onto the bed. Her body bounces slightly, and I watch, mesmerized, as her ass jiggles. My fingers quickly work my pants as I walk towards the bed. She spins around until her back is on the mattress.

I tsk at her, "Ass up, Rosa. I want to watch that ass jiggle as I fuck you." She pauses, and my knees hit the edge of the mattress.

I bare my teeth at her hesitation. My fingers curl around her ankles, flipping her over. I pull my pants and boxers down and climb onto the bed behind her.

"Ass up, now," I growl angrily. She obeys instantly.

I'm shaking with desperation by the time I settle behind her, my control hanging by a thread. Shit... I need to be inside her.

Hell, she's perfect like this... Ass in the air, pussy dripping for me like she was made to be fucked. My hands grip her ass, spreading her open, and a groan rumbles out of me.

My cock jumps with anticipation; the tip is dripping with precum.

I'm no better than an addict willing to do absolutely anything for his next hit.

My sanity has gone out of the window, and my mind is no longer mine to control. She owns every piece of me; one word from her, and I'll do absolutely anything, no matter what. She tells me to burn, and I'll fucking burn.

"I'm going to worship you and every inch of this beautiful body." She glances back at me over her shoulder, fuck... I lean in, brushing a kiss on the corner of her lips. "I will worship you for eternity, and even then, it won't be enough. It'll *never* be enough. You are in control of me. I am yours to take apart, to command, and to ruin. Do whatever you please with me, Rosa."

I grab the side of her head, gently but firmly pressing her face into the silk sheets. "Up," I demand, with a sharp smack to her ass. She moans and lifts her ass higher. My other hand spreads her cheeks apart, exposing her to me fully. "Fuck me..." I groan desperately as I stare down at her.

I shift my hips forward and place the tip of my cock at her entrance, and shivers run down her body as I do. I push myself in slowly, knowing the stretch will burn more in this position.

I grind my molars together, inhaling deeply, my nostrils flaring.

Her cries are muffled due to my holding her face in the sheets.

I'm trying to go slow for her, but I can't; the warmth and tightness of her sweet pussy clenching me like a fucking iron vice makes my control snap.

Fuck... *fuck*! Each thrust brings a new surge, and black sparks dance in my vision. I'm about to fucking explode.

Her tight pussy sucks me in deeper, begging for more of me, and I'm done, my hips slam forward with a loud groan passing through my parted lips. Her screams are loud, but I don't stop; she's so wet. It's weeping for me. I pull back, releasing my grip on her face, and look down between us at where our bodies are joined.

I watch my cock slide out of her pussy, soaked in cum. The sight is enough to break what little control I have left. I hiss between clenched teeth as I stare at her ass bouncing with each thrust.

"Fucking fuck, Rosa..." Her tight walls tighten around me as she orgasms, pulsating like she's trying to milk every drop out of me, and she screams my name. I'm right there, too close, and I'm not ready for this blissful feeling to be over, but she's squeezing the sanity out of me.

My hands start trembling as sparks of pleasure rush through me, heading straight to my balls. The euphoric feeling heating my blood becomes too much. Blackness seeps into my vision as I nearly pass out from the all-consuming pleasure.

"Fucking hell!" I roar as I spill deep inside her, cock jerking as the release rips out of me so hard my knees almost give out.

I stay inside her, refusing to pull out, not yet. I need my come deep inside her, exactly where it belongs. My fingers move up her spine as I drag my teeth over the tops of her shoulders, marking what belongs to me. "Look at you," I growl against her skin. "Full of me and ruined for anyone else."

She trembles, her body collapsing beneath me. "Tell me you're mine, Rosa."

She turns her head, cheeks flushed, eyes watery, so freshly fucked and breathtaking. "I'm yours..." she breathes.

"I don't fucking deserve you." I brush her hair back and gently guide us onto the bed, still holding her against me. Her silence is too much, so I wrap my arms around her waist, holding her tight like she might disappear if I blink.

"I'm yours regardless." She finally replies, my forehead presses against her shoulder as I release a shaky breath I didn't realize I was holding.

I hold her for a moment longer, savoring her warmth, before I finally slip out of her slowly, watching my come spill down her inner thighs. Something primal in me growls at the sight, completely satisfied, but there's something else... a need to take care of what's mine.

"Don't move," I whisper, kissing the top of her head. "I'm going to take care of you."

She hums in response, her eyes closed, completely trusting me.

I stand, heading to the bathroom. I grab a cloth, turn on the faucet, and hold it under the warm water. I wring it out, my hands shaking, not from exhaustion, but from the feeling in my chest I can't fucking name. When I return, she's still on her side, eyes closed. I love that I get to take care of her, and that I'm the only one who can.

"Baby?" I touch her hip. "Lie on your back." She shifts, legs parting for me. My nostrils flare, her thighs are glistening, with us.

Mine.

I kneel between her legs, one hand sliding under her knee, spreading her open gently. I want to take her again, but it's too soon. I press the warm material against her, and she gasps from the sensitivity.

"I know, baby." I drag the cloth over her, cleaning the mess we made.

My thumb rubs slow circles on her hip, soothing her as she watches me through hooded eyes.

When I'm done, I press a soft kiss on the inside of her knee.

I toss the cloth aside, pulling the blanket over our bodies, tucking her against my chest.

"Fucking hell, enough. Let's go, or I'm leaving you here." I snap, the corner of my lip lifting in a snarl. I'm only putting up with her shit because of Rosa, who I left sleeping in my bed, where I should still be.

"Who the hell do you think you're talking to?" Cassie fires back, resting a hand on her hip. My hand runs through my hair, and I growl, turning away from her, looking to Ian for help.

"You know how grouchy he is when he's apart from Rosa." Ian steps between us. "It's a mate thing, let's go. You have everything you need. If not, we can buy more there."

Cassie huffs, cheeks flushing, but when Ian says it's *a mate thing,* I see a slight flicker of jealousy and longing she tries to hide.

I'm not surprised; it's why she refused to be with Ian prior. She wants her own mate. I tried warning him, but he's too stubborn to listen.

"What's going on?"

We turn to find Damien standing tall in the doorway, and a genuine smile tugs at my lips. I am pleased to see him doing so well. It's why I left Rosa half an hour ago; she'll be so excited to see him healthy and awake.

"Ian's girl keeps overanalyzing and double-checking to see if she has everything she needs." I point behind me at her.

"Ian's girl has a name."

"Eleanor and I have been in the foyer waiting for the last fifteen minutes."

"I'm sorry, I guess I'm just nervous." Cassie's shoulders drop as she exhales.

"It's okay, we understand, right, Dimitri?" Damien looks at me, face stern, but his eyes are full of understanding. He still wants me to be the bigger person.

"Correct, but we need to leave." I grab two of her suitcases, Damien gets the rest, and Ian practically drags her out of the room. We follow close behind.

"How is she? Eleanor told me a lot, but I want to hear it from you." Damien asks, meaning he knows Eleanor only told him the good things.

"She has had a rough childhood, but she doesn't allow it to consume her; she uses it to make her stronger. Hell, Damien, she is amazing." I couldn't fight the smile. "She's smart, strong, and beautiful. You'd be so proud of her. It'll be good for her to have you all there, especially you. I want to teach her how to fight and to control her powers so that she can protect herself. She'll be unstoppable."

"Fuck, I didn't fight back because I wanted her to be safe and have a good life, but all I did was push her into another monster's grip." His voice cracks with guilt. "I hate that I wasn't there to protect her. Eleanor told me how powerful she could be with the right training."

He told Eleanor he didn't fight back, thinking that in the end, he would be protecting both Rosa and Eleanor.

"You couldn't have known. Don't worry, I visited the bastard, and I'm making sure he's paying for his sins in Hell."

"Good." He nods, lost in thought. "I also heard that you two are mates."

I clear my throat, feeling slightly uncomfortable, "Yes, sir. We are mates. I hope to have your approval, but respectfully, I don't need it because I'll never let her go, no matter what. I do swear I'll do everything in my power to protect her, love her, and make sure she's happy."

"Dimitri, I see you as my son. I love you, and it's weird, but she couldn't be in better hands. I wanted someone strong for her, and it doesn't get any better. I know she'll be protected and loved dearly by you, and as long as she is happy, it's all I could've wished for my daughter."

"Good," I nod, sounding bored, but the relief that rushes through me is... well, a relief. I feel like a weight has lifted off my shoulders. I fight the smile that threatens to come out.

Chapter Forty-One

Rosa

"A few more minutes," I grumble, rolling to my side, burying my face in the pillow. Dimitri pulls the blanket away from me.

"No, I have a surprise for you."

"Can't it wait?" I pout, stretching my body. "I'm exhausted."

"No, get up." God, he's so bossy.

I narrow my eyes at him, but slowly sit up. "Fine... but for the record, I'm mad at you." I head to the bathroom and lock the door, a little smirk tugging at my lips. I know damn well it won't stop him, it never does, but it'll piss him off. He had me up half the night, which I'm not complaining about, but he could at least let me sleep in. Everyone knows how grumpy I am with little sleep.

"Rosa, lose the attitude, or I'll fuck it out of you," Dimitri calls from the other side of the door.

I roll my eyes but can't help mimicking his words with a sly grin as I splash cold water on my face.

After brushing my teeth and my hair, I throw on a pair of jeans and a plain t-shirt. When I step out, Dimitri is leaning casually against the wall, arms crossed. I try to walk past, but a gentle hand on my elbow stops me.

"Don't be mad at me, the surprise can't wait."

I exhale, leaning into him. "I'm sorry for snapping. I'm just so tired. So much has happened, and I can use a break, one day to lie in bed all day. I just really wanted to sleep in with breakfast in bed as we watched TV."

He lifts a brow and pulls me into a tight hug. "Tomorrow, we'll stay in bed all morning. I'll cancel everything, no meetings, no distractions." His lips brush the top of my head as I melt into him, feeling both guilty and comforted. He guides my arms around his waist. "Come on, let's go. Your surprise is waiting."

It smells like bacon and eggs as we walk down the stairs, and my stomach grumbles loudly. Dimitri chuckles, and I whack him in the ribs with my elbow. That's when I hear voices; it sounds like everyone is having a good time. I look at Dimitri, but he doesn't look my way as he pushes me forward. We step into the kitchen, and I gasp when I see Cassie. I haven't realized how much I've missed her until now.

"Ahh, I fucking missed you! Bitch, you left without saying goodbye!" Cassie cries out as she shoves Ian out of the way; he nearly falls over. She collides with me, nearly knocking me over as well.

"I wasn't given much of a choice." I give Dimitri a pointed look. "A brute forced me. You literally saw him push me into the portal."

"Yeah, I know. I can still be mad for not getting to say goodbye." She lowers her voice, leaning closer to me. "Did you get my gift?" She pulls away, a playful grin spreads from ear to ear as she wiggles her brows. "I knew you were leaving, so I snuck it into your stuff while Dimitri was packing."

I laugh, shaking my head, when a deep, unfamiliar voice behind her makes my chest tighten. "Okay, Cassie. Can I see my daughter?"

"Oh, right, sorry." Cassie giggles, moving away from me. My breath catches in my throat. Standing behind Cassie is a man I've only seen in photos. Nothing like the man in the dungeons. He's nearly as tall as Dimitri, leaner, with dark brown hair that just brushes his chin. The strength in his stance is undeniable, but his smile, warm and genuine, makes me exhale the breath I didn't realize I was holding.

"Breathe." He chuckles, the sound is full of joy, and it feels like home.

I stand as still as a statue, not knowing what to do as my throat burns. Do I hug him, or do I cry? I honestly feel like doing both. I want to say something meaningful, but my brain isn't working. "You look way better than the last time I saw you."

Humiliation slams into me, that's what I say? It's not meaningful at all. I can't believe I sound like a socially awkward girl in front of a man I've dreamt of meeting my whole life. My inner voice screams at me... *Really, that's what you say? What the hell kind of compliment is that? Out of every possible sentence, that's the winner? Can we do a redo?*

"Well, I sure hope so. I was in pretty bad shape." His eyes hold a slight twinkle as if he finds the conversation amusing.

"I meant..." I wave my hand down the length of him, feeling awkward. "I know you look better, but how do you feel?"

"I'm tired and still need rest, but I feel better than I have in a long time."

"Good," I nod. My lower lip starts trembling, so I press my lips together, but then my eyes water. I blink rapidly, fighting back tears. I'm a mess, and I can't hold it back.

"Come here," he says, all teasing gone as he holds out both arms; he's teary-eyed, too. We both step forward, arms wrapping around each other in a long-awaited hug. I press my cheek to his chest, and it's as though every scar, every ache of the past, melts into the warmth that surrounds me. My tears soak into his shirt, but he doesn't care. He just holds me tighter, whispering, "I've missed you more than you'll ever know. You're safe now. I've got you."

This is everything I've always waited for and craved. A simple hug from my own father, there's one thing that is missing.

I pull back, searching the room, and my eyes land on Eleanor—my mom, my heart stops for a second. There she is, crying in the kitchen. I hold out my hand.

"Oh, Gods," she cries out as she rushes into our arms. "I never thought this day would ever happen." The three of us cry as we hold each other tightly. A family that was lost and is now reunited. Our bodies shake with the intensity of the moment.

I have a family now...

My stomach rumbles loudly, and Dimitri steps forward, pulling me away, "Let's eat."

"Good idea." My dad nods, his gaze soft and warm as it lands on my mom. There's so much love in the way they look at each other. God, even saying simple words like 'Mom' and 'Dad' still feels strange, almost unreal.

"You had me feeling jealous." Dimitri's lips move against my ear, teasing, but I hear the seriousness in it.

"Don't be ridiculous." I roll my eyes, laughing.

"Yeah, trust me," he whispers, pressing a soft kiss against my temple. "I know they're your parents, but that didn't stop the jealousy and possessiveness threatening to claw its way out. Don't laugh at my misery."

"I'm sorry, baby. Don't worry, I'm all yours; you have nothing to be jealous of." I pout, looking up at him.

He groans, dragging a hand down his face. "Fuck, don't call me that in front of your parents. It turns me on." His eyes turn toward me, dark with something I can't quite name, and my cheeks heat.

He pulls a chair out for me at the long ten-person table, then takes a seat at the head of it to my right. The food is already laid out, with different types of fruits in the center, and each of us has a plate full of eggs, bacon, and pancakes.

"It looks so good." Cassie sits next to me, and Ian sits on the other side of her. My dad is directly across from me, and next to him is my mom. They are both smiling gently as they observe the group. I take a bite of the pancakes, and I close my eyes to savor the flavor.

"Ian, have you taken over for your father yet?" My dad asks as he cuts into his food.

Ian clears his throat, straightening in his seat. "No, I have not. I asked for some time away before I took his place. It's time, though. My brothers and I are having a meeting after breakfast."

"He doesn't want to take over and is trying to find a way out of it." Dimitri jumps in.

I blink at him, "Dimitri, that's not something for you to say."

"But it's true." He shrugs, taking a slow sip of his coffee.

"It doesn't matter if it's true," I reply, frowning. "If he wanted to say that, he would be the one to say it. Don't be rude."

"Is that true?" Cassie ignores us, eyes locked on Ian. Ian's shoulders slump slightly, exhaling, and nods. "Why didn't you tell me?"

The room goes silent for a moment. I glance at Dimitri, who is watching me with an unreadable expression.

"I don't know. I've only told Dimitri; no one else knows. I prefer living in the human realm and having free rein to do what I want." I feel bad that Dimitri outed him, but I am glad he did. Cassie deserves to know where he stands, especially before he marks her.

"I understand that," Cassie says, voice mixed with hurt and anger. "But I have the right to know if I'm going to be a part of your future."

The room is now full of heavy tension, so I clear my throat. "Are you planning on rejoining the council?" I ask my dad.

"No," he answers, glancing at Dimitri. "We were actually going to talk to you and Dimitri about that."

"What is it?" Dimitri sets his mug of coffee down and rests his elbows on the table as he leans forward.

"Eleanor and I think it's best to step down." My dad continues, "We want to enjoy our second chance without the stress of the council, but as you know, to step down, we have to find replacements as strong as us or stronger. Dimitri, I know you don't want to be part of the council, but I am hoping you and Rosa will take over. It's only temporary until we find full-time replacements."

I see the desperation on their faces. They really want out, to spend time with each other, which I understand.

"It's a big decision," Dimitri answers, as his hand moves to rest on my thigh. "I need to explain the responsibilities to Rosa first. This is something she and I need to discuss in private."

"If you're okay with it, then I'm willing to do it. Temporarily, that is."

Dimitri shakes his head. "No, you need to hear the responsibilities before making your decision. After that, if you want to or even if you don't, I'll stand by your decision."

"No," I push back, feeling determined. "I don't care what the responsibilities are; they need this, and they deserve it. I want to do this for them."

Dimitri stares at me for a few moments. Searching for any type of deception in my words. When he doesn't find any, he nods. "Whatever you want. We will take your place temporarily."

The sudden slam of a door makes us all turn. Alastor strides in, full of confidence, like he owns the place.

"Good morning, beautiful," he greets me, dipping his chin respectfully.

"Alastor," Dimitri warns sharply.

Alastor shakes his head and continues, ignoring the warning. "I am here to fetch my brothers. Yes, that is including the bastard."

I push my chair back, stand, and poke him in the chest with my index finger. "Don't call him that."

He chuckles, holding up both hands in surrender. "Feisty, I like it. No problem, I won't call the bastard a bastard."

Dimitri grabs me around the waist and pulls me against him. Ian whispers something in Cassie's ear and places a sweet kiss on her cheek before stepping forward.

"I'm coming with," Cassie announces, springing up. Alastor's gaze locks on her, his eyes dilate, turning black. My lips lower into a frown as he stares at her with pure hunger. His fangs extend, and he steps closer. Dimitri grabs me and pulls me out of the way. His body is stiff as a board.

"No," Ian shakes his head and steps in between Alastor and Cassie, blocking her from view. His face is pale, full of horror and shock.

I open my mouth to ask what was happening, but Cassie beats me, "What's going on?" Her head comes into view when she looks over Ian's shoulder. Her wide eyes look at me and then at Dimitri.

"Who is she to you, brother?" Alastor demands, eyes on Cassie.

"She's mine, my girl. The one I told you I'm marking."

Alastor inhales deeply, and the exhale is part growl. It's like he's trying to keep his control. I can see his rigid body is trembling slightly.

"Then she shall choose, brother." Alastor's voice has an animalistic growl to it. I look to my parents; they're watching from the table, gripping each other's hands.

"She is not choosing anything." Ian's voice is still calm, but there's a demand to it mixed with a plea.

"She is right here, and he is right. I'll be choosing, but what am I choosing?" Cassie steps from around Ian, arms crossing. Her gaze pinballs between the brothers.

"I am your mate," Alastor confesses.

At the same time, Ian snaps, "Nothing."

Cassie and I both gasp, fully understanding. Alastor steps closer towards Cassie, his hands twitching at his sides as if he's itching to grab her and pull her away from Ian.

Ian snaps and attacks, a loud snap of bone breaking echoes around us as Ian's fist slams into Alastor's jaw.

"It is fate, brother." Alastor throws an uppercut, and Ian hits the marble floors. Comparing sizes, Alastor is bigger than Ian both in height and width. Having been around Ian these last few weeks, I know he's strong, but he's not a fighter, and I have a feeling Alastor is a lot stronger. Ian gets up, but Alastor is faster; his fist slams into Ian's chest, and the blow sends Ian flying across the room into the wall.

Alastor stalks towards him and slams his fist into the side of Ian's face. Ian is holding his arms in front of him, trying to block the blows, but he's not doing so well. Alastor is relentless, fighting for what belongs to him.

"Stop, Alastor, please!" Cassie cries, and Alastor's fist freezes mid-swing. Ian sways and collapses to his knees as he pants heavily. "I need time, I don't know... I just need time to think and some fucking air." Cassie turns and bolts to the glass doors leading out back.

I glance at Dimitri. He nods, but mumbles, "wait," then blows out a loud whistle.

I arch a brow, but I don't question it. I am too anxious to go and be with my friend who desperately needs me. Plus, she went outside, and I'm not sure if Dimitri or Ian told her the rules about staying inside the fence area.

A minute later, Cerberus and Gwyllgi rush into the room. "Go with Rosa and do not leave her side," Dimitri demands, and the hounds move to my side. I don't waste a single second.

The hounds flank me as I sprint outside. "Cassie?" I call out. She doesn't reply, but I do hear a faint sniffle behind a large grey tree.

I step towards it to find Cassie sitting on a metal bench across from a small pond. I sit beside her, not saying a word, and she rests her head on my shoulder. The hounds stand by the tree, giving us space.

"I used to think finding my mate would be the best day of my life. Why couldn't I have met him before I fell for Ian?" Cassie begins, "It was a dream of mine too, you know, finding my other half. But I am also in love with Ian. How do I choose?" She looks at me as if I have the answers she needs, and I truly wish I did.

I pause, thinking carefully. "Don't decide now. Spend a few days with Alastor. Really get to know him before you decide. My choice was clear on the first date, but I wasn't torn between two men like you are."

"What? Stay at his place? That's... I don't think it's safe. He could be a murderer."

"True," I agree, staring at the pond. Cassie lies down on the bench, resting her head in my lap. I gently stroke her hair, an idea forming, "Tell Ian to go home, the one he owns here. You and Alastor stay here."

"Dimitri won't like that idea," she protests. "Remember, he hardly gets along with his brothers. Plus, Ian... I'll feel bad for hurting him."

"Dimitri wants me happy; he won't like it, but he'll do it for me. Ian won't like it, but you need to make a choice, and that's the best way for you to do it."

"No." Dimitri shakes his head, crossing his arms over his chest. I can feel the intensity radiating off him even before he speaks.

After a long talk, Cassie and I came inside. The brothers had all left for the meeting. We spent all day together. My parents left the house midday to explore. Ian and Dimitri came back after dinner. Cassie went with Ian, and here I am telling Dimitri our plan.

"Give me one good reason." I mimic his stance.

"He used his thrall on you and touched you. That's reason enough." I frown and sink into the chair behind me, exhaling. That's a very good reason. "Two, I don't trust him around you. He's not as bad as my other half-brothers, but he's no saint."

"Okay, but it's not like he'll want to touch me. I mean, his mate will be here. His every waking thought would be about her."

He inhales deeply; he knows my argument is a solid one. "I don't know, the house is already crowded with your parents here. Cassie was supposed to stay at Ian's place. He won't even agree to it."

"He doesn't have a choice, and I know the house is already crowded, but..." I run out of things to say, but I am not opposed to begging. "Please, Dimitri, she's my friend, and I know you two don't get along, but she's like a sister to me. She needs this, and she can't go to his place. It wouldn't be safe." I blink up at him with a small pout. "Please."

His eyes soften, but only slightly. He's weighing the options.

"Fine," he grumbles.

I spring up, gripping his broad shoulders, jumping up, and wrapping my legs around his hips, lips slamming into his. His hands slide under my thighs, holding me close.

"You're impossible," he growls, voice thick with desire, pressing me lightly against the wall behind us.

I laugh softly, letting my fingers curl into his hair. "You love it," I murmur.

"You're lucky I'm in a generous mood." He grinds his hips into me.

Chapter Forty-Two

I laugh as Dimitri dips through the air, causing my heart to skip a beat. I look towards him, and he's staring straight ahead, wearing a lopsided grin. The wind that tears past us is cold, but Dimitri's arms are like a furnace around my body. He's carrying me bridal-style in his arms.

My hand reaches out, and I touch the black feathers of his wings at the base. His muscles flex beneath me as his massive wings flap through the sky. He shivers slightly, goosebumps rising from his neck and disappearing down the neckline of his shirt.

They are flapping at a steady beat, the deep whump... whump... whump is surprisingly soothing. His arms tighten around me, my gaze shifts, and I meet those solid black demon eyes. They hold more tenderness than any human can ever imagine, like I hung the moon, with so much love, like having me and loving me is a privilege he'll never get over.

He had some business to take care of and didn't want to leave me alone with Alastor in the house.

It's been three days, and Alastor has been around Cassie every waking minute, trying to make his time count. He's sleeping in the living room, with a single mattress on the floor, but he doesn't mind at all.

Yesterday, Cassie and Ian tried going out together. It went horribly, he lashed out, wounded and defensive. In other words, he was mean as hell to her.

He even said, *'If it's that easy for you to move on, then you should pick Alastor. I don't want an easy woman.'*

It broke her heart.

This morning, she chose to leave Ian, but she didn't pick Alastor either.

She said she wanted to get to know him before making a big decision, so they're dating and taking it slow. I'm glad that she's not jumping into it. He's leaving the house later today, and he got her a phone to keep in contact with him, and they planned their first date. I'm excited to see where it leads.

"We're here," somehow, I hear his low rumble, even with the roaring winds and the loud flapping of his wings. I turn away from his piercing gaze and towards the town down below. I saw a glimpse of it before, but we were further away.

From here, it looks alive. The streets are paved in deep brown brick, the cottages a warm sand color. The grey bushes with blood-red and black flowers in every yard make everything seem beautifully eerie. It's a strange, dark, but romantic scene.

Most have their lights on, which seems necessary here; no matter the time of day, the world is always draped in night as if the sun can't quite reach this place. You can tell the difference between day and night. During the day, the skies are light grey, with a red hue to it like a bad storm brewing. At night, it's so dark I can hardly see in front of me, but the red hue is brighter.

Dimitri lands in the center of town. The impact of his boots sends a faint tremor through the brick road. Demons stop mid-walk to stare; some gasp. They all stare at him and then at me with a mix of awe and fear.

He sets me down gently, takes my hand, and just...keeps walking, like this is normal. I decide to wait till we're alone to ask him about it.

Gwyllgi and Cerberus catch up with us, their paws clicking against stone. The crowd parts for us, like we were the evil ones.

I can't blame them. Dimitri towers over seven feet tall in demon form, wings outstretched wide, shoulders broad enough to block out the torches behind him. His tattoos glow faintly against his darkened skin, swirling across his chest and arms like living snakes. Add the two massive Hellhounds flanking us, and yeah...it's terrifying.

I turn away from the staring crowd and toward the familiar market I noticed last week. Wooden shacks with double doors wide open reveal their goods inside: bottles of glowing green and blue potions, blades forged from blackened steel, crates of black fruit, metal jewelry, and fabrics dyed in wine. Demons haggle, laugh, and argue. It feels alive, thriving.

Honestly, I can't wait to look around. My chest swells with happiness. This is a lot better than I expected, and it doesn't feel like I have to worry about large monsters everywhere I turn.

My fingers thread with Dimitri's, and he looks down as I smile widely at him. He returns it, pulling me close. My arm wraps around his lower back, right below his wings, my fingers caressing the feathers. I love his wings, they're gorgeous. He groans, like he does every time I touch them. I've learned they're very sensitive.

"I know you don't like crowds, but I want to explore later. If that's okay."

He stops, leans down, and kisses me. "Whatever you want. I just want you to be happy."

Warmth fills my chest. "I love you, Dimitri."

His chest rumbles as he says, "I love you too, Malyshka."

"You know, you've never told me what that means."

"It means baby. My baby girl. If you don't stop, we'll be late, because I'm about to take you to my office and fuck you on my desk."

I laugh, rolling my eyes.

"I'm being serious." He smirks, fangs sharp as his dimples wink at me.

"Come on, big boy." I step away, and we start walking once more. Everyone is staring at us. I turn away from them and look up at the castle that sits on the hilltop above it all. It's meant to be intimidating, and it is.

We walk toward the giant metal gate that separates the town from the castle grounds. The guards bow deeply and swing the gates open, but instead of going up the stone path toward the castle, we turn sharply left, circling the hillside.

A building comes into view as we cross the hill, and it impresses me the most, aside from the castle, of course. It's surprisingly modern compared to everything else I've seen. It appears to be made of black marble, with towering windows.

"This is where I work. I designed it myself." Dimitri turns to me, sounding proud.

I smile, of course, he did. It looks just like his—our—house, dark, elegant, and deadly.

"It's beautiful and intimidating all in one."

"Prince Dimitri," Two guards bow, one turns to open the door. We step into a long hallway that has black marble veined with white floors. There's a door on either side of the massive hall, or you can go straight, which has a set of double doors.

Dimitri gestures to the left. "Council chambers, it's where we hold private meetings." Then to the right. "Holding chambers, souls wait for judgment there. Alastor's been helping me the last few weeks."

He pulls me forward with our hounds following close behind. He pushes the double doors open, and I gasp.

The judgment hall is massive and shadow-soaked. Two black velvet thrones sit at the far end, trimmed in gold. The stone floor is thick, uneven, and ancient. Flames roar behind the thrones, rising against the back wall like a curtain of fire. Tall gothic windows stretch up the sides, letting in the muted grey glow from the skies outside. It's dramatic and screams power, but of course, it does.

The path leading up to the thrones looks like a corridor of *death*, with torches on either side flickering orange and casting monstrous shadows across the floor. This massive room is different, not at all modern. It's more gothic.

"We added your throne yesterday; it's one of the reasons I came," Dimitri says casually, like it's not important information.

"*My* throne?" My voice goes embarrassingly high, echoing off the stone.

He smiles like he enjoys the sound a little too much. "Correct, as my mate, you will sit beside me during judgments and council meetings since we are taking over. Your first judgment is about to start, but you may watch and learn until you're confident. I always shift into demon form for them."

"My first judgment is about to happen. Like right now? Oh God, Dimitri, why didn't you prepare me?"

"Don't use that name here," he warns softly. "And truly? I didn't think to warn you." He walks up the stone steps to his throne.

My mouth drops open. "You really need to work on communication," I scowl, mostly because I'm panicking and he looks far too relaxed, reclining back in his throne like a dark prince made from sin itself. Cerberus settles at his side, looking lethal. Gwyllgi brushes against my hip, nudging me forward.

"Sit, Malyshka, the guards are bringing the souls." I stare at him in disbelief until he raises a brow. I roll my eyes, but climb the steps slowly and settle into the smaller throne beside him. I sit upright, careful, aware of its cold velvet pressing against my back. I lean forward like the chair itself is dangerous, and I cross one leg over the other, my pulse hammering. Gwyllgi settles beside me.

Thank the gods I wore a dress. Not fancy, but it feels right now. Deep burgundy, high neckline, a keyhole cut down to my sternum showing just enough to make Dimitri feral. Two high slits trace the outside of both legs. I chose it because it was the least dramatic gown in my closet and because the way Dimitri looked at me in it could have started a war.

"Holy hells..." Dimitri groans. My eyes move to his to find him staring at me, eyes dark and full of lust. "Malyshka, I knew you'd look good in my throne, but fuck, you look sinfully sexy. You command the space and my attention. You were born to sit here and rule at my side." His gaze drags slowly down my body, darkening even further.

He leans forward as if he's about to stand, but the double doors open. He growls lowly, hands tightening into a fist at the interruption. I bite back a smile, which has his eyes narrowing in response.

He looks forward, but not before mumbling, "Later, my sweet mate."

Souls file in, silent and pale, forming a perfect line before us, and there are guards now stationed around the room. I was so engrossed with Dimitri, I didn't even hear anyone come in.

"You may step forward," Dimitri commands, his voice booms through the chamber, full of impatience and dominance.

The first soul that steps forward, kneels, then stares up at Dimitri. But his stare wanders towards me, and when it does, it lingers.

Dimitri definitely does not like it, even though his stare is full of remorse and not desire. "Do not look at her, she will not help you!" he shouts, making everyone in the room jump, including the guards.

"My apologies, my prince." His gaze is now on the stone floors beneath him.

"We shall begin," Dimitri states.

The guard steps forward and reads the file, "This soul murdered his brother for sleeping with his wife. He is now here because he committed suicide after the murder took place. Before the events of that fatal night, he was an outstanding man, no broken laws, no crimes of any sort. It seems like he snapped."

I swallow hard as the guard tells the man's story; it's horrible, and I'm not sure what I would decide if I were in Dimitri's shoes.

Dimitri stares down at the man's soul for a while, and he taps a single claw lightly against the arm of his throne. He looks like the prince they talk about, the deadly executioner.

"He is to be damned here in the Underworld. No redemption." Dimitri states coldly. "You are dismissed."

The man sobs, "No, please, I can't stay here! I am a good person! I won't survive down here!" His voice cracks on every word as the guards drag him across the floor. His heels scrape against the obsidian tiles, leaving faint streaks of ash behind.

Black gates appear, gothic designs carved into the metal, and they open with a loud groan—the gates to Hell. The guards toss the soul into the darkness beyond.

Dimitri doesn't react. Not a blink. Not a muscle twitch. He stares ahead with the same cold, dark expression the Underworld carved into him long before I met him.

My stomach twists as I watch the gates disappear. I know the man's sins matter. I know justice is why he's here… but hearing the horror in his voice makes the room tighten around me. The walls carved from black stone feel like they're leaning closer. I try to breathe through it, but my breaths come thin and uneven. That's when a large, warm hand wraps around mine. My trembling stops immediately. I look up, and Dimitri is watching me.

And then he does something that shocks the entire damned chamber. The Prince of the Underworld rises from his throne and kneels in front of me. Gasps echo around the room.

His hands cup my cheeks, and in a gentle voice he only uses for me, he says, "Shh, it's okay, if you need a break, I can take you to my office."

I shake my head, managing a weak but determined smile. "I would prefer to stay. I need to hear this."

"Okay," He nods, brushing his thumb across my cheek. "If you need to leave, just say the word." He straightens, but not before kissing my forehead.

"Carry on," Dimitri demands. The guard snaps out of his shocked state and clears his throat before speaking. "This soul is here because he raped and murdered six females and was murdered by the seventh. Before these incidents, he was always breaking mortal and supernatural laws."

It went on. I listened and watched the way Dimitri reacted, but he gave nothing away. The scraping sound of bodies being dragged across the stone, and the pleas, will stay with me. I might even have nightmares. Three souls were granted clemency. Their bodies glowed faintly before disappearing from sight. It was a beautiful thing to watch. The other souls who were damned were dragged away, then swallowed by darkness the moment the gates opened.

The last soul steps forward, and the guard starts. "This soul is here because he shot and killed a man. Before this incident, he was a good person. He only broke two petty laws and paid for those crimes."

I already know what Dimitri will say before he does. "He is to be damned here in the Underworld for his punishment."

The man breaks, collapsing to his knees. "Please! I'm a good man—that man deserved to be murdered! He raped and killed my baby girl!"

My breath catches; those words hit me hard in the chest. He's sobbing so hard he can barely breathe... Dimitri doesn't so much as flinch; he just watches as the soul is forcefully removed. The dark gate appears as they grow closer, but something in me snaps. "Wait!"

The guard freezes, blinking in surprise. I'm sure it's because I sat here the entire time, not saying a single word. Dimitri stiffens, turning slowly toward me. His eyes sharpen and are calculating. "What is it?"

"I want to hear this soul's side of the story." Dimitri's jaw ticks as he stares at me. I can see that he is debating what to do. Silence hangs in the air like everyone is holding their breath.

"Prince Dimitri?" the guard calls out, unsure of what to do.

"Bring him in," his voice low. "My mate wants to hear what he has to say. She shall have what she wants."

The guard allows the soul back in, and the soul kneels in the same spot as before, but instead of looking at Dimitri, he looks at me.

"Thank you," he whispers. "Thank you for hearing my side of the story."

I smile, leaning forward. "What did you mean when you said the man raped and killed your baby?"

He exhales, eyes tearing up. "The man I shot, he raped and killed my daughter. She was only sixteen and had her entire life in front of her. His father had money and connections. He would've walked free, laughing while my girl went into the ground." His hands shake violently. "So, I did what any father would do. I avenged her. I made sure he never hurt another girl."

Dimitri turns to me, eyes darkened, but full of pride and something else I can't pinpoint. "What do you say?"

I can't believe he's letting me decide. I swallow hard. "I... I think he should be granted leniency under the circumstances." I'm surprised at how confident I sound.

"What are you waiting for? You heard what she said! He goes above." Dimitri snaps when the guard hesitates.

"Yes, of course." The guard bows twice, once for Dimitri and then once for me.

The chamber empties slowly, but the weight of the father's story lingers. My chest aches with it still, that pure girl and father.

Dimitri watches me closely, at every flicker of emotion on my face. He's too still and too focused. Like he's struggling between dragging me into his arms... or dragging me straight out of the room to keep me from ever being here again.

When the last guard leaves, he exhales through his nose and crooks a finger at me. "Come here." His voice is a deep plea, full of emotions he refuses to show anyone else. I stand and move towards him. Gwyllgi follows me.

The second I step between Dimitri's knees, he grabs me by the hips and pulls me onto his lap. I cross my leg over the opposite. The hounds are sitting on either side of the throne. My heart pounds with a rush of heat and adrenaline still left over from the judgment.

"That," he growls against my throat, "was so fucking sexy, watching you take control. Watching you override my ruling."

His hand rests on my bare thigh, forcing me to uncross my legs, his fingers slowly move their way up, pushing them further apart. His hand stops when it is on the edge of my panties.

Heat radiates off his demon form, tracing up my skin like fire. The throne beneath us hums faintly, reacting to his rising desire, runes flickering like embers. The shadows at his feet coil with anticipation, mirroring the hunger in his eyes.

He pushes the damp fabric aside and slips his fingers up my soaking pussy slit, then spreads me apart, circling my clit with slow and confident movements.

A quiet gasp escapes me, my body tugged tight between pleasure and the electric pulse gathering in the room.

His touch is devastating, too slow, too knowing. The heat of his fingertips dragging through my clit makes the sensation even better, making my legs tremble.

I arch my back, moaning, but it doesn't stop my next words. "We can't, not here, anyone could walk in. What about the hounds?" My fingers curl around his wrist, stopping his movements. My eyes turn to Gwyllgi, but he's staring straight ahead.

"No one comes in without permission." He tells me, "Gwyllgi, Cerberus, leave us." His dark stare doesn't leave mine, holding me captive with those intense eyes. I hear the soft footfalls of their paws hitting the stone floors, and then the sound of the doors swinging open and shut.

My hand slowly uncurls from his wrist without shying away from his darkened eyes, and his fingers start moving in slow torturous circles once more. My lips part as the pleasure in my stomach slowly unravels, turning into something strong and dangerous. I still don't look away. I start moving my hips, keeping up with his quickening pace.

The room fades and narrows to the rhythm of his fingers, the heat of his palm, the deep rumble in his chest vibrating against my ribs. Every circle feels like it pulls me deeper into him, into the fire.

It's still not enough; I need more. I need his cock stretching me. "Take me. Show me who I belong to." My voice is low with seduction.

A deep growl is the only response I get. His hand disappears, and I whimper as my pussy throbs painfully with the need to be stretched. He grips me by the waist, lifting and spinning me on his lap, so that I'm straddling his hips. With quick and jerky movements, he unbuttons his pants. Leaning back and moving his hips forward, pulling them off until his cock jumps free, smacking his abdomen.

As I assumed, in his demon form, he is larger in length and girth, even more than I imagined. I swallow; it hurts when it's his human form... this is going to kill me... how will *that* fit?

He grips his hard length with his hand and reclines back, looking up at me, "Ride me, Malyshka, use me."

I swallow my fears, remembering that I am made for him, all of him. I need to please him in both forms. I move my hands, one pushing his hand away so that I'm gripping his cock, and the other settles on his shoulder for support as I move my hips closer, lifting them slightly until the tip of his cock is at my entrance. My pulse is racing as my nerves try to get the best of me, but I won't allow it. I need him.

I can't breathe as I slide down his enormous cock. I cry out, my hands gripping his shoulders tightly, nails leaving marks in their wake. I close my eyes, the stretch burns, but I force myself to keep going until he's fully buried inside me. I try to take a deep breath, but it's too much.

"Rosa..." Dimitri grunts almost painfully; he's trying to let me control the pace.

I move my hips slowly, working myself up and down. It's overwhelming, the pain, the pleasure is all too much for me, but at the same time, it's not enough. I push myself to go faster and harder.

Gods, being on top of him like this feels like riding a storm. His demon form radiates heat, a slow furnace warmth that rolls through my thighs and settles low in my stomach. The throne beneath us vibrates faintly with every shift, humming with ancient power. I swear I can feel the magic etched into the stone brush over my skin like ghost-fingers, the runes pulsing faintly under Dimitri's thighs.

Dimitri watches me with those intense dark eyes pinging between the spot where we're joined and to my breasts, to my face, not knowing which sight he prefers. It's intoxicating.

His hands turn into claws and are now clenching the arms of the throne, leaving marks in the dark stone as he tries to maintain control. I don't want his control. I want him to snap.

His wings twitch behind him, feathers brushing the stone as his breathing turns ragged, with each exhale a low demonic rumble that vibrates straight through my core.

I push myself back, releasing my grip on his shoulders and reaching for the buttons on the back of the dress, yanking on either side, and popping the buttons off. I pull down the straps, and my dress falls forward, and my breasts bounce free as I start riding his cock faster, sliding up and down his thick length. I moan his name; it echoes around the room.

Dimitri makes a sound between a moan and a groan as he watches them bounce. He finally snaps, pushing himself forward, his claws disappear, and his hands cup my breasts. His lips wrap around my left nipple.

"Holy hell, Dimitri." I cry out, his hands and lips on me are exactly what I needed. My pleasure rises, higher and higher. I can almost taste my orgasm.

My breath hitches, I'm on the edge. Nonsense spills from my lips, pleading with Dimitri for more. He obeys; he grips my hips to hold me still as he starts thrusting beneath me. His thrusts are hard and merciless.

My eyes blur as my pussy spasms and my body shakes as the orgasm violently takes control and waves of intense pleasure smack into me as I fall. I'm mumbling something as my body calms from the high. Dimitri roars my name, and I feel his cock start throbbing and then a gush of warm come. He's saying my name on repeat as he buries his face into my neck. Dimitri slumps back and takes me with him, my head resting on his chest.

He breaks the silence. "I love you, Malyshka."

I smile. "I love you, Dimitri."

"*Fuck*, say it again."

I laugh, my lips pressing against his before leaning back and looking into his eyes that are now the brilliant blue I fell in love with. "I love you, my sexy demon."

"Hells, I'm hard again." He groans, pressing his erection against my sore pussy.

The end...

Note to Readers

Thank you to all my readers! You have all helped me make my dreams come true!

Thank you to all of my family who've helped me through this amazing journey.

I couldn't have done this without my husband; he supported me and never let me give up on my dreams. He is my rock and my own knight!

You can find me on Instagram @Jstangauthor or email me at janethlala@icloud.com

Thank you!

About J. S. Rodriguez

J.S. Rodriguez lives in the beautiful countryside of Pennsylvania with her amazing husband and their four wonderful children. A lifelong romance enthusiast, she proudly calls herself a romance junkie who is fueled by strong coffee, good music, and the occasional spontaneous dance break.

Born in California, Rodriguez spent much of her childhood moving from place to place. Those early experiences sparked her deep love of reading and storytelling, eventually planting the dream of becoming an author. As she grew older, that dream only intensified, shaping her passion for writing heartfelt, imaginative romance.

Rodriguez now enjoys life in a spacious farmhouse, where the peaceful view of the creek from her front porch often inspires her stories. When she's not writing, she loves baking with her family, unwinding during cozy, lazy afternoons, and cherishing quality time with the people she loves most.

Please visit online at: https://www.instagram.com/j.s.rodriguez_author

OTHER BOOKS BY J.S. RODRIGUEZ

Wicked Little Witch

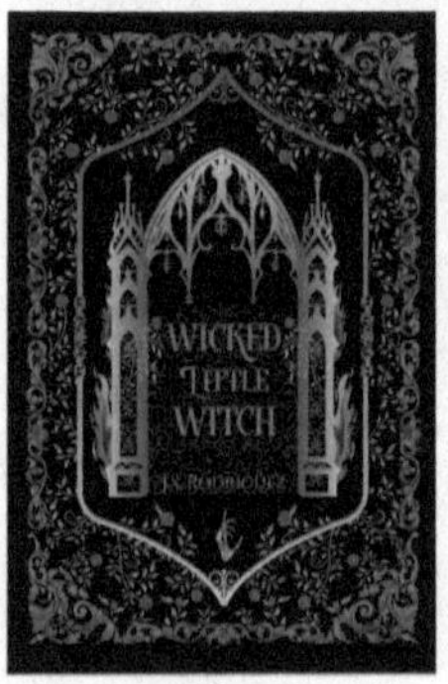

Azrael

Fuck... I need to do something I have never done before... pray and pray that I will not give in to her wicked spell. She is made straight from the devil himself, made to be a temptation you cannot fight, and she will cause you to sin for a simple little taste of her sweet nectar. She has me feeling things I have never felt before. I will not give in; I hate her and everything she is.

Bella

My mom is dead, and now my sister and I are on the run, hiding in the shadows so my own father doesn't find us. My life has been turned upside down after having met Azrael. He helped me, now I'm in his debt, and he will not let me leave until I hold up my end of the bargain. God, I hate him... or at least that's what I keep telling myself.